The Donegal Woman

The Donegal Woman

By John Throne

The
Drumkeen
Press

The Donegal Woman
First Published July 2006
by
The Drumkeen Press,
35 Springtown Road,
Derry, BT48 0LT,
Northern Ireland.
Email: thedrumkeenpress@hotmail.co.uk
Website: www.thedonegalwoman.com
Reprinted September 2006

Copyright © John Throne, 2006
ISBN 10: 0-9553552-0-6
ISBN 13:978-0-9553552-0-2

Printed in Ireland by Beta Print

"He leaves nothing out."
MRS MARY HAMILTON. DEPUTY MAYOR OF THE CITY OF DERRY.

"An unadorned, searing tale that reclaims from the often brutal and brutalizing conditions in remote rural Ireland the buried history of one woman's struggle to survive and rear her children. The Donegal Woman pulls no punches. It is a just memorial to courage and perseverance, shot through with sunbursts of innocence, love and natural beauty. A disturbing, unforgettable portrait." - GERALD DAWE

"John Throne, in this important and moving book, brilliantly conveys the real Donegal of a century ago."
- A DONEGAL READER

"This is the story of a child who loses her childhood to a brutal, dehumanizing system. It is also the story of the man to whom she was 'sold' for her labour and for the money to buy a cow. Readers will readily sympathise with her as she battles to regain her humanity, but his story, too, is told with extraordinary insight. We see how his spirit is fettered by the need to serve the landlord class as their agent and informer and how this links with his compulsion to control everyone else in his world, especially Margaret, his wife. We are drawn in with sympathy and despair as he fights the terrifying desires which threaten that control. The accuracy of John Throne's analysis gives authority to an unorthodox tale.We look at the landscape of Donegal, its bogs, fields and cottages, with a new understanding." - BRIDGET O'TOOLE

*In memory of my
grandmother and mother*

FOREWORD

This book comes out of a conversation I had with my mother one night in her home in Lifford, County Donegal. She was in her eighties, and coming to the end of her life. Thinking about it later I realised that she had been working up to the conversation for many years.

At that time she lived with her sister, also in her eighties, on their small farm. I respected both of them very much for their long lives of hard work and I owed my mother a lot for bringing me into the world and feeding, clothing and looking after me.

Whenever I looked at my mother I saw her back stooped with the years and her hands worn with work. One of her fingers was bent from where it had been broken breaking sticks for the fire and it had not set right. Whenever I listened to my mother, I heard her try to understand the world with the twisted ideological tools provided to her by the conservative organisations of her time. My heart would threaten to break for her, and I would have to turn my head away. She was a very intelligent and strong woman but the system she had been brought up in and lived under was a crushing burden on her back.

Her views could not have been further removed from mine. And yet the harshness of her life, including the confusion and difficulty her ideas brought her, were powerful elements in what made me a Socialist. I looked at how the existing system had made her life so hard and concluded it had no right to exist. My mother, so strongly opposed to my becoming a full-time socialist organiser was, para-doxically, one of the main reasons I took that road.

My mother was a very determined person. She never gave up try-ing to get me to change my ideas and way of life. When totally frus-trated she would refer to a bad head injury and concussion I had received when I was young and she would say, 'You were never right since you got that batter on the head.' This was her analysis of my commitment to my ideas and work.

Whenever I visited her she always had a list of things for me to do. Fix this door, re-hang that gate, fix the fence between these two fields. She was good at drawing up lists, and also good at heaping on the guilt to try and get me to carry them out. It had taken me years of my youth to learn how to ignore her guilt offensives.

On this occasion, in the late 1980s, I had called to see her on a winter night. I had driven up from Dublin on my way to Derry going the long way around through Sligo. I was tired. My mother started to talk as I sat and drank tea and ate her home baked bread and a couple of duck eggs. Then I sat up and listened. I realised that she was talk-ing to me in an entirely different tone from normal. And there were no lists and no guilt. Instead she was telling me something she espe-cially wanted me to know. I realised it was important to both of us that I should listen.

Perhaps, I thought, she wanted to tell me what was on her mind before it was no longer there. Whatever it was, it was clear to me that something different was going on, that my mother was trying to tell me something that was important to her and that I should pay atten-tion. What follows is what my mother told me in a few brief moments that night and is what provides the basis for this book.

'John, you know when Mother was young she was hired out at Allen's over at Rushey. Well what you don't know is that she had a baby. Allen was the father. Then she was taken from Allen's and

Father married her. It was very hard for Mother, John. She had a baby every year after that.'

Then my mother hesitated and looked up at me before she went on. 'And the other thing John, Father was not good to Mother. So you see John. Look at the kind of people we were.'

As my mother told me this her face was twisted up in the most terrible pain and sorrow. I could see she was desperate but also terrified to hear my response. She always spoke of her mother in the most respectful terms and she made clear she loved her with all her heart. But those who ran the ruling institutions of society in which she believed had got her confused and she could not separate the issues properly. She could not always allocate the blame to where it properly belonged.

She loved her mother and did not want to say a wrong word about her, but she had been taught that her mother had done wrong and had sinned. She had been taught that any woman who had a child and was not married had done something wrong. She had been taught that a woman who had a child and was not married was a bad woman. So she said to me with this terrible pain and look of betrayal in her face, 'Look at the kind of people we were.' She was devastated that she was saying this about her mother, but she also wanted to tell me what she saw as the truth about our family.

As I listened I was overwhelmed and humbled by her determination to tell me this. She did not have to tell me anything. She could have just kept quiet. But she believed so much in being honest and facing up to what we did in our lives that she was going to tell me no matter what happened. She was going to tell me that her mother, my grandmother, had a baby whose father was Allen and she was going to tell me that her own father, my grandfather, was not good to her mother.

I thought about what she had said and then replied in the most sincere and strong tone, 'Do not be saying these things Mother. Your mother was a great and wonderful woman. She was sent out there to that Allen animal and he raped her. All the blame, all the sin - I say this Mother because you believe in sin - it is all his. She was able to recover from that terrible injustice and assault she suffered, and have her baby and on top of that endure being given to your father, my grandfather, and have a baby every year from then on. And she brought up all her children to have good hearts. Mother, your mother was a great woman, a true heroine. She was a great person. Wallace, Allen, Campbell, those men are to blame. It is the system that is run by the powerful and rich men that is to blame here. Your mother was a great woman. I wish I could have met her. I wish I could have met my grandmother. She was a great woman.'

My mother did not say any more. But the pain and suffering was reduced in her face. She was very glad to hear this from me. She loved her mother. Her heart broke in thinking about her. The churches and the ruling institutions of society in which she believed, condemned her mother, pushing her herself to condemn her mother. It was a great relief to hear a different view from me, to hear me standing up for her mother, to hear me defend her mother so unconditionally.

She was very glad to hear this different view from me, to hear me stand up for her mother. She most strongly opposed the socialist views I held but it was these very views which allowed me to believe what I did about her mother's life, to take the position I did which comforted her and supported her mother. It was not any sin of her mother's. It was the crime of a rotten system.

This book is dedicated to two people. One is my grandmother. A real heroine who as a very poor young woman, caught up in and sav- aged by the hiring-out system, survived the brutal oppression of that system in rural Ireland at the beginning of the last century, brought her children into the world the best she could and brought them up to have good hearts. It is also dedicated to my mother who loved her mother and all her life kept this love alive in spite of what the established institutions tried to tell her. And who also believed she should tell the truth no matter how hard this was and how it hurt her to speak it.

Inevitably, every episode and detail in this book is not factually accurate. I am also not using the real names of the three men involved. It is not necessary after all this time. It is built around the very basic and limited framework of what my mother told me that winter night in her house outside Lifford and what I understand life was like at that time in that part of the world.

My hope for this book is firstly the belated tribute it pays to my grandmother and the voice that I hope it finally gives her. But I also hope that anybody who reads it will reflect more seriously on the hard, brutal life working class and poor women lived in rural Ireland in the past, on the system and the forces within it that dominated and controlled their lives, and from this, will see how far we have come today. But also see how far we still have to go. There are still those with great power and those with little or none.

The Donegal Woman

CHAPTER ONE

'Aw God save me. What did I do to deserve this? What did my wee girl do? Aw God save us from this. My wee Margaret to go over there now and work from morning to night and sleep in a barn and live in dirt and squalor, and who knows what else might happen to her before it is all over. She is only twelve. She does not know how things work. He says she is only another mouth to feed. But I could do with more help here myself. But sure it all comes down to money. He wants what she can earn. Sure things are tight but we could get by. In under God my heart is breaking, Margaret, Margaret, my wee girl.'

The tears ran out of Mary's eyes as she stood there in her helplessness, in her inability to help her daughter Margaret, in her rage and hatred at her husband and at the world and system in which she lived.

Margaret lived with her mother Mary, and her father, in a thatched cottage in the eastern foothills of the Donegal Mountains. Her two brothers lived there also when they were not hired out. The cottage was made of stone, wood, sods and rushes. Everything was from the surrounding fields. The only rooms were for sleeping and eating. There was no toilet. They went in the fields and hedges nearby. At twelve, Margaret was the youngest in the family and the only girl.

Her brothers and father worked in the couple of rocky fields the family owned, in the few acres of bog they rented, and when they could get the work, to the wealthier farmers in the area.

Margaret helped her mother in the house, doing the cooking and washing for the family, helped in the fields and the bog when things were busy and helped look after the few animals they had. She had left school able to read and write the year before. Margaret's mother worked harder than anybody else in the family. Margaret was being trained to do the same.

Margaret was a small, thin, fair skinned child with light brown hair. She had the habit of holding her head to the one side as she examined everything around her. She wore the same thing everyday. This was a dress her mother made her which hung straight down from her shoulders and stopped around her knees. She was very observant and saw the way her mother had to work nonstop. She was expected to do farm work and at the same time she had to slave for her father and brothers in the house.

Sometimes, when her mother was not looking, Margaret would look at her carrying on exhausted and try and understand why things were as they were. She would try and get the answer from her mother's face. If she was caught doing this her mother would shout: 'What are you dreaming about? Get out there and do something'. Margaret felt terrible when this would happen. Was she making it worse for her mother? But how could this be, she was only trying to understand so she could help her.

But this particular morning it was not Margaret who had annoyed her mother. It was her father. He had ordered Margaret and her one brother who was at home out of the cottage so he could talk to Margaret's mother alone. Mary knew she was going to hear news she did not want to hear.

'Mary, when I was in Convoy at the fair yesterday I talked with

Allen again. He still needs a hand and says he'll take Margaret.' Mary did not answer.

She was stunned by the thought of seeing her daughter hired out, of being sent to that brutal life. Encouraged by his wife's silence, Margaret's father went on.

'Sure Mary, she is only another mouth to feed around here. She's twelve. She should be out there earning her keep. And Allen is a good man. Look at the big place he has over by Rushey. He must have over fifty good acres there. He is a decent man. And sure he's one of our own.' Seeing that his wife could not get up the strength to resist him Margaret's father went on, 'Where is she? I'll go and tell her. She can go today.'

Margaret was playing in the field with her youngest brother. She loved all animals but their donkey was her favourite. It looked round at her and her brother as they took turns climbing on its back and slid-ing off. In between times it ate the grass and weeds around its feet. The family dog lay in the warm sun with its head on its front paws watching them. It was a sheep dog that helped with the animals.

The donkey, the dog, two cows, a few sheep, chickens and ducks made up the family's livestock. Margaret hugged the donkey's head and felt the soft skin beside its nostrils and put her cheek against it. She laughed as she slid off the donkey's back. It was a warm day in the autumn of 1910. Margaret had no idea that these were the last carefree and happy minutes of her life.

'Girl. Come here.' She did not like her father. He was always shouting at her or at her mother or talking rough to them and giving them orders. He was not much different with her brothers. And he did not smell good. He always had a smell of the animals on him and something else too. She did not know what it was. And she remem-bered the times he would come home drunk and shout at them all: 'I do everything around here, without me there would be nothing on the table, we would not have a roof over our heads. Aye, you are close to good for nothing,' and on and on. Margaret's heart broke for her mother who worked her fingers to the bone. She did not like her father and she was afraid of him.

But she turned towards him to see what he wanted. She always obeyed his orders. She knew if she did not he would either shout at her or hit her. And anyway it did not occur to her to disobey his orders. 'Girl, it's time you earned your keep. You are only another mouth to feed here. I spoke to Mr. Allen today. He needs a yard hand. He is willing to take you on for six months and see how you work out. You know Mr. Allen, you see him at church on Sunday. He's one of our own. You'll be all right with him. He's a good man he has a big place over by Rushey. He has over fifty good acres. The hard work will be good for you.' The savage brutality of his decision and the way he announced it passed her father by.

Margaret could not absorb what she was hearing. She was only another mouth to feed? What did that mean? She was being sent away? But her mother, what about her mother? She would not let this happen. She was her mother. To Allen? Being hired out to Allen for six months. Allen was one of her own. A Protestant. Not a Catholic. What did this mean? She was being sent away from home. From her mother. From the donkey and the dog and her brothers. From the nights sitting around the fire. From her home. She could not speak. Her heart was breaking. Her chest was squeezing it into nothing.

And she was terrified of the unknown that was opening up in front of her. She thought she had some idea about what the loss of her home would mean. But even here she could not absorb the terrible loneliness and suffering this would bring with it. She was leaving all that she had known all her life, all that was familiar to her, even if it was far from being all good. But at this time she remembered the good things best. Like her mother and the nights with all the family round the turf fire. And the donkey and the dog and.... But what was she going to? This was totally unknown to her. She was terrified. The terror felt like it was smothering her.

Margaret had no knowledge of the hiring out system. Young people and workers of all ages were hired out to the local wealthier farmers for a fixed amount of time, usually six months. They lived in the farmer's barns or, if they were very lucky, their houses. They got no pay until the end of their contracted time and if they left before their time was up they got nothing. Many farmers tried to make conditions so terrible towards the end of the contract time that the workers would not be able to stick it any more and would leave. They would then get no wages at all. This put the worker under the absolute control of the farmer.

'Well, you might as well be on your way. There is no reason to be hanging about. Here, I will tell you the way. Just listen to me and think about what you are doing and you will be grand.'

Grand? The word stuck in Margaret's head. It would never again mean anything to her but being put out of her home.

'Look. Walk down to the crossroads. You know it because we take it to church. It's about three miles. Then take a right up the road to Rushey. About two miles up on the right you'll see a tree that fell in last year's big wind. Two fields past that is the lane up to Mr. Allen's place. You will be there by evening if you start right away.'

He turned and shouted over his shoulder. 'Come on out Mary, Margaret is leaving.' At the sound of her father's shouting her brother came out of the byre and stood with his father. Her mother came out of the house. She was white in the face. She carried two thick slices of dry bread in her hands which she gave Margaret for the road and along with that Margaret's only other dress.

She wanted to scream her opposition to Margaret's going. Her wee girl. But faced with the father's control over her life and the widespread acceptance of hiring out, and the father's ownership of the cottage and land and she owning nothing, she said nothing but a couple of words to Margaret.

'Be good now, girl.'

That seemed worse to Margaret than what her father had done. She had expected her mother to help her. But she had not, she had not stopped her father sending her away, had only told her to 'Be good now, girl'. Then she turned and went and stood by the cottage door. What kind of a thing was that to say? Margaret was not being bad. What kind of a thing was that to say? Why did her mother not help her?

Margaret and all of them stood fixed to the spot. Nobody said a word. They all stood unmoving, held quiet by what was taking place. The brutality of the system in which they lived momentarily froze the family in place. They could not breathe. Margaret was only a child and she was being sent from her family into a vicious workplace environment by an economic and political system that none of them understood. They could not identify the enemy so they could not act against it. They were paralyzed. And for a few seconds all were equally victims.

Margaret looked from one to the other of them to be saved, the rest of them looked at Margaret unable to understand and see a way to fight this system that was placing them in this pain and heartbreak and paralysis. So faced with their pain and ignorance threatening to make them passive in front of the system, they acted to remove the most immediate and obvious source of their crisis which was Margaret. The father took the lead. He was going to see life would go on. No realistic alternatives existed in his way of looking at things. There was no time for standing about, there was work to be done. Margaret had to go.

'Be off with you now, girl. It will take all the time that's left in the day for you to get there.' And he pointed in the direction of the road.

Margaret's habit of obeying her father was well drummed into her. She turned and began to walk slowly towards the dirt road, which ran alongside the gable wall of the cottage. She dragged her feet and hoped something would happen, that she would get sick and die, that she would collapse with a broken leg and be unable to walk.

Her mother joined her father and brother and they walked in silence across the yard after Margaret who was walking toward the opening onto the dirt road. Margaret was holding the bread and her dress in front of her in her two hands. She did not look around as she slowly moved out onto the road. She was barefoot. All she wore was her rough woollen dress, ragged and stained. It came down to her knees. The mother could not keep quiet. 'Be good now, girl' she said again in another desperate effort to show her love.

When she was about twenty yards up the road Margaret stopped, turned and looked round. She could not understand what she was seeing or what was happening. They were her family. There was her mother. But they were sending her away. She held the two slices of bread. Who was Allen? One of her own. A good man. He had over fifty good acres. She could not speak. She turned again and walked slowly away from her youth and happiness. Her family turned and went back into their yard and back to their work. The dog which had followed Margaret part of the way down the road, looked at Margaret leaving and at the family going back in to the cottage and again at Margaret and it whimpered. Then it too turned and went back in.

CHAPTER TWO

Margaret could not stop thinking about what her mother had said. 'Be good now, girl'. What kind of a thing was that to say? Especially at this time when her life was shattering around her. 'Be good now, girl'. She had done nothing bad. What did she mean? Why did she say it? What kind of a thing was this to say? She had not been bad.

Margaret did not understand that at this time the Protestant peasantry from which she and her mother came, could see no way to change their lives. They could only see the need to fit in with the orders and demands of what they considered their betters, the richer farmers, the landlord class and the British Protestant regime that ran the country. So, as she was being sent off to be hired out, Margaret was being instructed to fit into this nightmare system, not to rebel, not to object, but to 'be good now, girl' and accept her lot. Henry Joy McCracken, the great Protestant leader of the 1798 rebellion, was long forgotten.

The land sloped downward in the direction Margaret was walking. Her family's cottage and few fields were located at the top end of the scrubby grassland. A few hundred yards further up and the green of the fields gave way to the brown and black of the bog where everybody around cut the turf for their firing. This sloped on upward toward the top of the mountain. The last half mile up to the top of the mountain was gray and brown with rocks and heather bushes.

The hedges around Margaret's home were made of rocks stacked on top of each other and every now and then gray rocks stuck their noses up through the grass. As she walked away from her home and further down the mountain, the rock hedges gradually changed to small hawthorn bushes and the fields were no longer punctured with so many rocks. There was more soil on top of the rocks the further down she went. This meant better crops, better food, better lives.

In spite of Margaret's family being Protestants, they did not live on this better land lower down on the mountain. To try and keep the loyalty of the Protestant peasantry, the British rulers tried to give them the better land compared to what was given to the Catholic peasantry. Margaret was not aware of any of these realities. Nor was she aware of why her family, in spite of being Protestants, had rocky land. The truth was Margaret's grandfather, like some other Protestant peasants, could not be fully accommodated by this system of privilege and division and fell through the cracks in the system.

He had been one of a large family the oldest son of which had got the family farm with the better land lower down the valley. The rest of them except Margaret's grandfather who had a bad leg, had gone to America. Margaret's grandfather had picked up a few skills that were handy working about the big house of Brown. Brown was the agent of Lord Taverstock, the largest landowner in the area, and a big landowner himself, and from his contacts with this Protestant landlord. Margaret's grandfather had managed to work his way into the few rocky acres up the side of the mountain which was now the small holding of her father. With this, and the few other skills he could provide directly to Brown, he and the family survived to hold onto this small piece of land.

As Margaret walked she at first did not think of eating the bread. Her head was not working. It was frozen by the shock. She had been put out of her home by her father and all her family. Her mother too.

Her mouth was dry with the terrible pain and trauma of it all. She just held the bread and her dress and walked. She held them out in front of her with her two hands like she was going to give them to somebody eventually. Her anguish was terrible. For a second she thought about the soft skin on the side of the donkey's nostril. But it already seemed to be so far away that it was no longer real.

After two miles Margaret had to go. The physical needs of her body forced her out of her paralyzed mental state. She looked around to see there was nobody about and then climbed in over the hedge that ran along the side of the road. Hunkering down behind the hedge she defecated and urinated. The familiarity of these actions helped her feel some normality again in her head and her body. The mental paralysis was leaving her. She picked some grass, making sure there were no thorns or nettles in it, and wiped herself. She threw the soiled grass on top of her waste. And picking up the bread and dress from the stone she had set them on, she climbed out onto the road again and walked on.

As Margaret walked, her rough dress scourged her legs and the skin on the inside of her thighs was being rubbed raw. It seemed like her misery was increasing with each step. She watched the dirt between her toes get darker as it mingled with her sweat. Without thinking she began to eat the bread. It was dry and stuck in her throat. But she ate it anyway. When she was finished she bent over the stream by the side of the road and drank.

The water was cool and clean. It was so different from everything else in her day. Its contrast with the rest of the day and the rest of her life shocked her but she could not understand in what way. She walked on and as she did so she eventually came to the big house where her grandfather had worked for most of his life. Margaret had only heard about his life there in the most general of terms.

The Browns lived in it. Margaret knew they were rich. The house was surrounded by tall trees with great thick trunks showing the occupants had been there for a long time and were not scarce of firewood for most of the time. Oaks and chestnuts. There was enough soil on top of the rocks here to let them put down deep enough roots to support themselves. The Browns sat in the front seat in the church. Were they her own kind too, she wondered?

She had been up to the big house once with her mother, but they had only been at the back door. They were not asked in. She had seen into the big kitchen with the copper pots and piles of food. The kitchen was as big as her family's whole house. There were servants. Her friend Rachael's mother worked there. She didn't sit at the front of the church with the Browns. She sat at the back with Margaret and her family.

The Browns had a wee girl about Margaret's age. She saw her now and then going past on the horse and trap when she herself was walking to church. She always had on white dresses and white bonnets. They were always clean and bright. Margaret thought with surprise she must have white things to wear under her dress too. It occurred to Margaret that she herself had nothing to wear under her dress, white or otherwise.

The wee Brown girl had shoes. She did not get dirty toes, nor scourged thighs rubbed raw by a rough dress. She did not even have to walk. She would never be sent away to Allen's for six months. She would never have to go behind the hedge. She thought more about what her friend Rachael had told her about what went on in the big house and the wee Brown girl.

There was one woman working in the house who had nothing else to do but look after the wee girl. Day and night she looked after her and did whatever the wee girl's parents told her to do for her. Margaret tried to imagine this in her mind. One woman to do nothing but look after her. Margaret thought why her mother did not have somebody to help look after her children when they were young.

Rachael had also told her that there were two women who worked there who did nothing but wash the clothes for the wee girl and her parents. Both what they wore and what they used. Margaret's mother washed the clothes for everybody at home. And at the Browns' there were four people who worked in the kitchen cooking and serving. And on top of that the mother had her own servant and the father his own and there was that butler man too. Margaret was not sure what he did.

As she walked past the house Margaret wondered about this and why she had to be out there walking with nothing while they had so much, why her mother had to be slaving at home seven days a week and the Browns had so many servants that they did not have to work at all. She did not put this into clear thoughts in her mind but Margaret felt in some way that it was not right. But also part of her wished she were the wee Brown girl. Her heart was breaking.

Margaret came to the crossroads. She had been here before many times when she walked to church every Sunday morning. The church was a place of threats and fear, strange music and a man in a strange costume always telling them what to do and threatening them with hell. The only good thing about it for Margaret was that it was where she saw Rachael and other girls her own age now that she had left school.

The man in the strange clothes told her that if she did not do right she would never get to heaven; instead she would burn in hell forever. She had a vague feeling that doing wrong was some way connected to her being a girl. It did not occur to Margaret to turn left and go to the church for help in her pain and loneliness and fear. Churches were not places where people like her, in situations like she was in, could get help. If it would tell her anything at all it would tell her what her mother told her. It would tell her to be good, it would tell her to submit and to go to Allen's. Keep doing what she was told and to be good.

So, turning right and off the road that would take her to the village and the church, she headed for Rushey. It was the first time she
had been on that road. Night was only a couple of hours away. She
was frightened so she tried to pick up her step and hurry. After an
hour walking she came to the tree that had been blown down in the
big wind. Past it to the lane. Up the lane. She wished she could find
some way not to come to the end of the lane. She felt panic but she
stifled it. The house stood up straight. It was not anything like as big
as the Brown's but two storeys and three or four times bigger than her
family's cottage. For some reason Margaret wondered if they had an
outhouse where they went to the toilet. She had never seen an outhouse, only heard about them.

When she came to the house she saw that a dog was tethered to
an old cartwheel at the side of the house. It began to bark. He must
be a bad one, Margaret thought. She would have to watch for him. A
fat woman came out of the back door of the house. The house made
up one side of a square of buildings, which included a barn, stables
and byres. The fat woman looked at her with hard eyes that assessed
her. Her look was without pity.

She looked at Margaret like she was a thing. 'You must be the
Wallace girl. Hey, Robert, the Wallace girl is here.'

Margaret thought that maybe the woman would help her. After all
she was a woman and Margaret was a girl. But the woman looked at
her, sneered, then scornfully laughed at her and went into the house.
A fat man came out.

He was dirty with the dirt of the soil and animals and himself. The
front of his jumper was stained with food mixed up with his own saliva,
which had become mixed together over a prolonged period and turned
the front of his jumper into a hardened surface. His stubbled face was
not clean. He sucked at his teeth and Margaret could see the hollows
between them were filled with old dirty food. He did not look kind.

'You are the Wallace girl. I hope your father told you. You'll be here for six months. At the end of that we'll see how you do. There'll be no time for playing about. You will be working here. The only way there will be a place for you here is with hard work. Your father needs the money. I've plenty for you to do. Come on.'

Like she was used to with her father and like she was trained to do when she was at school, Margaret said nothing and followed the order.

CHAPTER THREE

Margaret walked after him as he crossed the yard and climbed up a set of rough stone steps to the first floor of a barn. Inside was almost dark. She made out a partition about three feet from the gable wall. It was made of boards that were worn down and warped and had spaces between them. He pointed behind this partition. Old sacking had been stitched together and filled with straw to make what passed for a mattress. There were holes in it with straw sticking out.

'You sleep here.' Two cats lying on it leapt onto the partition and sat on its top looking down. 'Don't mind the cats. They keep it warm. And anyway they chase away the rats.' He laughed as he said it, but in a cruel way.

She looked at her sleeping place. She would not be staying in their house. She would be sleeping in their barn. But her father had said he was one of their own? What did that mean when she was to be sleeping out here with the rats and the cats? She was silent in front of this new shock. But look at the size of their house. She did not think they had any children. Allen pointed to some old sacks hanging on some nails. 'If you are cold they'll keep you warm.' That was it. A straw mattress and sacks in the barn. It did not occur to her there was nowhere to put her things. She did not have any things except the dress she wore and the other she had with her.

She stood stunned before this new brutality. 'Come on then, girl. You might as well get started.'

What was he saying? After that walk she was not even going to get to rest. He led the way down the steps again. She left her dress down and followed. He led across the rough yard on which there were piles of manure outside the doors of the byres and the stables, and opened the bottom half of a door, the top half of which already lay open. The smell of pigs was strong. There was a sow and a dozen or so wee pigs inside. The sow was lying on her side and the wee ones were poking and sucking at her.

'Take that grape and clean out that pen. Throw the dirt out that hole in the wall there. Then come to the house for the feed. Get in there, don't be feared of her.' He turned and left.

But Margaret was very afraid as she took the grape, pushed the door to the stall further open and edged in. Her family had no pigs and so she had never worked with them before. The wee pigs looked at her and ran around squealing. The sow looked at her and grunted a warning. Margaret's bare feet sank in the pig dirt and it squeezed up between her toes. Her nostrils tried to reject the smell. The old sow stood up and looked at her, grunting. Margaret slowly tried to scrape the dirt from around her. She threw it out the hole in the wall. The dirt and the smell got on her dress. The old sow, assured she was no threat, gave a soft grunt and gave her a nudge with her nose. It was the first friendly thing that had happened to Margaret that day.

When she was finished Margaret went to the house and stood outside the back door. She did not know what to do so she just stood there. The woman came out with a large bucket full of boiled spuds.

'Mash these up and mix this Injun meal in with them. Give half to the sow, half of what's left to the two cows in the field beside the lane and the rest to the two horses. Get going now, girl.'

Margaret could not lift the bucket of spuds. It was too heavy. So she began dragging it across the yard. It cut into her hands. The woman shouted at her. 'Don't drag that bucket. You'll pull a hole in it.'

She went into the house again and Margaret tried to drag it more quietly.

She could not find a spud pounder so she squeezed the spuds with her hands. They were hot. She mixed in the Injun meal. Then she dragged it to the pig house. The sow and the wee pigs grunted and squealed with delight and welcome. They were hungry. The cows took half what was left and the horses the rest. She left the bucket down in the yard by the back door and stood and waited again. The woman came out. The expression on her face said that she knew Margaret had not done right even before she looked to see what it was.

'You did not clean that bucket right. Look, there's still spuds in it. Clean it out and give what's left to the horses. There's to be no waste here. You mind that girl, there'll be no waste here'.

Margaret did as she was told and cleaned out the bits of spuds. She then went back.

'Wash that bucket, girl.'

She did so in the stream that ran past the house and down the side of the lane. She went back to the door.

'That's better. Mind you do that right from now on. There's to be no waste here.'

Margaret was to come to learn that this was the central slogan of this woman's life. That she saw her job in life as making sure that there 'would be no waste here'.

Margaret was too young to understand that this did not refer to her own life. It could be wasted as far as the Allens were concerned. In fact it was there to be wasted. To them it was not worth anything in the first place. The man came out.

'It's getting dark. Go to your bed. I will be getting you up early in the morning. Gone now.' And he went in and closed the door.

After a minute she went up the steps to the barn. She was terrified. Twelve years old, and going to sleep alone in a barn in a strange place.

Rats. The cats. Her eyes became accustomed to the dark. The cats were sitting on the bedding looking at her. She went towards them and they leapt off and sat watching from the top of the partition. Her exhaustion fought with her fear. But the trauma and work of the day, overpowered her fear. She went to lie down. The pig dirt was wet and dirty and smelly on her dress and against her legs. She realised she was hungry and she ate the two pieces of dry bread the Allen woman had given her. Why had she not eaten some of the spuds she'd fed the pigs? She was also thirsty.

And she also had to go. But where would she go? She had been so concentrated on doing what the Allens had been telling her to do and so frightened and disorientated, she had forgotten her own needs. Where would she go? She could not go in the barn. She was afraid to go outside in the wrong place in case they saw her and they would think she was dirty and stupid. But she had to go. She was only twelve. She wished she was home. Her mother's voice was in her ear. She stood for a while. The cats were watching.

She had to go. Slowly she went back out and down the stairs. She crept quietly around the corner. The dog started to bark. She hunkered down and went. And returned quickly up the steps again. She was wet and dirty, both from her own waste and the waste of the animals. She wished she was home where she could get help from her mother. But her mother had not helped her when she was being put out.

The cats were back on the bedding. She lay down as quiet as she could. 'Wee pussies,' she said. She was shocked to realise that it was the first time she had spoken since her father had told her she was going. She spoke to the cats mainly because she wanted them to stay and keep the rats away. They went to the side of the stall and watched. She slowly lay down. She was hungry. She wished she had eaten a spud. She smelled herself. The cats watched. She thought about the old sow and its friendly grunt.

'Wee pussies,' she said again. She wondered about her speaking. She was surprised in a way that she still could. The blows she had received one after another all day had knocked the voice out of her. But now she realised it was coming back, it was still there. She could still speak. She felt better when she thought about this, when she realised this. But she was still afraid of being alone and of being in the dark. She stopped thinking about her ability to speak. She was also tired. Her exhaustion dragged her down into sleep where her body and spirit would get a rest.

She began to drift off and the horrors of the day began to slip away. As she did, the cats crept back and slept on the bedding, curling against her for the heat. Their heat in turn comforted her and she fell asleep and dreamt she was back home playing with the donkey. Her dreams also took her into the big house of the wee Brown girl. These dreams gave her mind a rest. They healed her mind and spirit a bit. But they did not last long and the morning came too soon. Allen called her awake with his harsh cruel shouts bringing her back from where she had been in her dreams, back to where she was still lying on the straw mattress in Allen's barn and still smelling of pig dung. The dreams had gone. She wished she was dead.

It was a few days later, a Sunday morning, and Margaret heard the Allens arguing. 'Look she's not ours. If Wallace wants her to go to church then he should have sent her with more clothes or she should have washed that dress. He cannot expect us to get her one. She has only been here less than a week. She will have to stay home. That's all about it. I will go and tell her what to be at when we are gone.' Margaret could hear the woman's words as she washed the bucket in the stream that ran down the side of the yard and the lane. Then she heard her come out of the house and approach her.

'Girl, we're off to church now. You have that pig house cleaned out when we get back and clean out the two cows' stalls in the byre too. Don't you be doing nothing, girl. We'll see your father and we don't want to be telling him you're a bad worker.'

The woman turned on her heel and went round the corner of the house to where Allen was waiting with the horse and trap. Margaret heard the horse's feet on the lane as they left for church.

It was Margaret's first Sunday away from home. She had been at Allen's now nearly a week. To that moment she had not thought of going to church. Now it was all she could think of and it made her isolation at Allen's even worse. Now all she wanted was to get away from Allen's for a while, to get to somewhere that was not Allen's, to get away from his and his wife's orders, to get away from the byre and the pig house and the work. Her heart was breaking. Why didn't they take her to church? She wanted to get away. She wept and the tears ran down her cheeks.

Chapter Four

As she wept, it struck her that the woman was talking about her dirty dress which smelled of pig dung and cow dung and sweat. After the first day she had left her old dirty dress aside and worn the second one not thinking. Now she had two dirty smelly dresses. People would be smelling her and looking at her and they would not want to be near her. That was what the Allen woman was shouting at her husband about. She was telling him that they would not buy her another dress and so they could not take her to church. When she realised that it was her dirty dress which was the reason they were saying they would not take her, she was not sure if this made her feel better or worse.

She turned and went into the pig house where the dung squeezed up between her toes. The old pig grunted at her and she put her hand on its back. It looked up into her eyes and grunted again. The wee ones ran around squealing with a mixture of fright and delight. They pushed and bit and dunted each other as they fought for the sow's teats. The sow had a quietness, a contentment, about her and as she no longer saw Margaret as a threat she was happy to let herself be scratched. Margaret in turn felt a comfort in scratching her.

But then she thought this would make her even smellier. She pulled her hand back from the sow. She pulled her feet out of the dung. She stepped back out of the pig house and into the yard still facing into the pig house and looking at the sow and her wee ones. She began to breathe deep. She was in turmoil. She felt comfort in scratching the sow and touching and being part of the sow and her wee pigs' lives. When she was with the pigs and the other animals this was now the only time in her days when she had some warmth and comfort in her life, some feeling of caring, some feeling of belonging.

But this was making her dirtier and dirtier and this in turn was cutting her off even more from getting to go to church and seeing other people and maybe even some of her family. She knew her mother would not be there. She stayed at home to work. Margaret stood outside the pig house and fought with herself. She wanted to go to the church and see other people. She had to. She could not stay here. Margaret began to weep.

As she wept she sank down onto her knees in the yard. The tears ran down her cheeks. Her desperation was terrible. She had to get a clean dress and go to church. Nothing could be allowed to stop her. Her weeping merged with rage and determination to do this. She would get a clean dress and go. She would not allow herself to end up only friends with the sow and the animals. She would get a clean dress and go. Her weeping rose in volume. It came from the very stomach of her, she howled as she hurled her weeping defiance at the injustice and cruelty of it all. The sow looked out the door at her with concern in its eyes. And then gradually her weeping subsided. She had exhausted herself. She lay forward on her knees making only the occasional sob. And she lay for a long time, she lay until there was nothing left in her but exhaustion.

The old sow had been watching her through the open door. Now she came forward and nudged Margaret with her nose and grunted in a low tone. Margaret scratched her on the head and felt one of her ears. The sow pushed herself against Margaret's dress. Margaret reached for the grape and walked further inside the pigpen. Her feet sank in the pig dung. She looked down passively as it came up between her toes. The smell got stronger. The wee pigs ran over her feet and squealed. She sank the grape in the mixture of dung and straw and threw it out the top half of the back door that was open to the back yard. She was more at home here with the sow and the wee pigs.

She no longer felt it in her to care about the smell or to put up a fight against it. She was part of the smell now. It was not getting on her anymore. She was part of it. She no longer felt the need to keep herself clean. It was impossible and too late. The smell of the animals and Allen's farm was now her. If she did not accept this she could not go on. Not only that but the only warmth and kindness in her days now came from the animals and this came with their smell. She could not afford to think of it anymore.

What church? What dress? She was the pig house and the byre and the stable and the animal's dung. Life was only bearable if she subsumed herself in this and stopped trying to fight her way out and not always be thinking about getting a clean dress. She did not think of this and church much anymore. This was strengthened in her when Allen came home from church and told her he had spoken with her father and her father had said it was okay for her not to go to church. This made sense. Her father would go along with Allen and getting his money.

Margaret's work at Allen's was not only a question of getting dirty. It pulled and tore at her muscles and skin. The worst thing was her hands. After a few hours the first day she was there, they were torn and bleeding from dragging the bucket and using the grape and wheeling the barrow. There was never any thought of doing anything to heal these wounds. This was the way working people got hard hands; the way people got the calluses on their hands which were the protective covers for the softer skin. But the pain of Margaret's skinned hands stung her twenty-four hours a day. She could not get to sleep at night for the pain. Her feet were okay. They had become hardened over the years as she had always walked barefoot and working at Allen's was just more walking. But her hands were being torn to bits by the new work she was forced to do.

The Allens never said a word to her about how they could help with her skinned hands. The only comment she heard was between themselves when she heard Allen saying to his wife 'That will harden her up, sure we all had to go through it when we were her age.' When she was at the stream washing the bucket she would always wash her hands, let the cool water run over her hands. The cool clean water seemed to be the saving of her every now and then. She did this at night also before she would go to bed. She did it first to relieve the pain but gradually she realised that it would probably be good to clean the wounds on her hands, the skinned parts of her hands. For some reason every time she ran the water on her hands she thought of the wee Brown girl and that she would never have skinned hands.

She tried to lessen the pain by dragging the bucket using a different part of her hands and holding the grape and the shovel with a different part of her hands. For a few brief moments this worked but all it meant was that new areas of her hands got skinned, the pain spread, there was no way around it. It took over three weeks before the skin began to callus and harden, before her hands began to evolve to deal with the jobs they were being forced to take on, before they began to adjust to the friction and to produce the calluses that could stand up to the bucket handle and the shafts of the grape and shovel. Margaret gradually felt the pain subside and over time go away altogether and, as it did, she could see her hands had changed into the rough hard hands of her mother.

'Right, girl. It's time for you to start taking on the milking. There are only the two cows and you will be fit for them easy. Come on over and we will get you started'.

Margaret followed Allen towards the byre where she had put the two cows a few minutes before. Up until then it was either the woman or Allen himself who milked the two cows. The other man who worked as a day labourer on the farm, only did horse work and helped Allen look after the sheep on the hill. The cows were chained and standing in their stalls. Bringing them in and chaining them up had been her job since she had been there. Now Allen was saying this was about to change. She was going to have to milk them too.

'Get that stool and get over here.' Allen pointed to a three legged stool made from crude rough wood. 'Put it down there and get down and get started.'

Margaret had seen the cows getting milked many times so she knew what to do. But she did not know how to squeeze the cow's teats and she was also afraid, as the cows would kick at times. So very timidly she moved forward towards the cow.

'Come on, girl. She won't eat you.'

Margaret moved forward, placed the stool on the ground beside the cow and level with its udder. She placed the bucket under the cow and slowly sat down on the stool.

'Pull in closer and put your head against her side and take a hold of her.'

The cow looked around to see what was going on. This was new to her also. She had a new milker. Margaret sat there.

'Come on, girl. Get a hold of those teats and get started.'

Margaret reached forward and grasped the two front teats of the cow and squeezed.

'Now don't be too hard on her. Give her a chance. Squeeze one at a time and you will slowly get the hang of it.'

Margaret squeezed but nothing came out. She tried with the other hand. Again nothing came out. She squeezed again. The cow moved on her back feet. She was not happy. She switched her tail and hit Margaret on the head with its dung-encrusted end. When this happened, the long hard fine hairs of the tail whipped round her face and the pain was sharp. The cow moved again from one back foot to another as she showed her annoyance and discontent.

Margaret kept trying to squeeze some milk out of the cow's teats. Nothing was coming. Allen was standing glowering at her. She kept trying. Her hands were able to go around the teats and squeeze but something was wrong. She tried to squeeze them from the top down and push the milk down towards the end and out into the bucket. But it was not working. She squeezed again trying harder and this time she could feel the milk go down the inside of the teat but she was simultaneously squeezing the bottom of the teat and it could not get out. This hurt the cow and she drew her back foot forward, kicked back, knocking over the bucket and throwing Margaret back against the wall.

Allen never even asked if she was all right. Instead he spoke with impatience and annoyance.' It's a good job there was no milk in that bucket. I would of thought that your father would have taught you how to milk. Here, let me show you. Let me have that teat. Here look. Take it and squeeze it from the top down but at the same time leave the bottom open and this will allow the milk to get out. That is the way to do it. Do you see now, girl? Try it now yourself. And another thing, don't put the bucket on the ground. She will kick it over again. Pull yourself in closer to her and put your head against her flank and hold the bucket between your knees.'

Margaret was afraid of the cow but she did what Allen told her. She was also for the first time very conscious of how Allen was so close to her and the smell of him. She did not like it. She did not understand it. But she took the teat in her hand again and tried to squeeze from the top down as he said. A dribble of milk came out of the end of the teat. 'That's it. Now you will soon get the way of it if you keep at it. I will be back in a while to see how you are doing.' Margaret sat at the side of the cow and squeezed her teats. She moved from the front two teats to the back two and back again to rest her hands as they got very sore after a minute or two of squeezing.

Her hands were not strong enough for the job. But she had no choice. She had to do what she was told. She had to milk this cow and the other one. She kept at it, kept squeezing the teats. As she thought about her situation, she thought less about her squeezing and she squeezed the top of one of the teats too hard so that the milk went down the inside of the teat and could not flow easily out of the hole at the bottom. This hurt the cow. She gave a roar and kicked out again.

Her kick caught Margaret and the bucket and threw them both out onto the ground. Margaret herself hit the ground and skinned her arm and leg. She was dazed and confused. Sitting up she looked at the cow which had turned its head around and was looking at her. Margaret tried to gather herself to get up. But she was not able to do so before Allen came in.

'What is going on here? I heard her roar. What happened with this? Why is this milk spilled? This is a waste. There is to be no waste here. What happened here? This is not good. Get up and get in there again and be more careful this time. We cannot have you spilling the milk. Get up and get back to the work.'

Again not a word about was she hurt or was she able to get back to the work. Not a word about her hands being strong enough. Not a word about her ability to squeeze the teats correctly to get the milk out of them. Not a word of concern for Margaret. It was only about the milk and that there would be 'no waste here.' Margaret dragged herself up to her feet and lifted the stool and set it back on its legs by the cow and very carefully sat down and grasped the teats again and slowly began to squeeze them, this time keeping close attention so that her squeezing did not hurt the cow and result in her getting kicked again. Gradually Margaret got a rhythm going and the milk began to slowly rise in the bucket.

Allen came in again with another larger bucket and told Margaret to empty the milk into that one so that it would not be wasted if she was kicked again. Margaret kept doing that regularly as she milked the cow and gradually the cow's udder became slack and her teats empty and the larger bucket filled up. Margaret got up and moved on to the other cow. Her hands were hurting her as they were not used to the work but she had to keep at it. Allen came back to check on her and he looked at the larger bucket that she was emptying the milk into. Then he came close to her and looked into the bucket that was between her knees.

Then he reached in and touched her thigh as he looked to see how much was in that bucket. 'Aye you are getting the way of it. And your hands will soon get the strength into them.' Then he laughed in a sneering cruel way, 'Aye, and that will be good if you would ever need them for another job too.'

Margaret did not know what he was talking about but she felt that there was something dirty and dangerous about his tone and the way he touched her and the way he looked and how he spoke.

This feeling was even more strengthened as Allen stood close and watched her milk the second cow. 'There you see. Take it like that. Squeeze from the top down. Then the milk will get out.' He laughed again sneeringly and looked at her. 'You will know enough about all kinds of milking before you are finished. You are not too young even now for a bit of milking of a different kind. I will have to keep an eye on you.'

Margaret felt dirty and frightened at his words.

Chapter Five

And this was the way things went day after day, week after week, month after month. Working every waking hour, sleeping with the cats, getting abuse and orders from the Allens. The only kind words were from the sow and the cats and sometimes one of the cows which she had been taught how to milk, gave her a kind look. The only time she was not in anguish was when she was asleep, and sometimes not even then. She no longer cried. The brutality of her life had dried up her insides.

'Girl! Girl! Wake up. It's morning. Get up and get them cows milked, the houses cleaned out and the animals fed. Your father is coming today. Your six months are up. He will be here for your money. Even though you have not been as hard a worker as you could have been, I will pay him. But it's only out of the goodness of my heart mind you. Get up now girl.'

She could not believe what Allen was saying. Her father was coming. She would see her father. She would be going home. She would see her mother, her brothers, the donkey, the dog. For the first time in six months, she had some life in her step as she went down the steps and crossed the yard. She fairly flew at her work. The old sow did not know what was wrong. Margaret hardly gave her a pet that morning. She felt like smiling but she didn't from lack of practice.

At midday she heard them calling her. 'Girl! Girl!' She ran out of the byre and saw her father at the door of Allen's house. But there was something different about him as he talked to Allen. He was not giving orders. He had a funny smile on his face. His voice had a high tone. She wondered was he sick. No, it was not that. He seemed frightened of Allen. She did not know how to approach this man who was her father but not like her father. He was not giving orders. He was subservient to Allen.

He heard her approach. Then he was like himself again when he turned and spoke to her. His voice deepened in tone and became louder.

'Girl, have you been working hard for Mister Allen here? Have you been doing what he says? Mister and Missus Allen have been good to you. You're taller. Now look Mister Allen has given me the money. This is going to be very useful to us. Your mother says you're to be a good girl. She will be glad to hear Mister Allen is looking after you so well. Here I brought you a dress. Your mother sewed it. Now you can wear this and come to church on Sunday if Mr. Allen can spare you.'

What was he talking about? Was she not going home? What was he talking about? Margaret thought she would be crushed there and then. Driven down into the ground. She looked at her father. What was he saying?

'Now then I must be off, girl. You keep on working away here and do what Mister Allen tells you.'

Margaret watched her father walk away down the lane. He had the money in his pocket. She held the dress in her hand. It was worse than when he had come to her in the yard at home six months before and told her she was only another mouth to feed and sent her away. She wished she could die.

Instead, standing there in that moment, she closed off and shut down another piece of herself. She killed off another piece of the hope and joy in herself. And a big piece. It was too painful to hold on to the hope that she would have an enjoyable and good life. That good things would ever happen to her. She could not endure the disappointment. She was not going home. She had to stay with the Allens for six more months or for how ever long her father and Allen decided. She could not endure this if she still had hope close to the top of her head. It had to be buried deep or killed off.

'Now, girl, go back and finish cleaning out that byre. You heard your father, you are to do what I tell you. Go on now.'

Margaret went back. She continued her work. The rhythmic repetitive work acted like a mechanical movement in her brain. Her pain and anguish seemed to be made bearable by this. She no longer hurt in the same terrible way. It was replaced by a kind of dullness of her spirit. But she never felt hope or happiness and joy and laughter never passed her lips. And she never spoke a word to a human being from one day's end to the next. And in spite of the dress, she never did get to go to church. There was always some work that the Allens made her do on Sundays.

Her second six months came and went and then her third. At the end of each six months her father came and took the money and told her that her mother said she was to be good and do what she was told by Mister Allen. She had not seen her mother in nearly two years. She had been working every day over this time. Her hands were rough and hard like a grown labouring man. Her body was dirty. Her feet were permanently caked with dirt. She smelled of pigs and cattle and horses and herself. But she was not aware of this now. She was used to her smell. The patterns it left on her nose and brain were familiar and no longer offensive to her.

It was getting to the autumn of 1912 and she was fourteen. As usual she had gone to her sleeping place and covered herself with a sack. She was no longer hungry at night as she had been when she had first come to Allen's. To the porridge for breakfast, the slice of bread and spuds at midday, and the two slices and two eggs in the evening, all handed to her at the back door, she added a few spuds and Injun meal that she took from the animals feed without the Allens knowing. She drank water out of the spring by the side of the house. She fell asleep with the cats beside her.

Sometime in the middle of the night she awoke. Something was wrong. What was it? She listened and sat up, all her senses searching. What had wakened her? What was wrong? She sat motionless. Then she became aware of some wetness between her legs. What? She put her hand down and felt wetness on the inside of her thighs. She had wet herself. But it didn't feel right. What? She brought her hand up but she could not see in the dark. She smelled her fingers.

That part of her she had always been made to feel bad about. She never touched herself there. She never washed herself there. She smelled there. She had no place to wash anyway but her mother had only ever told her to wash her face and hands. Once she was scratching herself down there and her mother had told her so sharply never to touch herself there that she was frightened off for good. 'That's bad,' her mother had said. There was something about the church and that part of her. But she did not know what. But why was she wet? And it felt sticky.

After a while she lay down again and tried to sleep. But she could only lie awake in fear. It slowly became light. She lifted the sacks and looked. Then she saw that it was blood! It was blood! She was bleeding. Why? Was she dying? Was this it? Was she dying? But she was not bleeding now. She had been bleeding. Maybe she was not dying but what was it? She tried to think. Then: 'Girl! Girl get up! It's time for work.' But she was dying. But she could not tell him when it was down there. She pulled the sacks over herself. He looked round the partition. 'Get up!'

She cleaned the worst of the blood off her legs with the sacks and got up. She slept in her dress so it was stained too. But it was not too bad. It was dark brown and dirty and the stain was not too noticeable. She could wear it. Her blood felt wet and dirty and cold on her legs. She went down in shock and worked that day, waiting to fall down and die. And several times she had to hide in the byre or the pig house and clean more blood off her legs with handfuls of straw. That night she did not sleep as she waited to die.

For three days of fear the bleeding lasted. After the first her dress was too bad to wear. She put on the dress her father had brought at the end of her first six months. Already, as it was worn out, she had had to throw away one of the other two dresses she had brought with her. She would never go to church now. Her bleeding had ruined the clean dress. There was something in her mind about the bleeding from down there ruining her church dress and stopping her going to church, but she was not sure what. By this time she had seen that the bleeding was coming from her inside. What was happening? Had this something to do with her being bad, with that part of her being bad? With the church? Was that it? Then, just like it started, it stopped.

She could not believe it. On the fourth day she did not bleed anymore. She tried to wash the old dress and she hung it out. She wore the new one. It was dark brown also and the bloodstains on it were not too bad. She was almost happy that she had not died. But what was it? Was she sick? Had she done something wrong? Was God punishing her? What was that blood? But it was stopped now.

A month later, it came again. Like the first time she woke in the night with wet and sticky legs. This time it stained the bedding. For three days she was in agony with stomach pains and fear that she was dying. After three days it stopped again. She was still alive. Gradually she came to expect it every month and to expect it to go away after three days. This was what began to happen regularly. Her terrible fear lessened. But she was still afraid. What was it? What was it?

Some months before the first bleeding, she had begun to grow hair around her down there, at first just a little down, but then real hair. And under her arms also. What was this? She felt it under her arms in the night and wondered. She felt it between her legs once and took her hand away quickly. From what her mother had said she was sure it was not right. She was afraid to touch herself.

Around this same time her chest had begun to change. The little brown circles had begun to get pointed and her whole chest to swell up. Then two large round swellings began to grow. She became curved. And her hips too became curved. What was happening? She was bleeding every month and she was changing shape. She was becoming curved. But she had not died. The monotony of her work, the orders of Allen, the friendly noises from the sow, the feel of the cats sleeping with her, these kept her from spinning into madness as these new things came to her and she did not know what they were or why they came.

Then one morning Allen did not shout from the steps first. She awoke to feel his hand on her shoulder, then on the curve of her chest. It seemed to be shaking her. Or was it feeling her? She awoke. She was afraid and confused. This was the first time he had ever touched her in this way. What did it mean? Was it good? Was it kindness? What did it mean? 'Get up, girl.' His voice was thick and deep. 'Get up, girl.' He took his hand away. Margaret felt funny. Disturbed. She felt the touch of his hand on her front throughout the day. It did not feel good. She felt dirty, and nauseated, she felt an internal kind of dirtiness.

It was three mornings later. She awoke to feel him on top of her. He had one leg between hers. His smell sickened her. His dirty teeth were bared. Hatred was in his eyes but more, something frightening. Not exactly anger. It was worse. It was aimed at her. It was saying it wanted to do something to her and it did not care what she wanted. What was he doing? She held her legs closed but his leg was between them. He felt her curved chest. What? What? She was afraid to speak even in her distress. She had never spoken to him before. She had been brought up to know her place and keep quiet. She was not allowed to make a noise never mind scream. It was like she was dumb. She was only another mouth to feed.

Fear and confusion and pain flooded her mind. Was he killing her? But this was Allen. He was one of her own. He had over fifty good acres. He was a good man. He went to church. But what was he doing? He was pulling at her. She lay tight into herself holding her legs tight but his leg was already between them. Her arms bent up across her chest and held tight into herself. Her teeth were clenched and bared against his attack and against her own screams which stayed tied down and silent inside her. All her training told her to stifle her screams rather than let them out and direct them at him and fight back.

But what? He was pulling at her legs with his right hand. She held rigid. She was strong with work. She was young. He could not get her legs pulled apart. The cats were motionless on the top of the partition watching. He could not get her legs pulled apart. Why? What? What? She was stronger than him. But then he hit her. Drawing back his right hand he clenched his fist and hit her on the side of the head with the flat of his fist. The shock was terrible.

It weakened the core of her. The shock shattered her cohesion, the centre of her. She was not able to concentrate on keeping her legs and arms tight and her teeth clenched. While this trauma of being hit uncoiled her, he hit her again. She pulled her hands up and tried to turn. That is when he pushed his other leg between hers. He hit her again. She struggled in a desperate silence. Was she going to die? Was he going to kill her? He hit her again.

Then she felt his bare skin against her. And something hard, like a stick. And like a shock, she thought it's like the donkey's thing. But then his hand was between her legs and the hard, his hard thing was poking at her. She was terrified and frozen and dry with fear. But he was breathing hard and snarling at her. 'Come on, girl', come on girl, who do you think you are?" And he was driving at her. 'I'll get it,' he snarled to himself. "There will be no mistake about it, I'll get it." She wept. What was it. Why was this? What was this? Why was there nobody to help her? She began to weep uncontrollably and shudder silently as he tore at her.

She became weak. He took his hands down and tried to part the skin between her legs. She was dry and closed to him. He took his thing and pointed it at her. Then he thrust and thrust again and again. And a pain that she had never imagined was in her. She was being split open. What was this? What was he? What was this? What? She could not even cry out in her pain and fear and ignorance. One of her own, a good man, over fifty good acres, he went to church. All this that she had been taught to respect and defer to was on top of her and splitting her. She could not scream and swear and fight back against all this. She was only another mouth to feed, only a pair of hands.

She could feel blood. He drove away at her. His dirty teeth clenched and his breath smelling like something rotten and dying. She wept. The brutality of her life with the Allens' had dried up the tears in her. Now this new increased brutality had brought her tears back. He held and squeezed one side of her chest in one hand and with his other he held her neck and choked her. He had now beaten his way inside her and his thrusts became harder and faster. He began to breathe very fast and loud and his hand choked her tighter and tighter.

He drove again and again into her. Then he began to shake and held her neck and her chest in a terrible grip with his dirty nails digging into her. Then he gave a muffled roar and stopped pushing into her and his grip loosened. His lips covered his teeth again. Then he lay down not moving on top of her. Then slowly he began to lift himself up off her. Then he grunted to himself, 'That will teach her.' He pulled back from and out of her and reached down to cover himself and button his trousers. She realised she had not seen him open them.

He got up and turned. 'Aye, that will teach her,' he repeated to himself as he walked towards the door. Then he turned. 'Get up now, girl. There's work to be done. Don't be lying there. Get up.' He went out.

She was so used to obeying, so beaten down by the world in which she had been reared, that she got up. The pain was terrible. She looked at herself. There was blood on her. There was something else leaking out of her, something slimy. What was it? What had he done to her? She hurt. She did not know what he had done. Why had he hit her? Why had he put his thing in her? Her eyes widened as she thought in disgust and fear of him and what he had done. She wept quietly in case the woman would hear her and she would get into more trouble. What was it he meant when he said that this would teach her? What was it supposed to teach her?

From then on the mornings were terror. She never knew when he would come and hit her and attack her and leave her bleeding. Every two or three days he would come. She would clench herself and hold herself tight but he would do it. He was the boss. He was a good man, over fifty good acres, went to church, one of her own. He was a good man. Over fifty good acres, went to church, one of her own. How could she stop him when he was all these things, how could she resist all these things? She owned nothing but a couple of smelly dresses, she was only another mouth to feed, only a pair of hands. She smelled. She bled regularly and maybe was dying. How could she stop him and all these things that were him? He did it to her whenever he wanted to.

Then one day she realised she had not bled for many weeks. Maybe she was getting better. Maybe she would not die after all. She had not bled. Even when he attacked her now she did not bleed. She thought what she might do if she did not die. She was tempted to be happy for a second. But then she realised that she was already doing what she would be doing if she did not die. Life was a sort of dying. She was dying. That was all there was for her. She had no land, no house, nothing of her own. Dying was all there was for her.

Around this time she noticed she was getting fatter and her chest was getting bigger. Was she eating too much? Would they give her less food if they noticed? One day she saw the woman look at her and then go into the house. She heard her and Allen shouting. The woman came out and over to Margaret in the pig house. Her face was clenched and red. She came up to her. And she hit Margaret in the face with her closed fist.

'You dirty animal you. You led him on. You will be out of here. Look at you, you smell like a pig. You led him on.' And she walked away leaving Margaret lying in the pig dirt in the pig's stall.

He hit her to make her do it and she hit her for doing it. The old sow watched her and then gave a friendly grunt and came and nudged her with her snout. Margaret rested her head against the sow's cheek. It never hit her. It never attacked her and made her bleed. It never looked at her with hate and anger and fear or hit her and made her bleed, and left slimy stuff leaking out of her. Margaret put her hand on the sow's back and got to her feet. She was heavier and sometimes she got tired, and sometimes she was sick in the morning. She carried on with her work throwing the pig dirt out of the hole in the wall. If only people could be more like pigs.

CHAPTER SIX

'It's a message from Bishop Wilson, Elizabeth. He would like me to call and see him when I get a chance. I wonder what this is about?'

'You will just have to call and see, Charles.'

Charles and Elizabeth Brown lived in the big house that Margaret had passed on the way to the crossroads, the day she walked to Allen's. He was the chief land agent for the London based owner of the land, Lord Taverstock. They were the parents of Jenny, the wee Brown girl. He himself was also the owner of the largest piece of land in the area after Taverstock.

Taverstock had been given this particular piece of land by the British rulers after they had invaded Ireland, killed large numbers of the local people and stolen it. He was still managing to hold onto it despite the land acts of the last few decades. Unlike the previous owners, the Irish Clans, who had owned the land collectively, this land was now owned privately. In this case, it was owned by Taverstock. Brown's job as Taverstock's agent. was to keep the original owners from getting the land back, oversee the rental of the land to these original owners, see to the upkeep of the big house in which he lived, which was also Taverstock's, and to collect and transfer the rents to Taverstock in London. Taverstock paid his dues to the British crown from these and other rents. Being the overseer of the transfer of the seized surplus to London, did not make Brown a popular man amongst the tenants.

'I have to go down to see about other things so I'll call in today and see what the Bishop wants. Do you need anything, Elizabeth? I will be taking the horse and trap and can get anything you want at Burnside's store.'

'No. I have everything. The servants brought everything on Saturday. But wait, maybe get some nice sweet chocolate for Jenny? She has been very good lately.' Jenny was so watched after and spoiled she could hardly be anything else but 'good'.

'Good day, Charles,' Bishop Wilson greeted Brown as he was shown in by the servant. Landlords, the top land agents, like Brown, preachers, they all lived in the big houses that were dotted across the land. The rest of the people lived in hovels of one degree or the other. 'Come in. Come in. It's lovely weather we are having. How are you keeping? I suppose you have your hands full with those tenants as usual?'

'They do not want to work. They would rather get the land for nothing. Well what can be done? Lord Taverstock is a good man. Charges them a fair rent and still they complain.'

This was the normal exchange between the ruling circles. The peasantry were lazy and did not want to work, the rents were more than reasonable and yet they complained about them, unless the boot was kept on their necks they would do nothing. There was never much talk about the history of slaughter and oppression, which had preceded the stealing of the land by the landlords, such as Taverstock, and their associates, Brown and Wilson. Wilson was the man of God who accompanied the sword and helped the conquering and the suppression.

Behind where Wilson sat, was a coloured portrait of his son Robert, who was an officer in the Royal Enniskillen Fusileers. He was at present in India. On the other wall was a portrait of his other son. He was a missionary in Kenya. Wilson saw Brown looking at the portraits.

'My boys, yes, I am proud of them. Both doing the Lord's work. Robert was nearly killed last year. There was some sort of trouble in Northern India. They had to shoot a lot of the chaps. After all his Majesty has done for them. No gratitude. No gratitude.' So spoke the man of God.

'Anyway, Charles, I am talking away here. Matilda and the two maids are in Londonderry or we could have had some tea and sand-wiches. But here, have a little glass of port. I will have one myself. My brother sent it to me. He is in the diplomatic service, in His Majesty's embassy in Buenos Aires. He's doing well there.' Wilson's family were scattered across the world helping hold together the British Empire with its plunder and oppression. Wilson poured two glasses of port, handed one to Brown and both men sat down. Wilson was well connected.

The room was furnished with beautiful antique furniture. The leather in the chairs was soft and almost silky to the touch. A large rug from India or Pakistan covered the floor. Fine china was exhibited in dressers around the walls. And thick expensive curtains hung by the windows. If Margaret had been there she would not have recognized any similarity between this and her place in Allen's barn. There were twenty-three rooms in the preacher's house and there were no sacks sowed together for mattresses.

'Well, Charles, I wanted to see you because we have a delicate matter I would like you to help me solve. A small problem we need to deal with. You know the wee Wallace girl, Charles? She has been hired out now for some time to Allen who has the place up near Rushey. Over fifty good acres he has I think.'

Charles was beginning to see why he had been invited to visit.

"Well, Charles, that wee girl has not been behaving herself.' Wilson spoke in an aggrieved and pious tone like it was a personal injury that Margaret had deliberately done unto him.

'Yes, Charles, she has not been behaving. And what has happened, it appears, is that she is now in the family way. She has not been out of that place for over two years now. Some say Allen is involved. I do not know. But anyway, it looks very bad. I mean Allen is one of our own. And he has a good place there. He comes here to church every Sunday. It looks very bad. She is only around fourteen.'

Charles looked up. 'Yes, it is not helpful. Everywhere you turn now there is talk about politics and land. Just last week I heard Brennan, who rents a piece of bog from his Lordship, complaining to O'Donnell, his neighbour, about the rents. O'Donnell said that his Lordship had no right to the land anyway. I can feel it when I meet them. They won't look me in the eye. There is an anger developing. It's not good when one of our own kind brings shame on us in this way. It only makes things worse.'

'You are right, Charles. But what are we going to do? That wee girl cannot stay there. It will only bring trouble to the house and between Allen and his wife. What we need is to see if there is some-body that we know who needs a wife and who would be able to take in this young girl, marry her I mean, and be able to provide for her. This is why I asked you here. There is somebody I have in mind but I want your opinion of the situation and if we think it would work, then I would want you to approach him.'

Charles wondered who was he thinking of?

'The man I have in mind is Campbell. You know him. He has a few fields up near Moneymore and he lets the bog for yourself and his Lordship.'

Charles considered the idea. Campbell was at the bottom end of the remnants of the landlord system that remained. The bog was too poor to keep a full time agent so Brown contracted with Campbell to rent the bog lots to those who wanted them, for a small commission. Campbell also worked his own fields. He belonged to Wilson's church. He was in his thirties, an unfriendly, surly man but he always did his work and reported to Brown.

'Yes, he might do it. He has nobody belonging to him. He has that few fields and a bit of an income from the bog commissions. Yes, he might do it.'

'Very well then. We will get this problem dealt with and all will be well.' With the business done, Wilson gradually ushered Brown out the door.

On the way home Charles got the chocolate for Jenny. The problem, pregnant Margaret, only another mouth to feed, a pair of hands, something for Allen to put his thing in, was cleaning out Allen's byre. She was not consulted. She did not know her future had just been decided by people she had never spoken to, who ran a system she did not even know existed.

Brown decided to go and see Campbell right away. The sooner he got it over with the better. Brown also knew that if he dealt with this efficiently it would get back to Lord Taverstock and this would do him no harm at all. Wilson was well in with his Lordship. He would be sure to tell him. It was all in the interests of keeping things quiet. Keeping things stable. That was his job, get in the rents and keep things quiet, keep things stable. His job was not so much different from Wilson's. Keep things quiet and stable and the tenants willing to pay the rents. Brown did his work with the threat of eviction and Wilson with the threat of hell. Both threats were based on living conditions and locations.

He found Campbell digging a drain in one of his fields. He was trying to let a spring run off and get a bit of extra grazing from what was now a piece of boggy swamp.

'Hello there, Campbell. I see you are hard at work.' Campbell looked up at Brown. 'Aye.' He said no more. He waited. He knew that Brown was here for a purpose.

'What you need, James, is a woman to help you out. That's why I have come to see you.' Brown did not need to be overly diplomatic as Campbell depended on him for the bog renting work. 'Do you know the wee Wallace girl who has been hired out to Allen up near Rushey? Well, she has not been behaving herself. She is now in the family way. She would make you a good wife, James.' Campbell was quiet for a while. Then he asked what her father thought.

'He is all for it. Bishop Wilson has already talked to him. What do you think now, Campbell?'

Campbell stood for a few minutes in the wet ground and looked out over the valley. He sniffed and then blew his nose with his thumb, out on the grass. He felt a little power in his relationship with Brown for once. Brown wanted something from him that could not be given by many others. He looked back at Brown. They came to Campbell for the dirty jobs. Rent their worst land. Stay after their worst off tenants. Live on next to nothing himself. Now clear up their mess, put a good look on things with Allen and the Wallace girl. They would not come to him if it were their girl who was in the family way. Campbell was angry. But not a hint of this showed.

'Well I suppose I could do worse. But you say she's in the family way. A wean. What about?' He looked up into Brown's eyes. 'Maybe there would be something to help me get started. She's with somebody else's wean. I will have to feed and clothe it.'

Brown recognized the bargaining. 'I am sure this could be arranged. I am sure Allen would be agreeable to that.'

Campbell looked up at Brown again. 'I mean after all, Allen has had his time out of her. He should not begrudge a bit of money when I am taking her and the wean off his hands.' Margaret was being bargained over like any other commodity.

The next afternoon Brown rode down in the horse and trap to Wilson. This time he was not asked in. Wilson with his connections in London had more clout than Brown and he was not averse to showing it. They talked at the door.

'A good job, Charles. I am sure this will be all for the best.'

'Well he did ask for some money. He said that Allen should give him something.'

'He did, did he? Well I can see Campbell thinks a wee bit above his station. But then after all it's a small price to pay to have this problem dealt with. We don't want a scandal. It's a good job she's one of our own. If she were one of the other kind they would make a whole issue out of it. I will get a message to Allen and tell him what he has to do.'

Brown was glad to get home. Elizabeth met him at the door. And Jenny took his hand and skipped alongside him into the sitting room. The servant brought him a glass half full of scotch whisky. He sipped it and looked at Jenny. She was twelve years old now. Next year she would go to boarding school in England. They could only do it because Lord Taverstock was going to help. He could afford it. He had over a thousand tenants paying regularly between here and his rental buildings and lands in England. Overall he had over a thousand families working and paying him a portion of what they produced in rent. Legalized extortion on a mass scale.

'Can you tell me about it, Charles?' Elizabeth sat down by Charles after Jenny had gone up to bed with her personal servant.

'It's the wee Wallace girl. She has been hired out to Allen for the past couple of years. She has been misbehaving and she's now in the family way. I am sure it's Allen's. But Campbell is going to take her. Allen will give Campbell a few pounds and everything will be all right. The father is good with it. It's a good job the wee Wallace girl is one of our own. If she were a Fenian they would make a whole issue out of it.

'Remember the wee Wallace girl? She was at the back door here once years ago. I saw her looking in. Her eyes were like saucers as she looked at the kitchen. She's only around fourteen now. But she will be fine. Campbell is a hard worker and he has a couple of fields and I can give him a few more lettings to handle. It will be all right. But it makes us look bad. I mean it's all right for the other kind. They believe in nothing. But we are running this country and it makes us look bad. Allen!' He sniffed in disapproval. Then, putting things back in the order that allowed the control to hold, 'Well, that wee girl should not have been misbehaving.'

'But, Charles, that Campbell is a brute. Remember last year we came upon him whipping that little donkey he goes around with. There was no pity in him.'

'Elizabeth, you have to get these sort of things out of your head. It's not Jenny you're talking about. Sure the Wallace family has only a few acres. That Wallace girl has been working for Allen for over two years. And I am sure that what she earned was taken by her father. They are not like us, Elizabeth. They don't have feelings like us. Like Jenny would have. The wee Wallace girl is not Jenny. She's lucky that Campbell will take her. The wee Wallace girl does not have feelings like Jenny.'

Elizabeth did not feel right about it. But she looked down at the expensive rug on the floor and sideways at the curtains and the paintings on the wall. Then at the expensive and beautiful china in the dressers. She thought of her own expensive clothes. She thought of Jenny going to school in England. All these came from their position with Lord Taverstock. This was too much to risk. Maybe Charles was right and they did not feel like better people. And anyway, she and Jenny and Charles lived well. His Lordship looked after them well. And Charles did not like her arguing with him. She rose, went upstairs and looked at Jenny asleep on white sheets. Elizabeth kissed her and smelled her fresh clean skin. Jenny had been given a bath by Martha. Martha really was a good servant. She worked hard and never spoke unless she was spoken to. None of this could be risked. Elizabeth had to keep this in mind. None of this could be risked.

As Elizabeth was looking at Jenny, four miles further up the mountain road Campbell was entering McDaid's pub by the cross-roads. McDaid looked up in surprise. This was unusual. Campbell seldom came in here. He was not popular. McDaid's was a mainly Catholic bar. Many of his regulars rented bog through Campbell and he was a mean cheap bastard.

'What will you have?'

'A wee half.' Campbell grunted.

Hah, he has something on his mind when he is paying out for a wee half, McDaid thought.

Campbell took the wee half and went and sat at a small table by the door. They came to him when they wanted to get rid of her. He was not as good as them. Allen had had his way with her. They were feared of a scandal. Allen and Brown and the Reverend. Campbell was the solution. Well, he would get a few pounds out of it. And a woman. She would know how to work if she was with Allen for over two years. Aye, she would be able to work. Well that would suit Campbell. He would give her plenty of work.

Maybe he could get a cow now as she would be there everyday to milk it. He thought he would have enough grazing for it. If not he could put it on the long acre, along the side of the road. She could watch it. He was away with the bog lettings a lot. He sat there in his dirty clothes in the smell of his own dirt and thought how this woman could help his situation. Yes, now he could get a cow that there would be somebody there every day to milk her. And maybe she could do a bit of work to Brown or some of them big farmers and earn a bit that way too.

He determinedly pushed the memories of the last time he had a woman to the back of his mind. She was dead and gone. She was gone. And this time, unlike the last time, he was not responsible for this woman having a wean. It was Allen who had done it and if anything went wrong, it was his fault. There was no point in thinking about it. It was over. Aye, this one would make a good addition to the place. She would be able to milk the cow, he would get the cow from Allen for taking her, she would be able to earn a few bob working, she would do the work around the house, and a bit in the bog. Aye, this would work out well. He drove his memories down into the bottom of his head with a vicious determination.

The whisky made him warm inside. He would have another. After all he was getting a woman, and money with her too. And he'd get a cow. It was not every day. Another whisky. As he ordered it the door opened and in came Brennan and O'Donnell. They stopped and looked at Campbell and then at McDaid. What? Campbell was too busy with his thoughts to give them much heed.

They ordered two stouts. They were worried because out back they had five salmon that they had taken on Taverstock's land and poaching was illegal and Campbell was an informer, if ever there was one. They drank. 'Two more stouts.' McDaid put them up because he knew they had the salmon and he would buy them from them. 'Don't be starting nothing now boys,' he told them. They laughed and looked at Campbell.

O'Donnell began to talk in a loud voice so Campbell could hear. 'Aye, his lordship over in London. Living in a big house. Never lifts a hand. Over here we do the work and pay the rent. And then there are those who do his dirty work here. He tells them they are better than us. They are all the same kind he says. Protestants. Well, there's Protestants and there's Protestants. There's his Lordship in London who never lifts a hand, there's Brown in his big house with his servants, there's Allen with his fifty good acres and there's that wee Wallace girl slaving at Allen's for over two years. And now to be in the family way and to be put out. And by one of her own kind too.'

Campbell went red with anger and humiliation. How did they know so quick? Aye, how did they know so quick? He threw back the Scotch and stamped out of the bar. McDaid looked angry.

'You are a bad one, O'Donnell. What are you talking about that made him so mad?'

'Did you not hear? That wee Wallace girl is in the family way. Allen fixed her. Campbell is taking her.'

'How do you know this?'

'Sure Brown's kitchen maid is sick and my sister is working there for the week and heard it all through the door.'

'O'Donnell, you had better be careful. I know you're thinking you would like to be in with them boys above in Dublin. Them boys that want another war here. Be careful with Campbell. You do not need any more enemies.'

Campbell walked home and pushed open the door to his cottage. It was the same size, maybe a little smaller than the one the Wallace family lived in. He threw himself down on the old bench that served as his bed by the fire. Well it did not matter. He was getting a woman. Another pair of hands. He would be able to get a cow. And he would have help with everything else too. She must know how to work being with Allen for over two years. Aye, it's true she would be another mouth to feed but she'd also be another pair of hands. He was still trying to figure what he would get out of the deal, still wrestling with this base calculation of his coming marriage to the wee Wallace girl.

CHAPTER SEVEN

Margaret heard her father's voice shouting for her. She had no idea he was coming. She was in the byre cleaning it out and she came out the door.

'Come on, girl, you are coming home.'

She was stunned. She had been so long at Allen's and so beaten down she had lost all hope of leaving.

'Aye, come on.'

But what about Allen? Would he let her go? The door to the house was closed and it was never closed. She looked at the door of the house with anxiety and fear.

'Don't worry about him, Margaret. He has already given me the money. Come on, it's a good walk home.'

Margaret wanted to go and see the sow and its new litter of wee pigs and to see the cats before she left. But she was afraid to get her father angry so she followed him. But she felt terrible not to be able to go and see the pigs and the cats. They were her main comfort for the years. Not only had her father dropped her here and left her, but now he was dragging her away without letting her say goodbye to her friends.

But she was afraid to challenge him and afraid to take any chance of not getting away from Allen. She did not look back as she walked down the lane away from the house she had not left for nearly three years, and where she had been hurt and attacked and worked to the bone. She thought of Allen and his dirt and him saying that will teach her and the hurt she felt when he hit her and put his thing in her. She clenched her teeth in rage thinking of Allen as she walked down the lane.

They went down to the crossroads and turned left up past the Brown place. She thought of the wee Brown girl again and had anybody hit her and put his thing in her since the last time she had walked past her house. They then went on up the sloping hill towards her home. She wondered about her mother. How was she and what would she say? What about the donkey and the dog? For the first time in years she felt like smiling. Then she realised that she was very tired. Why was this? And she saw her fat stomach. What was it?

'Come on, girl, don't hang back. We want to be getting home.' Her father and his orders again.

The dog barked and her mother and brothers came to the door. Her brothers were bigger and older. But her mother was changed most. Not only was she older but she was worn down since Margaret had last seen her. It was as if she had been carrying a terrible heavy load all the time since Margaret had left. Her eyes and face were exhausted. She tried to smile as she saw Margaret.

'How are ye Margaret? Are ye all right? Come in and have a cup of tea and a bite of bread. You must be tired.' Her mother looked at her stomach and looked away.

For the first time in almost three years, Margaret was in a dwelling house and sitting by a fire.

'Not so loud, she will hear you.' It was night and Mary looked over her shoulder to where Margaret was sleeping in the wee side room. Then she turned to her husband.

'What are you saying? That Margaret was misbehaving? That this is what happened? It's Allen that did this. It's him is to blame. He is a

68

grown man. Margaret is just a child. I am going to ask her what happened.'

'Well don't go and disturb anything. I have the problem solved. Campbell is going to take her and she will be fed and housed with him.'

Mary looked away in anger. Her inside twisted with the dirty brutal injustice of it all and her own impotence to do anything about it.

Next morning Mary let the men go out to the bog. 'Margaret, stay here with me this morning. I have not seen you for so long.'

Margaret and her mother sat by the table in the kitchen. The dog came in looking for scraps and wagged his tail at Margaret. And two hens looked around the door. Margaret and Mary both had a mug of tea in their hands and some buttered bread. The turf fire burned and a pot hung over it from a chain and hook. Mary did not know where to start and Margaret had not spoken to anybody since she had left home almost three years ago.

'Margaret, you know why you were brought home, don't you?'

Margaret looked up but said nothing.

'You are going to have a baby. That's why you are getting fat and why you feel tired and sick.' Seeing the incomprehension on Margaret's face her mother said again 'You are going to have a baby. I had four babies. Your brothers and you and one who died. It will be all right. But how did you get this way? Who touched you? You know somebody must have touched you.'

Margaret still had the look of incomprehension.

'Margaret, some man must have put his thing in you. That's how you are having a baby. That's how your belly is getting big. The baby is in there.' She saw Margaret's expression change very, very slowly.

'Some man must have put his thing in you.' Mary's heart felt like it was breaking as she saw the beginning of understanding on her daughter's face. Then Margaret began to weep, first quietly and then great sobs that shook her body and twisted it in pain and grief.

'What happened. Margaret?'

For the first time in almost three years, Margaret spoke to another human being. 'It was Allen, he hit me and every two or three mornings he would come and hit me and hold me down and put his thing in me. My thing was bleeding. He would make me bleed.'

Margaret wept and sobbed. She wailed in her pain. 'He did it to me. He said that would teach me. He hit me.' Margaret spoke more in this minute than she had spoken since she had left home almost three years ago. She looked up at her mother.

'Well, Margaret, that is how you got pregnant. Now you are going to have a baby. Allen's baby.'

Margaret tried to grapple with this news, She wondered why it was that every big change in her life had been told to her in a few minutes and came as a great shock. She was never prepared for these things. Nobody prepared her for these things. Why did nobody prepare her for these things?

A baby. She looked down at her stomach. Her stomach was swelling. She looked again at her mother.

'You are maybe four months gone and you will probably have your baby in five months time. It will be hard, Margaret. Having a baby is not easy. But that's what we women have to do. We have things planned and they will be all right. A man wants to marry you and he will look after you and provide. He has already been talked to and he has agreed.'

Margaret was reeling with shock. In a few minutes she learned she was pregnant, that this was because Allen had put his thing in her, and now some man was going to marry her. He had already agreed. Who? What? What? She was going to be married. Everything happened to her. She never happened to anything else. Margaret, for the first time, began to question why she had no say in her life. But this was just a flash. It went as quick as it came. She had no control over

70

her life. Some man was going to marry her. It did not occur to her to ask who it was. She saw no basis in her life on which she could stand to question things.

'His name is Campbell. He has a few fields up there near the bog. He rents out the bog for Brown who is Lord Taverstock's man. He will look after you Margaret. He is one of our own. He belongs to the same church but he does not often go. He will be coming here tonight to see you and make arrangements. Now you will have to get yourself cleaned up. I have a dress for you I sewed. Come on now, help me make a bit of bread so we can have it for the night.'

Behind this calm explanation to Margaret, Mary was filled with anger and rage and pain. That Allen had done this to Margaret was hitting her hard. Put his thing in her. Forced her. Hurt her. Something should be done to him. 'I wish...' But he had over fifty good acres. Margaret thought of their own thirteen acres and it mainly rock. It wasn't right. He should not get away with it. But what could she do? There was nobody with any power in the place that would stand up for Margaret. They would all side with Allen or cover up for him. They would all side with Allen and his over fifty good acres. It was not right. Mary could see no way but to go along with the plans.

They were all sitting round the fire that night when the dog began barking. Margaret was in the dress that her mother had sewn for her. She was waiting to see what would happen and who was this man. Her father opened the door.

'How are you, James? Come on in. Don't worry the dog will not touch you. Come in. Here take this seat by the fire. The turf is burning well. It is from the bank at the far end of the bog. You know it, we rent it through you.'

Campbell sat without speaking and without looking at Margaret. He was not much interested in her looks as long as she could work.

The mother fetched him a mug of tea and some bread. He made

a noise as he drank the tea. He ate the bread in huge mouthfuls. He kept looking at the fire. There was a silence for a while. Then the father spoke. His voice was ingratiating, like Margaret had heard it when he had spoken to Allen. 'Well, James, we are sure glad that you are wanting to take Margaret. She is a good girl. A hard worker. She will be a good pair of hands for you.'

James did not speak.

Margaret sat in silence taking only one quick glance at this man who had come to look her over to see if he would marry her, before sitting looking down at her hands in her lap. He was over twice her age. He was tall and broad. He did not look kind. He did not laugh or even smile. Just drank his tea in deep slurps and ate his bread in great noisy bites and looked at nobody.

'Yes, James, we are very glad. Bishop Wilson said that next Saturday morning around eleven would be fine with him. We will have Margaret there at the church at that time. And everything will be taken care of. Will this be all right with you?'

James did not say anything.

After a few minutes he rose. 'Aye' he grunted.

Margaret's father did not know what this meant. Was he not going through with it? He stalled for time.

'Well, James. Will you not have another cup of tea?'

Campbell did not answer just went to the door and outside.

The father followed. He held out his hand. 'Well, we will see you there on Saturday about eleven.'

Campbell grunted aye again and keeping his eyes on the ground turned and walked away. The father sighed with relief. At least he had said aye.

'Well, there you are, Margaret. You will be married on Saturday. That was your husband that you just met. He's a fine cut of a man is he not? Mary, tell Margaret she is a lucky girl. Campbell has a wee cottage, a few fields and he makes a few shillings letting his lord-ship's bog for Brown. You could do a lot worse, Margaret, in your condition.'

Margaret sat there and looked at the fire. She had no understand-ing of what it would mean to be married to Campbell. Or even to be married.

'Well, get off to bed now, Margaret. You will need to be resting. Mary, tell her things will be all right but she has got to pull herself together. Show a wee bit of welcome to Campbell when she gets mar-ried on Saturday. She cannot just sit and say nothing.'

Margaret looked at her mother. Her brothers sniggered in the dark. 'Come on now, Margaret, off to bed.' Margaret rose and went into the side room and lay on the feather filled bedding on the floor. Her mind was empty of any rational thought. She just lay there.

Campbell walked home. On the way he had to pass McDaid's pub. He wanted a whisky. He had only enough for two wee halfs. He pushed the door open. There were half a dozen men there. McDaid was behind the bar. 'A wee half.' It was set up in front of him. He could hear the men's talk at the far end of the bar round the fire. He sat by the door by himself. He thought of the young one. She was strong enough looking. She was beginning to show. But she would be able to work.

The father was mad to get rid of her. Maybe he should ask him for a few shillings also. After all he was doing them a favour. Doing the girl a favour. Without him she might end up on the road or in the workhouse. Aye, maybe Wallace would give him something. But Wallace had next to nothing himself. But even a few hens. That would bring him a few eggs regularly. He would have to think about it. Wallace was mad to get rid of her. Aye, she would be strong enough to milk a cow.

Campbell sipped his whisky making it last. He had nobody about him. He had been brought up by his father after his mother had died having him. His father was hard. They had lived in the cottage he was in now. His father had beaten the hard work into him. He had beaten his hatred of the Catholics into him. He had beaten his obedience to those above him into him. He could still hear his father shouting at him as he beat him.

'Look, boy, you had better learn to respect your betters. It's the Lord Taverstocks, the Browns, the Bishop Wilsons and the police and army that run this country. Keep right with them and you will never go too far wrong. You may not have much but you will have enough to get by. Look at me. I have this wee cottage and the few fields and the bog lettings. Don't be thinking like them Fenians. They want to fight the powers that be. Look where it gets them. The workhouse or the boat and that's if they are lucky. For some of them it's the jail or six foot under. We may have little but they have less.'

There was that one time he defied his father and went away. That was a time of it. He had defied him and went and married that young one and moved into her place over near Glennfinn. Then that all went bad. That night. That night. To hell with it all. He could still hear the... That was not... He pushed the memory down again. Aye, he had defied the father for that while but it ended very badly. He had gone back to the father after that.

And his father made sure that Campbell learned his lesson well. He obeyed the powers that be from then on. He did what he was told and what the father told him. But he always looked to get a wee bit more than they wanted to give him. Now he was solving a problem for them. He was getting something from Allen. Maybe he would not ask Wallace for something now but there would be later. And he would make the wee girl work. Campbell was not going to let anybody put one over on him. Maybe he would ask Wallace for a few hens to bring with her.

'Well, it's yourself, Mr. Campbell. Sure I hardly saw you there sitting in the dark way back from the fire.' It was O'Donnell and he had had a few drinks. 'Sure how are you keeping?' Campbell snorted at him and turned away. 'Well, good luck to you, Campbell, on your coming wedding. You're a lucky man. Sure there's many here would give a lot to have a young one like the wee Wallace girl for a wife. Sure you must be a great man altogether to be able to get her.' O'Donnell taunted Campbell. Then he joined the crowd around the fire. They laughed. Campbell left without a second whisky.

'Look at him' O'Donnell said. 'He's gone up there trying to figure out what kind of a deal he is getting. Is he being done or is he getting the better end of things? You know even though that wee Wallace girl is not one of our own kind I feel sorry for her. From that father of hers, to Allen to Campbell. Sure I am not saying things are any better on our side either. The Allen and the Campbell types are plentiful on our side too. There's few of them would not bow the knee like Campbell if they thought it would get them something. Sure this is a terrible country altogether. I am close to having had it with the whole place. Aye, our own kind are no better.

'When I was in Dublin I got into some business with the rebel boys down there and the transport union men. I went to a meeting where a man called Connolly spoke. You know what he said! He said that it made no difference what religion the boss was or the rich farmer was, they all had the same aim, that was to get as much out of the working man and woman as possible. He said that to do this the landlords and the rich people keep us poor folk divided; keep us Catholics and Protestants against each other. He says that poor folk have to forget about religion and unite against the rich folk.

'Look at the way them better off Protestants treated that wee Wallace girl. She will be a slave all her life. And look here, not one of you can tell me that this would not happen amongst our own kind.

Look at your man Murphy over the hill there. He fixed that wee servant girl he had and put her out on the roadside. And our own priest had not a word to say about it. She had nothing, her folks had nothing so that's why she was treated like that. The priest wanted to keep in with Murphy and his over a hundred and fifty acres and his money so he kept quiet. Very like the Wallace's who have next to nothing. Allen has over fifty good acres so the rest of them want to keep in with him. That wee Connolly man is right, it's all about money.'

CHAPTER EIGHT

Shanks and Katie Curran lived up on the side of the mountain past Campbell. They knew Campbell well and also the wee Wallace girl. They were sitting at the fire talking about the coming marriage.

'What kind of a time is that wee girl going to have with Campbell, Katie?' Shanks asked. 'I mean you know him. He'll have nothing for her. Will he even think that he has to make any kind of a change? And himself, Katie, I know he's not much of a person but he might do damage to her or to himself. What do you think? I don't think I am far out here, Katie.'

'Shanks, I know you feel obliged to Campbell ever since he helped us with the cow. But what can you do?'

A shout came to the door. 'Hello there, Shanks. Are you in?'

'It's Quinn, Katie, it's Quinn, Come on in, Quinn.' The door opened. In came a disheveled man with a face red with drink and his eyes and voice full of wild laughter.

'How are you all doing? Jesus sure that's a great bit of a fire you have there. You will not be cold anyway. Shanks, you are a sore man on the turf. Hello there, Katie. How are you doing?' Quinn made a whole commentary on the evening and on Shanks' and Katie's lives in a couple of sentences.

'Quinn, sit down there. Pull up a chair to the fire. Have you been down in McDaid's? That drink will be the death of you yet.' Quinn laughed and his laughter gurgled in his throat. 'And your poor mother up there by herself worrying about you. Anyway, now that you are here I want your advice. You know Campbell. Does he not belong to the same church as yourself, the Bishop Wilson's? You know I feel obliged to that Campbell and I am worried.'

'Obliged to Campbell. Obliged to that dirty latchico, that dirty cur. Obliged to him? It couldn't be.' Quinn was aghast that anybody could feel obliged to Campbell. Katie got up and went over to the fire.

'Shanks, tell Quinn about the cow while I make him a cup of tea and get him a bit of bread and try to get him sobered up.' At this Quinn jumped up in outrage at Katie's suggestion.

'You are a terrible woman altogether, Katie, trying to get me sobered up. It took me three weeks to get this drunk and now you're trying to get me sober. Anyway, Shanks, what about the cow and Campbell?'

'You were working in Scotland at the tatie hoking at the time, Quinn. It was late in October. The grass was scarce and we had the cow on the long acre. We forgot about her and when I went looking for her I found her in a bog hole. She was up to her oxters, Quinn. She was lying there with her tongue out. She was far gone. I ran down for Katie. There was nobody else about in the bog or the roads. Me and Katie could not move her. The old thing was exhausted.

'Then I saw Campbell coming down from the upper bog. I was not happy because I thought that I would have liked to have seen anybody but him. He saw us and took the bank down to where we were at. He could see what was wrong. Now I do not have to tell you, Quinn, what that cow means to us. The wee bit of milk, the wee bit of butter, and every year a calf. Many's a one had to take the boat when they lost their only cow. Man, I was in a terrible state.

'Campbell had the wee donkey with him. Katie had brought up a rope with her. I got my shoes off and down to my shirt and trousers.

Campbell had a wee rope on the donkey. He reached the end of it to me and I tied it round my waist. Man, there was no bottom to that hole. I got down into it and pushed our rope down behind the cow's front legs and threaded it across and pulled it up the far side. We pulled it tight in a loop and then we all got on it and tied it to the donkey and we pulled. The old beast tried her best but she was beat. She had been in too long.

'We could do no more. I was in a wild state and so was Katie. We were fit to be tied. I mean, Quinn, if we had lost that old cow we might have had to take the boat or head for the workhouse. Campbell was standing with his hands on his hips, he had tried his best too, Quinn. He half turned to me and said: "You still chew that tobacco?" I did not know what to think. What kind of a question was that at a time like that? "I do, Campbell" said I, shifting a wad of it from one cheek to the other. Everybody calls him Campbell as you know.'

"Get up here to her head. You" and he grunted at Katie, "come back here. Take this stick of mine. Wait to I get that bit of a plank from over there." Katie and him were at the back of her, Katie with a stick and Campbell with a bit of a plank. "Get ready. We will have to be ready to give it to her. And now, Shanks, get in close, get a good mouthful of tobacco ready. Get down close. Lift up her eyelid. Hold her eye well open. Spit that whole tobacco chew into her eye."

'It took me a while to figure out what he was saying. Then I understood what he was saying. When that chew would hit her eye the pain would be terrible. She would make a wild effort to struggle to get away from it. We took his orders. He was right, it was the only chance we had. But also we could not have disobeyed him if we had wanted as we were in a state of shock. This was more words than we had ever heard Campbell speak before. We were in a state of shock.'

Katie laughed as she remembered. Shanks was excited on the chair. 'Well, I got down. I got the whole chew ready. I held her eye open. And I let go. Right in her eye. Dead on target. A cow's eye. Heh. Heh. Heh. Well, when that tobacco hit her she gave a plunge. The pain must have been shocking. Katie and Campbell laid into her with the sticks and the plank. And me and the donkey pulled. Well, she rose up and gave a plunge and got her front legs on the hard bank and we all pulled and shouted and gave it to her. And what do you know but out she came. She was on the hard ground.

'She stood there shaking herself. She was cold and shivering. We stood there looking at her. Campbell too. We were quiet. I looked at Campbell. There was a look on him I never saw before or since. He seemed at peace. That meanness was gone out of him. It was like we were all together and he liked it. You know that what O'Donnell talks about now and then? What's the word, Katie? Solidarity. Aye, Solidarity. Working together. That's what it was that was making Campbell human. He had helped us. Worked together. Solidarity. He's not all bad, Quinn.'

'Well you may be right, Shanks. But I have no evidence myself to back that up. Thanks, Katie. Even though this drop of tea will only sober me up, you are a good woman. What were you talking about Campbell for anyway?'

'You know he's getting married on Saturday, Quinn. That wee Wallace girl.'

'Aye, I know all about it. It's a shame. I'm shamed the way she has been treated. And Allen will get away with it because he has over fifty good acres. It's not right.'

'Well, Quinn, here is the thing. What do you think that wee girl is going to go into? Campbell will not think about getting some things now that he will be married. That house of his is in a terrible shape. He lies on an old bench at the fire. The second wee room that should be the bedroom, there is nothing in it but dirt. Quinn, don't you have an old bed frame up there in your barn? I saw it when I was up for the spuds. You don't need it, do you? We have an old set of springs here and we have an old feather mattress.

'Here is what I think. You bring down the frame. And me and Katie will take it and the springs and feather mattress down to him and set it up in the wee room. It's the only way she will have a place to sleep and they will both be together like man and wife. You know he lets us about the place not like yourself. He thinks that we owe him so much because of the thing with the cow that he will never be obliged to us. It will be like a present for him. I will tell him we were going to throw them out. I won't tell him the frame is yours or he won't take it. He would think he would owe you something.'

'If we don't that wee girl will come in and have nowhere to sleep. Campbell won't know what to do. Man, I cannot think of it.' There was a silence round the fire. They were all in their own thoughts. 'Aye, that Campbell man. What made him like that? What kind of a country is this? Hah, A grown man and he.... That poor wee girl and her to have a baby in a few months and it's not even Campbell's. Where is the clergy when they... But then they are part of it.'

'Quinn, will you have another cup of tea?'

'Naw, I'm grand, thanks.'.

The tears were in Katie's eyes.

'Campbell, Campbell. It's Shanks and Katie. Are you in?' They chapped on the door. It opened and Campbell grunted at them. His dog barked on the floor beside him. 'Campbell, Katie and I are happy for you. We have brought you a present. It's ours, we had it in the house and we have been trying to get rid of it. But we want you to have it. You know that without you helping us with the cow we might have been out on the roadside. Can we bring it in?'

Campbell still holding the door in suspicion, half moved out of their way. The fire was down to a few embers and the cottage was dirty and smelled of dog and dirt. Shanks had the bed frame in his hands and Katie balanced the springs and the feather mattress on the ground at the doorstep. Shanks pushed in and Campbell moved aside. They moved fast as they did not want to give him a chance to change his mind. Shanks went straight to the wee room. The door was open. He pushed in. 'What about here Katie? Wait, I will put this here and give you a lift.'

Campbell stood there unable to take any active role. Watching. Trying to come to some decision. But Shanks and Katie moved fast. 'Campbell, how are the bog lettings going this year? Are there any spare banks? Is Mr Brown still keeping that far bank for himself?' Not stopping to let Campbell get time to object and distracting him with talk of other things, Shanks and Katie set up the bed. 'That's a good bank there Campbell. Mr Brown knows his bogs. But then he has you to guide him.'

By this time the frame was up and the springs were mounted on it. Shanks and Katie struggled with the feather mattress between them. It took a lot of hens and geese to be plucked to fill it. Shanks' mother had worked at it over the years. It was not a bad one. The only thing was when you sunk down into it you could hardly move again. But it would do Campbell and the wee Wallace girl. It was either that or nothing. 'Well the best of luck now, Campbell' and the door closed behind them.

They both let out a sigh of relief as they set off up the road towards their own place. They had just carried out an extremely skilled operation. They were in and out quick. They gave Campbell no time to think and refuse. They distracted him with talk of the bog and Brown as they moved fast. And as soon as the bed was in place they were out of there. Campbell would have three days to get used to it before Saturday. If there had been any justice in the world Katie and Shanks would have been awarded a medal.

The wedding on Saturday did what it was supposed to do. Legally it gave Margaret to Campbell and made him responsible for her while at the same time it made clear that they were so far beneath the minister and the authorities of the church, that this did not have to be said. The Bishop Wilson who had set up the whole thing, never even appeared. Presumably he was too good to preside over a wedding for somebody like Margaret who was already pregnant. The whole affair was beneath him once he had made the fix.

His junior assistant preacher carried out the ceremony. They were kept in the back of the church and married there. The preacher did not look either of them in the eye once. Campbell grunted his agreement to the marriage. Margaret did not respond at all until nudged and ordered to by her mother. Even then she sort of moved the top of her body forward and a groan came from the back of her throat. She was not accustomed to being asked to give her agreement to anything. Then it was over. They were outside the church again with the doors locked on them. The preacher stayed inside and then left by another entrance.

They set off to walk home. Campbell's cottage was two miles further up the same road into the mountain from the turn off to Margaret's family's cottage. Campbell never said a word to Margaret or any of them. He walked on ahead and Margaret walked with her mother and father and brothers. They did not talk. Campbell's back silenced them. They arrived at the turn off to Margaret's family's cottage. It was a relief. Margaret's feet were skinned. Under pressure from her mother Margaret's father had bought her a pair of shoes. She wished she could take them off.

'Well, come on over then and have something to eat,' Margaret's father asked Campbell as they came to the turn off.

But Campbell walked on past the turn off and did not answer.

Margaret stopped with her family. What was happening? Campbell stopped ten yards up the road with his back to them. He never turned around nor did he speak a word. They all stood. After a moment's silence Margaret's father looked at her.

'Well, go on then with your husband, Margaret. Good luck to both of you now.'

Margaret did not move.

Her father pushed her forward. 'Gone now, Margaret. Gone.' Campbell walked and slowly Margaret began to follow him. Campbell in front and Margaret behind, and not a word between them.

This was the second time her father had sent her off to a stranger. First it was to the Allens, now it was to Campbell. Margaret thought about all that had happened to her since the last time. She held out no hope that this time would be any better than before. She had no control over her life and it seemed that it was always men with their big mouths and big bodies who decided what she did. What form would it take this time with this man Campbell who never spoke? Then she thought about the church. That was again more men sending her off to do what they told her.

'Wait, Wait.' Her mother ran up from the track that led to her family's cottage with a package. She had heard about what Shanks and Katie had done. She gave the package, which contained two sheets and a long filled bolster, to Margaret. 'There now, Margaret. Be good.'

Margaret turned and slowly walked after Campbell. The family watched and Margaret turned and looked at them. She thought again about the last time when she had been sent away, then it was to Allen's, This time it was with Campbell. Once again her mother had told her to be good. Did nobody have to be good but her? Then her mother had sent her off with a dress, this time with bedclothes.

Campbell's dog barked a greeting when they turned into the yard. It was the same as her family's cottage, maybe a wee bit smaller. It had glass in the windows. Campbell pushed the door open and went

84

in. The dog ran out and barked and then sniffed her and wagged its tail and gradually came close. Margaret touched its head. It licked her. She stood outside the door until Campbell grunted at her and motioned at her to come into the cottage. It was already getting dark. It was hard to see inside.

Campbell sat down by the fireplace on the bench. The fire was dead. There was an old worn stool by the wall. Margaret did not know what to do. She stood waiting for her orders. It was better than the barn at Allen's. She stood and Campbell sat. After minutes had gone by Campbell grunted at her again and pointed to the stool. Margaret went slowly to it and sat down still holding the sheets and bolster. She was tired and hungry.

The fire was out. They sat for a while and did not speak. The newly wed couple. Then Campbell lay back on the bench and lifted his feet up on it and turned his face to the wall and began to breathe slowly. Margaret never moved. The dog lay on the floor. It looked at her and wagged its tail. Campbell began to snore. Margaret sat on holding the sheets and bolster on her knees. Slowly she began to feel sleepy.

She very carefully turned her head and looked in the wee room. She saw the bed and the feather mattress. Where would she sleep? Where was she supposed to sleep? He had not said. He was snoring. But she had not been told where to sleep. Maybe the bed was for somebody else? Maybe she was supposed to sleep in the outhouse like at Allen's? But he had told her to sit on the stool inside the cottage.

What was she to do? She did not know this man and she was in a strange house. But she was tired. She sat for a while longer. The dog moved over to her feet. She put her hand on its head. This gave her courage. She looked at Campbell again. He was still snoring. Very carefully she rose from the stool. She was desperate not to make a noise and wake him. She moved noiselessly to the wee room. She was too afraid to make the bed properly. The mattress was stained and smelled musty.

She spread one of the sheets on the feather mattress. She placed the bolster across the top of the mattress. The other sheet she spread on top. She took off her shoes. What a relief. But her feet had been bleeding. She did not want to get the sheets dirty. But she wanted to sleep. She thought of bleeding in the barn at Allen's. She turned her head sharply to put this memory away. She bent over to lie down. Aggh Naw. She had to go.

She could not put it off all night. She had walked to the church and back and not gone. She could not go to bed now and not go. But she must not wake him. The dog it must not bark. She held her hand out to it. It wagged its tail. She crossed the floor in her bare feet. The cold stone flags felt good to her bloody feet. She opened the door a fraction of an inch at a time. She was relieved it did not catch or squeak. She slipped out. The dog watched her but stayed quiet.

But where was she to go? There was no toilet. She walked down to the stream. She did not want him seeing her waste in the morning. She hunkered down over the edge of the stream and went. Then cleaned herself with grass. She would have to find where he went. Maybe some people drank from the stream further down? She put her feet in the water and washed the blood from them. It felt clean and cool. Not dirty or giving orders.

It was a good night. The clouds moved across the sky toward the east. There was a wee breeze. The Atlantic Ocean lay thirty miles to the west. Margaret had never seen it and never thought about it. She could glimpse the moon every now and then between the clouds. She was alone. He was asleep.

The door made no sound as she went in. The dog did not bark, instead it licked her hand as she passed. Campbell kept snoring with his face turned to the wall. She went into the wee room and very slowly without taking off her dress, which was still her only clothing. she very quietly lay down on the bed. She slowly fell asleep. Campbell snored on the bench by the dead fire. It was their wedding night in the late summer of 1912. Margaret was fourteen and Campbell was thirty-four.

CHAPTER NINE

Margaret was wakened in the morning by the sound of the door closing after Campbell. She lay thinking. She did not know what to do. She had been given no orders. What work was there for her to do? She sat up in the bed. She went out to the kitchen which was the main room of the cottage. There was no fire on. What was she supposed to do? It was almost worse not being given orders than being given them. What would he think when he got back? Her life had become so accustomed to being one of work and getting orders that she could not think of any other way to go through the day.

After a little while, Margaret went to the door and then to the window and looked out. She could see nobody. What was she supposed to do? After standing for a time she then went back to the stool she had sat on the night before and sat down. Was Campbell gone or just outside? She did not know. She was frightened that when he came back he would be angry if she had done nothing but she did not know what to do.

By this time Campbell was well on the way to Allen's. He was going to get his money for taking Margaret. Campbell was not a man to be taken advantage of. It was midday by the time he got to Allen's back door. It was open. The woman came out. She glowered at him but did not speak. 'Allen?' She pointed up to where Allen was looking the sheep. Then turned and went back into the house. Campbell headed up the fields.

'So it's yourself, Campbell. How are you doing?' Allen asked him in an effort to soft soap him.

'I'm here for my money. The Bishop Wilson was to speak to you about it. I'm here for it.'

'You're not a man to let the grass grow under your feet, Campbell. You just got married yesterday. Well the best of luck to both of you. She's a hard wee worker that wee Wallace girl. She is that. You could have done worse. Well, here's a pound to help you get started.'

Campbell looked at the pound with an expression of rage on his face. 'That's no good. Allen. You have had your way with her. She has your wean. I will have to feed and clothe it. I want ten pounds. Or if you do not have that then I will have one of your two cows. A pound is no good to me.'

Allen went red in the face. 'Ten pounds? It is more than she's worth no matter what way you take her.'

Campbell was not shaken, instead he continued: 'Maybe we should go down to the house and talk it over with Mrs Allen.'

'Naw, naw. We can settle this here between us two men'. Allen grinned slyly in phony male solidarity. Campbell left with eight pounds in his pocket. It was not bad, considering.

On the way back he went down to the village and into the farm of Willie Roberts. 'Well it's Campbell. How are you doing?'

Never a man for small talk Campbell said 'I hear you might be wanting to sell one of your cows. Which one is it?' Roberts lead him through to his byre. He pointed to a roan cow with a large udder and horns.

'There she is.' Campbell bought her for seven pounds. Taking her by the halter he set off home. A woman and a cow all in the one week. It was not bad. It was late afternoon by the time he arrived back at his place again.

Margaret heard the dog bark and knew it was him. She did not know what to do. Other than go outside to relieve herself she had just sat in the kitchen on the stool. That was the only order she had got since she had arrived. Sit on the stool. She was frightened as she waited for him to come in. She heard him shouting at an animal and wondered what was happening. The dog was barking. The door was pushed open and Campbell came in. He did not look at her. He looked at the fire which was as dead as it had been when he left.

He went over to the shelf by the fire and lifted the lid of a tin can there. He took out a half a loaf and broke a piece off. He began to eat it. She had not eaten any of it. He turned and headed for the door. Margaret stood looking down. Then he turned around again. He grunted and gestured to Margaret to follow him. He stopped and pointed to the tin bucket that was on the table. She brought it with her.

The cow was tied in the lean-to shed by the gable of the cottage. There was a pile of hay in front of her and she was eating. Campbell pointed to the cow and then at Margaret and the tin bucket and again back to the cow. Then he grabbed Margaret's arm and pushed her forward to the cow. Then grunting to himself he turned and walked out of the yard and off down the road. He still had one of Allen's pounds in his pocket.

Margaret found a piece of block that Campbell had cut off the end of a tree stump. She put this on the ground by the cow for a stool and sat on it. She put the bucket between her knees and reached in for the cow's teats. She was hoping that the cow was not a kicker. Slowly she began to milk the cow. It looked around at her and seemed quite contented eating at the hay. Gradually the bucket filled up. Margaret was less stressed now that she knew what she was supposed to do.

She carried the bucket of milk into the house and set it on the table. Her experience at Allen's, where she used to take some of the animal's feed, came back to her and she drank some of the milk. She was starving. She wondered if she could risk taking a bit of the bread from the tin can. She was so hungry that she decided to risk it, pulling small bits from around the edges hoping he would not notice. She was hungrier than ever but she was too frightened to take more. It got slowly dark and she went and lay down on the bed and tried to sleep.

By this time Campbell was in McDaid's. What was wrong with her? She never lit the fire. She must have sat in the house all day. This was no good. She was going to have to work. She had better have that cow milked when he got back. After three whiskys Campbell headed for home. He still had money in his pocket.

He pushed open the door of the cottage. It was dark. He went to the press on the other side of the fire and felt around and got a candle and matches and lit it. The cottage took on a dull glow. Margaret watched him from the bed and then sat up stiff waiting for her orders. He looked at the bucket of milk. Then took a tin cup from the shelves by the fire and drank some of it. Then he blew out the candle and went and lay down on the bench. Margaret sat down on the bed and waited. When he gave her no orders she lay down and after a while went to sleep.

She awoke in fear. What was it? Something was at her, pulling at her. Then she realised it was him who was pulling at her. He was feeling her chest. He was grunting to himself. He had no trousers on, just in his shirt-tail. He pulled her legs over to the side of the bed. She did not know what to do. They were married, what did it mean? She held her legs closed. Visions of Allen were in her mind. She did not want this. She did not want this. He snarled at her. He pulled at her legs. She held them together.

'Married' he snarled. 'Wife' he snarled. This confused her. What? Did this mean she had no right to hold her legs closed? Again he snarled: 'Married. Wife.' This time more aggressively and put all his strength into pulling her legs apart. 'Married. Wife,' he said again.

Hearing these words again and not knowing what they meant she could do and not do, increased her confusion and weakened her resistance. They were also related to the power of the church which had married her and made her a wife. These words, married, wife, backed up with the power of the church, had the same affect as Allen's blow. They weakened her resistance. He got her legs apart. His thing stuck out. He pulled her to the side of the bed and he was standing between her legs. He pushed his thing at her. She felt the pain again as he put it into her body. He was holding her and breathing hard and pushing at her.

It did not last long. He pushed hard and then shook and then stopped. Then he pulled out from her and turned away and went back and lay on his bench facing the wall and soon his snores told her he was sleeping. She lay there. What? She felt, like with Allen, something leaking out of her. What did this mean? Her mother had told her that when men put their things in women they get a baby. But she already had a baby from Allen. She did not move, just lay there listening to him snoring, glad he was asleep.

And so it went. By grunting and pointing at her Campbell made clear she was to get up in the morning and make the fire and make him tea and stirabout from the oatmeal. This and bread, milk, and spuds was their diet. He bought flour at McDaid's and grunted at her that she was to make bread. This was perhaps the one job she did not resent. The kneading of the flour and the baking of the bread over the hearth fire and watching it rise, and the colour of it, and the smell and taste of it. It was the closest to art that her life allowed her. Except for the flour, salt, sugar and stirabout everything else they ate they produced from their own fields and the cow.

After making the fire, the tea and stirabout, she had to milk the cow and store the milk in the bucket on the shelf away from the fire. During the day, she had to bring in turf from the stack behind the cottage and make a pile beside the fire. She also had to bake bread from the flour. She had to milk the cow again in the early evening and make his tea when he came back. And if he wanted to get up from his bench and go to her where she lay in bed, she had to let him. He never slept with her. He always went back to his bench by the fire.

Halfway through the second week there was a change in Margaret's routine. After breakfast one morning he grunted at her and signaled for her to follow him. He walked off down the road and she came behind. They walked the three miles to Brown's house. The road to Brown's house went past the turn off to Margaret's family's cottage. She could see the top of the tree behind the cottage but the cottage itself was in the lee side of the hill. Margaret yearned to see her mother. They did not see any of her family. Margaret was almost five months pregnant and she was tired when they arrived. Campbell led her to the back door. The cook came out. 'Aye, you can leave her here.'

She was put to work polishing the silver in a corner of the harness room. She liked the smell of the polish. Sitting on a small stool she polished away. The repetitive nature of the job was almost soothing. The silver was expensive. One piece would have been a month's wages for Margaret. After a while bending over to polish the silver her stomach hurt. Her child in her stomach was being pressed into an unnatural position and she was hurting. But it did not occur to her to say anything. Her life at Allen's and Campbell's had taught her that there was no good in complaining about work.

That evening she walked home and found she had to milk the cow and make him his food as usual. The next day she had to walk to and from Brown's again and clean more silver and this time also clean windows. The following day she had to take the rugs and hang them out the back on a line and beat the dust out of them. Margaret enjoyed this as it allowed her to get some of her anger out, but it exhausted her.

The cook, who was her boss, never spoke to her other than to give her an order. It was clear the cook thought Margaret was beneath her. She never saw the wee Brown girl or her father or mother. They lived at the front of the house and upstairs. She forgot that she had ever wished she was the wee Brown girl. One blow after another until she lost any thinking that she could change things for the better, the idea of wishing had dropped away from her mind. Life had settled into an exhausting and brutal monotony. Everyday she would walk to and from the Brown's house. Every Friday Campbell would come to Brown's house and speak to the cook and get Margaret's wages and pocket them.

Up in the morning, light the fire, milk the cow, walk to Brown's, work, walk back to the cottage, milk the cow, boil spuds for Campbell. She would eat some of these and drink some milk. Every few nights let him put his thing in her. Lie and listen to him go to sleep snoring on the bench. Go to sleep herself and never have a dream that was not full of fright or punishment. And all through this just like at Allen's, a man, first her father now Campbell, would come and take the money she earned and put it in his pocket.

'Well, it's yourself, Campbell.' Margaret's father greeted Campbell who had turned up in his yard. Since the marriage had already taken place Margaret's father did not feel the need to be so polite to Campbell. 'How is married life?'

Campbell did not answer instead he looked at Wallace. 'I took your girl even though she was in the family way. I need a couple of hens to get a few eggs.' Wallace did not really understand for a moment what was being said. 'You have more than a dozen here. Three or four would not be missed.'

Wallace did not know what to say so he tried to stall for time. 'They will be the devil to catch and which four?'

Campbell on the other hand did not slacken. 'Aye, four hens

would be grand, any four. She is well gone now she needs more feed. Spuds, bread and milk is not enough. I have to clothe and feed her and she has another man's wean. It's not right.'

Campbell looked at the hens scratching in the yard. He held out the sack he had been carrying to Wallace. Together they rounded up the hens from the front of Wallace's cottage and put them into a shed. They then caught four, put them in Campbell's bag and he headed off up the road again to his own place.

Wallace looked over his shoulder and saw that his wife had been watching what had gone on. He felt he had to explain. 'Campbell came and said he needed some hens. He said he had taken Margaret in and she needed more feed and we owed him. So he wanted four hens. So I gave them to him.' Wallace turned away when he said this as he realised that Margaret's mother was looking at him with disdain for his capitulation to Campbell. But it was not only disdain that Mary felt. She was also confused herself because she felt that at least by Campbell getting the eggs Margaret would get some more to eat.

Margaret sat in the cottage as Campbell left. She did not feel that she was a person. She moved through her days with things happening to her. The work at the cottage, the work at Brown's, Campbell putting his thing in her, these things happened to her. There was no resistance left in her because she did not feel that she was a person with hopes and dreams and pleasures for which it was worth resisting. The last few years had left her without a personal centre.

She was becoming physically bigger and bigger every day. It was harder than ever to walk to and from Brown's place. It was not easy to milk the cow as she had to bend over her big stomach. When Campbell came to her he sometimes lay on her afterwards and this hurt her. But she did not think of pushing him off. After he would go to his bench she would turn over and lie on her side and rest.

When she was first at Allen's she used to think about the future when she would leave. But that soon left her and she just existed from day to day. It was no different here. Life was not measured by her on the basis of how much pleasure she would have, how much control she had over her life, any aims she had for the future. These things never entered her head. Life was not measured for her at all. She just existed.

In this state hope was not only difficult but it was impossible so it had died. Laughter did not come at all. Laughter would have had to come from her and things did not come from her, things happened to her. It was even worse for her than at Allen's in some way. There she had made friends with the pigs and some of the animals. But now even this was not in her anymore. She did not even wish to die as this would have demanded an individuality that she no longer had and an ability to desire which had long died.

CHAPTER TEN

It was Friday. He had come to Brown's, collected her pay and left. As usual he never came to see or speak to her. It was as if she did not exist. Only her pay existed. He came for her pay. He left with her pay. He did what he liked with her pay. She stayed where she was polishing silver or beating rugs. She never saw her pay. She was half way home. Her belly stuck out in front of her and pulled her forward. Her back hurt. The stool they gave her to sit on was too low. As she walked she held her hands on her haunches and tried to pull the top of her body back. Pain was what was now happening to her. And she was cold too.

She was exhausted. She trailed her bare feet. The dust clung to them. She stumbled when she stepped on a sharp stone, fell into the grass verge and rolled down into the bottom of the hedge. She wanted to get up but she also wanted to lie there. She was tired and empty of resources. She made a weak effort to rise and then fell back again. She gave way to her exhaustion and lay there. She felt sleep coming. It was a comfort to think that maybe she would not wake up.

It was there Shanks and Katie came on her. 'It's the wee Wallace girl, I mean the wee Campbell girl. That is who it is. Hey, what, are you all right? Waken up.'

'Is she? Shanks, is she?'

'Naw, she is just sleeping.' Shanks shook her by the arm. She opened her eyes. But other than that did not move. 'Come on now, girl, you cannot lie there. You'll get your death. You will have to get up.' Katie joined him and together they armed her up and onto her feet. 'Are you all right, girl?'

She looked at them. They could see she was exhausted and the size of her belly. 'Come on now, we are going home and we will walk you up. Are you on your own? Where is your husband? Where is Campbell? Is he at home?' She did not answer them, just slouched along beside them with her head down. Shanks and Katie glanced at each other behind her back.

It took them an hour to get to Campbell's house. They did not go in, just watched her walk to the door and push it and enter.

'My heart is breaking for that wee girl, Shanks. Look at her with that baby coming and working everyday and walking up and down. She was lying sleeping in the hedge. They have her worked to the bone. It's not right.'

Campbell was not home when she went into the cottage. She got the milk bucket and went out and began to milk the cow. It got harder and harder. She had to bend over her big belly and reach in to get a grip of the cow's teats. The milk began to stream into the bucket. Tnis Tnis Tnis. Each squirt made a noise as it hit the tin. The bucket began to fill up.

Margaret was not so alert as usual. She squeezed the cow's teat too hard too near the top and the milk was forced out of the hole at the end of the teat too strongly, forcing the opening too wide and hurting the cow. She drew back and kicked Margaret, knocking her off the makeshift stool and spilling the milk over her dress. Margaret was exhausted worse than she had ever remembered before.

She lay there in the dirt and put her head down and lay there and lay there. That was all she did. No thoughts crossed her mind. She surrendered to exhaustion and to her oppression and lay there. She lay waiting for sleep or some end to it all. She had no will or desire left. The cow went on eating its feed. She lay in the dirt with the wet milk seeping into her.

Over half an hour passed by and Campbell, not finding her in the house when he got back, came to the byre to look for her. He grabbed her by the arm and shook her.

'Get up! Get up! Look! All the milk is spilled.'

This was the most words he had ever spoken to her. She did not respond. He pulled her up to sitting position.

'Look at the waste here of this milk. You are useless. You are useless! Get up!' She did not move.

Then he hit her with his open hand on the back of the head. She bowed her head forward. He hit her again. 'Get up!' He was getting more angry by the second. This was the first time she had not obeyed his orders. He shook her. She did not respond, just sat there on the byre floor with her head hanging forward and her eyes shut. He started to shout at her. 'Do what you are told. Get up, finish the milking, and then get into the house!'

When she did not respond again he hit her again, this time with his closed fist on the side of the face. She fell over. He lost his temper and he dragged her like an animal by the back of her dress out of the byre and into the rough yard. Pulling her in great rough jerks across the yard and with each jerk shouting at her. It never occurred to him she was half unconscious with exhaustion. All he could see was his pair of hands were not responding to his orders.

In the cottage he let her fall on the floor and went to sit on the edge of the bench. Then he got up and took some bread to eat. He sat looking round every few minutes at Margaret. He was enraged. She would not work. She spilled the milk. She would not obey. She was lying sleeping on the stone flag floor. He leaned over and stretched out on the bench and went to sleep.

Margaret awoke and regained consciousness. She was lying on the floor. Her dress, wet with milk, was cold on her. She smelled. She looked around without moving her head. He was snoring. He must be on the bench. She began to drag herself slowly to the bed and, with a great effort, managed to crawl up on to it. She fell asleep and after an hour awoke to find she had wet herself.

She lay there, inert and without hope, unaware of herself other than the exhaustion and the wet and cold clothes. Campbell slept on and snored. The dog came over and looked up at her on the bed. Campbell awoke. He was standing beside her in his shirt-tail. His thing stuck out. She did not care. To care would have needed some kind of consciousness and regard for herself.

He pulled her legs over to the side of the bed. Then he felt the wet. At first he thought it was the milk. But it felt too hot. Then he realised. 'You have lay there until you pissed the bed. You dirty pig you.' She lay there and began to go to sleep. Campbell went back to the bench.

When she awoke she was frozen with the cold and hunger and her wet clothes. Campbell was gone, she could see this from the bed and the dog being gone. She rose herself up and then stood up. She was cold and wet and dirty, smelling of stale milk and her own waste. She went to the door and went out and relieved herself. She looked at the clear stream and the water rushing down it. Then she turned to go back into the house.

Campbell was back, standing at the door looking at her. 'Girl, listen to me. You need to learn your lesson. He approached and shook her. Her head slumped forward and she did not answer. You need to learn your lesson.' He approached and shook her. Her head slumped forward and she did not answer. He shouted at her. 'You have to learn your lesson. You are here to work.'

He let her go and turned and walked out of the yard and down the road. The night before and that morning he had spoken more words to her than ever before and they were all to tell her she must obey and she must work.

Margaret sank down to the ground. She lay there and then the rain started to fall in a mizzle. It began to wet her clothes, hair and face. But she did not move she did not care, she was at the end of her feelings. Where he had hit her was painful but while she felt the pain it created no emotions in her. She was too tired and beaten down for these. She fell asleep.

She dreamt that she was a bird. A wee sparrow fluttering around her nest and her mate was sitting on a branch watching her work. He was chattering and so was she. The lightness of her feet and her wings could lift her up in the air. She could not fall. She could fly. She jumped in and out of her nest. The eggs would come soon and there would be wee ones.

Margaret dreamt that she was sitting on a branch fluffing her wings and feathers with her bill and her mate was doing the same thing. It was an evening in the summer. Peaceful. There was no cold in the air. They sat side by side and chattered and sang and worked on their feathers. There was a companionship, an ease, no blows, no orders. Margaret dreamt she was a sparrow with her companion and life was better.

It was the dog that woke her. He was whimpering for her and pawing at her dress. Slowly she came awake and the dog was down on his front paws looking at her. There was anxiety in his eyes. He whimpered, then wagged his tail when her eyes opened and he licked her face. He was happy to see her come alive.

Margaret closed her eyes and tried to go back to sleep and her dream. But she was cold and the dog was pawing at her. Slowly she came fully awake. The wet dress lay on her and the cold got worse. Her bruises hurt. Her big belly lay in front of her. The cold drove her up on her hands and knees. She stayed there for a while and rested. She then dragged herself into the house changed her dress, climbed onto the bed, and fell asleep. She had not thought of going to Brown's that day.

Campbell was walking to the pub. She has to learn she is here to work. My father made me work. If I do not work I have nothing and it's the boat or worse. Everybody knows this. But women don't think right. She has to learn. I have to teach her. My father beat it into me. She needs to get it beat into her. I have to teach her her place.

'A wee half.' He took his whisky back to the seat at the door away from the other customers. He turned his face away from his own thoughts when the picture of his fist hitting her face came into his mind's eye. For a moment compassion tried to push to the surface of his thoughts. He jerked his head around again pushing the image and thought away. She has to find her place. I have to know my place. If I don't then they will give me the fist. It will be the boat or the jail cell. That is the way it is. Naw, it's no sense in not knowing your place. She has to know hers. She has to do what I tell her, like I have to do what Brown tells me. That's the way it is. This will teach her.

Margaret was trying to sleep. Everything happened to her. They sent her to Allen's. He attacked her and put his thing in her. Her father took her pay. Allen gave her a baby. They got her a husband. He made her work. Took her pay. Put his thing in her. Hit her. Took her pay. She felt a dull overpowering helplessness. She lay there slowly and began to doze. She had no desires left. They had beaten them out of her. She just was, just had things happen to her, she dozed. She had reached rock bottom.

When he came home he pulled her legs apart and put his thing in her. She hurt. He pushed and grunted and smelled of whisky. He shook and pulled out his thing and went and lay on the bench and began to snore. She lay as he had left her with her legs apart. She had no power left in her. Neither anger nor joy nor hope. She felt the stuff leaking out of her. She may have lay like that all night, bare to the world, if the cold had not got to her and she covered herself up.

This time she dreamt of the days before they sent her to Allen's. It was sunny and warm. She was with the donkey. She stroked its soft muzzle. It nudged and nibbled at her with its lips. She hugged its head. Her brother climbed on its back and slid off, she followed him. The dog lay in the sun and watched them. The hens scraped at the back door of her house. 'Girl! Girl!' She heard her father shout and come towards her. It was the end of her happy life.

Then she dreamt of a man's thing inside her. It was attacking her. It was looking inside her to see what it could do to her. It was searching looking for the best place to beat her inside. It was beating at her. What did it want? What was it looking for? Why did men's things not leave her alone? Why did they attack her? All they brought her was pain and a man insulting and abusing her. That will teach her. She has to learn her place. Put their thing in her. That will teach her. She has to learn her place. Put their thing in her.

Then she dreamt again of the sparrow on her nest with her companion. Chattering and flying around with the wind in her feathers. Chattering together. No orders, no hitting, no pain. In the nest, it was a summer's evening the wind was from the west. It was a soft wind with the feel and smell of rain in it. She felt it on her cheek. She lay back in the pleasure of it.

Then she awoke. She was wet and cold. He was snoring. There was no soft wind with rain in it, only the smell of the cottage, the turf, the dog, the clothes, whisky, her own smell and the smell of stale milk. She lay still, only moving her eyes. The less she moved the less likely to get hit. The less she existed the less likely to get acted on. She lay there without moving.

But she could not achieve this total stillness that she thought was best for her, because every now and then there would be a little movement inside her. For the past few months now she had been feeling little movements in her belly. She wondered was something wrong? Was something broken inside her? Was she sick? She wished it would stop. It scared her. She wished everything would stop. But no matter what, this movement inside her kept on happening and growing stronger.

CHAPTER ELEVEN

'Shanks, what can we do? It's not our business. Shanks, they won't like us pushing our nose into their business. You know what they are like. They think they are better than us.'

'That wee girl could die, Katie. She does not know anything about having a baby and that gulpin he is worse. She could die up there some night. Her own clergy just fixed her up with that man and they want nothing more to do with her.'

'What day is it, Katie? Is it not Wednesday? This is the day Campbell goes to Convoy to see Brown about the bog lettings. He will be away all day and late into the evening.'

'I will have nothing to do with it, Shanks.'

'Come on, Katie, we have to help that wee girl.'

'What about her own ones they just live over the side of the hill?'

'But they will do nothing unless they are pushed. Come on, Katie, come with me.'

Sometimes Katie had just about enough of Shanks. This is what she was thinking as she set off after him down the mountain road. It was really nothing but a rough track. She clenched her teeth and glowered at his back as they walked. She knew he was a good man. More than anything else it was this that drew her to him. For years she had seen him destroy himself with the drink. There were times that he was lying outside McDaid's on the side of the road full drunk.

He was a shame to the whole place at that time. When they were only barely out of their childhood they had been friends and played together. But then with the drink this ended. She remembered the day she had been walking up from McDaid's with some groceries. He was lying there drunk with his back propped up against the bank of the hedge. As she approached he sat up and tried to focus on her. And she remembered her astonishment as he spoke to her. 'Katie, I want to marry you.' The anger went out of her as she remembered and she unclenched her teeth.

She thought again what happened after he had said he wanted to marry her. No sooner had he said he wanted to marry her than he started to slide down the bank and it was clear that he was falling asleep. But the shock of her answering him woke him with a start. He pulled himself up. 'What did you say? Say that again.' He had not heard her properly. Katie remembered so clearly what she then repeated to him. She had said 'Shanks, if you give up the drink and stay off it and act like the decent man you could be, then I will marry you.'

Katie smiled to herself as she hurried after Shanks. She was as surprised at those words that had come out of her mouth as Shanks was to hear them. He always had been known for having the gift of the gab. But this time he was struck dumb. She had stopped and looked at him as she had spoken. She looked at him and he looked at her. She realised then for the first time how much she had missed his friendship. How these words must have been forming in her and leading to this challenge to him. She said no more but walked on.

Shanks never touched a drop of drink from that day on. Katie's mother died the following spring. Shanks worked at odd jobs here and there as he always did. A year and a half after the proposal and the reply and giving up the drink, they were married. Katie never regretted it. Whatever had been driving at Shanks and making him drink seemed to turn into the drive, that she saw in him now, to help others.

That was it, she thought. He wants to help Margaret now. And he is dragging me after him into who knows what down at Wallace's. Then she felt the anger going out of her and she smiled to herself. It's a lot better than him being on the drink that is for sure. She looked at him and felt the power of her affection and love for him. Shanks was a very good man. She was a very lucky woman.

They passed Campbell's cottage and some distance on took the turn left up to Margaret's family's cottage. Mary, Margaret's mother, was out in the yard washing a bucket of potatoes.

'Hello there, Missus Wallace.'

'Hello Shanks and Katie. How are you doing?'

'Grand, and yourself?'

'Agh, grand too.'

'Missus Wallace,' Shanks got straight to it in case he lost his nerve. 'We had to help your wee girl Margaret home the other night. She was lying in the hedge down near Brown's. She is working too hard I think. We are worried about her.'

Katie said nothing just looked off into the distance. Mary did not know what to say. Who were they to be worried about Margaret? And a couple of Fenians too. Margaret was her wee girl.

'Campbell is away today, Mrs Wallace, and Katie and I are on the way up home and we are going to call and see Margaret. She will be home milking by now. Maybe you would want to come up with us and see how she is?'

Mary was angry but she knew herself how she had been worrying about Margaret. She must be in her sixth month now. She might be in trouble. 'Okay, I will come.' They set off together. Mary's mouth was a thin tight line across her face with anger and shame as she thought about Katie and Shanks having to come to get her.

Margaret was in the byre milking the cow when they arrived. She had her back to them. For a few seconds they all stood and watched her. 'Margaret, your mother is here to see you,' Shanks said and he and Katie went outside. Margaret turned round and saw her mother. She thought and felt nothing. They had become disconnected by Mary's passivity when her father had sent Margaret away. And for all the suffering in between, Mary had not been there. Margaret said nothing and went on with her milking.

'Are you all right, Margaret?'

Her mother noticed the bruise on her daughter's face. She stood there wordless. The brutal events of the past years had built a wall between them. She had let her daughter go to Allen and let him get away with attacking and raping her. She had not stood up to her husband as he treated her daughter as only another mouth to feed and sent her away. She had not stood up to the clergy who got rid of Margaret by giving her to Campbell. Her shame and anger gagged her. She could not see clearly who was to blame for all this and so her rage filled the air around herself and Margaret threatening to explode and damage the both of them.

Margaret got up with the bucket full of milk. Her mother could see she could hardly carry it with her big belly. This at least Mary could do for her.

'I will carry it, Margaret.' And she took the bucket from her hands. Margaret walked to the door and out and into the cottage. Shanks and Katie watched them go and they left the yard and headed for home. They both felt more at peace.

'What happened your face, Margaret?' But Margaret did not answer. She pointed to the shelf for the bucket and her mother put it there. She then sat on her bed with her head down facing out into the room where her mother stood. The turf fire was the only warmth in the cottage. Minutes went by and they did not speak. Her mother stood where she was. She could bear it no longer. 'Margaret, are you all right?' But there was no answer. Margaret sat looking down and waiting for this to pass as she had grown to wait for all things to pass.

Then she jerked and for a second there was some life in her face, a surprised and anxious questioning. Her hands moved to the side of her big belly. She laid them on herself. She gave another jerk and her expression gained more life.

'What is it, Margaret?' Her mother then understood. It was the baby. It was moving in Margaret. She was maybe more than six months gone. Who was to know? She was very big for only to be six months gone. She might be even more.

'Margaret lie down,' Mary said and pressed her back on the bed. 'Did you feel a kick there? In your belly? Did you feel a kick?' Margaret jerked again and held her belly. 'Margaret let me see,' and she lifted up her daughter's dress and held her hands to Margaret's belly and there it was. The baby was moving and kicking inside. Mary could feel it and see it.

'Look, Margaret, your baby is moving. It's alive and okay. Look down, you can feel it and you can see it. Look, there it is pushing against your stomach. Look, look.' Margaret looked down and she could see the outline of the baby pushing against the side of her belly. 'Margaret, your baby is moving. It will soon be here. Your baby is moving.'

Margaret had endured too much to be excited with this news. She had lost all hope and desire for herself. She could see and feel the baby moving but it did not seem to be related to her as a person. It was related to her as a body. But not as a person. She had given up feeling as a person. So the baby could not find her. She looked at her belly and lay there. Her mother did not know what to do. She was happy to see the signs of her daughter's baby. But her daughter was not. There was something wrong.

'Margaret, Margaret. It's your baby, it will soon be born. You should be happy to be having a baby. It is God's blessing. Margaret, it is God's blessing.' Margaret lay back on the bed and turned on her side with her back to her mother and lay there.

At that point Campbell came in the door of the cottage. He was tired with his walk from the village and his day's work. He looked at Margaret's mother, did not speak, went to sit at the fire which Margaret had lit earlier. He sat down on the bench with his back half turned to Mary. He just sat there. She stood. They did not speak for a minute.

Then Mary pulled herself together. 'James, I was just calling to see if Margaret was all right with the baby coming and all.'

Campbell sat at the fire and did not respond in any way.

Mary did not know what to do. She was afraid for her daughter. She was afraid of Campbell. She wanted to leave but she was worried about her daughter. She had abandoned her too many times. But she could not see what she could do. 'Well, I will be off now, Margaret. I will come by and see you now regularly because the baby will soon come and you may need help. Cheerio, James'. Campbell sat there motionless and unanswering as she left.

Margaret lay on the bed with her back to the main room and to Campbell. Her legs were curled up as she lay like a foetus. She was confused. She realised that she wasn't able any longer to sink into the passive despair in which she had lived for the past years. Something was bothering her. Something was prodding at her. She tried to sleep. Then she felt the baby kick again in her belly. She held her breath. It kicked again. She held her breath and listened and felt her senses becoming alert.

Then it was still. She lay quiet waiting. Nothing happened. She lay waiting. But nothing. Slowly she relaxed a little but she was still waiting. Then it happened again. She felt it. She felt it. She felt a feeling of life in herself. She became more alert than at any time in years. She was alive waiting for it. She felt it again. This time she put down her hands. No longer passive. She wanted to feel it with her hands.

'It's in me. It's moving in me. It's my baby,' she whispered to herself. And for the first time in years Margaret began to realise that she might after all want a future.

She lay there. Campbell was snoring at the fire. He knew nothing of this change that was at work behind him. He knew nothing of Margaret feeling alive and interested for the first time in years. He snored on. Margaret listened to him, glad he was asleep. The baby moving was hers. It was hers. He would not know. She would now have something of her own. She was holding this baby in her belly. For once she was doing something to another. She was not passive. She was giving this baby life.

She thought of it. She looked down at herself. Only moving her eyes as she did not want to waken Campbell. She wanted to be alone and to keep this new part of her life to herself. She lay there holding her belly hoping to feel the baby again. There it was. It was the baby kicking. She could feel it. She could feel it with her hands. She realised that for the first time in years she wanted something. She wanted to have and to see the baby.

Along with this new feeling of concern for and interest in her baby, she felt her passivity begin to fall away. She began to think how she would survive the next months and how to keep her baby alive. It was like a whole new place had opened in her and from it was coming a different person filling out her body and mind. She held her mouth closed and narrowed her eyes. She was barely breathing.

Like a creature in the wild, she held herself motionless and tensed. She looked into the future, searching for the path to take that would best allow her to overcome her enemies and survive. A new person was coming into being as she lay in her dirty bed in her dirty clothes with the bruises on her face and Campbell snoring at the fire. A new person, a fighter who would do whatever it took to bring her child into the world and look after it.

She felt the dog's nose on her back. It was standing on its back legs with his front feet on the bed. It had never done this before. She turned to look at it. A look of concentration was on its face. Concern and affection for her was in its eyes. It sensed something new in Margaret. She turned away again and gently pushed it to the floor as she did not want Campbell to see and maybe understand that something was changing. It was better he thought she was the same person. She was already thinking tactically to hide what was going on from Campbell.

She lay there holding her belly and every now and then feeling the baby kick and push. She began to relax. She began to feel at ease hugging her baby in her belly. She began to breathe more deeply. She began to feel drowsy, a gentle drowsiness. She felt like stretching. She felt like lifting up her head and standing up straight. She let her breath out with a rush. For the first time in years she felt a smile in herself. She hugged her bellied baby. She smiled secretly inside herself. The past three years began to slide away behind her. For this baby of hers that was moving inside her she wanted to live. She wanted to live. She wanted to live. She wanted a future.

Chapter Twelve

The knocking at Mary's door was loud and a man's voice was calling to them. Wallace got up and shouted:

'Who is there?'

'It's me, Campbell, she's having the wean.'

Mary threw on her clothes and gathered up a few cloths and a bucket and was out the door. She was not intimidated by Campbell for once. She did not even think about him. She headed up the lane half running. Margaret, she had to be all right. Was she alone? Had he left her alone?

It was a beautiful spring night with stars shining and a light breeze from the west. Mary ran slipping on the rocks on the dirt road. She would help Margaret this time. She would not let her down this time. In the past months, from the time she had first went up, she had gone back every other Wednesday when she knew Campbell would be gone. Margaret had never talked to her but a change had taken place in her attitude. She was no longer passive and silent. She was still silent but she seemed to be alert and thinking about things. She almost appeared at times to be plotting.

Mary was almost bursting in her rush to get there. She had not helped Margaret in the past three years but now she would. She would be there for her from now on. She felt her heart pounding and her breath coming in gasps. She was afraid she would have a heart attack and die before she got to Margaret's. She tried to slow down. But she could not hold back. She began to run again. She would not let her down this time.

Campbell came behind her walking without any great haste. Let the women handle it. She was her mother. Let them handle it. He had enough on his plate to worry about. It wasn't his wean anyway. Let them handle it. He had gone down for her, wasn't this enough? And he had been through this before. He tried to push the memory away, but it threatened to rise up in his head bringing with it a terror. He pushed it down again.

Margaret was lying back in her bed and her body felt that it would break open. Every minute or so a great spasm and pressure would go through her. It felt like the bones in her pelvic area were being driven apart and as if her skin was being stretched to where it was going to rip and tear. She tried desperately to make no sound but now and then a muffled groan would escape from her.

She lay there in the dark and held on. Her mother had told her that this would be what would happen when the baby was trying to be born, to come out of her. So she knew what was happening. But she had no idea the pain would be this bad. Again she clenched her teeth and stifled her screams as she was shaken with a new enormous pressure.

She had been lying there in labour, in the dark, on her own, for over three hours. Campbell had left the house and never said where he was going. She was not afraid. She had slept for nearly three years in Allen's barn alone. She had been beaten and attacked by both Allen and Campbell and she had survived on her own. And she was now stronger than ever. Since she had felt her baby moving in her she had got new strength and a desire to live.

The door burst open. It was her mother. 'Margaret, Margaret, I am here. It is all right.' The fire was on. This was good. Mary put a pot filled with water on the chain hanging over the turf. She turned over the turf to let the heat up and put on a few sticks that were lying there. 'Margaret, it will be all right. The baby will soon come.'

Three hours passed. Mary sat and held her daughter and Margaret lay and laboured with great wracking shudders and stifled screams, and feeling as if the pressure inside her would either burst her apart or would kill her. The baby fought to be born. Margaret fought to bring it out of her body into the light. But what happened if it could not? For the first time Margaret thought that maybe something could go wrong. She had a vision of the baby's body being stuck inside her and her not able to get it out.

She felt each time her spasm came that this was what was happening. All the mothers who died having babies they must have died because the baby could not get out. The mother's body must have burst. Or maybe it could not burst and the mother and baby just killed each other. The baby exhausting the mother trying to fight its way out and the mother exhausting herself and the baby trying to bring it out but not being able to. Margaret thought what a terrible way to die.

But she tried not to think of this. Her spasms were coming more frequent now. Something was changing in her body, it felt that there was an even greater increase in pressure, a greater force. Her mother held her and then felt down between her legs. This shocked Margaret. She thought it was evil to feel between her legs. The dim candle was not enough to see what was happening but Mary sensed that the baby was making a move. Then, for the first time, Margaret screamed out loud, screaming in her pain. Then she began to move and reached out to her mother to catch her arm.

Her mother cried and talked to her. 'It will be all right, Margaret. Come on hold me. Hold me.' Margaret lay back in the bed with her legs raised and pushed. Her mother stood beside the bed between her legs and the candle sat on a stool beside her. After screaming, Margaret's spasms very temporarily lessened in intensity.

But then they began again. Worse than ever. She screamed and felt again the terrible increase in pressure in her body. 'Come on, Margaret, it is coming. Its wee head is trying to get out. Push, push, push, some more and it will soon be over.' And that is what happened. The baby slid out of Margaret with Mary holding its head and catching its body as it came forward and slid into the light.

The baby cried. Mary cut and tied the umbilical cord. Then she pressed on Margaret's stomach to help the afterbirth to be expelled. Fortunately for Margaret this slipped out intact a few minutes after the birth and Margaret lay spent and exhausted. Mary dried the baby and lifted it up and gave it to Margaret and then went on to dry Margaret herself. Margaret took the baby and held it to her cheek and to her breasts.

Then Mary turned back to Margaret. They had spoken to each other and held each other for the first time in years. The wall that had been built by Mary's helplessness in the face of the crimes done to Margaret, was being breached by the baby's birth and Mary's help in this. Mary helped Margaret position the baby with its mouth to her nipple.

But it did not end there. It was as if Margaret herself was being healed from the wounds of the past years. The touch of the baby's mouth on her nipple was so soft and gentle. She had never experienced such gentleness before. It was like the sweetest kiss that could ever be given. Then the baby raised a little hand and let it rest on her breast beside her nipple. The tenderness of its touch threatened to make Margaret faint.

She lay back exhausted with the baby sucking her milk, holding her nipple in its mouth, and resting its tiny hand on her breast. A kindness came into her, a warmth. This was her baby. Her baby wanted her, wanted her nipple, her breast, her milk. She sighed with the enormity of her pleasure and feelings. She felt human again for the first time since her father had come to her in the yard when she was playing with the donkey and sent her away to Allen's.

'It's a girl, Margaret,' her mother said. To that moment Margaret had not even thought if it was a boy or a girl. She took in the information but she did not care. Her baby was with her. She was helping it. She had given it life and now she was feeding it. Everything was no longer happening to her. She was now the mother of the baby and she was giving the baby life. She was no longer a beaten down victim.

Mary went to the bucket by the wall and took a tin cup and filled it with water and Margaret drank it down and another one on top of it. Then she took some bread from the box and brought it to Margaret but she would not eat it. She shook her head and lay with her baby. As the baby fed Margaret drifted off into a gentle sleep.

She dreamt again that she was a bird. But not a sparrow this time. She was not sure what kind of bird. But in the dream she had blue feathers and a long tail. And she was very aggressive as she strutted around. She defended her territory and her baby against all comers. Hopping around and spitting out her claim to her place and her little one. The sun was shining. She flew up into the air in the sunlight. Her wings lifted her. Then she just lay there in the sun and the breeze held her up. She was gliding.

Her little one took off after her. Up in the air it came. The breeze held it up and it glided along over the hills. They came to this great water. Great waves were rolling in from the horizon and crashing up on the beach. They landed. The sand beneath their feet was warm with the sun. The ocean was in Margaret's dream though she had never seen the ocean. She stood on the sand looking to the ocean with her little one standing in around her. They were together.

In Margaret's dream she was the blue bird with her little blue bird.

Walking along leading it by the ocean. Cackling to warn off any attackers they walked along the beach. The beauty of the ocean was to their left as they walked. The great noise with all its calming was around them. The salt was in the air and on their feathers and feet and bills. They walked along by the sea. It was beautiful. In this dream Margaret was in a world of wonder and strength.

Then the dream changed. Margaret was herself again. She had her baby in her arms. It was hers. But her father appeared in the dream shouting 'It's just another mouth to feed. Allen says he will take it.' Margaret's scream brought Mary running. 'What is it? What is it?' Margaret turned in the bed toward her mother. Holding her baby to her breast with her left hand she reached out and caught her mother's arm with her right hand.

'It's my baby. It's not just another mouth to feed. It's my baby. Allen cannot have it. I will feed it.'

Her mother held her in her arms. 'It's all right, Margaret, Allen will not get your baby. It's your baby. It's not just another mouth to feed. It never will be. Margaret, I am sorry. I did not try and stop your father sending you away to Allen. I am sorry.' Mary wept in her daughter's arms. 'I never did anything to Allen for what he did to you. Margaret, I am sorry.'

Margaret did not answer just put the baby to her other breast. Margaret almost fainted again as the baby's mouth and little lips took her other nipple and held and suckled it. And as its wee hand touched her. She lay back and her mother watched her and this time Margaret fell asleep and did not dream.

Her mother settled the baby in Margaret's arms and sat on the side of the bed and watched them both. She herself was tired but she had found her daughter again and nothing could prevent her this time from staying with her until she was able to handle things. She had found her daughter again.

She looked at the baby as it slept. It was Allen's. What kind of a life would it have? What would Campbell do? Would he resent it? Well it was here now. Mary remembered her own life. The birth of her own first baby, the three boys and then Margaret. She had never had anymore after that. She did not know why. Maybe she had been damaged having the others.

She remembered their gentleness and delight and joy when they were wee. Now they were grown up. She did not see them ever show delight. What was wrong? Why not? She supposed that their jobs were too hard, that they had nothing to look forward to but poverty. Their father believed in nothing but keeping in with the powers that be. He was teaching the sons the same. Such an attitude did not bring out the best in people. There was no place for delight and joy in that approach to the world.

Mary watched Margaret in the light from the candles that were burning. She smiled to herself as she saw the peace on Margaret's face. She wondered what would happen to Margaret's baby, what would happen to Margaret herself before she grew old and died. She thought of all the men around them.

The men, all they did was put their things in the women. But it was the women who had to have the baby inside them, who had to get the baby outside them, who had to feed the baby. How could men know anything when they had so little to do with bringing about new life? It was women who made the world carry on. Mary jumped in shock and fright as she thought about what was going through her head.

But she could not stop thinking about those close to her. She thought about her sister who had gone on the boat to America. That was twenty-three years ago and she had never heard from her again. Where was she now at this minute? What was America like? Was her sister alive? Had she any children? Had she fallen into bad ways? Or had she died? She hoped not. She remembered her sister and herself playing in the fields when they were small.

Her sister was called Victoria. She sat and cried as she wondered where she was. Maybe Margaret would call the baby Victoria. She would like this. She missed her sister. She looked around the cottage as the first rays of daylight made their way in. New day light and the new baby. But the walls of the cottage were bare and dirty.

She thought of Brown's place, which was the only rich person's home that she had ever seen. They had beautiful carpets and curtains and furniture. They had beautiful paintings hanging on the walls. Everybody should have these things. Margaret should have beautiful things too. Everybody should have beautiful curtains, furniture and paintings. Mary gave a start looking around her as she realised what she was thinking.

If anybody knew, if her husband knew he would be angry. He got angry and frightened any time anybody talked about the better off and about ordinary people having better lives. It seemed he took it as a criticism of himself but even more so, he seemed afraid that he would get into trouble with the powers that be if anybody ever heard about such talk.

She had heard her eldest son say that he and his brothers should get better wages. But his father had almost hit him, telling him that Kilgore, one of our own, had given them jobs and that they should be grateful. The father had said after all Kilgore could have given the jobs to Fenians but he didn't, instead he gave them to his own kind.

Mary did not know what to think. She was tired being poor. Her heart was broken that she could not give her children more, give them beautiful things like the wee Brown girl had. She herself could not read or write. Nor her husband. Her children could but what good was it to them with the jobs they were being offered? Why could her children not at the very least have enough for a good life?

Margaret stirred in the bed. She held the baby in her arms. And settled down deeper into sleep. Mary lay down in the bed beside her. She would stay here and see everything was all right. She did not know where Campbell had gone and, for the moment, she did not care. She slowly drifted off to sleep beside her daughter and her granddaughter and she dreamt that she had windows in her cottage and she and Margaret had curtains and paintings on their walls. It was April 1913.

CHAPTER THIRTEEN

Campbell was not a contented man. It was September, over five months now since she had the baby. She was not able to walk to work at Brown's anymore though she was doing the work around the house and milking and doing a bit in the bog. He missed the money from Brown's. It was a good job he had got the hens from her father.

The breakfast was stirabout and tea, the rest of the day it was spuds and eggs and bread and milk. She fed the baby herself. She had got better at baking the bread so this saved him a bit. But one night when he had a few drinks, McDaid got round him and he bought a few yards of cloth for bedclothes and for her to make the baby's clothes and covers. She had made a dress for herself out of it as well. This made Campbell mad. Out of cloth he had bought with his money. She had made a dress for herself.

But that was not what was really getting at him. It was something else. Something had changed in her. She did everything he told her as before. She obeyed his orders and did what she was told. Even when he went to her and entered her she lay there and let him do this as before. But there was something different. Whenever he gave her an order or when he put his thing in her. It was different.

He could not tell exactly what the difference was. She still did what she was told but it was not the same. There was something different and it had come with the baby. She had control of some part of herself that she never had before. Some part of her was her own and he was not able to touch it any more. His ability to control her, to hurt her was reduced. This angered him because this part of her might grow and nobody would know then what would happen.

He pushed open the door to McDaid's. 'A wee half,' he grunted and took his seat by the door as usual. There was O'Donnell and his crew by the fire with himself holding forth. They looked round when Campbell came in. O'Donnell raised his voice so Campbell could hear. 'Look at them bosses in Dublin. They are trying to make them men work for nothing. They have locked them out of the work. They are trying to starve them.'

'What is it about, O'Donnell?' Brennan asked. Brennan was giving O'Donnell a chance to get at Campbell.

'The men only want a decent wage and to be able to join Larkin's union. That's all, and for that they are locked out of their work and some of them even have been killed. That Murphy who owns the tramways is at the head of it and all the other bosses and the churches and the English are backing him. It's not right.

'Look at that Murphy. He is one of my own kind. And he has the full backing of the priests and the bishops of my own church. There is no difference between them. No matter what church, they are all for the ones with the money when it comes down to it. Did you see where the priests won't let the children of the strikers go to England to get fed because they say their souls will be in danger? But their bodies are in danger of starvation here. They don't care about that'

O'Donnell was well on at this stage. He had been angry ever since he had heard about the lockout some weeks ago. Campbell had been told about it by Brown but had not given it much thought. O'Donnell moved down to confront Campbell.

'What do you think, Campbell? Should these working men not get a decent wage? Should they not be able to join Larkin's union? Surely a working man like yourself would support this. Just like my church, your church is against the working man.'

Campbell turned away from him and grunted. He was not going to get drawn into an argument and maybe a fighting match. 'What do you think, Campbell? These men should have a decent wage. Larkin and Connolly are fighting for these men to have a decent wage. Is this not right? It is not religion here. Murphy and many of the employers are my own sort, many of the other employers are your sort. It is not religion here. Should the men not have a decent wage?'

O'Donnell was no longer taunting Campbell for sport. The more he spoke the more angry he became. The more he felt the truth and justice of his words. He also felt frustrated because he knew of no way to help the Dublin workers. Campbell as an agent and informer for the bosses in the area was a good enough target for him. If he could not help in Dublin he could give it to this bosses' agent here in Donegal. O'Donnell was hoping Campbell would say or do something that would give him a chance to give it to him.

But McDaid intervened. He did not want to lose money by losing Campbell as a customer nor did he want any damage done to his property. And anyway he did not like the sound of these Larkin and Connolly boys and people wanting more wages. 'O'Donnell sit down and leave Campbell alone. He never said anything to you. He was sitting there minding his own business. Come over here and sit down.' O'Donnell stood where he was hoping that Campbell would say something and give him an excuse. But Campbell threw back the remains of his drink and left.

He headed up the road for home. His anger was near boiling point at the humiliation he had suffered at the taunts of O'Donnell. And she was up to something at home. She was plotting something. She was not under his control like before. He did not like it. Now there was this other thing in Dublin. Control was slipping everywhere. He snorted to himself. They will not get away with anything with me. She will still have to work and do what I tell her, and these boys like O'Donnell will still have to rent bog and pay on time. That was what he was hired to make happen, that was what was going to happen, and that was why he was Lord Taverstock's man. That was what he was going to make happen.

Campbell was strong and healthy and had the few fields and the bog lettings and a woman and a cow. But he was never at ease. He was always ready to explode. The things he had to control were always trying to slip away from him, her at home, and the crowd that rented the bog banks. The problem as Campbell saw it was that these people were stupid. They did not see it was no use trying to change things, that it was better to go along and know your place.

Look at himself, the insults he had to take from Brown and the Reverend and the better off, even Allen. Wasn't he rearing Allen's wean? He accepted this, he accepted his place. When they insulted him he took it. That was the smart thing to do in his place. But in spite of himself, and trying to convince himself that he had it worked out and he accepted his place, as he walked towards his home and thought of these things he could feel his rage building at the way they treated him.

The blood rushed through his veins, his breath came shorter and more shallow, his fists balled up, the skin on his face felt like it would split across the bones and his teeth felt like they would splinter they were clenched so tight. His whole system was in high stress as he felt the rage at the way he was treated. But he knew he had to take it. His father had beat that into him. There was no way out upwards. There was no way out by trying to fight those above him, those who had control, no way out by trying to change the system.

He knew that the way was to find a wee niche he could stand on and turn his anger instead against those beneath him. This was the way to do it. Those above him controlled him, so it was his job to control those beneath him on behalf of those above him; keep those beneath him beaten down further and this would give him a bit of slack. He would see that as far as possible those beneath him knew their place, the way out was to control those beneath him not challenge those above him. And her at home. She would have to learn her place too. His anger came to focus more and more on Margaret. Her he could control. She would be there when he went home. She he had control over. He would teach her her place. And her young one too.

And as he walked he thought that was it. It was the wean. That was what had changed things with her. The wean coming had given her thoughts above her station. It was this had done it. He did not know why but that was it. Well he would just have to put an end to it. She would have to learn her station again and he would be the man to teach it to her. Everybody has to be taught their place.

It began to rain. His clothes soaked it up and the cold seeped into him. Aye, Allen and his offer of a pound. Her and her wean. Her and her change and her no fear of him anymore. He regretted taking her on. He would have been better by himself. But then he had got the cow. It was not all bad. But he also had to feed her wean. He weighed the transaction up and he was not sure who had come out ahead, Allen, the Reverend, Brown or himself? The uncertainty added to his rage.

He pushed open the door of the cottage. The fire was low with only a few red embers of the turf showing and he was cold and wet. She was lying in the bed covered up and with the wean with her as usual. She was probably feeding it. When she had that wean in her hands she seemed to be even more out of his control. He seemed unable to touch her no matter what he did to her. His control was slipping away. She lay there with her back to him.

He went to sit on his bench by the fire in his wet clothes. It was too much. As he sat there he felt himself losing control of his rage. The fire was nearly out and she was lying there ignoring him. He turned and went into the room where she lay. He grabbed her by the arm and pulled her half over on her back to face up to him. The baby was suckling at her right breast with its eyes closed. He pulled Margaret further back. She showed no fear, just held her baby tighter. Her control enraged him completely.

'Look at the fire, girl. It's nearly out. Where is the tea? Who do you think you are lying there with that wean and me out working and nothing for me when I get home. I did not take you in with Allen's wean to have you lie about. Get up!' Losing control entirely he tore at her with all his strength and half pulled, half threw her out of the bed onto the floor with the baby still held in her arms.

She was so determined to protect the baby she held both arms round it and had nothing to break her fall. Her head hit the flagged stone floor and split open. The blood ran down her face from the cut on her forehead. But she ignored it and drew herself up to her one knee with her two hands still wrapped around the baby. Nothing else mattered to her.

The baby was crying but she could tell from the sound that she was only frightened. She rose to her feet and with one hand holding the baby she turned over the turf embers in the fire, threw on a few sticks and more turf and pulled the hanging pot of water over the flames that were rising. She reached up with her free hand and took down the bread tin. Into another pot of water she put two eggs and hung them over the flames.

Meanwhile the blood was running down her face and down into her clothes. But she acted as if the cut had never happened. She took his cup from the nail on the wall and set it on the bare table and put a spoonful of tea leaves in the tea pot. She set a knife beside it all, then went and sat on the bed and watched the fire to see when the water would boil. All the time she held her baby in her arms.

All this time Campbell stood rooted to the one spot with his breath coming in deep gasps as he watched her. The sight of her bleeding sobered him and dampened down his rage. He stood there as she made the tea, took his two eggs out and put them on the table with the bread and butter. Then he went and sat down. 'That's it' he grunted as if his violence was justified by her setting the boiled eggs, the tea and the bread on the table.

Only then did Margaret take a bit of cloth from beside the bed in her room and wipe the blood off her face. By this time the flow had slackened and almost stopped. She held the cloth to her head and the baby to her breast. It had stopped crying by now and gone to sleep. She was at peace and calm because her baby was safe. The heat and softness of it at her side comforted and warmed her.

She did not lie down in the bed again because she did not want to give him an excuse for a new rage. She sat on its edge holding her baby. She looked at it breathing with its eyes closed and asleep. She felt its life in her arm. She felt her whole person become more alive and almost smiling as she thought of the little life that she had brought into the world and how her daughter was lying there sleeping and content. And most of all, how she had protected it. Yes, how she had protected it. She felt stronger than at any time in her life. And prouder. She had protected her baby.

Campbell took off his wet outer clothes and lay down on the bench by the fire. After a while he slept. His snores always told her when he slept. They were like an all clear sign except it was never all clear. She lifted her baby to her face and kissed its cheek, then kissed it on the mouth, then held its cheek to hers and felt its softness, its warmth and its life against her own face. She would protect her baby. It was the only good thing in her life. She loved her baby. She felt like she might burst with the power of her love for her baby.

After a little while she lay down softly on the bed and with her breath in time with the baby's, she fell asleep. She dreamt that Campbell had died and that she lived in the cottage alone with her baby. She dreamt that she was dancing round the kitchen of the cottage holding her baby in the air and singing. She was laughing and singing and talking to the baby.

In her dream she was no longer round shouldered. After being sent to Allen's she had slowly become slightly hunched forward in the shoulders. Waiting for the next disappointment, waiting for the next blow, she had developed a protective stoop. It pulled her head down away from blows. And she had lost all the spring out of her step. But in her dream she was straight and lithe and nimble, dancing on her toes with her head up.

In her dream there was some kind of strange music that she danced to. It seemed like great waves sweeping this way and that. Then great surges of noise, great explosions of sound, it seemed to be played by many people together, this was like no music she had ever heard before. Then it would go down sometimes until it was almost nothing, down to an extreme tenderness. At these times she felt her fingers and her toes stretch out and reach for the sound.

Then it would change. Then the music would become like the fiddle playing she had heard passing McDaid's pub once. It was the Fenian music. She was not supposed to like it. It was their music. But she heard it in her dream. Then there was their wee half drum that they played with one hand. The beat of it gave her strength and energy and power. She felt it in her feet and in her lower stomach and in her spirit.

Then it was the terrible loneliness and cry of the bagpipes. This stopped her movement but inside her she felt a powerful searching and feeling. She wanted to know. What was it this sound, this movement in her inside, a feeling that she was more alive than before?

Why did the bagpipes bring this to her? She reached up one hand and held her head as feelings and thoughts that she did not know rushed through her.

She awoke with a start. What was it, what? Then she realised it was him, he was pushing at her with his thing pointed at her. There was no music anymore. Not the great sweeping sounds, not the fiddle or the wee drum, not the bagpipes. No music came with this thing pointing. His thing, like Allen's, came unaccompanied. She let him part her legs and put it in her. As she did she held the baby in her arms. He stood and thrust and thrust into her. Then he was finished and went back to his bench and his sleep.

She closed her legs and turned on her side holding the baby tight. She felt the baby's tenderness and its need for her. She knew that she would do anything to help and protect and love this wee life. She remembered the dream and wished she could bring the great sweeping music to her baby so that it could grow up with its head up, its shoulders straight and with laughter and a spring in its step. She herself grew stronger as she drifted off to sleep with her baby in her arms.

CHAPTER FOURTEEN

It was Wednesday and Campbell was on his way to Brown's for his weekly report on the bog lettings. 'Well, Campbell, come on and we will see how things are.' As usual Campbell was not asked into the house. They went into the harness room and sat on rough wooden benches. Campbell had not much new to report from the previous week. He need not have worried as Brown wanted to speak to him about something else.

'Campbell, you have heard about this lock-out business in Dublin? I have talked with Bishop Wilson. He has heard from Lord Taverstock. His Lordship says to keep an eye out for anything unusual, any sign that there might be any trouble here. He says there must be no letting up on these boys for any back rent from the bogs. If there are any far behind then throw a few of them out. Take the letting from them. They must see that this Dublin business changes nothing. They must see that there is no slackening, that we are still in charge. And let me know what they are saying about this Dublin lock out business. And especially if they are talking about either Larkin or Connolly the leaders of this trouble.'

Brown got up, turned his back on Campbell, opened the door and went out. 'Well I will see you next week Campbell. How is the young Wallace girl, ah I mean your wife, getting on? I hear she has had the baby. You are a lucky man, Campbell. A family now, that's the job.' Not waiting for an answer Brown went into his house and closed the door. Campbell headed up the road for home. 'Aye,' he fumed, 'that's the job.'

'Elizabeth. Are you there?' Brown joined his wife, sitting across the fire from her on a large soft deep armchair. She sat in an identical one.

'I am frightened, Charles. This business in Dublin is scaring me. I think we should get Jenny off to England to school as soon as possible. Who knows where this all may end. I am frightened.'

'Now, Elizabeth, there is nothing to worry about. The authorities in Dublin are in control. His Majesty's government will not let an ignorant mob take over. This will be ended in a few weeks. The leaders of this treason will be dealt with and things will be put back in order. Anyway the whole thing is in Dublin, there is nothing up here. Don't worry, everything is all right.'

'But still, Charles, I would like to get Jenny off to England as soon as we can.'

'Of course, Elizabeth. Of course we will do it as quickly as we can. I will write to Lord Taverstock tonight. And I will also speak to Bishop Wilson because he sometimes hears from Lord Taverstock through the telegraph system which comes to the RIC station. I will talk to Bishop Wilson. In fact I will go down there tonight.' Brown was getting worried himself as he listened to his wife's fears.

He knocked at Bishop Wilson's door and waited. The butler came to the door. 'Good evening, sir. I will ask Bishop Wilson if he can see you.' Brown was angry at not being shown in right away but did not show it. 'Come in. Bishop Wilson will see you in the front sitting room. Can I bring you a cup of tea, sir?'

'Yes, that would be nice.'

'Well, Charles, how are you this evening? I am glad you called.

I was wanting to ask you if you had any indication of what people are thinking out there about this Dublin business?'

'I just talked to Campbell. He says there is not much excitement about it,' Brown answered.

'Well, that's good to hear. It's a bad business. Those people are traitors. They will have to be dealt with. It will be the Lord's will.

'But we must be on the alert, Charles. There are many problems out there and you never know when some hothead can get the wrong idea and try to change things. Make sure Campbell and all the others we can trust, are keeping their ears open. I would be surprised if we have seen the end of this yet. These Larkin and Connolly gentlemen will have to be dealt with. I see they are even getting support in Belfast from our own kind. This is not good.'

Brown saw his opening. 'I am sure you are right, Bishop. Elizabeth and I were just talking about this very thing. You know that Jenny is to be going to school in England. Lord Taverstock has helped arrange it. We are wondering if we can get her off sooner rather than later. We are worried if there might be any trouble. I was wondering if you are in contact with Lord Taverstock if you could mention this to him.'

'I will be delighted to, Charles. Leave it to me I should get in touch with him and hear back from him within the week. I can see no reason why Jenny cannot go earlier than planned. It would do her good to spend some time with Lord Taverstock's contacts and friends over there. It would broaden her horizons. Just leave it to me now.

'Before you go, Charles, did you see that the leaders of those people in Dublin, Larkin and Connolly are socialists? You know they want to take people's land and property away from them? Apparently Connolly is the worst of them. He was a troublemaker in Scotland where he was born and in America where he lived for some time. Keep your ears open if you hear anybody talking about him in particular.

'The good thing is that it's not only our kind who are against them. William Martin Murphy, who owns the Dublin tramways and the Irish Independent newspaper and who is one of the other kind, also has it in for Connolly and Larkin. And Rome is also against Larkin and Connolly and their mob. This is a good thing. Of course Rome has a lot of wealth and land and property too. And they would not like to lose control over that or their people to some socialist. So I think we will come out of this all right. But, Charles, be sure and keep your eyes and ears open for any sign of trouble here.

'I mean to say, look around you.' And Wilson swept his hand around the room with its expensive furnishings. 'These people like this Larkin and Connolly, only common working men, and that mob they lead, how could they run things? Civilization would be destroyed. They have seen nothing but poverty and bare walls all their lives. Its people like us, Charles, who hold things together. If we were ever to lose control then there is no telling what damage would result. The Lord put us here for a purpose, to run things.'

Brown rode his horse back up the road to his house. The Bishop was right, these people could not run things. But why was the Bishop talking so much about the trouble in Dublin? It was as if he knew more than he was saying. Well he would keep an eye out and he would get Campbell to do the same. It would not be good if he missed something that later turned into trouble.

He saw three figures walking ahead of him. It was Shanks and Katie Curran but who was the third? It was an old man. Oh yes, he had heard about it. This would be Katie's father who could no longer work and therefore had to leave the Wilson place where he had laboured for over fifty years. Michael was his name. He had had to come to live with Katie and Shanks.

They turned as they heard his horse approach. 'Hello there, Shanks and Katie. Hello there' to the old man. 'Hello, Mr Brown.' The old man did not speak.

'It's a lovely evening to be taking a walk. It is terrible that every-body in the country are not minding their business as we are. I am sure you have heard of this business in Dublin. This mob that is refus-ing to work. Sure everybody has to work.' Brown wanted to see what Katie and Shanks thought. 'It's a terrible thing altogether,' Brown repeated. 'Sure, I hope the trouble is over soon.'

Shanks was giving little away with his reply. 'I hope so too.' Brown put his heels to his horse's sides and trotted on leaving them walking.

The three walked on in silence for a bit. Then the old man burst out.

'Listen to him. A terrible business. This country has been robbed by him and the likes of him for centuries. Look at me. I have worked all my life for the like of him and now I cannot work anymore they put me out and you have to look after me. I don't know all that is hap-pening in Dublin but it is time something is done in this country.' Shanks and Katie were surprised and frightened by the old man's words.

He went on. 'Look, from what I hear these men in Dublin are out for better wages and to be able to get together to try and get things a bit better for themselves and their families. I don't see what is wrong with that. These Larkin and Connolly men might be more right than wrong.'

'Father, you must not be talking that way. You will get us all in trouble. Don't be saying such things outside of ourselves.'

The old man said nothing. Just walked on with his head down and bent forward looking at the ground. Katie and Shanks walked silent-ly on each side of him. All of them were thinking of the old man's words and laying them alongside their own experiences. Shanks and Katie were frightened by how their lives and the old man's words corresponded.

They were passing the opening into Campbell's place before any of them spoke. And then it was because the dog came out barking. 'He's all right he won't bite us.' As Shanks reassured them Margaret came out of the door of the cottage and threw a bucket of water out across the yard. As she turned to go in she saw Shanks and Katie and the old man. She stopped and looked at them.

In spite of her new found strength she still did not speak to others. She looked at them and turned to go in. 'Margaret, Margaret, we are very glad to see you looking so well. How is your baby? We hear it is a good strong baby. Margaret, could we see her? We would like to see your baby and wish her and you well.' Katie's face was lit up thinking about the baby.

Margaret did not know what to do. She usually waited for things to pass when she was not sure what to do. She usually stayed quiet and waited and things passed. But she was torn here. She wanted to show her baby to them. Shanks and Katie had helped her home and she knew it was they who had gone and got her mother to come up. They were good people. But she could not move. She was paralysed by her past experiences.

Shanks and Katie could see this. But they could also see that there was new life in Margaret. That when Katie asked to see the baby she had to struggle to hide her pleasure. She wanted to show it but she was afraid to. Shanks pushed in past Katie and walked across the yard to Margaret. 'Margaret, we have heard that the baby is a great looking wee girl. We will just have a wee look at her and go.' He walked on to the cottage door. He knew that Campbell was in the village that day.

Standing outside he looked in. 'Margaret, come on, girl dear, and bring her out to us.'

Margaret was in a terrible confusion. She wanted so much to show them her baby but her past told her not to act but to wait and let things pass.

'Come on, Margaret, we would love to see her.' Katie smiled and her eyes shone as she spoke. 'Come on, Margaret. We won't stay but a minute.'

Margaret still stood. Then Katie and Shanks went to her and together put their arms around her and moved her to the cottage door. 'Come on, Margaret.' The feel of their arms around her almost overcame Margaret. But it also made things easier. It was they who had made her move. Once started she was all right. She went in and came out with the baby in her arms. It was a lovely wee girl with Margaret's eyes.

Katie touched her face, then she said. 'Margaret, can I hold her? For luck. Please, Margaret.'

Katie took the baby from Margaret's arms. Margaret was in a state of panic and terror as she saw the baby in somebody else's arms. She had not even let her mother hold her yet. Katie and Shanks talked to the baby and laughed and petted her. Gradually Margaret lost her terror and began to hear what they said. Inside she began to soften and warm with their words.

'She is a beautiful baby, Margaret. She is a beautiful wee girl, Margaret. You are a lucky woman and she is a lucky child. Here, Margaret', and they handed the baby back.

Margaret held her tightly to her breast to be sure she was safe. She did not speak and her face was tight hiding the conflict of emotions inside her.

'Well, we will be off, Margaret' and the three of them made their way out on to the road again and walked up the hill towards their own place.

'What's wrong with that girl?' the old man said. 'She never spoke.'

'Daddy, she has been badly treated. She was hired out like you were. The farmer put her in the family way and then they fixed it so she would marry Campbell and he is no prize. That wee baby is the only good thing she has I would say.'

'But she never spoke,' the old man said. 'She never spoke to you. What is wrong with her? And look at her face. There is some sort of scar on her face.'

'Do you remember that dog we found at the crossroads just after we were married, Katie? Remember it was starved. The ribs were sticking out of it. Its leg had been broken and it had set crooked. Its tail was down all the time. It had been badly done by. But the main thing we began to notice was that it could not bark. Remember, Katie? We thought there was something wrong and it had no bark.

'But we had it for a couple of years and we treated it well, fed it well and never beat it. Slowly it began to improve. At the beginning it would only ever cower when we spoke to it or went near it. Gradually it realised that we were not going to hit it and it stopped the cowering. But it still never barked. We just thought that it had no bark like a person who cannot speak.

'Then one day, it must have been about two or three years after we had it, and it was after a rat in the backyard. The rat was down behind the turf stack and the dog could smell it but could not get at it. We were watching it. For a couple of hours it was at it, digging and sniffing and trying to get at the rat. As we watched it got madder and madder. It was in a terrible rage altogether.

'And then it stepped back, looked at the turf pile, and then raised up its head and it was like a miracle. A sort of a snort at first, then a half growl, then the semblance of a bark came out if its throat and then it began to bark and not just bark but howl with rage at the rat. Remember, Katie, how happy we were? It could bark. It could bark. We realised that it had not barked before because it had been so mistreated that it tried to disappear, to escape the bad treatment. Part of disappearing was not making a sound.

'It's the same with that wee girl, Michael. She has been so mistreated. First by her own father, then by Allen, then by Campbell, that she has tried to disappear. Part of this is not talking. She has made her voice disappear. She never speaks to my knowledge. I bet that she has never spoke to Campbell who is her husband. She never speaks.'

'Yes but Shanks, I bet that when she is alone with the baby and sure nobody is around that she speaks to the baby.'

'You are probably right, Katie. I would like to hear her speak. But she is not like our old dog. We treated it well and it got back the confidence to speak. She has got nobody to treat her well. She may never speak again to anybody but her babies and then only when she is sure she is alone.'

The father walked along in silence while Shanks and Katie talked. 'That wee girl has nobody to treat her well enough so she can feel confident enough to speak again. This is a terrible country altogether.' As he said this the old man walked on full of anger.

CHAPTER FIFTEEN

Margaret sat out on the grass looking down over the stream and on to the valley below. It was a late October evening and the air was clear and unseasonably warm for that time of year. She held her baby at her breast and felt a relaxation in her. She knew that Campbell would not be home as he had to go through the Gap to Donegal Town on some business for Brown and would not be back until tomorrow. She knew because he made her make him so much food. She was very glad.

As she sat the events of the past months filled her mind. The baby whom she had called Victoria at her mother's request had changed everything. She now lived for the baby. The baby made her want to live. As she sat there she could feel this knowledge seep through her. It was as if by just sitting there and letting this knowledge stay in her mind she became stronger and more whole.

She also liked to sit outside because of the clean fresh air. Like the other women in the area, all she had to keep Victoria from wetting and dirtying herself and the bed and the cottage, were the thin flour bags she got with the flour and washed out and used and doubled up again and again. These did not work and Margaret and Victoria shared a regularly wet and dirtied bed. The cottage also smelled of this. Margaret wished she had some way to deal with this and also she thought of what it would be like when she had two, four, five children.

Margaret's evening of consideration and peace did not last long.

'Margaret. Margaret.' It was her youngest brother's voice.

He was calling from the roadway. She had not seen him since the day she was married to Campbell. All the closeness that had existed between them when they used to play together as they were doing the day her father sent her away, had long ago been destroyed. She looked at her brother coming towards her with no expression on her face.

'You had better come back to the house with me. Mammy is sick. She has been sick for the past three days and now she is worse. She is coughing up blood and since last night she has been unconscious. You should come back with me.'

Margaret stood up with her baby. She went into the cottage and got a shawl and wrapped it round her and the baby. In this way the baby was carried in the shawl. She never answered her brother, just followed him.

In less than an hour she was on the road approaching her family's cottage. She had not been on it since she was married. It was a rocky dirt road running through boggy fields and bits of bog land on each side. Her brother walked ahead of her and did not speak. It was as if there was something wrong with her and they ignored her since she had come back from Allen's expecting the baby.

Margaret did not feel much as she walked. Her mother had helped her have the baby and that night they had held each other and cried together and celebrated the birth of the baby. But things had not developed since then. The next time her mother had visited, the warmth of the birth night had gone and they were back to Margaret not talking and her mother not able to talk for both of them.

In the weeks that followed, her mother had visited regularly but they could not talk about the injustice of their lives and they could not therefore overcome the past. Her mother was locked in guilt at her inability to save Margaret from Allen and being hired out and from being unable to see that Allen was punished. Being poor and with a husband who was locked into servility in the face of those better off than himself, she was not able to protect Margaret or make Allen pay. Margaret and her mother were not able to over come this obstacle to their relationship.

Her back was sore carrying the baby but her brother did not offer to help and she would not have let him carry her baby if he had. The cottage came in sight and her family's dog ran out barking to greet her. He was always glad to see her. She petted his head as he ran along beside her. Her baby was awakened by his barking.

Her brother pushed open the cottage door and went in. She followed. Her father and two older brothers were sitting round the fire. The door to the bedroom where her father and mother had slept, was open. She could see her mother's feet push up the bedclothes.

Her father turned to Margaret, 'You are too late girl. You are too late. She is dead girl. She's dead. Just an hour ago. She was vomiting blood and she just gave out.'

Margaret walked into the bedroom where her mother lay on her back on the bed. She was gray in the face. Margaret went up close to her and stood looking down. This was her mother. The past years had taken their toll. Margaret's feelings for her mother had been driven deep underground. Mother. She spoke silently to herself. Mother. Mother. Experimenting with the word and seeing what emotions stirred in her.

Her father's voice sounded in her ear. 'It's a terrible thing, Margaret. Your poor mother. Your poor mother. She was a hard worker all her life. She was the mother to all of you. She was a good woman.' Her father's voice was full of whining guilt and calculation.

'Aye, we sent for the Bishop Wilson but he has not come yet. Its a terrible thing to happen.'

Without speaking a word Margaret turned and walked out of the bedroom across the kitchen floor and out of the cottage with her baby in her arms. She crossed over the yard and out onto the dirt road and set off for home. Her father came out after her.

'Margaret. Margaret. Where are you going? We need you here to help. Margaret your mother has to be laid out. We need you here. You can even come back for good if you want. We will need somebody to look after things about the place.'

Margaret walked on alone along the road and made no answer. Her mother was dead. Her father and brothers were sitting whining and trying to explain to themselves and anybody who would listen that they had done everything they could. For the first time since she was sent away to Allen's, she did not wait for things to pass. She had walked out of her father's house. She had acted to make things happen.

Her mother's death had made it impossible to hide from the lies and hypocrisy that was the world of her father. But what was different this time was that she did not wait and let things happen and listen to him. She had taken action. She walked out and by this decision, this decision which she had made herself, she had ended her participation in their filth of emotions and words. Her baby's birth, her mother's death, and she had acted.

She was going back to her own cottage. In spite of Campbell and his brutishness there was more of a place there for her and her baby. Her father said she could come back. But to be what? To be a servant to him and to her brothers. She was no longer just another mouth to feed it seemed. She was now another pair of hands again. It was strange how the different circumstances her father found himself in led to him seeing her in different ways.

When her father had enough people to do the work for him around the cottage she was just another mouth to feed. When he did not then her mouth seemed to lose its importance and she became another pair of hands. Well this time she was not going to be what her father decided she was, based on his needs. She was her daughter's mother first and foremost, even if that meant she had to serve Campbell, had to be a pair of hands and a place to put his thing in.

They could have sent for the doctor. But her father would have been weighing up the cost. They could have sent for the doctor. Her mother was dead. Her mother was dead. They wanted her back to work for them. It was too late. She would have a better chance with her baby with Campbell.

She lay with her baby in the feather bed. She was exhausted with the walk to and from her family's house. Her baby was asleep. But she could not sleep. Why did they not send for the doctor? But if she was vomiting blood then she had tuberculosis and it would have been no good anyway. But that was not the reason they had not sent for the doctor. It was because they were too mean to pay the doctor.

She remembered one time when she was only five or six years old. Her mother had taken her up to the lough in the mountains above the cottage. It was the late summer and the water was warm. Her mother had taken her by the hand and together they had gone into the water up to their knees. They paddled together. Her mother laughed as the water tickled them and held Margaret's hand and they laughed together.

Margaret remembered this as the only time when her mother did not have to work and was light hearted and laughing without fear. It was only the two of them. They paddled in the lough's warm water. They laughed together. Margaret remembered with surprise that she had also laughed at that time with her mother. She began to cry as she lay with her baby. She began to sob and cry and her pain came out of her in great lamentations. Oh she wished she could paddle in the lake and laugh again with her mother. She wished to do something to bring her mother back to life and to that day.

But she could not, so she was crying for her mother and the terrible life she had. Only once in the years of Margaret's life had she and her mother ever been able to laugh without fear. This was when they had gone to the lake together. Her father had not been there and this was one reason why her mother could laugh and play. Her father was always on top of her mother. Holding her down. Making her do what he ordered. Controlling her. Margaret suddenly realised that she hated her father.

Hated? Hated? But how could she hate? How could she hate? This was her, Margaret. How could she be important enough to hate. Strong enough to hate? But she could love. That was it. It became clear to Margaret in a flash. Her daughter had made her able to love. This love had made her strong. And this meant she was strong enough to hate as well as strong enough to love. She hated her father. She bared her teeth and began to breath in great deep gasps as she allowed her hatred for her father to express itself in her mind.

But it did not stop there. She also hated Allen. And she hated Allen's wife. She felt the energy rise in her, her heart beating fast, her breath coming in deep gasps. She became afraid. She was going to explode. She hated Campbell.....She fought for control. Her baby. Her baby. She had to keep control. She pulled back from this next step. Hatred of Campbell. She stopped short. She could not afford to hate Campbell in the way she hated the others. She had her baby to bring up. She needed to be able to tolerate Campbell. For the baby's sake. Poverty and lack of control over her own life still dictated whom she could afford to hate and whom she could not.

She fought in her mind to get things under control. She could afford to hate her father. She might never see him again. She could afford to hate her brothers she might never see them again. She could afford to hate Allen and his wife for the same reason. But she could not afford to hate Campbell because if she did she could not endure to live in the same cottage with him and what would she do then to bring up her daughter. It was a thing when Campbell was the best option for her Victoria.

Margaret kissed her daughter and held her little check to hers. The great feelings and energy welled up in her and she almost burst with love for her daughter. The hatred she could have, but could not act on, for Allen and her father and brothers, the hatred which she could not afford to feel for Campbell, all the energy of this hatred got turned instead into the love she had for her daughter and the kisses she gave her daughter's tiny face. Her hatred of Campbell would have to be buried somewhere deep inside her for the time being.

It was morning and Campbell was not yet home. Margaret did her work around the cottage and in the byre. She worked hard and her mother's memory found a place to rest in her. She remembered the day at the lough and tried to forget the bad times. She remembered the night of her daughter's birth and tried to forget the harsh words and treatment her father had dealt out to her mother. She tried to let slip into the past her mother's inability to keep her from being sent to Allen or to punish Allen.

'Margaret. Margaret.' This time it was Shanks and Katie. 'Margaret, we are going down to your mother's wake. Will you come down with us? We will help you with the baby.'

Margaret went into the cottage and closed the door. Shanks and Katie stood motionless in the spot

'Katie, what is it about?...Katie, what is the matter with that girl? Katie, there is something wrong with this country. Katie. Katie. Katie. I do not know. But there is something wrong with this country.' They stood and looked at each other. Then Shanks said, 'Anyway, come on and we will go down.'

Margaret listened inside the door but Shanks and Katie did not try to come in. She could not go down to her family's cottage and be with her father and brothers and they alive and her mother dead. She would explode if she tried to. She could not look at them. In the best of times she could not speak to anybody so she could not go there and be spoken to by all the people who would come to her mother's wake.

'How are you, Shanks and yourself, Katie? Come in. Come in.' Margaret's father opened the door wide for them. The cottage was full of people.

'I am very sorry for your loss, Mary was a good woman. To die so young too.'

'Aye, Aye, It's terrible altogether. Mary was a very good woman. Sure she was such a hard worker and she looked after us all. I do not know what we will do now. Who is going to do her work around the house and look after us all?'

'I could not stay there any longer, Shanks. Listening to him about how good a woman Mary was and the next word was what was he and his sons going to do without somebody to do her work. Maybe that's why Margaret could not come down. She could not listen to her father. Shanks, I wish we could help Margaret more. But what can we do? She won't say a word. What do you think it is that's wrong with her, Shanks?

'Shanks, I do not know.' Katie was answering her own question. 'But look what she has been through. Now to lose her mother. I think that she is a good person. And very strong too. She survived that father of hers, the poverty, Allen, Campbell. She is strong. And now she has the baby this will make her even stronger. She will be living for the baby. Did you hear Wallace complaining that he had asked her to come back and she had not answered him?

'Imagine that. After he sends her away to Allen and then to Campbell because he does not want to feed her. Now when he has no woman about the place he asks her to come back. I think this is right, Shanks, that is why she won't go down to the wake. She is too mad at her father. I never thought I would say it but she is better off with Campbell. There she only has one man to look after, not three, only one man to put up with.'

'Are you back then?' The old man was sitting at the turf fire when Shanks and Katie came in. They told him what had happened and what they were talking about. He sat there by the fire with his head lying forward on his chest. They thought maybe he had not heard them. But then he turned and looked at them and his face and eyes were full of the most intense painful anger. He looked at them and they looked at him and then he turned and looked into the fire.

Down the road a bit Campbell had returned. He had been told by a neighbour on his way home about the death of Margaret's mother. He was surprised to see her in the cottage when he returned and all the work of the day done. He stood and looked at her when he came in the door. She was lying with her baby on the bed. He almost spoke to her to ask her about her mother's wake. But he did not.

To speak to her in any way other than to give her orders or to criticise her for not carrying out his orders correctly, was threatening to him. By asking her to give her opinion, and especially to talk about her feelings, even on such a topic as her mother's death, would be to treat her as a real person not a pair of hands. Or a place for him to put his thing. This would then make it more difficult for him to keep control over her, to keep treating her as an object to be used.

She got up and made him tea, boiled some eggs and laid these out with bread on the table. He sat and ate. When he was finished he rose and left the cottage. Margaret could hear him leave the yard and head down the road. He was on his way to her mother's wake. As he walked he thought of Margaret. He did not like it that she was not at the wake. It was another example that she had a mind of her own. He was not comforted by the thought. A mind of her own. That was not a good thing. A strong back was one thing. But a mind of her own, a strong mind, that was another thing altogether. He would have to watch her.

CHAPTER SIXTEEN

Margaret's body was well filled out with her new and second baby that was growing in her. On her own at night she hugged Victoria with one arm and the baby in her belly with the other. Another baby, this would be good. She even smiled occasionally in the dark and privacy of her bed as she thought of this. Victoria was not yet six months old and Margaret was well pregnant again.

Campbell said nothing if he noticed. The same ritual continued. They never spoke together. He would sometimes grunt an order at her. But they never talked. Since the night he had split her head he had not hit her or roughed her up again. He still would rise in the night and put his thing in her. He never did this immediately they would lie down. He always lay for some time and she would usually be asleep when he would come to her. It was as if in this way she would be less of a person to him.

The two would have gone to their separate sleeping places, they would have been separated. Whatever relationship existed by her making his food and putting it on the table was dissipated by this act. They never ate together. She knew he would not want it. It would put her too much in front of him as a person. He might have to see her as a person eating. She always ate either before he came in or after he had left.

The truth was that she did not want to eat with him either. To sit with him, to reach out and take her food, and put it in her mouth. Chew it and feel some pleasure at its taste. And all in front of him. This was too intimate to share with him. This was to expose too much of herself to him. She wanted to do this in private or with her back to him. She did not want him to see the movements of her face. Her face needed to be always closed to him for her own protection.

In the evenings he would go and lie on his bench without a word. She would go to her bed and fall asleep and he would lie down on his bench with his face to the wall. Later he would rise in the dark and come and put his thing into her heat and push and shake and pull his thing out of her. All in the dark. He did not see her, or talk to her, or feel any obligation to her. At night in the dark she was only a thing to put his thing in.

Campbell was walking home. It was early December. Things at home had changed over the past year and he did not like it. And things had changed in the country also and he did not like that either. Since this Dublin lock-out business started Brown was on to him all the time about what was going on. It was like he was frightened of something. Campbell, what are they saying? Campbell, keep your eye out for things. Campbell, make sure they do not get any ideas above their station. Campbell, what are they thinking?

He wanted a drink. In the bad light of McDaid's pub he took his seat at the door. Up by the fire there was the usual crowd. O'Donnell was at the centre of it like always. Campbell wanted to hear what he was saying. He could tell Brown and this would get him in the good books. He strained his ears to listen but this was not necessary as they had had a few drinks and were talking very loud.

'O'Donnell, you are always on about something. What are you saying about this business in Dublin? Sure those men are only cutting their own throats. They are locked out and getting no pay. They would be better to go back and let Murphy and his boys have their way. Sure you cannot beat the big boys. They have everything going for them. Sure they have the money, and the government and the police, they all back them up.'

'Look, those men have a right to a wage they can live on. They have a right to organize together if they want. What kind of a country is this if people are starving or if people cannot get together and talk? This Larkin man is right. Working people have to stand up for themselves. Look at around here, sure labourers cannot live on what they are paid. This is not right. The big farmers are like the Murphy's and the bosses in Dublin.'

'But the priest last week said that Larkin and that other boy Connolly were Socialists and they wanted to take everything we had away from us. That is no good. And that they were not Christians, that they did not believe in God or Jesus or the Holy Mary.'

O'Donnell was challenged for a minute. He did not want to go up against the priest. But he did not want to say that Larkin and Connolly were bad either.

'Look, maybe the Father was mistaken. Larkin and Connolly are for working people that is what I know.'

Campbell could not believe his luck. Here he was getting what Brown had asked him for. What they were thinking, but not only that, Brown had also asked about anybody talking about these Larkin and Connolly men. He would get back to Brown with this and this would help him. Campbell drank back his whisky and nodded at his glass when McDaid was watching. The fill up came and Campbell threw it into him.

But his good mood did not last long. For who should come in through the door but James, the eldest of the Wallace boys. Herself's brother. He did not notice Campbell as he went to the bar and then joined O'Donnell and the crowd around the fire. The talk stopped as they realised that James had not seen Campbell but that Campbell had seen him. The young Wallace boy looked at them to see why they had stopped talking.

He saw their eyes go to the door. He looked round and then he saw Campbell. He turned and threw his head back. 'O'Donnell, how are you doing? What have you heard about the boys in Dublin? You were telling me they were out for better pay. That is what me and the boys here need. Better pay. What about these Larkin and Connolly men? They seem like good men. Maybe they would take up our case against these big farmers when they are finished in Dublin. We need a union here too.'

Campbell was enraged. He could see that all the credit he would get for his information to Brown would be for nothing when they heard that his wife's brother was for a union and was some kind of Connolly and Larkin boy. He got up and stamped out of the door. He should never have taken her on. She was bad news on all fronts. She was getting out of control. Her brother was involved in this union business now and she was expecting another baby. More mouths to feed and more money.

He fairly strode up the road to his cottage. She had better have things ready for him or she would pay. She had better not be lying in that bed with that wean and the fire dead. She had better have the milking done and everything in order. She had better have his bread on the table. 'Hey Campbell, Hey Campbell.' He heard his name being called from inside the hedge.

He grunted and went over and looked into the field. It was Shanks walking up inside the hedge with a couple of snared rabbits in his hand. 'Campbell, I was just wanting to say that we are sorry for your trouble. It was terrible, Margaret's mother dying so young.'

What was he talking about Campbell's trouble? It was her mother. He had only taken her in because he got a cow and an extra pair of hands out of it. It was not his trouble.

158

He turned and went on his way up the road to the cottage. He was angry at Shanks because he was confused now. His anger that had been focused on Margaret was now all over the place. That Shanks. He was always interfering. Why did he not mind his own business? He was always interfering. What was wrong with him and his wife anyway? They should keep themselves to themselves.

He pushed the door of the cottage open. The fire was burning bright. The water was bubbling in the pot. In ten minutes his tea and eggs and bread was on the table. It was like she knew and had everything ready quick just to thwart him. He could not complain, he could not attack her. He ate and steamed and ate and in vain tried to think of something to attack her for. He went and lay on his bench. He could not sleep. Her brother. He snorted to himself.

But he could not go and take his anger out on her by putting his thing in her he was so angry at her. It was like she was putting a spell on him. Twisting him this way and that. He wished he could get rid of her. But then there was the cow. He would have to get rid of it. And his tea ready, and the fire burning, and his thing. He lay and fumed with anger at her. She lay with Victoria in her arms and in her heart, content and smiling inside of herself.

He awoke early. He did not have to leave early but he had to get away from her. He headed down to Brown with his information. He would not mention about the Wallace boy being with O'Donnell. He had figured out how to deal with this if it came up. It was Brown who had got him tangled up with the Wallace crowd in the first place. It was Brown's fault, not Campbell's fault.

What was happening with her anyway? This morning she had got up and got his breakfast, milked the cow, looked after the baby. Everything. Nothing was missed. She was doing it just to get at him. That must be it. She was giving him no excuse. And she did not seem to mind doing everything. It was as if it was part of some plan of hers.

What was it? What was he missing? His mouth tightened and his eyes glared as he tried to figure it out.

But it made no sense to him. He was unable to understand that Margaret now had a centre to her life and a clear objective. Her baby was her centre and her objective was to see that her baby was brought up safe and sound. This was what governed all her actions. It was this which gave her the increased focus and discipline. She made the food, she milked the cow, she kept the fire burning, she let him put his thing in her. All this was so that she could have a cottage, and a fire, and food and clothing, and safety for her baby and the new one that would soon come, and safety for herself because the baby and the new baby needed her.

Campbell had such contempt for Margaret and all women that he could not imagine that she would be so clear in her objective and so disciplined in pursuit of it. He could not imagine that she could conclude what her actions should be in relation to him if she was to achieve her objective. And be so determined in carrying out the tactics which flowed from this. He could only imagine that she was deliberately confusing him and driving him wild with frustration.

When he left the house Margaret finished her jobs about the house and went into her room and lifted up the feather mattress. She took out some pieces of cloth that her mother had brought to her. She began to cut them and then sew them together. Gradually the shape became clear. She was making clothes for her new baby and for Victoria. She had been at this now for days.

These were the best minutes of her life so far. Sitting with Victoria asleep on the bed, a new baby in her stomach, Campbell out of the house, and herself making new clothes for her babies. At these times she would feel the stress go out of her neck and shoulders. She would take in deep breaths and then release them. Now and then she would let her hands fall still on her lap and pull her head back to where she was looking up to the sky. And she would then let thoughts, feelings, images play about in her mind. That is all, just let them play.

She did not have to close down her thoughts and imagination and feelings because neither her father, nor Allen nor Campbell was around to come in and hit her, or order her with shouts. The lifting of these threats, even if temporarily, came together with the love she had for her baby. The strength she had derived from having her baby and realizing that she had given her life and that she was needed by her baby continued to grow in her. So she could for a moment lift up her head and her eyes and her thoughts.

She looked around the cottage and through the window at the valley stretching down below. The sun was up in the sky and the valley was beautiful. In spite of it being winter the valley was still green. Margaret was only fifteen years old. But those years had contained such shocks and struggle that she was matured beyond her years. In spite of her isolation from the struggles that were taking place in society at large, she herself had developed conclusions and responses to cope with her situation. She had not been crushed, instead she had grown from her experiences.

Now she had Victoria and soon she would have another baby. She had a centre to her life, something to live for. This helped her put up with Campbell, the poverty, the daily decisions she had to make, the moods that would threaten to rise up in her. All these were now subject to the overall task of her life, the overall emotion of her life, bringing up and loving Victoria and soon her new baby.

She had a ballast in herself now. A ship would be blown in all directions and wrecked if it was empty on a rough sea with no ballast. But with ballast it could plough its way though the waves. With its keel held in the water by the ballast it could deal with the pressures of the wind and the storm. Margaret's ballast was her baby and the babies to come. Her keel was in the water. This was what gave her the calmness and confidence and strength that so frustrated and enraged Campbell.

Campbell himself had little ballast. Instead he was kept in line by the orders and pressures of those above him, those he insisted on obeying. It was as if the demands of the powers that be tied him like a ship is tied to a pier. This gave him a certain fixed character, a certain position and discipline, but unlike the ballast it made it impossible for him to rise and fall with the great movements of the ocean. Instead these external controls that determined his life were always threatening to wreck him against the pier or pull him apart as the pull of the ropes continually fought with the power of the sea. And when he would be free of these ropes and set to sea he would be thrown in all directions by the storms.

Margaret's centre and discipline, her love for her baby, her living for her baby, drew forth from her all the great positive emotions and qualities, courage, love for and with her baby, understanding, tenderness, sacrifice, internal discipline. Campbell's discipline on the other hand, which was accepting what the higher ups put on his plate, doing their dirty work, this drew from him all the negative qualities and emotions, subservience to those above him, cruelty to those below him, contempt for all around him, lack of sympathy, lack of solidarity, hatred, fear, selfishness. While Margaret's spirit grew and became richer, his shrunk into itself, stagnating, atrophying, dying.

Campbell could not allow his positive emotions to develop. To feel love would make it impossible to evict and threaten Taverstock's tenants. To feel solidarity would make it impossible to force them to pay the rent when they had nothing and were in rags. Campbell's relationship to the world around him brought all his negative emotions to the fore, all his self-destructive tendencies, hatred for others, contempt for others, selfishness, self-centredness. So he shrunk in on himself as the years went by. His spirit could not grow. All this was written on his face in a permanent sneer of hostility.

But Margaret was growing in all ways. As she had learnt to love her baby she had also learnt to hate what should be hated, such as the suffering of her mother and the oppressions of Allen, and her father and Campbell. Because the centre of her life was her baby and this drew out all her great life affirming tendencies, Margaret was growing stronger by the day.

She sat and looked out over the valley and felt more complete than at any time in her life. As she sat there, a rabbit and her young ones fed on the grass alongside the hedge by the roadway. Margaret watched them and smiled to herself as she watched the mother rabbit continually raise her head and sniff the air for danger. Margaret was glad the dog had gone with Campbell. She did not want that mother's life to be shattered by the dog killing her little ones and maybe herself. Margaret held her baby to her cheek.

CHAPTER SEVENTEEN

It was early March 1914. Katie and Shanks were sitting round the fire in the evening with the old man. He was becoming more angry and bitter by the day. The news he had got from O'Donnell who had stopped in one evening about the labour war in Dublin, was making him worse. His spirits had been lifted a bit when he heard that the workers had set up their own army to protect themselves. But the inability of the strikers to win, the church's role in stopping the children from going to Liverpool to be looked after, these had been too much for him. He did not speak much about it, just got more morose and sat with his head down looking into the fire.

'Shanks, we should do something about it,' said Katie. 'That McDaid gave me flour last week and it was less than the full two pounds. We should do something about it. I am going to go down to see him.'

'Ah Katie, what good will that do? Sure he will just deny it. It's better to let things lie and just watch him in the future.'

'And let him get away with it?' Katie was angry. She knew she had a man with a good heart in Shanks. A kind man. She would not change him for anybody. But she knew that he tended to try and avoid an open struggle.

The old man knew this too. But he could not say anything. Wasn't he staying in Shanks' house? That McDaid was a crook, a gombeen man if ever there was one. Somebody should pull him up. Katie was right. But Shanks would rather find some way to get round it. Some way to avoid a fight. Katie was far and away more of a fighter. The old man was proud of her and he wished he wasn't under an obligation to Shanks so that he could speak out.

There was a knock on the door. The dog jumped up barking.

'Who is it?' shouted Shanks thinking it was maybe Quinn or O'Donnell. It was Campbell's voice that answered.

'She's having the wean.

Katie leapt up from her chair. Running to the kitchen she gathered up a bucket and some cloths.

'I am coming. I am coming.'

Campbell made no answer as Shanks opened the door to him. He would not come in, just stood there.

Katie was out and down the road in a matter of minutes. Shanks watched her go. Not a word of thanks came from Campbell. He turned, walked out to the road but, instead of turning to go downhill, he turned uphill. Shanks could not believe it. He was not going back to the house where Margaret was having the baby. Shanks turned and told this to the old man who snorted in response. Grabbing his coat, Shanks set off after Katie. She might need help.

Margaret was in labour when Katie and Shanks got there. The door was open and they went in.

'Margaret, we are here. I will help you. Do not worry everything will be all right.'

Her presence seemed to give Margaret the go ahead to make her pain known. She screamed as the spasms hit her body. It was like the last time. She felt that the pressure would make her body break, that her skin would be burst apart.

Why did it have to be like this? Why did women have to go through this? He only had to put his thing in her. He liked that. There was no pain there. Why did she have to go through this? Why did women have to go through this? It was not fair, it was not fair and Margaret screamed in anguish as these thoughts raced through her mind.

'It will be all right, Margaret. It will be all right.' Katie comforted and held her and Shanks worked at the fire getting water boiled.

Victoria was crying in the corner terrified by her mother's screams. Shanks came to the door of the room. 'The water is boiling, Katie. I will be outside. Call me if you need me. I will wait outside.' Shanks could not bear the screams of pain from Margaret.

'No, Shanks, you will have to take Victoria up home and look after her. She is terrified here.' Katie lifted Victoria and handed her to Shanks.

Margaret saw what was going on. In the midst of her pain she saw her baby being taken away from her for the first time. She dragged herself up in the bed and caught Victoria's wee leg as Shanks caught her.

'No No No!' and Margaret broke into hysterical weeping. 'No, No, Victoria, my baby.'

'Margaret, she cannot stay here. She does not know what is happening. She is very frightened. Shanks will look after her well. Please, Margaret, let her go.' Margaret in her exhaustion and pain let go of Victoria's leg and fell back in the bed in hysterical tears.

The next spasm hit her and shut off the weeping with another scream of pain. It was like the last time. No better. Again Margaret went through the terror of thinking that maybe the baby would not be able to get out of her. Maybe it would get stuck. Maybe she could not open up enough for it. Maybe it would be too big. Again the millions of women who must have died this way, went through her head. She screamed as another spasm shook her. She was bursting and she could not burst.

This went on throughout the night. No man could understand the pain she was enduring. Men have the easy part Katie thought. The sky was clearing when Margaret felt a change in her body. As before something was changing position. Katie came to her and held her. 'It will soon be coming now, Margaret.' Katie touched her between the legs. 'Its wee head is trying to make it out. Keep pushing Margaret.'

'It is coming, Margaret. It is coming.' And like before Margaret felt the baby slide out of her. She lay exhausted as Katie cut and tied its cord and washed the baby down with the wet cloths.

'It is a baby girl, Margaret, and she is fine. Everything is all right. Hear her crying. Everything is all right.'

She passed the baby up to Margaret who managed to hold her and put her to her breast. Like before only not so powerful, she felt the gentleness of the baby's lips and need on her nipples and breast. She felt a healing from the pain of the past hours and the pain of life. She felt a powerful peace.

Unknown to them both Campbell had returned during the night and stood outside the cottage. Margaret's screams filled his head. He held his hands over his ears and after barely a couple of minutes he turned and made off back again up the road to the bog. He could not stand it. He could not stand it. The last one had died screaming. The one he had left his father for years before. She was having the baby and she screamed until she and the baby both died.

He could do nothing. He could only listen to her screams. But he could do nothing. His helplessness added on to the terrible nightmare of her screams and her pain. He was changed forever that night. Before that night he had smiled and sometimes laughed when he had looked at her. He had even kissed her on the mouth and even smiled when he had been putting his thing in her at times when he had seen the pleasure in her face. He had laughed with her. Then she got big with the baby.

Then she lay and screamed and died with the baby stuck partially out of her body. And the baby died too. He could do nothing. He was helpless and stood outside wishing he could hit somebody or kill somebody or do something. This helplessness was not the lot of a man. This total lack of involvement in the terrible struggle that was going on inside, the struggle of his woman and the two women who were helping her, was not endurable to him. Her pain, his part in making the baby, his helplessness, his nothingness in the process of her terrible death, all these came together to crush and brutalize his spirit.

When the screaming had stopped he had gone inside. He saw her body with the head of the baby half way out of her and blue in death like its mother. The horror of that sight never left him and threatened to destroy him, to drive him insane. He thrust it away. He turned and fled. He attended the funeral. Then he left and behind him tried to leave the sight her body and the baby's head. But what he did leave was all the affection, solidarity, sympathy and love he had ever felt. He could not lead life with these. He became Campbell.

His father took him back because he was a pair of hands. But he did not forget to taunt him about the failure of his attempt to escape and to have a woman and a family and some warmth in his life. 'I told you it would not be any good. I told you. You should have stayed and listened to me. I told you. But you knew better, you knew....' Campbell became more Campbell everyday with the brutality of his father's taunts and as the only way he knew to keep the memories beaten down.

When he reached the bog he lay down in a stack of turf away from the wind. He lay on his back and above him he could see the clear night sky. There was no moon but the stars were bright. Slowly the terror and the memories left him. He gradually fell off to sleep. When he woke with the cold half an hour later, things were back in their place. 'Aye, she will be well finished now. I will be getting back down soon. But give it a while. Then that Katie will be gone.'

Meanwhile, Shanks and the old man were sitting at the fire and the wee one, Victoria, was sleeping on the bench with the feather mattress beside them. She was asleep. 'I will be getting on up there with the wee one.' Shanks said. He was worried with the baby in the house with only himself and the old man. 'If she starts crying here she might exhaust herself. I will be getting back up,' and he rose and wrapping Victoria in the blanket she had been in, he left the cottage. The old man never answered.

It was quiet and Shanks hoped that everything was all right. 'Katie, Katie,' he called at the cottage door.

'Shanks, quiet she is asleep. The wee one has come and is all right and she is all right. Have you Victoria with you?' Katie came out the door and took Victoria and they all entered the cottage. 'Aye, she is all right, Shanks. Everything is all right. I will stay here with her until she wakens. Why don't you go on down home? I will be all right here on my own.'

Katie lay down in the bed beside Margaret and held Victoria who was sleeping in her arms. Katie was exhausted also. She dozed off. But she woke with a start after half an hour as Margaret came awake and tried to push herself up off the bed. She held on to her new baby but looked around in panic and opened her mouth as if to speak. But then she saw Victoria lying sleeping and the tension went out of her. She held out her other arm for Victoria.

Katie moved over to the side of the bed and placed Victoria on the mattress close up by Margaret's side. Margaret put her arm out around the sleeping baby. In her other arm she held her new baby who was sucking at her breast. The peace she felt after the struggle and pain of the birth was greater than she had ever felt before. Lying there with her two babies. She was at peace and content. The world seemed to be turning with her.

Where was Campbell? What was he doing? What a useless lump of a man. No good to his wife at all. Ran and hid every time there was a baby coming. What was wrong with him anyway? She shook her head. She was glad she had Shanks. He and her worked together as a team. She heard the door push open and saw by the bulk of the person that it was Campbell. She got up and rose from the bed.

'The baby is fine. Margaret is fine. It's a grand wee baby girl, it is a sister for Victoria. I will be off now and if she needs anything then run up and get us. I will come down at any time. Shanks looked after Victoria but she is back now also and they are all sleeping. Everything looks grand.'

Campbell sat down at the fire with his back to her. He never said aye or naw nor thanks or anything else. Katie stood for a minute and then pulling her coat around her she went out and closed the door after her.

She gave a start as she saw something move at the gate. 'Katie. Katie.' It was Shanks. 'I thought I would wait for a while and see if you were going to be coming. Then when I saw himself come out from behind the house and go in I knew you would not be long. Aye, he was somewhere in behind the house. What kind of a man is he anyway? It is good that Margaret has the two weans and she loves them otherwise what kind of a life would she have anyway? That Campbell man. He is good for nothing. Maybe getting her in the family way but that's about all'

'Shanks, Margaret is very content and peaceful with the two weans one in each arm. She is a great mother. You could not ask for better.' At that, something moved and darted across the road. It was a fox with its white nose and its beautiful full auburn tail.

'Aw look, Shanks, it's a fox. Isn't it beautiful? It is a sign of luck for Margaret and her baby.'

'Aye, it might be, Katie, and at the same time it might be a sign that it is going down to eat our couple of wee chickens. That is what it could be.'

Katie laughed and Shanks laughed and the tension of the night and the anger they felt at Campbell and the stress of the last twenty four hours all left them as they thought about the fox.

'I like foxes, Shanks. I know they eat the chickens. But they are so beautiful and smart and sneaky. Did you see that one on its wee toes as it moved across in front of us? It knew it was safe for the time being. The fox it is a sneaky one. Maybe it will go down and eat McDaid's chickens instead of ours. This would be better. That way we could get our own back on him for giving us short weight. And if it ate McDaid's chickens he might have to give us a better price for our eggs.'

They walked on in silence each in their own thoughts. Campbell what kind of a man....? Margaret with her two children now and only a child herself and a good mother and content, at peace. Was the fox a mother or a father? Katie's own father at home. What was he up to? Where was he when Katie was born? Did he help? Katie never knew her mother, she was too young, her mother had died after she had her.

'Go on in, Katie. I will be in in a minute.' Shanks walked down to the side of the cottage unbuttoned his trousers and began to urinate in the stream. He watched the curve of his water and where it hit the stream and blended and rushed down over the rocks. As he stood there he looked up at the stars which shone so bright he too was at peace. Katie was a good woman. He was a lucky man. Margaret now was a mother twice and she was a good mother. He shook himself and buttoned his trousers and went inside with the smell of the grass and the heather in his nose.

CHAPTER EIGHTEEN

Life went on in the cottage as before except that Margaret shared her bed now with two babies. Her increased difficulty in keeping the bed from being soiled did not in any way lead to her regretting the birth of her second baby. Her love for her babies overcame all the extra work and smells that came with the babies. The bags that came with the flour from McDaid's were used for trying to keep the children dry and clean. But they were only partially successful and the bed and the room and the cottage always smelled of the children's waste.

But the extra work and smells and washing she had to do, in some strange way strengthened her love for them and strengthened herself. The increased sacrifice strengthened her love and herself. In some way she felt that they were the love. She thought of the future when she would have four or five or more children but she put the thought off into her head.

Campbell slept on his bench and after a few weeks he began to come to her again. The babies slept through these episodes. Margaret lay there and let this happen. They were part of the price she had to pay for the roof over her head, the food in her mouth, the clothes on her back and the safety of her babies.

It was July, over a month since Margaret had had her second

child. Campbell was out of the house early that day and on his way down to Brown who had sent for him.

'Campbell, there you are, come on in.' And they went into the harness shed as usual. 'Well, Campbell, that Larkin business is over in Dublin. He and his mob have been well and truly beaten. This is a good thing for all concerned.' Brown was exaggerating the degree of victory of the bosses over the Dublin workers to keep up his own and Campbell's morale. 'We do not have to worry so much now that they have been defeated but at the same time take no chances. Keep everything up to standard. There is to be no slipping. These people have to see we are still in charge.

'You did me a real service, Campbell, keeping your eye out and your ears open for what people were thinking and saying over the past while. I am glad that you told me that some of them in McDaid's were talking about Connolly. This is always good to know. But him and his friend Larkin are people of the past now. They tried their best and were beaten. This will teach them a lesson.

'Just like these home rule people will be beaten too. You see the gentlemen of the British officers in the Curragh refused to do the government's bidding when they wanted them to disarm the loyal Ulster volunteers in Belfast. Aye, there will be no home rule here. We are part of his majesty's empire and this is where we will stay.' Campbell had not heard about the mutiny of the British officers in the Curragh camp so he did not know what Brown was talking about. But he nodded his head in agreement.

While this conversation was going on Margaret was at her work around the cottage. When she had moved in there had been no toilet. After Victoria was born Margaret found herself thinking more and more about this. With the birth of her second baby whom she called Mary after her mother, Margaret was determined to have a toilet. The ground on the west side of the cottage sloped down into a narrow gulley.

The byre for the cow and calves stood up behind the cottage on the same side of the gulley. The manure from the byre was thrown down into the gulley and made a midden.

Margaret now felt well enough recovered from Mary's birth to take the saw that Campbell had and walk across the fields to where there was a small grove of ash trees, hazel bushes and plants. She carried her two babies with her and left them down wrapped in covers on the ground while she went to work. She cut down eight long pieces of ash, stripped them of their fine branches and dragged them back. She leaned six of them against the gable of the byre sticking the pointed tops of them into gaps between the stones in the wall. Then she drove the other ends into the ground and fastened them all together with pieces of string. And the remaining two she tied across the others to strengthen them. She had herself the frame of a little lean-to.

A few old jute sacks had gathered up in the byre over the years. She gathered together her nerve and took some of these and draped them over her lean-to making holes in them with a knife. She then used pieces of string from the flour bags that they bought the flour in from McDaid's, to tie these to the poles. Then she hung what was left on the back and the front of the lean-to. She fastened the ones at the back and let the front ones hang loose. She rolled some heavy stones and leaned them against the bottom of the poles. She took one of the three buckets there was about the place and set it inside.

Campbell snorted at it when he came home and saw it. She heard him grunt 'a waste of a bucket' but he left it alone. But this was a major concession from him. Margaret used the toilet from then on. When the bucket was close to full Margaret would take it out and empty it in the midden. She had a toilet for the first time in her life. And she had a toilet for her children. It was not comfortable to sit on. Sometimes if she was sure there was nobody around she would pull back the sacking and sit and look out over the downward sloping hills. Campbell never used it.

Building this toilet gave Margaret greater comfort in her mind. She seemed to be more complete, more at ease, stronger after she had built it. She liked to go to it and see it and that it was still standing. She began to pull grass and leave little piles of this inside to wipe herself. She weighed this down with a stone. The stone, the grass, the toilet, they combined to give Margaret something of her own and her children's, something that she had made herself.

One day Campbell came back early from his work. He was accompanied by another man. Margaret knew him to be a farmer from closer to the village. He had almost as big a place as Allen. Campbell and him went into the byre and when they came back they were leading the young calf that the cow had given birth to nearly a year ago. They stopped outside the door and Margaret could hear what they said.

'Well, Campbell, I have given you a good price for this beast. You should be well pleased. I don't know if he is worth it but I will take a chance. I hope I come out all right.' Campbell grunted in reply. 'What do you think, Campbell, of that business that went on in Dublin? This striking business. You see where they were wanting more wages and to be able to organize together to force the employers to give them more wages. This was not good Campbell.

'And you know what I heard. That some of the boys here were talking along the same lines, of more money and organizing a union. These labouring men are getting above themselves. Sure we give them work, a place to sleep, food to eat, and now they are talking about getting more pay. About getting organized into a union. I tell you if there is any of that among my hands I will show them the road. I won't pay them more than they are worth. Sure we are doing them a favour hiring them at all. They should be grateful to us.

'And you know what is most dangerous about this, Campbell, is that some of our own kind are involved in this union business. I heard that these Larkin and Connolly men are preaching that Protestant and Catholic hands should get together to work for more money. That our kind's labouring men should get together with the other kind's labouring men. This is dangerous. If this were to happen then they would want more than they are worth. We have to see that this does not happen, Campbell.

'I mean to say. These boys should be grateful to have work, to have a place. If it was not for us hiring them out they would have to take the boat. Or they might have to take to the ditches like them tinkers. I heard that up in McDaid's one night you heard some of them talking about this. Who was it anyway? You have to keep us informed of this Campbell. You have a better way of getting around and hearing these things.'

Campbell grunted in agreement but gave no information. He did not want to admit Margaret's brother was one of these he had heard on about this.

Margaret heard this conversation from inside the cottage. What were they talking about, organizing a union? What was a union? She thought about what this man had said about farm labourers and they should be grateful to the farmers. She thought of Allen. Had she been a farm labourer? She was not grateful to Allen. She hated him. She had never seen her pay as her father had taken it and Allen had attacked her and put his thing in her. She did not know if she was well paid or not.

Margaret knew nothing about the cow that Campbell had brought home and that she milked everyday. She did not know it had been the price Allen paid for his rape of her. She did not know how much she had been paid at Allen's or at Brown's. She did not know that this calf which Campbell had just sold was part of the pay off that Allen had been told by the preacher to give to Campbell for taking her and her baby. Part of the pay off for her rape.

She heard Campbell walk across the yard and into the byre. Then she heard him come out and call the dog and she knew that they were heading off up the bog. She gave them a minute and then went out to the byre and sat down and began to milk the cow. Victoria was with her and Margaret set her inside a crate that was pulled across a corner of the byre and she could not get out. Mary lay sleeping on a pile of hay.

Margaret went over the conversation she had heard as she milked. Labourers should be grateful. They were paid enough. Joining a union. What was a union? And talk about all religions of working people should get together. One of our own kind. What about that? Margaret was not able to figure it all out. She felt that there was a lot more she should understand but it would not come to her. She felt that there was something she should agree with in the labourers getting together and unions but she could not get it clear in her head.

She turned away from these thoughts in her confusion looking instead to her two children both of whom were now sleeping. This was the best time for her, when she was alone with the two children. She felt the energy of her feelings for them rise in her and the confusion and thoughts she had felt arising from the conversation, sank into the bottom of her mind. She could see no way for her own life to connect with unions whatever they were and she did not get any pay of any kind. She was confined and isolated in Campbell's cottage but she was making headway there in her own struggle by her own efforts

It would not be long until she would have another baby. He was coming to her again. What would she do if there were four or five babies? Where would they all sleep? She got excited as she thought. She would have to try and make some sort of other bed for the room. The youngest ones would always sleep with her but as they got older maybe the oldest ones could sleep in another wee bed. She would have to start collecting filling for another mattress.

If she was stuck she could stuff it with hay. But this would bring old ticks and other insects. But she did not have enough hens to get enough feathers. What would she do? She could take some feathers out of the big mattress she had and make it thinner and make another one out of that. What about bed clothes? Could she ask Campbell to buy some? But she never spoke to him. She had never spoken to him in the nearly two years they had been together.

What about food for more children? She would have to dig an extra part of the field and plant more potatoes and carrots and cabbage. Maybe she could get more hens. Could she get a rooster and then they could hatch out new chicks? Yes, this would be it. But how could she do it? She did not speak to Campbell. She had no money to buy a rooster from anybody and anyway she did not know anybody to ask who had one. Shanks and Katie. That was it. She would ask them.

But she would have to speak to them. She would have to get over her wait in silence and it will pass approach. Now with the children and more to come she would have to speak and act to get by. The talk of the farm labourers and their demand for more wages flashed into her head. Where were those wages she had earned? Her father had them. She could go and ask him for a rooster. He had taken her wages.

But as the options came up one after another, Margaret was faced more and more with the one certainty. She was going to have to speak to people for her children to get by. She was going to have to move from the wait and it will pass to taking action. She sat a little stunned at the thought. It scared her. She was going to have to change. She looked round as she milked the cow, at her two sleeping children. She was going to have to speak to people. She could no longer be dumb. As she looked at her children she felt the determination to change spread through her.

Victoria began to cry as she woke and Margaret turned to see she was all right. Mary awoke and started to cry also. But they were all right. She knew by their cry. They were only hungry. She would protect her babies, she would do the best she could for her babies. Even if it meant speaking to Campbell, to Shanks and Katie, to her father, to anybody. Whatever she would have to do she would do to protect and look after her babies.

CHAPTER NINETEEN

It was a couple of days later and Margaret was out in the front of the house. She had been trying to see Shanks or Katie for the last days. This time she was in luck. They were coming up the road on their way home. She felt her chest tighten with stress and the sweat break out on her. She was going to have to speak to them. To speak and to ask them for something. She went over to the edge of the yard where it ran up to the road.

'Hello there, Margaret,' Shanks and Katie greeted her. They were prepared to carry on both sides of the conversation as usual. 'How are you doing and how are the weans? You are looki...'

'I need a rooster. I need a rooster.' Shanks and Katie were stunned. She had spoken. It was true not very much and not very polite but she had spoken. She needed a rooster.

'I have these.' She spoke again, pulling a small sack from behind the stone wall. It was half full with seed spuds. 'And I have this.'

And again from behind the wall she took another small bag of stirabout oats. She left this down on top of the bag of seed spuds. It had taken her weeks to decide to take these spuds and the stirabout because she was afraid that Campbell would notice and she would suffer. When she handed over the two bags she looked at Katie and Shanks. But only very briefly. She then turned away and stared out over the valley. And waited. She had spoken. She had told them what she wanted. She was finished speaking. The silence stretched out as Shanks and Katie tried to recover.

Shanks gathered himself first. 'A rooster, Margaret? You say a rooster? Oh I see you want to have some wee chicks. That is a good idea. What good having hens and no rooster? You would give these for a rooster?' And he indicated the two bags on the ground. 'Well, Katie, do we know anybody has an extra rooster? What about the Kelly? Does he not have a couple of young birds that are coming up? Margaret, we will ask him and see what he says.'

Without another word Margaret lifted the two bags and put them in Shanks' hands and turned and went into the cottage. She had done it. She had spoken. She had done it for her children. She went into the room and sat down with her children. She was drained of energy, utterly spent. Her back was sore with tension. She had spoken and given them the things for the rooster.

'Katie, you cannot expect everything at once. At least she spoke. It's like that wee dog that could not bark for a while. She will need a bit of practice. In the meantime she needs a rooster. I do not know if Kelly will take this for the rooster or not. We will have to tell him it is for her as he has no love for Campbell. And Kelly is a bitter boy. He might not want to give it to her. This could be an awkward one. But Katie, we have to help her.'

'Shanks, I tell you what we could do. We could get that rooster from Kelly and keep it ourselves and give ours to Margaret. This way would be a lot simpler.'

'Katie, you are a crafty one. Why did I not think of that? Sure that's the best way to do it. But will Kelly take these seed spuds and the meal for the rooster? Well if not we can offer him a few more spuds or something. After all we will be getting a younger rooster.'

'What made her speak, Shanks?' Katie went on to answer her own question. 'I know what it was. It is not any good treatment from Campbell. It is her weans. It is her love for her children that gave her the strength to speak. That's what it is, Shanks. The needs of her children are forcing her to speak.'

'You are right, Katie. The children also make her feel stronger about herself. Well let's get her a rooster and the next thing you know she might be singing.' They laughed together, happy that they could help, as they walked up to their cottage with the two bags.

And that is the way it worked out. Kelly's rooster replaced Shanks' and Katie's and theirs went to Margaret. When Campbell saw it strutting around the yard and scratching and glaring, he stood and stared. Where did that come from? It must have strayed from somewhere else. Well all the better. Let it stay. It did not occur to him that Margaret could have managed to get it. He was feeling good thinking he had got it for nothing. When he was sure there was nobody looking he grimaced greedily to himself at his good fortune.

It was early August. The first of the new spuds were ready. Margaret was looking forward to supplementing their diet with blackberries and other berries that were ripening on the hedges. She was watching a hazel grove across the fields for the nuts to be ready. The hay that they had cut from their couple of bits of fields was in the byre.

Campbell was on his way up from Brown's. He was increasingly edgy over Margaret's growing confidence and strength. If he had known that she had broken out of her isolation and spoken to Shanks and Katie and got the rooster he would have been even more concerned. It was always easier to control somebody when that person is isolated. But what made him even more insecure was that sometimes he found himself looking at her with interest in how she felt, who she was, what she was thinking.

The new animals about the place, the cow, the hens, the rooster were all connected to Margaret. The cow he had got in exchange for her rape, abuse and pregnancy. He took Margaret and her baby and her abuse off Allen's hands and off the conscience of the preacher. He had helped maintain the facade of respectable Protestantism and control. The cow was the price he was paid for all this. The few hens he had got by squeezing Wallace because he was taking Margaret and her baby off his hands too. Wallace would have had to feed them.

He did not know it but the rooster was in a different category altogether. The other trades were all at Margaret's expense even though she did not know it. The trade for the rooster was at his expense and involved Margaret growing stronger and being inspired by her babies. She had to speak in order to act to help her babies. To get the rooster Margaret had to heal some of the wounds of her oppression of the past years. The trade for the rooster was different. To achieve this Margaret had to grow stronger.

This is what Campbell felt and this frightened him. He had no use for a stronger Margaret. Except in the sense of her having a stronger back. But a stronger person. No, this was not what he wanted. She would start to think she was somebody and begin to think she could decide what to do and what not to do. The next thing would be she would want to have a say in how things were done.

It was not good when women got the notion that they could have a say in things. It only made for trouble. What did women know anyway? What did she know anyway? They knew nothing but about weans and making the food and milking and things. But about the things that were involved in making the real decisions they knew nothing. Aye, he was right. Women would only cause trouble if they had a say in things. He would have to keep her in her place.

And if the women got to have a say in things then who else would want a say in things? The ordinary working man and woman would then all be encouraged. They would all want a say in things. Control would begin to slip and the whole situation would go to hell. Naw, it was important to keep the women down so that the rest could be kept down and that things could be kept in control. Anyway the women did not know enough to have a say in things.

It was a lovely summer night. The moon was up. A few clouds drifted across the sky. There was no cold in the air. He thought of the time he had gone to Dungloe for that young horse for Brown. He had seen the sea. He could hear its waves crashing on the sand and see the big roll of them and the green water. He felt his spirit begin to soften. But then he thought of her again and the dying of her and the child. And he thought also of the need to keep control. And he hardened himself up again.

He needed a drink to settle his head. He stopped at McDaid's. It had been a few months since he had been there. The usual crowd was round the fire. O'Donnell at the centre of it. And, ah naw. Her brother was there too. That James boy. What was he doing hanging around with a bunch of Fenians? What was his father thinking about letting this happen? He should be put in his place.

Campbell had no trouble hearing their talk. 'Look, O'Donnell, because you can read and we cannot you have to keep us up to date with what is going on.' Seeing Campbell by the door O'Donnell saw his opportunity to taunt him.

'The best thing that is happening here from the labour war in Dublin is that us farm hands are getting organized. Look at the hours they try to make the hired men work. Some of them farmers try to make us work from six in the morning to eight at night.

'We should have the eight hour day. That's what we want, more wages and the eight hour day. All us farm labourers should get together and strike. It does not matter if we are Protestants or Catholics. Look, James,' to Margaret's brother, 'the Kilgores are not treating you right no more than the Murphys are treating Brennan here right. No more than that Allen treated your sister Margaret right.'

Campbell thought the rage would get the better of him. Instead he threw back his whisky and stamped out of the door. McDaid was angry.

'O'Donnell, I am warning you. If you lose any more customers on me or cause any more trouble I will bar you.'

O'Donnell laughed. 'I am only speaking the truth.'

'That's right.' Margaret's brother spoke. 'He is only telling the truth. Look at that Campbell. He got a cow from Allen and hens from my father as his price for taking Margaret and Allen's wean. O'Donnell, what about this organizing? Are you just talking or what?'

'It's not just talk, James. We have to get organized. Look, the situation is this. Things are changing in this country. The working man is not going to stand for things as they are any more. Very soon we are going to have to take some steps and get some of what has been taken from us. I for one am for joining Larkin's union and I for one am ready to strike. These farmers have been using us like slaves too long. Look what Larkin and Connolly and the boys did in Dublin.'

'That's right.' Brennan spoke up.

And James followed him. 'You are right, O'Donnell. Gilgore keeps us in that leaky barn, feeds us stirabout and spuds and makes us work twelve hours a day.'

'And Murphy does the same with us,' Brennan spoke in agreement. 'It will have to change. Things will have to change.'

McDaid turned away and pretended not to be listening. When they started talking about wages and hours and prices it made him nervous. But it was not only that. What also made him nervous was that talk like this made him think about what he did when he took the eggs and other produce he bought from the local folks, down to Stranolar to sell to Craig. In the back room of Craig's shop he would have a wee whiskey and he would recount the goings on in the neighbourhood and what the boys in the pub were talking about. Craig's

brother was the Sergeant of the police in Stranolar. All this information he knew was then passed on to him.

McDaid knew what he was doing. He had to look after business.
He had to be sure that the police knew he was a sound man. That he
could be depended on. This would help him if any trouble came up
for himself. Aye, it was important that he give Craig all the news he
had. When he would meet the Sergeant in the street the Sergeant
would always speak to him and call him by his name. He was letting
him know that he knew who he was and that things were in hand.

But McDaid was feeling a little nervous now about his talks with
Craig. Things were getting a little more serious. What with this labour
business in Dublin and with O'Donnell stirring it up in the pub. He
would have to be careful. Make sure that nobody knew what he was
talking to Craig about or even that he was going into Craig's back
room and talking to him at all. Come to think of it, he should mention
this to Craig to be sure that he knew that things had to be kept quiet.
He would have to be careful. But he would keep on with the wee talks
with Craig. He had his business to look after.

It was not only McDaid who felt the ground less stable under his
feet. Campbell was feeling some of the same insecurity. Everything he
had tried to keep simple was becoming complicated. He was Lord
Taverstock's man and if there was any organizing and they needed him
to stamp it out, he would be there for them. But now O'Donnell was
talking about herself being a labourer like him. And that James boy
was hanging out with O'Donnell. He spit on the road and stopped and
urinated and looked out over the fields. To hell with the lot of them.

She was lying in the bed with the two weans when he went in.
The fire was burning and his food was on the table. How did she
know he would be home at this time? She must be watching the road
for him. He was getting more angry by the minute. She was watching
for him. What else was she doing that he did not know about?

Anyway, it's a good job she was here in the cottage and could not get out of it with the weans. Maybe if she had another one this would help keep her in her place. She would have no time for anything else. This would teach her if she had to look after three of them. Aye, he would see to it that she had another one and more than that. With plenty of weans around her feet she would have no time for anything else.

What was she doing in that bed? He started to look up. Then he got that feeling of fear again. What difference what she was doing? He would tell her when he wanted her to do something and she would do it. This was the way it was. He did not need to know what she was doing, what she was thinking or what she was looking at. He gave the orders and she obeyed. He felt better but he was still uneasy. He could not ignore the fact that now and then recently he had been thinking about her and about her thoughts and actions and what she would like or not like.

This is what really frightened him. Thinking about what she would like and not like. What difference what she would like or not like? It was no concern of his. In fact it was no concern of hers either and it was better that neither of them thought about it. The way things were, and he would see they stayed that way, was that he gave the orders and she followed them. If either she or he began to think about what she liked and did not like then the whole system would collapse. There was no room for her wants and desires in the world they lived in.

He sat and looked into the embers of the turf fire. She was asleep in the bed with the two weans. To hell with her anyway. She was always making trouble for him in his mind. He knew she was not content. That she did not like his control of her. Well that was too bad. This was the way things were. She would have to learn this. He stirred the fire with a stick that was lying on the floor. Sparks flew up and he felt the heat rising.

He thought again of his father. He would not be sitting worrying about what his wife thought. He would not care what she thought. She had a place and it was his job to keep her in it. There was no more to it than this. Campbell bared his teeth at himself in anger and frustration. What was he thinking about her for and what she thought? He should not be thinking about her. This only made it harder to keep her in her place.

Campbell took off his boots. And his trousers. Then he stretched out on the bench. He never undressed further than this. It would have seemed to him to make him vulnerable to her. He waited for sleep to come. He would have to keep her under control. That O'Donnell and her brother and the mob in the pub. He would have to see they were kept in control. Those labour boys in Dublin they would have to be kept under control. That was the way it had to be.

What was wrong with these people anyway? They thought they could do what they liked. That was no way to think. It made no sense. He would be there when he was needed. To make sure that things were put under control. He had his cottage, his few fields, the cow and donkey and a few hens, the lettings and he had her to work. He was all right. He was all right. The thing was to keep things as they were. There should be no letting things slip.

With that he got up and went to her. He pulled the cover back of her and pulled up her clothes. The two children slept on every side of her. He pulled her legs round to they hung over the side of the bed. He put his thing in her, control, keeping things under control, he was just the man to do it, he would see it was done, there would be no slipping, and aye, control, aye, control, and he sent his sperm up inside Margaret. Aye, that's it. And he went and lay down on his bench and slept. That will teach her.

CHAPTER TWENTY

Campbell had gone to the bog that day. Margaret knew because he had taken the donkey and some creels. He would be away most of the day so she would be able to relax a bit. She was holding Mary and feeding her. Victoria was toddling around the kitchen. Victoria pointed at the table where Campbell had left some bread from his breakfast. 'Bread' she half whispered. Margaret looked at Victoria. Why does she whisper, why does she whisper? Is there something wrong with her voice? Is that it? Maybe she cannot speak right?

Margaret was frozen in fear for some minutes before it dawned on her. It was because she herself only ever whispered and when he was in the house she did not speak at all. Margaret was shocked as she thought about this. She had not spoken aloud for years. The one exception was when she had to speak to get the rooster from Shanks so she would have some extras for the children. But now it turns out this was not enough. If she kept whispering the children would whisper too. That is what they would learn because Campbell never spoke to them. She herself tried to never speak when Campbell was in the house. If she could not be invisible she could be inaudible.

But it was not good enough for the children. She realised now that she would have to speak out in the house also. She knew that she would have to risk his anger if she spoke aloud. But there was nothing else for it. Was life just one struggle after another? Was her life always going to be like this? Never any rest, never any peace. Now she would have to speak out loud and maybe have to pay the price from Campbell. But this would be better than her children never being able to speak properly. She sighed to herself and bared her teeth as she resolved to speak aloud.

Once she realised she had to do it she wasted no time. It was the morning after and Campbell woke on his bench wondering what had stirred him.

'Get up now, Victoria. Get up and help your mother.'

What was that? What? It couldn't be herself talking. But it was. But she never talked before. What was going on? She was getting above herself. This was what was happening. She thought she could do what she liked. Talking out loud around the house. He snorted as he got up and went out the door to relieve himself.

She had milked the cow and lit the fire earlier and when he came back in, his stirabout and tea were on the table. He was angry and frustrated. He could not very well tell her she could not speak. But he knew what was going on. She was getting above herself. That was what was happening. He would have to put that out of her. He sat down and ate and fumed at his impotence. He wished he could get up and beat the talking out of her. But what? But how? How could he tell her she could not talk? He cursed her in his mind for living.

When he finished eating he stormed out of the cottage and headed up to the bog. The excuse he gave himself was to see what the tenants were doing but the real reason was to get away from her. His jaw was shut tight, his mouth a line across his face, his whole body tense and tight with anger. He wished he had never seen her. Talking out loud. What would she try next? He should have hit her a box to the side of the head.

As he walked up the bog with its great black banks, its green and purple and brown heather, its deep holes, and its organic smell, some of the tension and anger began to leave him. He began to breathe again. After some time he stopped and turned around and stood looking out over the side of the bog and down to the valley. He felt his mind go blank off her. He stood and let the air and the feel of the land seep into him. After a while he went on his way upwards, surveying the banks to see if anybody had gone outside their area. He was going to keep control here.

Margaret meanwhile was feeding Mary and talking out loud to Victoria. She was glad Victoria was growing up. She was getting over the stage where she dirtied herself and the bed regularly. Mary would still be doing it for a while. No matter how she worked it with the flour bags, doubling or trebling them up and tying them in different ways, Margaret was not able to stop the children wetting and soiling the bed. During the day when it was warm weather she could let them run around in their dresses and just go where they stood and she would clean them after. There was a continual battle for cleanliness in her daily life.

Then there was a knock at the door. She saw a small man standing there with tins on a string which hung over his shoulder. 'Do you want to buy some tins, missus?' He was a travelling man. One of the large population of Irish peasants who had been evicted from their lands in the past but who had not been able to make it to the boat to emigrate or to the city and a job and who rejected the workhouse. They ended up on the side of the road making tins and selling them. As a result they were known by some as tinkers while some people mistakenly called them gypsies. Margaret looked at the man and said nothing.

'Do you want to buy some tins, missus?' Margaret stood there and thought of her children and how she would have to speak if they were to learn how to speak. The travelling man waited. 'Missus. Some tins?'

Margaret gave a start and took a step forward into a new phase of her life. 'I have no money.' For a second it struck her as strange that these would be the first words she would say to a stranger.

'Well, what about something to eat? I have had nothing since yesterday.'

'I have bread.'

He looked at her. 'And how about some tea?'

Margaret went to the fire and got the water boiling and put on an egg. The travelling man sat on the windowsill outside and looked out over the land as it sloped down to the distant valleys. He thought how much better his life would be if he only owned a couple of fields and a cottage. Margaret brought him out four thick slices of bread, a boiled egg, and tea.

'Thank you kindly, missus.' Margaret went back inside to the children.

Victoria pushed past her to the door and toddled close to the travelling man.

'You are a grand wee girl you are. Young one what is your name?'

Victoria smiled at the man but did not speak.

'Come on, wee girl, what is your name?'

Victoria went back into the cottage. Margaret had heard the man speaking and knew that Victoria either could not speak or was not confident enough to speak. She bared her teeth. She would speak out.

'Thanks, missus,' the man handed the cup in to Margaret and turned to be on his way.

'If I give you this scone of bread would you give me one of those tins you are carrying?' She pointed to one of the middle sized cans he was carrying.

'That is one of my best tins. Look at the work in it. I put a lot of work into this tin. What else have you got?' Margaret thought she had nothing else to give so she stood silent. The eggs were raw and he would have no way to cook them.

'Give me a drink of that milk there and the loaf and that will do then.'

Margaret handed him a cup of milk. He drank it down and swallowed loudly in appreciation. Returning the cup he took the tin she wanted off the string and handed it to her. She handed him the scone of bread. 'Thanks, missus.' As he left the yard of the cottage Margaret thought that she was better off than him. At least she had a roof over her head. He had nowhere to sleep but the ditch.

Margaret held the tin in her hand and looked at it. She had been wanting one to keep in the toilet with water in it to wash herself. She did not feel right doing it in the cottage. The birth of the children had wiped away the guilt she had about touching herself down there. How could it be bad when the children came from there? Her mother had touched her down there and Katie had touched her down there when her babies were being born. Now she had a tin she could keep full of water in the lavatory and she could keep herself cleaner. The children, it was all due to the children.

It was their birth that had made her think right about herself down there. It was their birth that showed her that her mother and Katie could touch her down there. This meant that she could touch herself down there. Now it was the children who had made her speak out loud. And this had made it possible for her to speak to the travelling man and make the trade with him for his tin. Now she would be able to wash herself in the lavatory in privacy.

The travelling man did not mind her speaking out loud. He even spoke civilly to herself and Victoria, which was more than Campbell had ever done. Where was he sleeping tonight? In a hedge or a haystack if he was lucky? Margaret thought of the tin in the lavatory and how the travelling man had made it. He was skilled with his hands but he had to sleep outside. There was something wrong about this.

She would carry on with her way of working. She would do the work about the house, she would look after Campbell, she would let him put his thing in her. But she would not stop speaking out loud, the children needed her to do this if they were to learn. She was not in a good situation but she was better off than the travelling man. He was in a worse condition than her. He had nowhere to sleep.

She was glad Victoria was growing up. Mary was still at the very young and helpless stage. Then there would be the new baby to come. And after that another and ..... Margaret stopped as the thought struck her for the first time. Wean after wean. She was already expecting her third. How many would she have? She was young. She could have up to twenty or thirty if she had weans until she was in her forties.

Margaret stood stunned as she thought of this. Twenty-five or more weans. How would she ever manage? He kept coming to her. But there was nothing she could do. He would not stop. If she tried to stop him what would happen? She needed him to provide for the weans. She needed his cottage and everything else he owned. She could not risk stopping him.

Was there anything else she could do? She knew of no ways to stop having weans. But to stop him. But she could not risk this. She looked down at Victoria and at Mary in her arms. She had to let him and have more weans so that the ones she already had would have a place to sleep and food to eat. She breathed out as she realised she was trapped. All her thinking that she was getting more control over her life came down to this. She had to let him and please him as he owned the cottage, and he owned the cow and he was paid for his work. She was not.

Every triumph Margaret secured, every new step she took, only brought her up against the realization of how much she was con-trolled by Campbell or some man. She would never get out of it. Her father, Allen, Campbell, the men that controlled her life. They all owned things. Houses, fields, cows. She was only able to stay in their houses if she pleased them. If she did not they would put her out because they owned everything.

She turned away from this thought. It was too demoralizing. She walked back to the cottage door with her children. She was going to speak out loud and teach her children to speak. She was going to have more children because she had to keep him content. She was going to work and do everything she had to so she could have a home for her children. She did not own anything so she had no choice except this choice. For her children then this was her choice.

CHAPTER TWENTY ONE

It was a few days later. Margaret was carrying Mary and Victoria was toddling by her side as they went down to the stream at the side of the cottage. They filled the tin they had got from the travelling man with water and then went round the back of the cottage to the lean-to lavatory. Margaret pushed aside the bag at the front and set the tin of water inside. She almost smiled as she saw how her lavatory looked so well. Soon the children would be able to use it also.

For some reason as she stood there Margaret began to think about her mother. She remembered the day they went to the lough and paddled in the water. It was only an hour walk away. Campbell was in the village seeing Brown. He would not be back until night. Why not? It was a beautiful day. Why not? She would take the two children and go up to the lough. If she left it much longer she would be too far gone with the next baby to walk the distance. Margaret felt liberated as she prepared to go to the lake. She was going to be doing something for her and her childrens' pleasure for the first time, something that was not work. What an incredible wonderful thing this would be.

Gathering up Mary in her arms, she took Victoria's hand and they set off. But she had made a mistake about how far Victoria could walk. After a short distance she began to cry and say she could not walk any further. Margaret lifted her and carried her along with Mary and the new baby forming in her womb. She walked slowly and deliberately as she made sure not to fall on the rough paths and hurt the children and herself.

It was warm and there was no rain. The heather and the grass and the trees soothed her as she walked along. Mary slept and Victoria looked at everything they passed in this new adventure for her.

'Those are trees. That is heather. That is the shugh.' Margaret continued with her speaking lessons for Victoria. 'Trees. Heather. Shugh.' Victoria repeated after her mother.

By the time they reached the lough Margaret was ready for the rest. 'Look, Victoria. Look, Mary. The lough. Look at how much water. Look. My mother brought me here and we went paddling in the water. Come on now, Victoria, we will paddle.' None of them had shoes or socks so with Mary in one arm and Victoria by the other hand they slowly walked into the shallow water. There were small stones and rough coarse sand on the bottom but their feet were hardened with going barefoot and they did not feel any pain.

'Mammy! Mammy! Mammy! Mammy!' Victoria was beside herself with excitement as she felt the water tickle her ankles and legs. Mary sat in Margaret's arms with her eyes wide open saying nothing. Then Margaret lowered her down until her feet and ankles were in the water and Mary too smiled as the water tickled her.

'There, Mary is that not nice? Victoria, my mammy brought me up here when I was a wee girl like you are, Victoria. Now I am bringing you here.'

Victoria's eyes shone with her excitement. She laughed and giggled as she splashed in the water. 'Water Mammy, water Mammy.' Margaret's spirit was lifted up as she saw the happiness of her daughter. Then she remembered her mother when they were here. And how her mother had laughed and how her spirit had been free for a few hours. Now her daughter was happy here too.

The peace of the place, the quietness, the ripple of the water on the stones and the feel of it on their legs all combined to soothe Margaret and make her think that this was the best day of her life. Alone, at peace, together with her two daughters. She paddled slowly with them back and forward. Suddenly the water was broken about twenty yards out as a large salmon leaped out of the water and then came back down with a loud splash. They all jumped with the breaking of the silence.

Then Margaret for the first time she could remember, laughed out loud in delight and wonder. 'Victoria, that was a fish. A salmon. It was jumping up to get the sea lice off its back. It will lay its eggs here and have babies in the lough. There are lots of other fish in the lough as well. If we could catch them we could cook them and eat them.'

Victoria looked up and said 'Fish.' Margaret was content she was taking her children where her mother had taken her and where she had seen her mother happy for the only time she had known her. And on top of that now Victoria was happy and learning new words.

Margaret vowed to herself to make a visit to this lake a regular tradition with every child that she had. To make it a regular event every year that she would come and have her soul and her children soothed by the quiet and beauty of this place. The water, the heather, the view of the mountains behind and then far away sloping down to the valleys in front, these lifted her out of her harsh day-to-day world. From now on this was to be a tradition in her life Margaret vowed. This beauty and peace that was here, she would come and bring her children to it every year.

By the time they got back to the cottage Margaret and the children were exhausted. It was time for Margaret to milk the cow and do the work around the yard and to get ready to make the tea for Campbell. She left the children in the bed and they both fell asleep. She put the bolster her mother had given her to the side of Mary and laid her between it and the wall. Victoria was too big for that and she was always in danger of falling out.

Margaret went out again and up to her lavatory. The long walk had moved all her waste and she sat and urinated and defecated and felt the peace that comes with that. As she did so she held back the bag that acted as a door and looked out over the valley. She sat and thought about the children. She would be able to keep them coming on all right. She would be able to feed them and help them to talk. The main thing was that she had to keep on doing enough of what Campbell wanted her to so that he did not put her out.

If only she owned a cottage and some cows and hens and things of her own. If only this was the case. But then women did not own things. It was always men owned things. Not all men. That wee travelling man owned nothing. Her brother James who worked over with the Kilgores owned nothing. But it seemed that no women at all owned anything. That whoever owned anything was a man. She wished that she owned what Campbell owned then she would not have to always be pleasing some man.

She was going to look for some way to make the toilet seat less painful. If she could get some flat pieces of board and put them on it. She would have to keep an eye out if she could find some. Now that she had the can for the water if she had this for the seat her toilet would be just about perfect. She sat there thinking about how she had made it and how it had been a good thing to do.

Then she was finished and took the tin full of water and she washed herself. She would get a cloth and hang it here too. But for the present she was drying herself with the grass that she kept in her lavatory. She went out and filled her tin from the stream and replaced it in the lavatory. She felt a security about her now that she had a lavatory and also a way to wash in it when she was finished. She was making progress.

She went to milk the cow and do the rest of her work. Sometimes it was a comfort to her to milk the cow. It had got used to her and had not kicked her since the time when she was pregnant with Victoria. But it left a smell on her and on her clothes. She had to lean into the cow with her head and her right shoulder to get her milked. This usually took her about fifteen to twenty minutes. Then when it was summer and there were flies about the cow would hit her with its tail as it tried to keep the flies away.

As a result Margaret would take the cow's tail and put it behind the crook of her knee as she sat on the piece of wood she used as a stool. This left her knee and leg dirty and smelling of cow dirt as the tail was always covered in it. Her hair, her shoulder, her clothes, her leg, for a minute she began to think of the wee Brown girl and how clean she would always be. But even more than when she left Allen's, Margaret knew that she would never have what the wee Brown girl had. So this did not occupy her mind for more than the fraction of a second. She could no longer afford to dream to be the wee Brown girl. She could only think about bringing up her children healthy and sound. This was now her ambition, her dream in life.

Margaret was back in the cottage again when Campbell returned. She put the water for the tea over the fire and stoked up the flames. He sat at the table where she placed the bread and a knife. Then she took the pot of potatoes off the hook by the side of the fire and put some out on the table. Campbell set about eating without saying anything and as usual Margaret said nothing to him either.

She went back into the room and as she did so Victoria toddled out and over to Campbell. She leaned with her hands against his leg as he ate. 'Water, water, fish, fish, trees, trees,' Margaret could hear Campbell almost stop breathing as he was faced with Victoria talking to him.

Then he went on eating and ignored Victoria. 'Water, fish, trees'

At this Margaret became worried that Campbell would do something to Victoria so she went out and lifted her and brought her back into the room and lay with her on the bed.

Water, fish, trees. What? What? What was she saying? She was speaking. Water, fish, trees. She was speaking to him. That was it. It was herself put the wee one up to this. She knew better than to speak to him so she was putting the wee one up to speak to him.

That was what was happening. He was not going to have this. If she started speaking to him she would want to ask for something. He would have to listen to her. He would have to think about her as a person with a mind. This was not going to be allowed to happen.

She would start to say what she wanted, what she wanted him to give her or do for her. This would only make her think that she might get what she wanted. He would not let her talk to him and she would not be able to tell him what she thought and wanted. Water. Fish. Trees. What was this? The wean was talking to him. What did she mean water fish trees. What was this? There she was in the room with the other one and this one was out here talking to him. He was not going to listen to any of them. He went on eating and Victoria kept standing leaning on his leg. He fought the gentleness that he felt rising in him as her little hands pressed on his knee. None of that. He would keep control here. None of that.

When he was finished eating he went out and headed down to McDaid's. Margaret heard him go and his footsteps on the roadway leading downhill. When she was sure he had left she got out the cloth and the knife and began working on more clothes for the children. Her mother had brought her the needle and thread before she had died. She had no money to buy these things and never spoke to Campbell to ask him to get them.

Mary was lying sleeping and Victoria was on the floor playing with a piece of stick that she had got from the pile by the fire.

Margaret stopped to watch her play.

'Victoria, what are you doing? What is that you have in your hand?'

Victoria held it up. She did not know what it was called.

'It is a stick, Victoria. A stick. Say it. A stick.'

Victoria did her best to repeat. 'Stick, stick, stick.' Margaret was bursting with pride to hear her learn.

Some time later both children were in bed asleep and Margaret lay beside them getting ready to sleep. She slowly drifted off and her dreams began to slip into her head. It was the salmon. She dreamt that she and the children were swimming in the lake. That they could swim underwater like the salmon. A big male salmon swam alongside. He turned and looked at them as they moved along.

Then he came closer and nudged Margaret with his side. He pushed her with his shoulder. Then he spurted ahead looking around to see if she was coming. She did not know what to do. She had not played for so long. The last time she had played was with her brother the day she was sent to Allen's. The big fish came to her again. And again he nudged her.

This time he did not go ahead but dropped back and went up alongside Victoria and Mary who were swimming along. He nudged them with his shoulder. He did it again. The children laughed and shrieked with delight. They began to reach out to touch and to play with the big fish. He in turn darted ahead, let them catch up, nudged them and spun them over and over in the water. Victoria and Mary never had such fun before.

Margaret wanted to join in. She was bursting with her desire to play. After all she was still only sixteen. She felt the terrible urge to swim over and nudge the big fish and swim off to get him to chase her. Her babies would love her to do this. She wanted more than anything to do this. Victoria turned around and shrieked. 'Mammy.

Mammy.' The water swirled around them as they played and swam and pushed and chased each other.

Margaret could not do it. It was too long since she had played. Her body and her head were too rigid. They were frozen with the suffering of the past years. The big salmon came back and looked at her and then nudged her over and over to try and get her to play. It was no good. Slowly the dream began to fade and she woke up to find herself in bed with her children. As she woke she heard Campbell approaching.

After he came in and laid down she began to drift off to sleep. But before she could get asleep he was at her with his thing. She was thinking of the big salmon wanting to play. If only she could play. But she could never play with Campbell. He could never play with anybody. He could not play. Then she thought about the dream. In it she could not play either. In real life she could not play either. The thought ran through her like a physical shock. She was not able to play. She was like Campbell. She was horrified, she was like Campbell. She could not play. He could not play. The country had beat it out of both of them.

With the shock of this thought she actually began to sit up in the bed with a start but Campbell had his thing in her and was standing between her legs in front of her. He did not know what was going on. He stopped. Was she rising up to feel his thrusts better? Maybe even rising up to reach out and touch him? This could not be happening. What kind of a woman was she? Was this why she had Allen's wean? Did she actually like it? Was that it? He pulled himself out of her and went back to his bench. What had happened? Margaret thought. That was the first time he had not finished by shuddering and shaking and grunting and leaving the slimy stuff in her.

Campbell was angry on the bench. What did she rise up for? Did she like it? Did she want more from him? What kind of a woman was she? Did she want to touch him? That was it. It was making sense now. First she was talking out loud. Then the wee one was coming to lean on his leg when he ate and she did not stop her. Now she was reaching up to touch him. He would have none of that touching business. Next thing she would want to talk, want to say what she thought, and then want to say what she wanted. This whole thing was about her trying to get doing what she wanted. That was it.

He would put an end to that. He would not put his thing in her. Or if he did and she tried to touch him he would stop her. He would put a stop to that business. There would be none of that touching business here. She was here to work. He would keep control of the situation, and there would be none of that talking business, there would be none of that touching business here. Not from her and not from that young one with her hands on his leg and her water, fish, trees business.

CHAPTER TWENTY TWO

Campbell was on his way back from seeing Brown. He was tired of hearing this 'keep them under pressure' business. Show them we are still in charge. After this labour business in Dublin they must see that we are still in charge. Every time he went to see Brown this was the refrain. It was almost as if he was near panic. With the exception of O'Donnell and his mob in the pub, Campbell could see no sign of any great effect that the Larkin business had on anybody.

Not only that but he was getting increasingly aware of how Brown would only talk to him in one of the outhouses and also how he would increasingly talk down to him and keep their talk, if it could be called that, to a few curt orders. Campbell believed in keeping in the good books of those above him but that was harder to do when those above him treated him as if he was dirt. They might think that but they did not have to say it or show it.

Look at what he had done for them. Taken herself off their hands. Kept his ears open for anything that might be starting. Did his work well and responsibly in the bog and with the lettings. But this seemed to count for nothing. Brown and his kind still saw him as way beneath them and deserving of nothing but whatever was necessary to get him to do what they wanted. Sometimes Campbell was worried that he had these thoughts but he could not stop them from his mind.

As he left Brown's he saw the two linen maids hanging out the linen in the back garden. There were two women with nothing else to do everyday but to wash the linen for the three Browns. The father and mother and the wee one. Or maybe it is only two now. He had heard the wee one had gone or was about to go to school in England. Two women with nothing to do but wash the linens for two other people.

Then there was all the others. The cooks. The silver maids. The ones who cleaned the house. The ones who repaired the clothes and sewed. The leather man and the horse man. The personal maid of the wee one and the mother, the valet of himself, the butler. It was almost a wee village with them all working for the top three. What kind of a setup was it anyway?

Where did they get all the money to pay all these? To keep themselves living in the lap of luxury? What was he talking about? Sure they got all this money from the share they got of Taverstock's rents and the rents they got off renting the smaller pieces of bogs and the other land and properties they owned themselves. He was one of the people that made them the money to pay all these servants. Campbell got even more worried the deeper he went into things. He had to stop thinking about how things worked if he was to do his job and to keep things in order and under control.

Campbell was dismissive of Brown's worries about any effects the Larkin business in Dublin might have had in the area. Only a few big mouths in the pub was his opinion. Only a few who would not work anyway. Campbell was totally unaware that his own increasing thoughts and anger at the Browns and their wealth and the way he was treated by them, resulted partially from hearing about the Dublin business in McDaid's and these ideas then germinating in his own head.

He was more than half way home when he saw Pollock coming

towards him in the distance. He had been trying to see Pollock now for weeks. Pollock had been cutting over his line in the bog. He was like that, always trying to get more than he was due. Well, that would not happen here. Campbell was in charge and would put him in his place. He would talk to him now.

'Pollock. Pollock, I want to talk to you about your spot in the bog.' Pollock looked at Campbell and answered.

'Sure It's a great day altogether.'

'Aye, it's a good day that's right. But, Pollock, you are way over the line there at the bottom cut of the first bank you are in. I will have to charge you more for that. There is no way that you can be cutting over the line. Sure you are well into that other cutting that I will soon be letting to somebody else.'

'I don't think you are right there, Campbell. I think I am well inside the line. I am not one to be cutting outside my bank or my cutting. Be God I know for sure that I am inside the line. I was up there the other day and I happened to see where you are talking about. No, I am well inside my ground. You are making a mistake there now, Campbell. You are making a mistake and that is a fact.'

'I am making no mistake now, Pollock. You are outside the line. I will step it when I am up next and I will be charging you whatever it is for the extra.'

'Now you will be doing no such thing, Campbell.'

Campbell walked on and left him on the road. He was angry. He knew what Pollock was up to. He was hoping that he would not notice he was over the line. Then when he did, Pollock was denying it and haggling in the hope that Campbell would get fed up with the whole thing and let it go. This is where they were at now. Then when Campbell would measure it and show that it was outside the line he would haggle again hoping to get away with having to pay only half. This was Pollock and it was non-stop.

Pollock spit into the hedge and watched Campbell head on up the road. 'There he goes. Ready to have a heart attack over that Lord's bit of bog. Heh, Heh.' Pollock spoke out loud to himself. Pollock had never liked Campbell, always considering him a humourless bastard. Pollock went over the line to see if he could get a bit extra for nothing but also just to provoke Campbell. Now he would have to go and measure it and come looking for him again. It was only what he deserved. Bastard.

Pollock had known Campbell's father. He was a hard mean bastard just like Campbell. But there was one difference. His father had a bit of craic in him. He had a bit of humour in him. This Campbell had none. Pollock did not like any man who could not tell a yarn or laugh at a good scheme well carried out. No, there was no craic at all in this Campbell man. It was good enough for him to have to go and measure it again. For that alone it was worth it. And then maybe he would get a bit for nothing or maybe Campbell would have a heart attack and die and Brown would never know Pollock was over the line and all would be well.

Campbell was going to stop at McDaid's but he was too angry and did not want to have to listen to O'Donnell and his mob. Or to have to look at that sleeked two faced boy McDaid. Aye, he could do without that. On up the road he walked towards home. That Pollock. Like all the rest of them trying to get something for nothing. Trying to get away with something with Campbell. Why did they always think they could do this? They should know by now that he was in charge and would not let them do it.

Campbell turned into the yard of the cottage and pushed the door open roughly. Margaret had heard his hob nail boots on the stones of the yard and was already at the fire turning over the turf under the pots for his tea and eggs. The fire was burning well and the tea and eggs would not take long. He threw his coat on the bench and sat at the table. In a few minutes she had his tea and eggs, bread and butter on the table in front of him. He started to eat.

'Victoria, do not push your wee sister. Here do not push her now.' Margaret was speaking aloud to Victoria. She was not going to stop pushing forward on as many fronts as possible just because overall control of her life was not possible. Campbell was eating and glowering at his food and the table and whatever his eyes lit on. What did she think she was at? Trying to pretend she was all helpful and speaking out loud at every chance she got. Margaret began to talk to Victoria and Mary again.

Campbell raged as he ate. She was trying to take a hand at him. That was what she was at. She was getting above herself. She was forgetting her place. He could hardly get the food swallowed he was so wrought up. This after having to listen to Brown and then to Pollock. Now her. She was talking out loud. Who did she think she was? She was pushing him. Trying to get something that she had no right to. Did he not give her a roof for herself and the weans and food to eat. That was more than enough.

Now she was wanting more. He was not stupid. He knew she was wanting more, that was what she was up to with her speaking out loud. They were all wanting more of him, Brown, Pollock, them all. Now she was wanting more. Trying to take a hand at him. Trying to get what she wanted. Trying to push him for more. That was it. That was it. Well it would not happen. It would not happen. He choked on the food in his mouth. Then he lost control over himself.

Jumping forward and up he pushed the table over and the food and dishes scattered across the floor. He ran and grabbed Margaret from the bed. 'Naw, that will not happen' he roared. The children began to cry with fear. Margaret enraged him further as she looked at him and said nothing and showed no sign of fear. He pulled her from the bed and from the side of the two children. Dragging her out into the room he shouted at her. The spittle was coming out of his mouth he was so angry.

'Who do you think you are? Do you think you are somebody? Do not think you are going to .....I put a roof over your head, food in your mouth. Do not think you are somebody.' He shook her and raised his hand to strike her. Holding her by the arm and the dress he shook her. 'Do not think that by speaking out loud this makes you something or will get you anything.' Then he struck her with his open hand on the side of the head.

Then just as quick as it exploded it died down. His hands dropped to his sides as he let her go. She stood there motionless. He stood motionless. They did not look at each other. A terrible shame for a second threatened to rise up in him. But he roused himself and turned and walked abruptly out of the cottage door. He walked over to the byre and up to the cow and young calf that was tethered with it. He felt the cow's udder. 'Aye, you are still giving plenty of milk there for this young one. You will have to get the bull next time you are running.' Then he felt the calf's back. 'Aye, you will be a good young stirk.'

That is the only way. They have to be kept under control. In their place. I treat her well and then she goes and tries to get above herself. I have to let her know her place. That is the only way. Women do not understand things like men. They need to be kept in their place. Her and her speaking out loud. She must think I am a fool not to see what she is up to. This will teach her. This will teach her.

When he got back into the cottage she had the food cleared up from the floor, the table back on its feet and what was this? He stopped in mid-step. She had a new pot of tea, bread and two eggs on the table for him. What was she up to? That was the question. Well it was only natural he reassured himself. It was her job to make the food. He went over to the table and sat down and began to eat. He felt the tension begin to leave him. He was putting her in her place. He was in charge.

She had obviously learnt her lesson. He had given her a good shaking. And a good slap. And here was the food back on the table again. This was the way to keep things in order. Campbell began to congratulate himself on how he had enforced control of the situation. He would soon get round to it with Pollack also. He had shown her how things would be dealt with. Things were back in order again all right.

'Victoria, Victoria. Don't push your wee sister. She has to sleep in the bed too you know. Stop pushing your wee sister.'

Campbell froze with a spoonful of egg half way to his mouth.

'Victoria, come on over here and leave Mary alone. She is your wee sister and you must not push her off the bed.'

Campbell sat motionless with the spoonful of egg still up in the air. But the terrible rage that was in him before was gone. The explosive anger was no longer in him.

He carried on with the egg to his mouth. Damn her. Damn her anyway. And he carried on eating. Let her talk out loud. As long as she does her work and what she is told this will be okay. As long as she knows what it is she has to do and does it. And if she gets above herself I will put her back in her place. She has been doing the work and looking after things well. Damn her anyway and her speaking out loud. But if that is all, she can do it.

Margaret lay with her children. She had cleaned up after him. She had soothed the children after he had frightened them. She had let him shake and hit her. She had let him away with all this. But she was not going to stop speaking out loud. She was not going to be quiet again. She was not going to go inaudible again. The children needed her to speak out loud to learn to speak themselves. He could do whatever he liked but she was not going to be quiet or speak in whispers again. This would harm the children. She would not do it.

She began to think of the travelling man. He did not mind her speaking out loud. He had spoken to Victoria in a civil way, something Campbell had never done. Where was he sleeping tonight? In a haystack if he was lucky and a hedge if he was not. He had made the tin in the lavatory. He was skilled with his hands but he had no place to sleep. Something was not right. There was something wrong with the way things were. That that wee man had nothing but the clothes on his back.

She would carry on the way she was doing. She would do the work about the house. She would look after Campbell. She would let him come to her. She would have as many children as came into her. But she would not stop speaking out loud. The children needed her to speak out loud. They needed this. Otherwise they would grow up not being able to speak right. No matter what, she was going to speak.

CHAPTER TWENTY THREE

'Katie, I am thinking of going down to get some things at McDaid's. Will you come with me?' Katie got her short coat and the two of them set off. They spoke of the weather and the shape of the land and the old man's health. As they approached Campbell's they saw that Margaret was out digging potatoes in the potato field with her children. Victoria was tottering about rising and falling and Mary was lying sleeping on an old piece of sacking.

'We'll go in and see her, Katie.'

'Margaret. How are you? How are the weans?' Shanks greeted Margaret and got only a look in return. But both he and Katie had no rush and so they sat down on the potato drills where Margaret was digging some out to boil for the evening meal. For some reason, Shanks was full of chat.

'Margaret, you are a terrible woman altogether. Out here digging. Campbell should be doing that for you. Now that you have the two weans and another one on the way.

'Digging spuds always reminds me of going to Scotland for the tattie hoking to make a few shillings. Those were some times. It was hard work. Sleeping in old barns, working from morning to night. But what am I talking about, Margaret, sure you had the same I am sure when you were hired out to Allen. That would have been no holiday either. That Allen would work the hind leg of an ass.'

Margaret was in a turmoil. She knew she had to speak out for the children's sake but she wanted to keep quiet like she used to do and hope Shanks and Katie would go away. But then the weans were there. They should hear herself, and also other people, speak as much as they could. Margaret therefore pulled herself together and replied with two words. 'At Allen's.' Shanks and Katie looked at each other and smiled. It was only two words but it was progress.

'Aye, that Allen. You know what he tried to do with the man that was there before you, Margaret? In the weeks before the six months were up he would try and make him quit so he would not have to pay him his money. One thing he used to do was he would put straw ropes down in the venals behind the cattle. Then when your man, what was his name, McCausiland, would clean out the byres, the straw ropes would be pulling everything with them. He would not be able to get the dirt into the barrow. It was breaking the poor man's back.

'That Allen is a mean one. He would follow a crow a mile for a spud. Aye, and herself, she is not much better. Have you ever heard Hughie Boyle on about him? You know Hughie, Margaret? He has something to say about everybody. He says that if Allen had a barrow full of pennies he would not give up two of them to close his dying mother's eyes. That Boyle he is some boy. He can come up with them.'

Margaret went on digging the potatoes and made no more answer. 'Katie do you know what Boyle was telling me?' Shanks was talking now mainly for Margaret's benefit as Katie had heard these stories many times before. Shanks went on. 'There was a terrible row down in McDaid's the other night. The Anvil was down there. You know the Anvil, Margaret? He lives with his mother over near the big rock. They call him that because he is so short and skinny he would not put down the one end of an empty scale.

'Well, the Anvil was in McDaid's and he had got a few shillings from somewhere. This was very unusual for the Anvil. He normally has nothing and drinks only an odd stout. But this time with the few shillings he ordered a double whiskey for himself. A double Powers. The whole bar stopped and looked at him when they heard him give his order. McDaid set it up on the counter. With all eyes on him the Anvil took his time. "Aye, the weather is good all right," the Anvil said to the whole bar by way of making out that the double whiskey was an everyday occurrence and he was in no hurry.

'"Aye," he said still ignoring the double whiskey, "sure the harvest and the turf will all be got in safe this year. I hear that they are cutting the wheat over near Brown's already." Nobody answered him they were all so intent on seeing him drink the whiskey. At last the Anvil reached out and put his fingers and thumb around the wee glass. But he did not lift it. Instead he just turned it on the counter. He was savouring it. He stood leaning forward on the bar with his two hands for a while. Then he repeated his fingering and turning of the glass on the counter. Still savouring it but also making the rest of the bar wait and water at the mouth.

'Then he shrugged up his coat on his shoulders, cleared his throat and turned and walked over and outside. He was going to clear himself out. Going to empty himself out so he would be proper prepared for the double whiskey. Aye, the Anvil was getting ready for it. For his double whiskey. Of course he was also showing the bar that drinking a double whiskey was an everyday event to him. No big deal for the Anvil. He was a man who could order a double whiskey, leave it on the counter, go and empty himself out and come back and drink it later.

'But inside the bar a babble of talk broke out immediately the Anvil left. The tallest man in the bar was big Johnny Thompson. You should know him, Margaret, he calls himself the Apache. He had heard of these fighters from somebody who had come back from

America and he liked the sound of them so he called himself the Apache. The name stuck and he became known as the Apache. He lives over near Murphy's big place.' Margaret did not know if she was supposed to answer or not so she kept quiet.

'Anyway, the Apache stepped forward to the bar where the Anvil's double whiskey was sitting. He reached out for it and as he did so he said, "That wee Anvil, that wee attempt at a man. Sure he has no use for a double whiskey. He would not be able for a double whiskey." And lifting the glass the Apache downed the Anvil's whiskey in two quick swallows. He left the empty glass back on the counter where it had been and stepped back making a noise with his lips and mouth.

'The bar went silent. It was in a state of shock. Just at that moment the Anvil came back in and went up to the counter where he had been. He was ready, he was prepared, he was set for his double whiskey. They would all be ready to see him drink it now. But what? But what was this? What the...? The Anvil could not take his eyes off the empty glass. The empty glass. The whole bar was silent, you could have heard a fox breathe. The Anvil was still except for his eyes. They searched the counter for his drink. This must be an empty glass some of the boys had set up to take a hand at him.

'But nobody said anything, Margaret. The Anvil stepped forward and looked over in behind the counter. McDaid was there but things had happened so fast he did not know what to say. The Anvil searched behind the counter with his eyes. But there was no drink there. He looked at McDaid who remained silent. Then he looked around. "Okay, who has it? Out with it. Where's my drink?" Nobody spoke for a minute and the Anvil repeated his demand. He was getting red in the face with anger. He could feel the pent up expectation for the drink rising in him. The Anvil's cool at getting a double Powers was now well and truly gone.

'At this the Apache stepped forward and spoke up. "Aw none of those boys have it, Anvil. Nobody has it. I drank it. A wee runt of a boy like yourself, sure you would not be able for a double whiskey, you would have no need for a double whiskey. Sure it might even kill you. I drank it." The Apache was laughing throughout this explanation. At this the Anvil went wild. But he is such a wee boy he could not reach up to the Apache. So he climbed up on one of the bar stools and tried to hit the Apache.

'But in doing so he overbalanced on the stool and the stool and him came clattering down on the floor with him still hanging onto the Apache. The Apache was laughing and could not stop. The whole bar was laughing by this time. The Anvil got up and made to have another go at the Apache but the rest of the bar got a hold of him and held him back. It was all they could do because while the Anvil is only a wee bit of a boy he is wiry and they were all weakened with the laughing.'

Katie and Margaret were intent on listening to the story and Margaret had even stopped her digging and had turned round and was looking into Shanks' face while he had been talking. She was caught up in the story and had temporarily forgot about whether or not she should speak and when and to say what. Katie instead gave Shanks a nudge. 'Well how did it end Shanks? How did it end?' Shanks was annoyed at Katie for asking this question as he had hoped that Margaret might have asked.

'Well, that is the best part, Katie. You will like this part of it. Apache claimed he had no money left. So the boys got round and got on to McDaid to put up another double whiskey for the Anvil. He refused at first. But they got on to him. They said he should have been watching his customer's drink. Eventually he could see no way out and he put up another drink for the Anvil. All of them were happy. The Anvil got his drink. Apache got a free drink, and all the rest of them had a bit of craic and were glad to see McDaid get caught. That Apache is a boy, Katie.'

'Aye, but there might have been a bit added on to that story you know how that is, Shanks.'

'Aye, but one thing is right and that is that McDaid got caught, that is for sure. A couple of other boys told me that too.'

Katie knew that Shanks was partly making the case for his idea of not confronting McDaid over the low weights he gave out. But she said nothing. She enjoyed hearing Shanks tell his stories and she enjoyed watching Margaret get so caught up in it for a while she forgot her problems.

'Margaret, you must have enough spuds dug by this time. Here we will give you a hand,' and with that Shanks and Katie bent down and helped gather the spuds into the creel which was made of willow rods which were bent round and round and in and out of a frame of thicker willow branches to form a creel or a basket. Margaret did not know what to say. Victoria helped her out. 'Spuds, Mammy,spuds'

'Aye.' Shanks said, delightedly 'Spuds, Victoria.'

Katie having figured out what Shanks was up to nudged him to keep quiet as she spoke to Margaret.

'Margaret, Victoria is a good wee talker. When did she start? When did she start?' Margaret swallowed and tried to answer. But she could not. She was so choked and silenced by the length of time it was since she had talked to anybody except the children.

'Here, Victoria, come over here and tell me some more words'. Katie held out her hands to Victoria.

'Margaret, how is your rooster getting on? Are things working out all right? Are you getting plenty of eggs? Are you going to hatch any out? Some of the hens should be sitting by now. That is what you need, a few more hens about the place. Margaret, how many eggs would you get in a day now?' Katie decided to try and get Margaret to speak. 'How many eggs a day, Margaret?' Shanks had taken the hint and kept quiet. Katie kept looking at Margaret as she held Victoria who was clinging to her legs.

'How many, Margaret?' Margaret got red in the face, then she thought of her children. She had to speak for her children. Victoria then spoke to Katie. 'Spuds, spuds,' and then she pointed to Margaret. 'Mammy, Mammy.' Margaret pulled together her resources and she spluttered in answer to Katie.

'About five, six.'

'That is good, Margaret, but when you get a few more hatched out and a few more hens then you will have even more eggs. Are Victoria and Mary doing well? They seem to be looking very well at any rate. Are they well?'.

Margaret again spoke. 'Aye'. With that she turned and lifting the creel of spuds she went down to the stream and began to wash the dirt off them with her hands. The fresh clay came off easy and left the pink skin of the potatoes showing brightly. Katie and Victoria played in the potato ground while this was going on.

When Margaret came back with the washed potatoes Katie picked up Mary and carried her towards the house and Victoria took her mother's hand and they walked slowly towards the cottage door. 'Well, we will be off now, Margaret. We are going down to get a few things at McDaid's. It was nice to see you. Cheerio now, Victoria. Cheerio. Say cheerio to us now as we are leaving, Victoria. Cheerio. Cheerio.'

At this Victoria said her own 'Cheerio'.

'What am I thinking, Margaret?' Katie said. 'Do you want anything from McDaid's? We can bring it up for you if you do'.

Margaret was stuck in the spot by the question. She had no money to buy anything in McDaid's. But she did not yet have the speaking confidence developed enough to respond to Katie and Shanks without admitting this and without being impolite. So she shook her head and went inside the door quickly.

As Shanks and Katie made their way down the mountain road Margaret put the spuds in the pot and went out to the stream to put water in them. But her mind was not on her work. She was thinking how she had not been able to speak better to them. How Victoria had spoken to them. How she needed to learn how to speak more easily and just about the day to day and minute by minute things. This was the way it would have to be if the children were to learn. She had to learn how to just chat. It was not enough to just answer questions and not enough for her just to talk to the children when there was nobody around.

What about what Shanks had told her about the pub? It sounded like all that went on there was drinking and talking. Old chat. It was no good to anybody. That was how her father referred to it. He did not like the men who hung out in the pub. But they never really talked in her house when she was at home. What happened was that her father talked and the others listened and answered him. She could see now that that was only one way of talking and she could also see she did not like that.

She could also see that this was not the way that Katie and Shanks went on. They talked to each other, they talked together. It was not one always talking and the other always listening and answering. Campbell never talked to her except every month or so and then to give her an order or to shout at her. She never answered in either case. And every time Campbell spoke to her she waited for the order or the threat.

It could not happen. She could not allow it to happen that the children would learn only the words and not learn how to talk. She would not let it happen that there would be no chat, no craic in their lives. But to do this she would have to make sure she did not back down to

Campbell. She would have to talk to them and them to her and to each other. She would have to have a lively house full of chat and also not afraid to laugh. The example of the pub was closer to what she wanted than where she lived at present. She stood still deep in thought at the enormity of the task she faced. But yes, she and the children would solve it. There was no other way as Campbell and her were never going to talk together.

She put more turf on the fire to bring the spuds to a boil so they would be ready for Campbell. She sat on the stool and held Mary while Victoria stood and clung to her knee. The turf caught and the flames lit up and the heat spread out to them. The smell of the burning turf also soothed her. She sat there and thought of her life. It was getting better. She had the two weans. Times like these when she was with them alone were the best times of her life. She took her breast and fed Mary. Victoria watched and her eyes became drowsy with sleep.

The flames from the fire leapt higher and the heat was great. They were at peace the three of them. Then she heard the dog bark. His hobnail boots striking the stones on the yard. She leapt up and took Mary from her breast. She went to the room and placed her on the bed. Victoria had toddled with her. She lifted her up onto the bed also. Then she heard his boots go past the door and on to the byre. She breathed a deep breath of relief. She had a few more minutes before he would be in.

She willed the spuds to boil quicker. That Shanks and Katie had held her up with their chat and now he would have to wait. Why did they not keep away and leave her alone? Then she caught herself. Katie had helped her with Mary being born. She should have spoken to them more. She had to speak more. She had to chat more. She had to let the children speak to more people than her. She softened in her mind as she thought of Shanks and Katie again. They were all right.

And she knew that she should be able to live to see that having a bit of a chat was more important than having the spuds boiled on time.

Chapter Twenty Four

It was August 1914. Shanks pushed open the door to his cottage. He was breathless. 'They've started a war. Did you hear? They've started a war.' Katie looked round at him from where she was standing at the pots hanging over the turf fire. The old man turned round and looked at him too. Neither of them spoke. 'Aye, they have started a war. They are going to fight the Germans.'

The old man spoke as he turned his head around again and stared into the fire. 'This will not be good for us poor folk.'

They all stopped where they were and stood silently in their own thoughts. 'Aye, its bound to be bad for us poor folk,' Shanks agreed with the old man. 'They will want us to go and fight.' Shanks calculated in his head that he was too old to be made to go. Katie tried to think what it would mean. What would a war mean to them? The old man shook his head and looked into the fire. A war. Shanks had heard about it from a couple of men in the bog. He could not see everything it meant for them but it would not be good.

The war had no immediate noticeable effect on Margaret's life. Things went on as before. The winter came and went. Margaret started digging the spud ground in April. Campbell had done it in other years. She kept her two children with her lying sleeping on the grass or in Victoria's case sometimes toddling and falling and rising. Her back ached day after day.

She worked up and down the ground parallel to the hedge along the road. She would take a three or four foot strip and work down it backwards. Facing up the hill she threw the upturned sod uphill. If she had done it the other way then after a few years the clay and the whole plot would have worked its way down to the bottom of the field. As she turned over the clay she wondered at the darkness of it. It was closer to black than the soil at Allen's. It was probably because of it being on the edge of the bog.

As she turned over each sod she broke it up by striking it with the edge of the spade. She would leave no piece bigger than her fist. The result was that up to nine inches deep, which was the depth of the spadeful she would dig out, the clay was broken into small pieces. She looked at the worms as she dug them up and wondered about their lives. What did they think about when she cut them in two or dug them up? Did they have thoughts?

The first day she got half way down the old square of potato ground along the length of the hedge. As she worked she thought about the small amount of spuds that was left and she remembered that last year there had not been enough. For a few weeks before the new ones were ready to eat they had had to live on stirabout and bread as there were no spuds left. Then it struck her.

Campbell was planting the same amount of spuds as he did when he was alone. Yet she was here now and also Victoria and soon there would be Mary eating and there was the new baby she was carrying. It was as if she and the babies did not exist. She only existed as a person when she could do something for him. Milk the cow. Make his food. Light the fire. Let him put his thing in her. She did not exist when he was thinking of what he had to do. She stood up straightening her back resting on the spade and looking out over the valley.

That was it, she only existed to give things to him, to do things for him. She did not exist when it came to him giving things to her.

So when he had to dig the spud ground it was the same size as when he was alone. When he had to buy something for the house he only bought things as if he was alone. Then she remembered him bringing the piece of cloth for the children's clothes and the bed. Well that was an exception. In most cases he only bought things or did things in the same way as when he lived by himself.

Well it was her was digging the spud ground this year. Not him as was usually the case. Now she was doing it she could make it bigger. She stood still hardly breathing as she wondered did she have the courage to make it bigger? Would he stop her? Would he hit her? Would he not care as long as she was doing the work? It would mean a bit less grazing for the cow and the calves and the donkey. But they would survive. She knew that. Would he stop her just because it was her idea?

She stood there with one hand on the spade and one hand on her haunch holding her back upright to try and keep the pain away. She realised she did not care what the repercussions would be. She was going to make the spud ground bigger. That was only right. There were more people to feed now that she was here and Victoria, and soon Mary would be eating spuds. She would increase the size of the spud ground.

She reached near the bottom of where the spud ground had finished before she had to decide how much further to go. She decided on another one quarter as far. This should be enough. If she went further this might provoke him too much and this would not be good. She kept digging on past the old mark and with every extra foot she dug she felt both more confident she was right, but also she felt more nervous about what he would do when he came home and saw what she was doing.

That night when he came home he said nothing. He seemed to be ignoring the whole thing. Margaret worked every day at the spud ground and by May it was finished. She then had to go over it all breaking it up into even smaller pieces. This took her another week. She had dug it, broke it up and enlarged it. It was ready for her to make the drills. She made these about twenty inches wide at the base tapering into nothing about fifteen inches high. She was proud of them, they were straight as she had worked parallel to the hedge.

All during this time Campbell pretended not to see her working on the spud ground. What was she doing? Did she think this would get her somewhere? Well that was what she was here for. To work. He would not let her get anything over on him just because she worked hard. He worked hard too. It will be good for her. Aye, it would be good for her. Anyway he would have to finish it for her. She would tire before she got it done.

But Campbell was wrong. She never said a word to him or gave any sign she needed help. He could see the pain and exhaustion in her at night. But she carried on and seemed content to do so. One night he was eating and thinking about these things when he started with a jump from the table and went outside. He stood at the gable wall looking out over the dark valley. He felt frightened.

So what if she had finished it? So what if she was a hard worker? It was going to make no difference. He would still see that she knew her place. He would still see that she did not slack. She need not expect any special treatment from him. He would still be sleeping on the bench. He would still go to her when he wanted. She was his wife. That was her job. Hah. He shook himself. Now that he had her pushed back down into that place where he need have no feelings for her he felt better, in control again. He went in and finished his food.

When Margaret had the drills made she then had to get the dung into them and spread. Using a grape she dragged the dung from the midden and spread it in the drills. It was rotted and easily broken up. The smell of it reminded her of her father's place when she had helped plant the spuds there and also of Allen's. The smell of fresh turned clay, the smell of dung that was rotted and spread and heated up by the spring sun. These were always to hold memories for her of the spud planting.

This was the hardest part of the job. She had to carry each grape full from the midden to the drills. She did not have the courage to ask for the donkey and cart. At its shortest it was twenty yards and at its longest it was over forty yards. This was the most back breaking exhausting work of all. Day after day she worked at it. She thought it would kill her. Victoria would watch her and call: 'Mammy, Mammy, what is that and what is this?' But she had not the time or energy to answer her.

At night she did not have the energy to do anything but make his food and collapse with the children in their bed. Campbell would watch her out of the side of his eye. Aye, she will have to get him to finish it. That's for sure. He could offer her the donkey and cart but it was better to let her have to ask. But again he was disappointed. She never spoke to him or asked him for anything. And at last she had every drill filled with dung and it spread evenly. Now she was ready for the dropping of the seed spuds.

She had seen him do it and done it herself at Allen's. She cut an old sack down the one side. She then had a sack with one side and the bottom still stitched together. She could tie it around her with a cord and so have a pouch hanging down in front of her which she could fill with spuds and walk along bent over dropping a seed spud every nine inches or so.

But would she have enough? She had thought of this earlier and then it had gone out of her head. She was worried especially as she had taken some of the seed spuds to trade for the rooster. Campbell knew nothing about that. She would have to cut the seed spuds to be sure. It would not do if Campbell were to find that out. Also the spud ground was bigger this year and more seed would be needed.

Taking a knife from the house she sharpened it on the stone in front of the door and she sat down at the pile of spuds that were covered in the corner of the byre. Then she cut each spud so that the buds on them were equally distributed in the two halves that were left after she cut. As long as there were a couple of buds on each half then this would do. Margaret sat and cut the seed with Victoria by her side and Mary lying sleeping in the straw.

'Mammy, what is that?' Victoria pointed at a crow that had landed ten yards or so away.

'It is a crow, Victoria. A crow.' Margaret liked crows. They seemed dignified and to know who they were. They seemed smart too. Margaret threw a half rotten spud to the crow. It jumped and flew a few yards away then looked and came back and took the spud and flew off. Victoria laughed with delight.

'Victoria, say it. A crow.' Victoria repeated after her. 'A crow.' Margaret was very pleased. Victoria was learning new words. 'Don't do that, Victoria. Don't eat that. It is dirty.' Margaret took the piece of dirty straw that was used to cover the spuds and threw it away. 'That is bad, Victoria.' 'Bad.' Victoria repeated after her.

When Margaret was working at cutting the seed spuds Campbell came up the road and into the yard. As usual he saw her but tried to pretend he was not looking at her. He went over to the byre and disappeared inside. Victoria spoke to her and pointed at Campbell.

'Who Mammy?' As Victoria learnt to speak more she was asking more awkward questions. Now she wanted to know who was Campbell?

What would she tell Victoria? If she told her Campbell was her father would Campbell be angry? If she did not say this would he be angry? What would Campbell understand by this if she said Campbell was her father? But what else could she tell Victoria? Then when Mary asked, what would she say if she did not tell Victoria that Campbell was her father? She could see nothing else for it but to tell Victoria that Campbell was her father.

'He is your father, Victoria.' Margaret was very frightened when she said this. What would Campbell say or do? Why did everything have to be so hard?

'He is your father. Call him father if you like.'

'What is father?'

Margaret was stumped. Then she said: 'I am your mother, Victoria. I look after you and feed you. He is your father he does the same. He is your father, Victoria.'

Margaret could not think what else to say.

Margaret finished up cutting the seed spuds in time to go and milk the cow and get the food ready for Campbell. He had gone out again heading up in the direction of the bog. She had seen him go out of the corner of her eye. She went in and milked the cow taking the milk into the house and getting the fire going and the spuds and water for the tea into the pots hanging over the fire.

Mary was very hungry and Margaret fed her from her breast. Victoria ate some bread and then some spuds mashed up in milk when they were ready.

'Good, Victoria? Good?'

'Good, Mammy. Good, Mammy.' She was a good eater now that she was no longer at Margaret's breast. Margaret was still breast feeding Mary when Campbell came in. She quickly got up and went to the fire to get his food.

The pot of eggs was boiling and ready. The spuds were also ready. She set them out on the table with bread. She set out a cup of warm milk also. Campbell said nothing to her. Nor did he look at her. He sat and ate. As he did Margaret went back to the bed and took up feeding Mary again. She did not notice as Victoria wandered over and balanced herself against Campbell's knee.

Margaret came alert with a shock. She sat upright and alarmed on the bed. Victoria held on to Campbell's knee.

'Father, Father,' Victoria said.

Campbell stiffened. What was this? What was this? He was not her father. What did she think she was doing? He was not her father. He began to get angry. Who did she think she was telling the wee one that he was her father? He was on the verge of getting up to go to her.

But what would he say? What was the wee one to think? What would he say to other ones if he did not let her call him her father? He could see no alternative. What was he to do? Again he felt that he was trapped in a situation where he had to allow herself to take liberties with him. But what was he to do? He could not stop her talking out loud. How could he say to this young one he was not her father? His shoulders slumped and he went back to eating. He would have to let it go. Damn her anyway.

Boiled spuds. Boiled eggs. Warm milk from the cow. And he would not have the cow without her. He could be coming home here and having to make his own food. But then he would have peace. But then he would not have the cow. Nor would he have the work she did about the house. Nor would he have her to rise to in the night. But then she was another mouth to feed and two young ones also. To feed. And maybe more to come. He was getting angry again. He did not know if he was coming out ahead or not. He was always falling into this base calculation.

But then the more he thought of it the more he was convinced he had got a good deal. If she would only go along with what he wanted and not try to be above herself. Why could she not keep her mouth shut and stop trying to speak out loud? What did she want to be speaking out for anyway? Now the wean was speaking out too. And calling him father. This talking from them would only mean trouble.

They would be asking for something next. That wee one would soon be asking him for something. If she would only learn that it was far better to keep her mouth shut. To only speak when she was spoken to and then only if it was necessary. Aye, this talking of hers was only going to lead to trouble.

CHAPTER TWENTY FIVE

It was a beautiful late spring day. He had gone early. Margaret got out the bag she had cut days earlier and tied it round her waist. She went and dragged the seed spuds in their bags from the byre to the head of the spud ground. She filled the bag around her waist. And then bending over she began to slowly move down one drill and up the next dropping a spud every ten inches or so.

It was back breaking work. Victoria watched her as she filled her bag and went, bent over double, up and down the drills. Mary slept. By early afternoon she had finished about one quarter of the ground. She then got the shovel and she began to work her way down the first drill separating the drills of clay half one way and half the other. In this way she covered over the seed spuds and the dung and she ended up with new drills inside which had the seed spuds sitting in their bed of dung and covered over with clay.

By the time she had this done the day was gone. And she was covered in sweat and smelled of dung, clay and sweat. The next day and the next and the next, it was the same routine. Dropping the spuds, covering them over with clay and working from morning to night. By the end of the fourth day she was finished. She had her spud ground dug, broken up, drilled, dropped and closed over. She had her spud ground planted. All it needed now was the weather and the time.

She had been worried at the start of the job that she would not have enough seed. But she had more than enough. She still had ones left over. She would give them to Shanks and Katie. They might need them. They would need more spuds now with the old man having moved in with them. And they had helped her so much that they deserved them. Shanks and Katie. She thought of the help they had given her.

Campbell said nothing when he came back at the end of the fourth day and saw that the job was done. She had his food ready. He told himself that that was all that mattered. That nothing had changed, that he did not care as long as she did what she was supposed to for him then it did not matter. Anyway look at the work she had saved him. Aye, everything was grand, she was working hard, saving him from doing it. He congratulated himself on teaching her well.

But he was not able to fool himself for long. Something was wrong. Something kept eating away inside him. It was not all right. He did not feel as in control as before. That was what was wrong. He realised that what he did not like about it was that she had done it without him giving his permission or giving her the order to do it and it showed also that this was another area in which she did not need him. This was not good. She was getting above her station. And now that she had done it she would be feeling even more above herself. This is what was eating at him. She had done it on her own.

That night he got up and went to her. He pulled her legs to the side of the bed even more roughly than usual, and parted them and lifted them. Holding each leg behind the knee he pushed his thing into her and began his thrusts. He stood up straight while doing so, pulling her into the position where he could do this. He was not going to move to suit her, she would move to suit him. He was in charge.

He held the sneer on his face while he was doing this. Putting his thing in her was his decision, He could take it or leave it as he wished, she had no say in it. He was in control. He was teaching her a lesson. That was it, he was doing this for her own good, to teach her a lesson. He could do this and would do this any time he felt like it. 'Aye, that will teach her' he said to himself, and he thrust his thing into her.

When Campbell had first rose to Margaret in the early days, she had remained dry and the pain was very severe. There was no pleasure in it for Margaret. As the months passed and especially as she had Victoria and then Mary she found she was lubricating herself. She still got no pleasure out of it but it seemed that she was allowing herself to get wet so she would not have the terrible pain that came with the dryness. Margaret also wondered did her love for Victoria and Mary and her knowledge that she would have more and she wanted more also have something to do with it. Letting him was necessary for her to have more children so it was no longer such an alien act.

Campbell built up the rhythm of his thrusts and tried to keep his arrogant sneer on his face, but the pleasure of holding her legs in his hands, the pleasure of her wet heat that surrounded his thing, the feeling of great purpose that he felt when he pushed himself into her as far as he could go, all these combined to dissolve the sneer off his face. It was replaced by an expression of emptiness and then by desire. He became bent over as he tried to enter her further. His thoughts were being overcome by the pleasures he was getting from her. The sensations of pleasure were pushing into his brain and pushing the sneering, controlling, arrogant expression from his face.

He could not control himself. He could not get straightened up again and put the arrogant controlling sneer of indifference back on his face. The feel of the soft flesh of her legs in his hands was too powerful. Then he put one hand on her breast. This was even more powerful. The softness of it. Then he put one hand under her hips and felt them. The soft roundness of them. His thing, oh the wet heat and grip of her around it. Then he felt himself sending his sperm up inside her. He bent over further as he thrust into her. His face was emptied of all superiority and filled instead with want and desire.

He straightened up and pulled his thing out of her. He was in a rage of conflicts. To hell with her anyway. 'That will teach her' he grunted as he went back to his bench. He was a man controlled by those above him, seeking to control those below him, and in the process having all human solidarity and affection driven out of him. He was now in a position where even the pleasure of putting his thing in her could no longer be enjoyed. Even it too threatened his control. It too was threatening his ability to control.

The more pleasure he got from her the more angry and fearful it made him feel. The more pleasure he got the more she was influencing him. But his entire physical being pushed him to take this pleasure. He hated especially those seconds when he put his seed in her. Then he knew he was out of all control, that he was in her control. Her and her thing. When he was doing that he was not in charge. He raged at himself for wanting to do it to her.

That night Margaret was so exhausted that she hardly felt him and just about slept through it. She turned over on her side when he was finished and put her arm around Victoria and Mary. This made Campbell even more angry. Even putting his thing in her now was no good. Afterwards he no longer felt in charge, in control, the boss. He was angry as he lay down on his bench. She had ruined this for him too. He snorted in anger as he tried to sleep. But his mind would not let go. He was losing control.

But how could he be losing control when he was still the man in the house, he owned the cottage, he brought home the money, he was a man and she was only a woman? How did she ruin everything? Even though he was still in charge he knew he was not in charge like before. Before he ruled her. His orders were what decided how she lived her life and how she felt and thought. She had been afraid of him. Now he was getting the feeling that she was just letting him get his way because this fitted into some wider plan of hers. She thought she was letting him instead of it being him making her. That was it, he no longer controlled how she felt and thought.

To hell with her anyway. She still did the work, she still made his food, she still lay there for him and his thing. He tried to get off to sleep but it would not let go of him. He knew he could still hit her and still make her work and still put his thing in her but then he understood more clearly what was wrong, He no longer controlled how she felt and what she thought. That was it, he still controlled what she did but not how she felt and what she thought.

He did not want to dwell on this sudden realization that had just come to him. He stoked up his anger instead. To hell with her anyway. To hell with her. Aye, she was up to something. That was for sure. She thought that she was letting him do these things when he was in reality forcing her to do them. Who did she think she was anyway? Thinking that she was letting him rather than him making her.

She was up to something. She wanted something. That was what the talking out loud was about too. She had figured out that to get whatever it was she was planning she had to let him do his thing and she had to work for him. He raged as he lay trying to sleep. He was the one to decide things around here. He did decide things around here. But she was still up to something. He would find out and put a stop to it. He would stop her. He would be ready for her when she asked him for whatever it was she wanted.

As Campbell was lying steaming and trying to understand what was going wrong, Margaret was coming awake. What woke her was the curve on her belly that she felt with her arm after rolling over from Campbell. She withdrew her hand from where she was holding Mary and felt her stomach searching for the feel of the child in her. But it was too soon yet for that. However she knew that she was pregnant again.

She lay holding her two babies and thinking. Another baby was on the way. Soon there would be three. Three babies. She sighed. She was happy with the thought of a new baby. But she was tired. She thought of the extra work. Victoria would have to help. She was glad that she had planted the extra spuds. This was good. She lay there holding her children and feeling her rounding belly. She would manage and she smiled to herself. And she fell asleep in peace.

Campbell hardly slept all night. He could not get the change in her out of his head. In the morning she made him his stirabout and tea and eggs and bread as usual. No words were spoken. This was also usual. He left the house and headed up the bog to get away from her. She went and milked the cow and stored the milk in the cottage. Victoria toddled after her and she carried Mary. Soon she would be able to leave Mary with Victoria and Victoria would look after her. But by then she would have the next one anyway.

Later in the day Margaret sat down with Victoria at the top of the spud ground. The sun was out and there was no wind. It was not cold. Margaret admired her work, feeling the satisfaction of it, and thought about the extra food that they would have next year. As long as there was no blight on the spuds they would have more than enough. She watched as the crows scratched and hoked around the drills looking for worms.

'Crows, Victoria, Crows.'

'Crows,' Victoria repeated after her. 'Mammy what that?' And Victoria pointed at a black beetle that was crawling across the ground where they sat.

'A beetle, Victoria.' Victoria repeated the word after her.

'Victoria, I planted the spuds here. See, all that work I did? I planted the spuds so that we will have enough to eat next year.'

'To eat, Mammy?'

'Yes, to eat.' Victoria looked up at her with a questioning expression on her face.

'Victoria, you will have to help me with Mary when I have my next baby. A little sister for you. You will have to help.'

Victoria just looked at her not knowing what was being said. She turned away and toddled and fell as she went toward the drills. Margaret looked at her and Allen came into her mind for the first time in weeks. That is Allen's child. But as soon as she thought that she put it out of her mind. 'No, Victoria is my child. I bore her and hold the pain of her birth in me and fed her. She is my child. Not Allen's.'

She fed Mary at her breast as she sat there in the sun and with Victoria toddling in the spud ground. It was the first day of the year that she could feel the heat of the sun penetrate through her clothes and into her skin and heat her up. It was the first real confirmation that winter was over. Margaret was glad. Winter was over. Soon it would get even warmer and it would be easier to look after the children, not having to worry every moment if they were too cold.

As Margaret sat there Campbell was on his way up to the bog. He was still raging with the previous night's thoughts. He saw two men walking towards him on the dirt road. They were far away and he could not make them out at first. Then as they came closer he saw that it was Pollock and O'Donnell. He ground his teeth together as he thought of that pair getting together. This was the last day he wanted to meet them too. But especially together.

'Well Campbell, how are you doing? It is a grand day altogether.' O'Donnell always spoke to Campbell in a tone of taunting challenge and provocation. Almost as if he was laughing at him. Campbell grunted in response. But it was Pollock that Campbell wanted to speak to.

'Pollock, you are over your ground up there. I checked it. You are over.'

'Not at all, Campbell. You have made a mistake. You will have to measure it again. I am not over.'

'You are over, Pollock. That is all there is about it. I will be charging you more.'

'Aw now that won't do, Campbell. I am not over and I am not paying more.'

'Well then you will not be taking any turf out of that bog, Pollock.'

'We will see about that, Campbell. Will you be sitting day and night to watch that I do not take my turf out of the bog? I don't think so. Maybe Taverstock or Brown will sit day and night to watch. Hah, I don't think so.'

It was here O'Donnell interrupted. 'Campbell you are a hard man looking after somebody else's bog. Sure you know that Brown and Taverstock care nothing for you. They are just getting you to do their dirty work. Up here at night you could be poaching the fish out of their rivers, taking an odd load of turf from their banks, making a few shillings for yourself. Sure nobody would know the difference. Sure you know they would be expecting you would be doing this.'

Campbell did not even answer O'Donnell. 'Pollock, you hear what I am telling you.' At that he walked on up to the bog.

'What is wrong with him, Pollock? That he has it in for you. You one of his own kind and all. No offence.'

Pollock looked round to see Campbell was out of earshot. 'That mouthpiece. He is as bitter and ignorant as his father before him but at least the father had a bit of a laugh in him. That cur has none.'

'Aye, but why is he after you now?'

Pollock looked at O'Donnell. They had been poaching salmon out of Taverstock's rivers and streams off and on together now for years. O'Donnell was all right. 'Look O'Donnell, I have no time for that man at all. He is an ignorant cur. Whenever I get a chance I put it to him. Sure I went over my ground there in the bog by about six foot. He noticed it. He is up measuring it and whining about it and getting on to me. I like to see him getting himself into this mess. I will keep on denying it. He will keep on about it. With a bit of luck he will have a heart attack about it.' They were both laughing when they heard Campbell shout.

'Pollock. Pollock.' He was coming running back down the dirt road. Her at home may be slipping her controls but Pollock will not. He was going to take him up now and show him where he was over his ground. 'Pollock, come up with me now and we will end this once and for all. I will show you where you are over.' Campbell was white in the face with rage.

'Sure now, Campbell, I have more to be doing than going up to the bog on a wild goose chase. I am a busy man.' The whole point to Pollock, as he had explained to O'Donnell, was never to end it once and for all.

O'Donnell, knowing better now what Pollock was up to, chipped in. 'Aye, Campbell, you should know Pollock here is a busy man. He has no time to be going off with you whenever you try to order him to. Pollock, Campbell here is like the bosses down in Dublin. They want to order the working man around and the working man would have no say in anything. He's like those big shots who want to conscript us all and force us to go and fight the Germans while they sit at home drinking whiskey. The days are over when that could happen. Campbell, why don't you just take it easy there? Go on about your business. Pollock is not over his ground.'

With that Campbell lost his temper. He lifted his fist and drew it back and swung and caught O'Donnell a glancing blow on the shoulder. Pollock grabbed Campbell by the other arm and held him. O'Donnell made a swing and caught Campbell in the ribs. Pollock shouted at O'Donnell and Campbell to stop it. Both men halted, frightened by their own violence. 'Pollock you are over your ground.' And with that Campbell pulled himself free and headed back on up the road to the bog.

Everywhere the control was slipping. Her at home. Pollock and his extra ground. That O'Donnell and his big mouth. Those labour men in Dublin that O'Donnell was always on about. Well, they would not get away with it with him. He would see to it that things were kept in order. If she put a foot wrong tonight then he would give it to her. After digging that spud ground she would have to get a good battering anyway at some stage as she would be thinking way above her station.

He would deal with Pollock too. And he would get a chance at O'Donnell. The next time he was with Brown he would report that he was going to cut Pollock back the six feet and take some of his turf. Aye, that is what he would do. Campbell stopped and urinated at the side of the road and spit into the rushes. Aye, he would keep control. She would have to be taught her place. They all would have to learn their place.

CHAPTER TWENTY SIX

Margaret was delighted when she began to find the extra eggs. The young chicks that she had hatched out after the arrival of the rooster, were now laying. Every day she was able to collect over a dozen eggs. This was more than they could use. She gathered a dozen together one day and when she saw Katie go past she went out and handed them to her. In spite of her decision to speak more she did not speak but just handed them to Katie. Katie looked at them and then at Margaret and explained that she had plenty of hens and eggs.

'Take them to McDaid's, Margaret. He will buy them from you and then you will have a few pence to spend. Take them down to McDaid's. He buys from anybody who has eggs to spare. Just go down with them and he will take them from you. He will gave you the going price. I will look after the children'

Margaret was almost stunned by the idea. She could sell them. For the first time in her life she could have some money. She could have money and for the children. She got ready to go.

But the children. She had never left them alone before. She knew it was with Katie. But even so. She was caught in a hard struggle. To get money for the eggs to spend on the children she had to go. But to go she had to leave the children with Katie. What would she do? What should she do? She felt the terrible tension in her as she tried to decide. But gradually she knew she would have to go. She would have to have something to spend on the children. Katie would look after them when she was away.

Campbell was away that day to see Brown. Margaret wrapped the extra eggs in a piece of cloth. There were enough for three days. Leaving the two children with Katie she set off for McDaid's. This had been a big step for her but she realised the benefits of having some money for the children and this strengthened her. Besides, she trusted Katie. It was a half hours walk. McDaid's door was open and she went into the shop which had a separate entrance from the pub. She set the eggs on the counter.

McDaid came out through the door from his kitchen and looked at the eggs in the cloth. 'How are you, Missus Campbell?' McDaid knew who she was as he had seen her walking home from her work at Brown's. She did not speak. 'You are selling these?' He handed her over the few coppers that he paid for the eggs. She was not to know but he doubled his money on the eggs he bought. 'This is what I pay for a dozen. Bring me more when you have them. I can use all you bring me'.

Margaret turned with the coins and went to leave.

'Have a look around. Maybe there is something you would like to buy.' McDaid never liked to see any money he paid out leave his place.

She stopped. She did not know what to do. For the first time in her life she had money in her hand. For the first time she could buy something. The value of her labour power and her surplus labour power had been stolen by the combination of her father and Campbell, Brown and Allen. But now she had a few pence for the first time in her life.

'There are some very nice wee biscuits I have got in. For yourself, or dipped in milk for the weans. See them there, the Rich Tea.' She did not move. He went over and took the biscuits down from the shelf and set them on the counter. Margaret stood without looking at him still faced towards the door.

She still did not know what to do. It was not that she was turning over alternatives in her mind. It was just that the situation had caused her mind to block. There were too many new challenges and far too many issues that arose from them all. She had too many decisions to make. McDaid filled a paper bag with the biscuits and put them on the counter. McDaid took half the money he had given her for the eggs out of her hand. He did not know what was wrong with her.

Now that the actual purchasing was over Margaret was struck with another thought. What would she do about Campbell? He would know she had been to McDaid's. He would know she had money. He would not like that. Like her father he thought any money in the house was his. She wished she could give the biscuits back and get her money back.

But especially he would not want her to have any money. This would be seen as a challenge to his control over her. She began to realise that selling the eggs was a whole lot more complicated than she had first thought. Having money threatened to change her relationship with Campbell. It left her again with the dilemma of whether to challenge him again for a bit more room for herself. It was like the time when she had to decide whether to speak out loud or not.

It came back to the children again. She wanted the money to be able to give something to the children. This was the heart of the issue. She realised this as she stood there. It was back to the children again. She would do anything for the children. She did what he wanted in terms of work and looking after his needs including putting his thing in her. These did not directly hurt the children. But this was different. This involved the children directly, like her speaking or not speaking.

She realised then that there was only one decision she could make. She was going to collect the eggs and bring them to McDaid's to sell and spend the money on the children. From this moment on it became only a question of tactics. He would know when he saw what she bought the children that she had money. Would he try to take the money from her? Selling the eggs was only the beginning. It was the easiest of the problems.

What would he do? Would he hit her and try and take the money from her? She felt the confusion in her mind clear away completely. She went over it again to be sure. It was like her decision to speak out. To let him put his thing in her. To do the work he made her do. It was all for the children. Without looking at McDaid she reached out and took the biscuits from the counter and almost ran from the shop.

On the road she walked fast and her breathing was coming in gasps. She held the biscuits so tight that she heard them break in her hand. They were in a small white paper bag. She loosened her grasp of them and began to slow down and to breathe more easily. Her frustration and anxiety and tension began to decline. As it did the thought of her children, of Victoria and Mary, came into the front of her mind.

She could see their faces. She began to feel warmth and almost happiness as she thought of how their faces would light up when they would taste the biscuits. But maybe they would not taste good? How did she know? She had never tasted a biscuit in her life never mind this kind. Maybe they would not taste good to the weans? She speeded up again in her anxiety. She had to get home quickly to see. She could not wait.

Katie had stayed with the children. This was the first time Margaret had ever left them. She had been so overcome with the idea of selling the eggs for the children that until this minute she had not felt worried about them. Now she did and she began to run. She saw the roof of the cottage, and the wall and entrance come into view. She turned in and the dog barked a welcome and ran to her. She ran to the door. It was all right. Katie was holding Mary in her arms and sitting by the fire and Victoria was tottering at her knee. They were okay.

'Margaret, how are you? Sure these are the greatest weans. They are just great. You have done a great job with them.'

Margaret rushed over and almost pulled Mary from Katie. She was breathing hard. Her face was tight with worry and fear. She held Mary close to her and too tight. Mary began to cry with fear at being squeezed. Katie understood what was happening and was not offended at Margaret's rudeness. She knew Margaret was frightened for the baby, that was all.

Margaret sat down and took the biscuits from the bag. Then she got up again and got a cup of milk. Then with Victoria and Mary she sat on the bed and, dipping the biscuits in the milk, she began to feed them. Katie was standing watching. Margaret reached over and held out the bag filled with biscuits to Katie. It was her first time to have a guest to whom she could offer something. It was a milestone in her life. Katie took one and began to eat it.

The women watched as the two children opened their wee mouths and tasted the biscuits dipped in milk. Their little faces tightened up, their wee mouths pulled together as they savoured this new sweet taste for the first time. Margaret held them and looked at them with love. They liked the biscuits. Without thinking she spoke out loud. 'They liked them.' And as she said this she looked up at Katie. 'They liked them, Katie.' She voluntarily spoke her first full sentence to another human being in her adult life.

Katie felt like her insides would melt. Margaret had spoken to her and called her name. They were friends. Margaret trusted her. Trusted her to look after her children and trusted her to speak to her and call her name. 'Aye, Margaret, they liked them. Sure they are good biscuits. Why would they not?' Margaret looked at Katie and then back to concentrating on the children. She took a bite herself out of a biscuit. She had never tasted a biscuit before. She liked them too.

A peacefulness settled on the two women as they sat. They forgot about the problems in their lives and the new ones that would lie ahead. They sat and fed the children and ate. They were at ease together. 'Margaret, these are great weans. You have done a great job. You are a great mother altogether. You should be proud of yourself.' Margaret felt almost as good as she had when Victoria had first taken her nipple into her mouth. She felt a healing from all the insults and bad treatments she had received in the past years. 'Margaret, you are a great mother. Don't let anybody tell you different.'

Katie got up to leave. Margaret rose to see her out. Victoria walked with her and she carried Mary. Before Katie could leave Margaret caught her by the arm. Then she ran back into the cottage and returned with what was left of the biscuits. She handed them to Katie. 'No. No keep them for yourselves and the weans, Margaret. Me and Shanks have plenty to eat in the house.' But Margaret kept pushing the biscuits on Katie.

Then she spoke. One word. 'Campbell'. She pushed the biscuits on Katie again. 'Campbell', she said.

Katie was confused. What about Campbell? Then she realised what it was about. Campbell would know Margaret had money if he saw the biscuits. Margaret did not want this. Katie understood the situation. Men like Campbell liked their women to have nothing, no friends, no money, no independence. This way they were better under control. Katie knew he would find out anyway, but to please her she took the biscuits and left for home.

At this time, Campbell was on his way back from the village. He went into McDaid's for a drink. He found himself doing this more and more. He would come in and have a drink and prepare himself for her and the house. He realised this was what he was doing as he sat down and ordered his usual, a wee half of Scotch. To hell with her anyway. What was it about her that he always had to think in advance before he went home to her? He savoured the Scotch. He was into his second and he could feel its effect on him.

Then McDaid came into the bar. His wife had been serving before. He saw Campbell. 'Well, Campbell, how are you doing? You are looking well.' Campbell grunted. 'Your wife was down here today. She is looking in good health too, Campbell. A fine cut of a woman. You are a lucky man. She sold me some eggs and bought some biscuits. Aye, you are a lucky man, Campbell.'

Campbell did not know what to say. He felt the rage build in him at a terrible rate. She was selling eggs now. What would she be at next? McDaid brought him down another Scotch. 'This is from me, Campbell. I never did buy you a drink when you got married and started your family.' Campbell looked at it like it would jump off the table and attack him. He did not trust anything that anybody gave him for nothing. There was always something behind it. He grunted at McDaid.

She had been in McDaid's. She had sold eggs. She had money. What would be next? He sat there with his anger. Every time he looked around she was at something else. He had never told her she could come to McDaid's. He had never told her she could sell eggs. Now she would have money. What did she need with money? She had her work to do and the weans. That was all she needed. Not to be gallivanting about with money.

He would take it off her and put a stop to her traipsing to McDaid's and selling eggs. Aye, she was not fit to have money. It was his job to have any money that was going. He nodded to McDaid for another scotch. He was having a fourth. That was unusual. McDaid did not realise that this extravagance was due to him buying Campbell's wife's eggs. Did not realise that, because of her connection with the market and money and the wee bit of independence that this gave her from Campbell, he was selling him another whisky.

Campbell sat wondering what he would do when he got back. Would he just straight out demand the money and that would be that? Would he order her to sell no more eggs? To never again go down to McDaid's? Would he hit her to show that he would not go along with her selling eggs? Aye, that is what he would do. But there was something niggling at him. He did not realise it but it was his better nature trying to come out. As with other times when this happened he beat it down with the help of taking into account the way the country worked. What kind of a state would things be in if she had money of her own and could do what she liked?

Aye, things were getting out of control everywhere. In Dublin and everywhere. The Fenians were getting out of control. And not only the Fenians, his own kind were at it too. Some of them were joining those unions and trying to do what they wanted. Everywhere would be in chaos if this was allowed to go on. Things had to be kept in control. And she at home especially. She had to be kept under control too.

His mind drifted back to a conversation he had heard a few months ago between the Sergeant and Brown. They were saying that somewhere women were wanting the right to vote. They laughed at the stupidity of the idea. They were right there. What would women, especially women like her at home, want the right to vote for? Sure all they knew about was weans. They would end up voting for things that would help themselves and the weans, not what was good for the country. What kind of a way was that to think?

They would not want a war, sure they would be afraid that their weans would be sent. Well maybe the Brown woman would be all right to vote. Them kind could get their weans out of going to war if they did not want them to go. But women like her at home. She knew nothing but work and poverty. They could not be trusted to vote. It was like having money, they could not be trusted to have money or to be allowed to vote. Their place was to do what they were told and keep their mouth shut.

Campbell sat sipping his whisky. After coming to all these conclusions and being sure that he was right he felt a curious emptiness in himself. Everything around him he had put in their place. The Taverstocks, the Browns and their kind, they would be in charge. They knew what to do. Her and her kind, the women who had nothing. They would do what they were told and keep their mouths shut. They knew nothing and had to be kept in their place. Them strikers as well. They knew nothing and they had to be kept in their place. Doing what they were told and keeping their mouths shut, the same for them.

For a second Campbell got a glimpse of what was ailing him, what was causing this emptiness in him, why he was always in conflict and rage and battle. There was not much of a place he had left for himself. He had left himself with no friends. Nobody who trusted him. His betters expected him to do what they told him and for him to keep his mouth shut, to speak only when he was spoken to. He was not good enough for them. Not good enough to be in their company.

But the ones he kept in control for his betters hated him. They did not want Campbell in their company either. His relation to them was to make them carry out the orders of those at the top. Most of them hated him. He was alone. Isolated. In the middle not of a cooperative collective, but in the middle of a war. And he was neither general nor private. He did not have the company of either the officer's quarters or the private's quarters. This is why he always sat near the door in the pub. His place in the pub was like his place in society. He was isolated. Nobody in the last analysis wanted anything to do with him.

How about her at home did she too...? His mind stopped for a second at this thought. Did she hate him too? Because he kept her in her place? Did she hate him also? Well that was too bad. She also had to be kept in her place. And he was the man to do it. He had to do it. But did she hate him too?

He sat forward with a jerk. His whisky was finished. He held the empty glass up to McDaid.

Jesus, what was wrong with Campbell tonight? He must have seen a ghost. It was a good job O'Donnell and the boys were not in. If Campbell got any more into the drink they might think they could give him a battering. He would have to keep a look out if they came in. If anything happened to Campbell in the bar or after he left, it could get a black mark against it as a rebel bar and this would not be good. It would be bad for business. His talks in Craig's might not be enough to help him out of the situation. He would have to watch out for Campbell and keep an eye on O'Donnell if he came in. Things could get out of control.

CHAPTER TWENTY SEVEN.

It was the first time he had done it. But before he left McDaid's he ordered a half bottle of scotch to take with him. He drank out of it as he walked up the dirt road to his house. After the drinks in the pub and now this he was beginning to feel serious effects. He turned into the yard of the cottage. He was tired and he was drunk. He stopped and looked at the spud ground that she had planted.

He went over and sat down with his back against the wall, which ran along the side of the field next to the road. He took another drink out of the bottle. Aye, she had money now. She was selling eggs. And she had put in all the spuds herself. Hah! he snorted. So now she was getting above her station. So that was it. Now she had money. She had planted the spuds. Now she thought she was somebody. Well he would soon put an end to that. He was the man of the house. He was the one who held the money.

But his mind drifted with the drink. He was having a hard time keeping a good anger focused on her. His eyes settled on the spud ground. She had done a good job. There was no doubt about it. She had worked hard and done the whole job herself. Not many women would be able for it. Not many would try it. It would be left to the man of the house. But she had done it all herself. And it was well done too. The drills were straight as you could get.

He was half way down the bottle by this time. His own controls were slipping as he thought of the work she had put into the spud ground. Aye, maybe he would say nothing about the egg money. Just leave it alone. She could keep it. He took another drink and leaned his head back against the rough stone wall. He looked out over the valley and the moon was bright and the whole place looked grand to the eye. Aye, she deserved it. And nobody need ever know.

That McDaid telling him about her buying the eggs. Trying to get at him. Then a thought struck him. Who was looking after the weans when she was down there? It must have been that Shanks and Katie. They were always poking their nose in where it did not belong. Aye, that is who it would have been. They would have been watching the weans. Then they would know about her selling the eggs and getting the money. And McDaid knew.

It was bound to get out then. The whole place would know that she was out selling eggs and that she was keeping the money. That was it then, he would have to take it off her. If he did not then the whole place would know that she was doing what she wanted. That he was losing control over her. He would be a laughing stock. That was what would happen. Then the rest of them would be trying something on with him.

Aye, that Pollock and O'Donnell would know and it would be over the whole country. Brown would know. Then Brown would begin to think that Campbell was not up to keeping things in control in the bog anymore if he could not keep control of his wife. She was getting money and keeping it. Pollock was getting away with extra footage in the bog. Things were slipping away from him too in spite of all his big talk. Who would know where it would lead? He would have to put a stop to it.

He took another drink. But then she was a hard worker. She did everything he wanted. Maybe he should forget about it? But that was not the way things were. The Taverstocks and Browns ruled from the top. Kept control from the top. Campbell was beholden to them. He was under their control. The Pollocks and the rest of the bog clients were under his control. She herself was under his control. That was the way the system worked. That was the way it had to be.

By this time he had finished the half bottle. He was drunk to the point of staggering and hardly able to keep his feet. He managed to get himself up by turning over on his hands and knees and gradually, limb by limb, rising. He steadied himself and looked down over the valley. Aye, she would have to be put in her place. Unsteadily he made it to the door and pushing it open, went in.

There was a dull red glow from the fire. But for that the cottage was dark. He made his way over into the doorway into her room. By the moonlight coming through the windows and the open door he could make out her shape on the bed. He reached out and took a hold of her upper arm. 'So that is what you are at, selling eggs in McDaid's and keeping the money? Who do you think you are?

'I know what is going on. You put in those spuds and now you think you are somebody. You think that you are above your station. Well I am telling you you are not. You do what I tell you and you speak when I tell you and you do what I say. And any eggs that are to be sold around here I will sell them and I will keep the money.' He pulled her up in the bed by the arm and leaned over her staggering as he shouted these words into her face.

The children woke at the noise and began to cry. Their fear made no impression on him. Margaret held her right arm out straight in the air over them where they lay, to protect them. He pulled and jerked at her until he had her out of the bed. She fell on one knee onto the floor. Then he drew back to hit her but he was drunk and this hampered him. His blow was a weak slap that caught Margaret on the shoulder.

'Where is the money? Where is the money? I want it now,' and he tried to hit her again. But he was so drunk that he could not hit her hard. Margaret remained on one knee watching her children who were crying but who were still in the bed and out of his reach. 'Where is the money? I want it' But by this time the drink was overcoming him and his anger was fading. He turned and left her and went and got on his bench, turned his back to her and dropped asleep.

She remained where she was until she saw him lie down. Then she got up and into the bed and holding her two children in her arms she comforted them. Gradually they stopped crying and drifted back to sleep. She lay there holding them and thinking about what had happened. He was trying to stop her again. He was trying to stop her doing things for the children, trying to stop her having a few pence for the children.

This was like when he had tried to stop her speaking out loud. This was the same. The children had to have a few things now and then from McDaid's that she could not make them at home. He had things from McDaid's, his drink. The children should not be denied things. She wanted nothing, cared nothing about having things for herself. But the children, that was different. They would have things. A few biscuits now and then.

But it was not only that. When they would get older they could not be kept in the house for ever. They would have to be able to take a walk down to McDaid's and see what there was for sale there. She would have to be able to take them out. She would have to have a few pence to spend on them. Margaret lay in bed with these thoughts going round and round in her head and with each turning she grew more confident that she was right.

She still had the few pence, that were left over after buying the biscuits, on the children's side of the bed. That way he would not feel them when he came to her. How would she handle this now in the morning? If she defied him openly then what would happen? The children would be awake and would see him hitting her. This would not be good.

Without being able to decide what to do, she fell asleep. And she dreamt with a vividness that was new to her. She dreamt that she was an eagle. One of the great brown feathered ones she had seen once when she was still at home. It had that powerful beak and feet and that fearless look. She was an eagle. She was fearless. She dreamt that she was flying over the mountains and the hills and the bogs and the valleys. Oh the wonderful freedom of it.

Then her dream changed. The eagle landed on a high craggy cliff side. Its nest was there. There were eggs in it. And crawling close to the nest were two weasels. They were after the eggs. The eagle struck and got one weasel in its claws and then went after the other with its beak. The one that was free fled and fell off the side of the cliff and went bouncing down over the rocks and shrubs until it disappeared from sight. The other one the eagle tore to pieces with its claws and beak.

Then the dream changed. She was no longer an eagle. She was a salmon in the lake again. She was swimming followed by her mate. She was up in the high end of the lake where the water was low. She found a spot she liked and using her tail she cleared out a shallow hollow in the sandy bottom. Then when she was content it was right she released her eggs into the hollow. Her mate held himself steady above the eggs and fertilized them. Then she covered them over with her tail to protect them from the predators that could eat them.

Margaret felt as if she had been dreaming all night when she awoke and saw the light of the morning. For some reason she had a certain peacefulness in her. It was as if she had resolved something while she slept. But she was not aware of any new decisions she had made. She got up and quietly worked around the fire getting it lit and trying not to waken Campbell. She no longer thought about what she would do about selling the eggs. It seemed no longer to be a problem in her mind. She did not know why. She put on the water for the tea, eggs and stirabout. Campbell woke and went outside to relieve himself. When he came back his food was ready on the table.

When he sat to eat, Margaret lifted Mary in one arm and took Victoria by the hand and went outside where they all went to the toilet and washed themselves in the stream. The children seemed to have no memory of the violence of the night before. They were their usual morning selves. The dog pranced around them and licked Margaret and the children. The children laughed delightedly as they felt the dog's soft tongue on their faces and hands.

She went back into the cottage to get the bucket to milk the cow. She took it from the shelf and, with the children still with her, she headed for the door to go to the byre.

As she approached the door she heard her own voice speak in a quiet but confident tone, 'I am selling the eggs and using the money but only for the children.' She had no idea she was going to say this. It just came out of her mouth.

But once it was done she never for a second considered taking it back. She felt completely confident about what she had said and did not want to take it back. She wondered that she did not even seem surprised she had said it even though she had no idea she was going to. She stopped inside the door as she said it. He was sitting eating at the table with his back to the fire. His mouth was full of eggs and bread. He had the cup of tea half way to his mouth.

They all froze there for what seemed a long time. Even the dog stopped its antics at the door where it was waiting for Margaret and the children to come out. Margaret stayed completely stationary and quiet. She had said her piece. She had announced her intention in relation to the eggs and the money. It was up to him now. She was waiting for his response.

He heard her clearly. He had no doubt what she had said. But she had never acted like this before. What would he do? He had a bad hangover from the drink. He was not in good shape. He thought of rising to her and beating her and telling her she was going to do no such thing. That she was not going to be selling eggs and keeping the money for the children.

But he did not have the strength of feeling in him to do this. Maybe it was the drink? Maybe it was that he had already beat her last night? Maybe that was it? He had got it out of himself. Maybe he would have to be sure and give her a much harder beating in future if this was what was going to happen? The next morning she speaks out loud and defies him. The thought of this, her openly and out loud defying him, motivated him for a second.

He moved to rise from the chair and the first sounds of an oath and a shout began to come from his mouth. But then he subsided back in the chair again. He did not look at her. He did not try to rise again. He just grunted at her again in a loud aggressive tone. But it was not really that. It was more that he grunted at the world in general. At the world that was changing around him no matter what he did to try and stop it.

Then Margaret found the same thing happened again. She did not plan it. She had not prepared it. Again the words came from her mouth. Not in an aggressive tone, not loud. Just clear and firm. 'I am going to sell the eggs and use the money but only for the children.'

She still did not move. Nor did the children. Nor did the dog. Nor this time did Campbell. Then he lifted a thick slice of bread in one hand and a bit of the hard boiled egg in the other and before he put these in his mouth he grunted again. It was still an aggressive grunt. But any power there had been in it was gone.

Margaret was so sure of her decision that she did not dwell too much on his grunts or his actions. She realised that she was telling him out straight and she was standing there to make sure that he heard. But more important she was standing there to let him do what ever he was going to do to try and stop her selling the eggs and using the money for the children. She was standing there to get it over with and she would then go on doing it. But it seemed that this was all that he was going to do. Grunt.

Margaret tightened her arms around the children and hefted Mary higher on her haunch. The bucket for the milk hung from her fingers under Mary. Without any reply and without any drama she moved on out of the door and walked across towards the byre. The cow was wait- ing with her udder full to be milked. She looked around at Margaret as she put down the two children and sat down to begin to milk.

Tnis. Tnis. Tnis. The milk hit the bottom of the metal bucket. The cow chewed its cud contentedly as she felt the familiar knowing hands on her teats and felt the pressure go out of her udder. The buck- et gradually filled up and the noise of the milk hitting the metal was replaced with the noise of milk hitting milk. Margaret was comforted by the sound.

Victoria and Mary lay on the piece of sacking that Margaret kept on the pile of straw and slept. They were tired from having been woken up during the night. The dog lay beside them with its head on its front paws watching Margaret. Every time she milked the cow and the dog was there she squirted some milk out onto the stone floor behind the cow for the dog to lick up. He liked this treat very much. This morning she did this twice. The dog was happy.

Margaret thought of Allen's and the work she had had to do there. And the terrible horror of him forcing himself into her and the crush- ing powerlessness of not knowing if she would be there all her life or what. She hated Allen and his wife. But this morning she was not thinking of this hatred. She had a contentment in her that was new and totally unknown to her. She thought about this as she finished milking the cow.

Lifting Mary in one arm, and with Victoria holding onto her skirt and with the bucket of milk in the other hand she made her way out of the byre and towards the house. As she approached the door Campbell came out. Buttoning his coat on him he whistled for the dog, looked in her direction and past her to the dog. It came running and the two of them headed out the gate and up the road towards the bog.

Margaret went into the house. She put the bucket of milk on the table, put the sleeping Mary on the bed and helped Victoria climb up along with her. In a second they were both asleep. She put on two eggs, water for tea and stirabout. When it was all ready she set it on the table in front of herself. Then sat with her back to the warm fire and slowly began to eat. As she did so she spoke out loud to herself,

'I am going to sell the eggs and use the money for the children.'

CHAPTER TWENTY EIGHT

It was November. Margaret was on her feet again after the third baby which was born in the early autumn. Another girl. She had called her Anne. Campbell wanted no say in any of it. Her name or anything else. Katie had helped her again. She was thinking of these things as she sat near the fire feeding Anne at her breast. The door of the cottage was open as there had been no bad weather yet. It was still mild. Then Margaret heard Victoria calling.

'Mammy! Mammy! Mary sick. Mary sick.' Margaret rushed with Anne in her arms to see Mary on the bed. She was lying on her side and she had thrown up. Margaret knew what it was. She had been increasingly getting her on to new foods in preparation for the new baby who would need all the milk she had. She had got some different biscuits in McDaid's when she was down with the eggs. They had all had some of these earlier. They had made Mary sick. She resolved to only eat the rich tea from then on.

As she cleaned the bed and Mary's mouth she was thinking how Victoria was now speaking well and speaking out. She was helping her more and more. Like this time calling her about Mary. She would be all right with having a baby every year. The children would all help as they grew up as Victoria was already doing. She would manage in this way. 'Victoria that was a good thing you did telling me about Mary.'

'Mammy, look hen hen.' A hen was looking round the door seeing if the coast was clear for her to come in. 'A hen, Mammy. A hen.'

'Yes, a hen. Here Victoria. Come and help me.'

Victoria came over. She was much more steady on her feet now. 'Victoria take this broom and sweep out the floor.' The broom was twice the height of Victoria but she struggled on with it. The sweeping was not great but she was learning to help Margaret.

All the size of her wee legs. All the size of her. Margaret felt her heart melt for Victoria, she felt a terrible fear for her future. She would never let her be hired out. That would never happen to her. But what would her life be like? Would she be attacked by some man also? Margaret had to look away as the image of this in her head was too hard to bear. She would protect Victoria, Mary, Anne and the rest to come.

But how could she do it? She owned nothing. She could not keep the children at home for ever. There would not be enough to eat for them. And she knew Campbell would be wanting the children to go out and earn him money. Maybe she would not be able to protect them. Her mother was not able to protect her. Victoria fell over the brush and Margaret helped her up and she was laughing about her own fall. Victoria was a good wee girl.

Campbell was away through the gap into Donegal Town that day. He would not be back for at least another day. Margaret could feel the weight of his presence lift off her shoulders. She could feel her body become less rigid. Her joints become more supple. Her muscles began to feel at ease with the rest of her. Not hard and unyielding as they usually did. How did it come that Campbell made these things happen to her body?

It was as if his threatening oppressive pressure was being registered in her body, in her joints, her muscles. She found herself taking a long deep breath every now and then when he was gone for a day or two. She found herself straightening up and looking around her at the sky and the countryside. Not like when he was there when all she did was concentrate on the work she had to do, to see it was done right and keep on the alert to protect the children in case he lost his temper and hit her.

Her body was a canvas on which his oppression, on which the experience of their relationship was registered. Holding Anne in her arms she leaned against the side of the door and looked out over the valley. Mary was asleep. Victoria was holding onto her dress. Anne was asleep. Margaret sighed deeply. How she valued the little peace when he was gone. But it was never long enough. She never had enough time to get fully relaxed.

She watched as some crows scratched and leapt around the end of the midden where it reached down to the stream. None of them was bent over, none of them seemed to be shaped by oppression. What was it about the animals that they seemed to be different from her? What was it that made her father and Allen and Campbell act the way they did and beat and shout and dominate and try to control her? She did not know.

As she stood there thinking, she heard a voice calling her from the road. It was Katie and Shanks. She was always conflicted when she saw them. She knew they were good to her. And she knew she need-ed to talk to them to help her talking and help the children talk. And Katie always looked after the children when she went to McDaid's to sell the eggs. But they always stressed her out as she could not relax and just talk to them. It was a big effort for her to think what to say and how to say it.

'Margaret how are you doing? I see that wee Anne is looking to be doing all right. How are you yourself, Margaret? Are you keeping well?' Margaret did not answer she just looked at them. 'Well, Margaret, are you keeping all right?'

This time Margaret felt she had to answer. 'I am.' She realised that her speech was as rigid as her body. Between her father and Allen and Campbell they had stiffened her up in every way. They had bent her over in the shoulders, stiffened her up in the joints and the muscles and speech.

'Sure it's great weather altogether for this time of the year, Margaret. I see you have got all the spuds dug and pitted. They are safe for the winter. That was a hard job for you over the summer with the wean coming and all. At least you had a bit of help towards the end.' Shanks was referring to the fact that Campbell had helped dig and pit the last half of the spuds when Margaret had got too big to do any more. Well at least that was something, Shanks thought.

'Did you have a good crop, Margaret? I remember all the work you put into planting them and getting the ground ready. Was it a good crop?' Again Shanks questions were too direct for her to keep quiet. It would have been too unmannerly.

'Aye, it was good.' Margaret was angry at herself for always answering the questions with the same words as the questions. She was going to have to try and use more words of her own. That's what she needed, a house of her own, fields of her own, words of her own.

Katie felt sorry for Margaret having to answer Shanks' questions even though she knew it was better to make Margaret talk.

'Margaret, next year you should put in a few carrots and cabbage. If you do not have the seeds you can get them in McDaid's when you sell the eggs. That will be good for you and the weans, keep you stronger. There is nothing like the spuds and a few vegetables and a bit of meat.'

'Aye, not that many of us can afford the bit of meat now with this war on and the price of everything going up. You know, Margaret, the only meat we ever have to eat is when Shanks snares a rabbit. Lucky for us he is good at it and we get a few every week. The odd fish too.'

'Well, Katie, Margaret does not want to hear about that.' Shanks interrupted Katie quickly because he did not want Margaret to hear about his fishing escapades as Taverstock had all the rights and Shanks was poaching.

Katie realised what Shanks was doing and kept quiet letting him speak. 'Aye, Margaret, there are plenty of rabbits around here you could get yourself an odd one. Even here in the spud ground I often see them. A lot of us snare rabbits. It helps with the old diet.' Katie got animated. 'Shanks tell Margaret about the Apache and Burns and the snares. That was a good one.'

'Aye Margaret you will like this. I do not know if you know but the Apache hates that Burns crowd that lives up there behind him. One time they informed on him that he was poaching salmon off Taverstock's place. You know the Burns, they are always trying to get in with the big shots. They would inform on anybody. Anyway that would have been before your time. But the Apache has it in for the Burns ever since. He is always trying to get back at them.

'Well old Burns he is not able to do the heavy work so much any more. And they are a terrible tight crowd altogether. So old Burns he started to do a bit of snaring. The Apache heard about this. So he lay up there in the wee wood and watched in the early morning until Burns went round to check his snares. This way he knew where they all were. So then for a week or two the Apache would get up early and take whatever was in them before Burns was out.

'He used to do well too. But you know the Apache he is never content unless he is up to some extra devilment. Cleaning out the snares was not good enough for him. He then took to another move. After he would clean out any rabbits that there would be in the snares he would move the snares. He would move them sometimes twenty or thirty yards and sometimes only a few inches or a few feet. Old Burns would notice this and was going mad. He began to wonder if he was going off the head. The Apache would be lying up there too watching him pushing back his cap and scratching his head trying to figure out what was going on.

'Then the Apache came up with another one. He began to leave a single rabbit in one of the snares but in a way that would get old Burns going. The first time he did it he got an old piece of red cloth from his house and tore a strip of it. Then he tied a strip of this round the rabbit's neck. Old Burns came along checking, the Apache was lying up to see what would happen.

'Well old Burns he came on the snare with the rabbit in it. He began to hurry when he saw it at first. But then as he came closer he slowed down. What the hell? He slowed altogether when he was a couple of feet from the snare and stopped. He looked for a while. At the rabbit with the red scarf on it. Then he looked around to see there was nobody watching. He stooped down and took hold of the rabbit.

'Taking it out of the snare he saw it was already dead. But with a scarf on it? He looked at it for a minute or two and again looked around and then he tore the strip of cloth of its neck, threw it away and hurried on. Burns was too mean not to take the rabbit but he tried to deny to himself that it had a red scarf on it.

In the meantime the Apache was a happy man. He let Burns go and then he slipped out of the hiding he was in and headed for home. He knew he was driving old Burns mad. He kept raiding old Burns' snares. Every few days he would move the snares this time just a foot or two or even a couple of inches. Old Burns was getting very worried about his memory and, ever since the rabbit with the scarf, about whether his head was going or not.

'Then the Apache left another rabbit in a snare but not with a scarf this time. Instead this time he had got his mother involved. She hated the Burns crowd too, she had been hired to them that is how she first came to this part of the country, so the Apache got his mother into it.

He got her to knit four wee things that looked like two pair of socks for the rabbit. He took the rabbit out, killed it and put a sock on each foot and put it back in the snare. Laughing to himself he lay up again to hide and wait.

'Burns came along as usual. This time he did not see anything wrong until he got right up to the rabbit. He reached down to take it out of the snare and then he froze. A rabbit with socks on it. What the ...? He drew back as if he was stung. He looked around to see if anybody was watching. A rabbit, not with one pair of socks on it, but with two pair of socks on it. He reached down again to take the rabbit out of the snare. But he drew back again. How could he take something that could not be? How could there be a rabbit with socks on it? How could he eat a rabbit that he found with socks on it?

'The Apache was watching and holding himself with the laughing. The old Burns man stood bent over for a while. He reached out his hand a couple of times and then drew it back. How could he lift a rabbit and take the socks of it? There could not be a rabbit with socks on it so he could not take them off it. It was impossible for there to be a rabbit with socks on it. He could not do it. If any body heard about it they would think he was mad. But what was he going to do, leave it there? He could not even tell anybody what he had seen. They would think he was mad.

'The end of it was that he left snare and rabbit and all there and hurried back the way he came. He did not even check the rest of his snares. That was the end of him snaring. He never even lifted the snares and he never mentioned the rabbits with the scarf and the socks. The Apache took the snares and has been snaring away with them ever since. But that was not the end of it. It gets even better. The Apache was not finished with him.

'He began to spread the rumour that old Burns was saying that he had snared a rabbit with a scarf and another with socks on it. Now

Burns had never mentioned what happened to a soul. But the Apache was spreading the story that Burns was saying this. It soon was all over the place. Old Burns heard about it from one of his sons. He denied it but the son could see from his face that there was something not right. That he was lying. The sons were a greedy lot. They wanted the old man out of it so they could have the whole farm to themselves.

'They were only too glad to believe the old man was mad. They tried to get him put in the mental hospital but they had not enough proof. The whole house got into an uproar over it and to this day the father won't speak to the sons. The Apache did well out of it. A whole set of new snares, plenty of rabbits, his own back on the Burns for informing on him and some good nights of craic down in McDaid's telling the boys about what he had done. That Apache is a boy.' Shanks shook his head and laughed.

Katie laughed along with him. But Margaret could not get a laugh out of herself. She had liked the story. Inside she wanted to laugh. But it had been too long. She could not laugh anymore. She thought of the Apache and his escapades. She knew that he could laugh, he could laugh. Why could she not laugh? Once in a dream she had almost laughed. But not since she had been sent to Allen's. No, she was not able to except on that one occasion when she had seen the salmon jump in the lake.

'Aye, Margaret, you should get a couple of snares and put them out there around the spud ground. There are plenty of rabbits about here. It would take you no time either. Shanks would show you how to put them down. You can buy them in McDaid's. They are not much. A dozen eggs would get you a couple. Then you could have some meat for the weans and for yourself. A bit of rabbit in a stew with some spuds and vegetables. There is nothing to beat it.'

'We'll have to go, Katie. Your father has to get his tea. Margaret, the wee girl is doing well. She slept the whole time we have been here. Cheerio, Margaret. Cheerio, Victoria. Cheerio, Mary.'

'Cheerio,' Victoria said. Katie bent down and kissed Victoria.

'Cheerio,' Margaret said.

Katie and Shanks both stopped for a second. This was the first time that Margaret had said cheerio to them. She was coming on every time they called to see her. She was speaking more.

Shanks and Katie walked up the road. They always were thoughtful after they left Margaret. They wanted her to get on and to do better. 'Aye, she is getting on, Katie. She is making progress. It's the weans, they are bringing her out of herself. That is what it is. The weans. It is not that Campbell lugan anyway. Imagine having to live with that boy, Katie. Imagine having to put up with that. That Margaret is a strong woman.' Both of them shook their heads as they walked along.

Chapter Twenty Nine

Campbell was not worried. All this noise about conscription and making all men go and fight the Germans. Aye, they were all on for extending conscription to Ireland. The bishops and all were for it. Well not for themselves. But he would be safe. He knew too much for Brown and Tavestock to let him go. They would never be able to figure out the bog without him, the measurements and who had rented what. Brown would be lost without him. He would be okay. Anyway the war was on for two years now. It could not last much longer.

And if they brought it in, this would be good. They would be able to get rid of those like O'Donnell and Brennan and Pollock. It would be good riddance. In Dublin those kind of people had already had to join up. After the labour war they lost their jobs and had nothing to eat. They had to go. The hunger had already conscripted them. It was good riddance to them. The country was well rid of them.

Things were going all right for him. It was true that her at home was too much above herself. With her talking and her selling eggs and keeping the money. But he had let it go. It was not worth it. He had let her get away with it. Even though he was not happy about it. She was doing her work and looking after the house and him. It was just not worth it to keep on at her. And since she had got keeping the egg money she had not come up with anything else since.

It had been a hard enough winter. But they had had enough turf and spuds and the cottage was well roofed. It had been all right for them. With the milk from the cow, what he got from Brown for doing the lettings, and the few sheep he had on the mountain and the calf that the cow brought him every year, he was better off than he had ever been. Aye, he had done well out of her. But if she would only keep her mouth shut and keep the weans' mouths shut and not be trying to run down to McDaid's and ......If she got too much of her own money you would never know what she would think she could get up to.

He snorted to himself as he thought of these things. It was the same old thing that was wrong with so many of them. She would not accept her place. Like so many of them she was always trying to get above herself. If they would only accept their place. If they would only accept there was no way out upwards. Then they would be more content. Then everybody would be more content. Keeping their mouth shut like he did with Brown, knowing his place like he did with Brown. That was the way.

Aye, sure it was true that there were times when Brown treated him like dirt. It was true that Brown thought he was so much beneath him that he would say what he wanted to him, do what he wanted to him, too bluntly and too viciously. But he did not let the anger this stirred in him find a way out. He knew his place. Even at times when the anger threatened to burst his heart he did not let it out. It was not good for him health wise he knew. But he knew his place. He did not try to change things. That was the best way. Don't try to change things.

This anger that he suppressed from Brown and the anger he had stored up from having to tolerate herself at home, these were driving him more and more into McDaid's every night. The whisky cooled his mind. It dulled the memories of these angers and helped him forget them for a while. It helped loosen up his body and helped him sit back in the chair and instead of being tensed ready to strike out, he could come closer to just sitting there. Just being.

When this would happen he would sometimes be able to sift through old memories. They all seemed less hurtful with a few whiskys. Some of them would even threaten to make him laugh. At least to bring a smile to his face. He would never let it show to the boys in McDaid's but he would feel it inside. He liked it. After listening to Brown about how he had to keep a close watch on things and thinking about herself at home talking out loud to the weans, he turned into McDaid's.

He was into his second whisky and feeling the softening coming over him when the door burst open. It was O'Donnell and one of the McGinns. They rushed in in a terrible excitement altogether. What was wrong with them? They did not even see him where he sat in his usual seat by the door. Everybody up at the bar and around the fire turned when they heard the noise.

It was O'Donnell who came out with what their rush was about. Shouting in a loud voice he gave them the news. 'Hey, they are fighting in Dublin. They are fighting in Dublin. Did you not hear? Aye, it's great. The boys are fighting the English. It's Pearse and Connolly and Clarke and the boys. They took over part of the city and they are fighting. It's great. This should have happened years ago.'

'Aye, it's great', McGinn joined in.

The bar went quiet. They sat in stunned silence for what seemed like minutes. McDaid recovered first. 'Tell us again. What do you mean? Who is fighting in Dublin?'

'It's the Irish Republican Brotherhood boys. They declared an Irish Republic and they are fighting to take over Dublin. I wish I was with them. I wish I was not stuck here in Donegal. I wish I was with them.' O'Donnell snarled in rage and frustration.

Nobody knew what to say. The news was too big for them to get their heads around it. The war was on and many men they knew were away fighting in Flanders for the English. What did this mean? Now the IRB was fighting in Dublin against the English.

O'Donnell was enraged at their lack of enthusiasm. 'What are you sitting there silent for? This is a great thing. Are you all cowards or dead or what? Now maybe we can get the English out and the country back.'

In his rage he noticed Campbell sitting at the door and moved towards him. 'What do you think, Campbell? What do you think? Is this not a great thing?' O'Donnell was ready to attack Campbell. He wanted Campbell to say something, anything that he could use as an excuse. If he could not join the boys in Dublin he could give it to this English landlord's agent, this informer, here in Donegal.

The bar went silent for a minute while O'Donnell stood waiting for Campbell to make a move. But McDaid intervened. This was not good news to him. He thought about his trips to Stranorlar and the information that he gave there. This fighting would only make things more dangerous. And it would only bring more trouble into the business. Here it was already. 'O'Donnell leave Campbell alone. He is not bothering anybody.'

Campbell threw back the remains of his whisky and with a grunt at O'Donnell pushed him to the one side and left the bar. As he walked home he thought about what he had heard. If it was true it was not good. Brown would be even worse than he was after the labour war. He would be nonstop about watching and listening to what was going on and the need to keep everybody in their place.

Back in the bar O'Donnell and McGinn were being pumped for more information but the truth was they did not have much more to give. They had heard about it from McGranahan. He had been down on a building job in Derry and had heard it there. O'Donnell and McGinn had met him when they were down in the village for a new scythe for O'Donnell. They had already told the bar all they knew. But this did not stop the speculation.

'What do you think will happen O'Donnell? Will the boys win? What do you think? What are they fighting for anyway? What are they fighting for?'

'They are fighting for the freedom of the country. What do you mean what are they fighting for? To get these British out. I wish I had known, we could have got it started here too.' McDaid was trying to keep quiet. In conversations like this he liked to listen and keep quiet. But he could not keep from speaking up here. 'Win? How could that scattering of men win against the English?'

O'Donnell was quieted for a minute. McDaid was used to being listened to. Then McGinn spoke. 'How do you know, McDaid, whether they can win or not?'

'Aye, that is right,' said O'Donnell recovering himself.

'When did it start?' McDaid asked.

'Last Monday. It's been six days already.'

'Maybe they are already beaten,' McDaid said. He could not keep quiet. He wanted them beaten as soon as possible. He did not want any risk to his business or to himself. That Stranorlar business where he visited with the Sergeant's brother, could bring bad trouble if the boys got heated up about this business in Dublin.

The bar became quiet. Every man there had been sobered and silenced by the news and by trying to figure out what it meant and what implications it had for them personally. They could not grasp it. Slowly they began to break up and head for home. They were quiet in their good-byes not like the usual noisy laughing farewells. Soon there was only O'Donnell and McGinn left sitting at the fire drinking two stouts. McDaid stayed behind the counter pretending to be busy.

'Look, McGinn, I will tell you what we will do. If we do not hear anything more at the Mass tomorrow then we will go down to the village and see what we can hear.'

McGinn shook his head. 'Sure they are all Protestants down there. It will be better to head over to Glennfinn and see some of the McHugh boys. If anybody has news they will have it. You know they have brothers in Dublin and they are all for the cause.'

'Aye, you are right. That is a better idea, McGinn.'

McDaid was thinking more about what he had said and regretting it. He had not been supportive enough of the fighting. They would think he was a traitor. 'Here boys, two more stouts.' O'Donnell and McGinn were speechless as McDaid handed them the stout. 'This is on me.' McDaid was not known for giving anybody a free drink. He pulled up a stool beside them and sat down. 'Tell me again what is happening down there in Dublin, O'Donnell.'

O'Donnell did not like McDaid. He thought he was a money grabbing bastard. The fact he was a Catholic did not change that. All he cared about was money. He knew that he overcharged the people and also that he gave short weights. But he wanted to talk about Dublin. 'Aye, it is the IRB boys and Connolly's boys from the labour war. They have joined together and are now taking on the English. Aw, McDaid, you have to acknowledge it, it is a great thing altogether. We are blessed to have lived to see it.'

McDaid was not going to make the same mistake again. 'Aye, you are right, O'Donnell. They are good men to stand up to the English that way. They are brave men all right. There are not many men like them in the country. But I am worried for them. That is why I said what I did earlier. About can they win. I am worried that they may all be killed. That would be a terrible thing to happen.'

O'Donnell and McGinn sat drinking their free stout and looking into the fire. McDaid went on. 'Look, boys, you know I am as good an Irish man as there is. I want the English out like everybody else. I just do not want them fine men like Pearse and Clarke and Connolly to be shot. To have their lives to be taken from them. Sure the country needs them too much for that to happen.' O'Donnell and McGinn sat in silence. In their excitement they had not thought about these men maybe being killed.

McDaid was not used to O'Donnell having nothing to say. He felt obliged to go on. 'Look, boys, be careful what you are saying now around here. There will be damage done to a lot of people over this. Maybe you do not want to be shouting so loud about things to you see how they turn out. I mean the walls can have ears you know. You never know who might be hearing you. You never know who might be passing on what you are saying.'

The two of them had finished their stouts by this time. 'Aye, well we will be off, McDaid. We will see you the morrow.'

'Aye, men, mind what I said now.' He shut the door after them.

That was better. He was not so worried now. He had told them he was for the men, that he was against the English. That was a good job. He breathed out a loud breath of relief as he went in behind the bar and in the door to the kitchen. His wife and the weans were in bed. He was relieved but he was still uneasy. This could turn out bad yet. He would have to watch. Especially about that Stranorlar business.

'Listen to him. Did you hear him, McGinn?' O'Donnell and McGinn were walking up the dirt road. The moon was bright and the sky cloudless. O'Donnell stopped and began to urinate in the stream beside the road. McGinn did the same. They both looked out over the valley lit by the moonlight. It was beautiful and peaceful. They were both with the men in Dublin in their heads. What were they going through while they were standing here in the moonlight looking out over this peaceful beautiful valley?

'Will you tell me Sean O'Farrell where the Rising's going to be, in the old field by the river so well known to you and me and the pikes they will be gleaming in the rising of the moon,' O'Donnell sang but he could never remember all the words to the old songs so he would make up his own. Tonight he wanted to sing about the men in Dublin, their heroism and so the lack of words did not stop him.

'Aye, did you hear him, O'Donnell? That bastard McDaid. He would sell his own grandmother. Him trying to convince us that he is for the boys in Dublin. Look, he is always pulling you off that Campbell informer. That McDaid does not want any change in anything. He is making his money, the drink and the groceries, he is making his money. He wants no trouble. He was only covering his back there trying to say he was for the boys. And the walls have ears. Aye, they might but they would not need them with him about. He would tell all in a minute to the English if it kept him in business.'

'Look, McGinn, tomorrow morning we will head over to Glenfinn. Is that right with you? We will see if they have any news over there about things. If it is still going on, I might try and get down to Dublin.'

'That is good with me, O'Donnell. Call down for me around ten and we will head off. The boys over in Glenfinn should know if anybody knows.' McGinn turned into his cottage and O'Donnell headed on up the road to his own place.

'Oh, I met with Napper Tandy and he took me by the hand. How are things you boy you, how are things in Ireland.' O'Donnell's singing trailed off as he could not sing and he could not remember the words. But he thought of the Napper Tandys and all the people who had to leave the land the English had taken from them. Left them out on the road. His own relatives were mainly in America. Where, he did not know. He was only still here because his mother had only had him. Only the one child. The few fields were enough to keep them and she needed somebody to help her. His father had died in Scotland in some sort of an accident when he was working there.

O'Donnell sat down on a rock. Aye, he would not miss this chance. He would join up with them boys in Dublin. He would try and get it started here in Donegal. Maybe the boys in Derry would start it. McGinn was a good man and there were more. But he would need to get some guns. Where could he get these? That would be the thing. He would have to get contact with Dublin. He hoped the Glenfinn boys would know how to make the contact. They are supposed to be in the know.

He walked on. Aye, tomorrow he would know a lot more about what was happening. Then he would be able to decide what to do. But one thing he was sure he would not stand back and do nothing. That McDaid pretending he was for the Cause. The only cause he was for was his pocket. That would be the way it would be. The ones with the money and the property would be against it even if they were Catholics and Irish. The ones that would be for it would be the people like himself, those with nothing or next to nothing.

CHAPTER THIRTY

'Ah, Campbell. You are on time. That is good.' Campbell did not
answer but he thought that he was always on time so what was Brown
talking about. 'Ah, you are on time that is good. Come on in here. I
must get that boy to brush up this harness shop more regularly. That
is the problem, everything is getting harder to keep in line, to keep as
it should be. The young ones they have not the same attitude as our
generation, Campbell. They do not want to work. That is a major
problem.

'But that is not what I want to talk about, Campbell. It is about
that business in Dublin. It always seems to be in Dublin. First that
labour war and now this treason. This stabbing of His Majesty in the
back when we are at war with Germany. I have no doubt the Germans
financed and organized the whole thing. But, Campbell, you know
how these people here are so simple minded. They might begin to
think that the Dublin treason was in some way connected to their own
imagined grievances.

'I know that the cost of food has gone up, that a lot of the young
men are abroad doing their duty and many dying, but this Dublin treason has nothing to do with that. It is just some German organized
business. But as I say, some of these people here might think it had
something to do with the high prices, their rents, their young people
off at war doing their duty and many of them dying. It is over now,

Campbell. The leaders are being shot and the rest of them are locked up and will be kept there. It is only what they deserve.

'But what I want from you, Campbell, is just like after the labour war, to keep an ear open for any kind of talk about the Dublin treason. Especially if anybody thinks it is a good thing. And keep an eye out for any signs of support for it. Along with that keep a good grip on things. Don't let anything slack. Don't let any slide in the rents. Keep a tight grip of things. We are still in charge no matter what about any Dublin rebellion, I mean treason. Have you heard anything at all? I know it is early days yet.'

Campbell weighed up what he would do. It was not that he had any qualms about informing on O'Donnell and McGinn it was just that he did not want to give Brown anything for nothing. And on top of that he was growing more and more aware that he did not like Brown and that Brown thought that he was a piece of dirt. But he thought it would help him better if he told.

'Aye, in McDaid's on Saturday night O'Donnell and McGinn came in very excited and supporting the rebellion.'

'Supporting the treason,' Brown corrected.

'Aye, the treason. They said it was a good thing and that now maybe the English could be driven out and the Irish could get the country back. But there was no support for it in the rest of the bar. They just kept silent and got up and went home. McDaid said the treason could never win.'

'That boy O'Donnell again. This is very good to get this information, Campbell, and the rest of the pub said nothing?'

'Aye.' Campbell grunted.

'Well that is good, it shows good sense on these men's part. Anybody who supports this treason will have a price to pay. This is a serious business. Attacking His Majesty's back while we are in the war against the Germans. There will be a price to pay for this.

'Well that is all, Campbell. I will see you next Wednesday but if you hear anything of value come down and let me know. We have to keep a tight grip on things.' Brown turned and walked out of the harness room and into his house. As usual he made no effort to bid Campbell goodbye or to show any courtesy of any kind. Campbell was increasingly aware of and annoyed by this.

As he walked up the road he considered this. It never made him this mad before. He did not know how long it had been going on. Maybe since that labour war in Dublin. Where Brown had kept at him all the time to keep his eye out and to keep tight control. Then there was herself. She was getting harder to control. Now there was this treason in Dublin. He was against them all, he opposed them all. But now he too found at times that he himself also wanted to rebel at something, to change something.

He heard a horse and trap in the distance. It was coming to meet him and as it came into view he saw it was McCausiland who had that big place over the hill on the road into Letterkenny. He was moving fast. What did he want? There must be some emergency that he was pushing the horse like that. As the horse and trap and McCausiland came up to Campbell the driver pulled on the reins and the bit between the horses teeth cut cruelly into its mouth and it was pulled to a halt.

'Campbell, get in here. I need your help.' McCausiland was close with Brown. It would be better for Campbell to go along. McCausiland held open the door of the trap. It never occurred to him that Campbell would do anything but what he was told. Campbell got in and McCausliand turned the horse and trap around and set off at a canter again up the hill road. 'Campbell, I have a cow down in the upper fields near the bog and she is trying to calf and cannot. I need you to help out.' Campbell grunted his assent.

'The head is out but the front feet are stuck. If she does not get it out soon then she and calf and all will be dead. I have a rope here and we can use that. I thought it would be closer to get somebody coming down this way than going all the way back into the home place. My own hands are working down in the lower fields near Letterkenny.

'Campbell, what do you think about that Dublin business? The traitors down there stabbing His Majesty in the back. There we are at war with the Germans and then this. Well it's over now and a load of them are being shot. It's only what they deserve.'

Two men could be seen walking in their direction on the road in the distance. They soon came closer as the horse was moving at speed. It was O'Donnell and McGinn. Campbell was sure that they were up to no good. 'Maybe we would need another man, Campbell. Maybe I should take one of these boys. It would be better to have too many hands than too few.' He pulled the horse and trap to a stop beside the two men. 'One of you men jump in here and come with us and give us a hand. I have a cow calving and need an extra hand. Get up here one of you.'

O'Donnell and McGinn stood and looked up at McCausiland. Then at Campbell. It was McGinn who spoke first. 'Give you a hand? Why should we give you a hand? When did you ever give us a hand? Anytime we worked for you you paid us next to nothing. Go on and look after your own cow. We are not like Campbell there who will do whatever you crowd will tell him to keep in with you. And I will tell you what, you see this Dublin rebellion, before it is all over you and your kind will be finished.'

O'Donnell found his voice then. 'Aye, you will be all put out of the country. That is what will happen to you all. You should never have been here in the first place. Give you a hand? Who do you think you are talking to? Before Connolly and the boys are finished with you, you will get a hand all right. You and your big place while the rest of us have to get by on a couple of acres or have to leave the country to Scotland or America. Those of us you do hire you pay us nothing.'

McCausiland was shocked into silence by the open defiance of the two men. That they would stand there and tell him this to his face was something new to him. He did not know what to say.

Then they started on Campbell. 'Aye, and look at you, Campbell. It was Allen, who is another boy like McCausiland here, with a big place, while the rest of us have nothing, who worked your wife to the bone and abused her. And here you are nothing but an ass kisser for them. Doing whatever they tell you. And look at your wife's brothers slaving over there at Kilgore's for a few crusts of bread.'

McGinn joined in. 'Aye, if we had something wrong at our place, McCausiland, would you come running and help us? Hah. You would not even notice us on the road if you did not need something. And you look out, Campbell, when you get over there it will be you that will be doing all the dirty work and the man pulling to get that cow calved. McCausiland here will not be doing it. The truth is that the McCausilands, the Browns, the Allens, the Kilgores think no more of you, even though you are a Protestant, than they do of us.'

With that O'Donnell and McGinn walked on down the mountain road. After a minute when he tried to recover himself McCausiland started up the horse again and headed on up the road. 'Well did you ever hear the like of that, Campbell? Those boys need to be taught manners. They need to be horse whipped. You know what it is. That labour war was the start of it, then with all the men off at war there is a shortage of hands in the country, and then this rebellion, I mean this treason in Dublin. These boys are getting away above themselves. They will have to be taught a lesson.'

Campbell made no answer and the both of them stayed silent as the horse broke into a gallop and pulled them up over the edge of the mountain and down towards the fields where Campbell knew

McCausiland's cow would be. 'She is over there. Do you see? There, Campbell, there. Below the big tree.' Campbell could see a cow lying on her side. The horse and trap drove in the open gate and in minutes they were beside the stricken animal. They both jumped down.

The cow did not move. She was exhausted and the calf's head stuck out of her back end. 'Try and see if you can get the front legs out, Campbell, and we can get this rope on them and see if we can get it out.' As Campbell got down on a knee beside the cow and pushed his hands up inside the cow beside the calf's neck and felt around for the front legs, he remembered what O'Donnell and McGinn had said. Aye, he was doing the dirty work all right. He felt one of the front legs and then the other. And putting his shoulder against the calf's head and pushing it back he managed to get the two front legs out a few inches.

McCausiland reached him the rope. He put this in a sliding loop around the two legs and got to his feet and began to pull at the calf. It was still alive. This was good. Maybe everything would be all right yet. He pulled and the cow began to push again as she felt something changing in her. She roared with the pain of it. Campbell pulled but he was not making much headway. After a few minutes he was sweating and egged on by the words of McGinn and O'Donnell he looked around at McCausiland who was directing him.

He looked directly at McCausiland and anger and frustration were in his eyes. McCausiland could see this and thinking also about the words of O'Donnell and McGinn and thinking of the loss it would be to him if the cow and calf died, he moved over behind Campbell and took a hold of the rope and the two of them began to pull. It did not escape Campbell's notice that McCausiland had moved to take hold of the clean end of the rope, the part furthest away from the cow.

After ten minutes of pulling and extra efforts by the cow, the calf slid out onto the grass. The cow got to her feet and began licking the calf. The afterbirth slid out of her onto the grass. Campbell and

McCausiland stood getting their breath back. 'Well thanks, Campbell. Without you I am not sure if I would have managed it.' Already McCausiland was playing down Campbell's role. Without Campbell he would have a dead cow and dead calf. But it was never good to give people like Campbell too much credit. They would be expecting too much in return. They would get above their station.

'Campbell, I will mention to Brown the service that you did me. I am sure he will be glad to hear how helpful you have been. And when you think that those two boys would have left me on my own and the cow and the calf would have been.....' He stopped. He did not want to say that Campbell had saved his cow and calf. The calf by this time was stumbling to its feet. Campbell stepped forward and directed it into the cow's udder and put a teat in its mouth and it began to suck the mother's milk.

'Well, Campbell, I will stay here with her for a little while and then I will have to be down to see what those boys at the bottom fields are at. You know yourself if boys like that are left on their own they will not keep at the work. You have to keep on them. I would give you a ride up again if it were not for that. But I will tell Brown how helpful you have been and he will be glad to hear that. Watch yourself on your way back. Keep an eye out for those two boys. They are not good boys.'

Campbell lifted his coat from where it was lying on the grass. He put it on as he turned and began to walk towards the gate out of the field and head up the side of the mountain towards home. He was enraged and in an inner struggle with himself. O'Donnell and McGinn had described exactly how McCausiland would treat him. Look now he even had to walk back home again. Campbell was only a pair of hands to be used whenever they wanted them and then ignored.

But to think like O'Donnell and McGinn. That was impossible.

They were always looking for some kind of trouble. They were always getting above themselves. Trying to change things. Just what Campbell knew was no way to live. It never worked trying to change things. The powers that be would be the powers that be. Campbell raged in himself at the two of them for so accurately describing what would happen. Then he raged at himself and at McCausiland for treating him like dirt. In his anger he went back and forward between McCausiland on the one hand and O'Donnell and McGinn on the other.

The walk up the mountain, the rhythm of it, the familiarity of the fields changing into bog and rocks. Up over the top and down the other side. Here he was in familiar territory as it was Taverstock's bog. He cast an eye out over it. Noting the divisions and seeing if he could catch anybody over their line. That Pollock he would have to deal with him. But with that exception things looked in order. Aye, he was keeping things in order. Brown knew that he was a good man at keeping things in order and getting in the rent. Campbell felt his superiority over the O'Donnells and the McGinns and herself and her folks with his position as the on-the-ground agent for the bog for Brown who was the agent for Taverstock.

He began to get things in order in his mind as he saw the order he was imposing on the bog. Aye, McCausiland was who he was, but then what did you expect. The big boys were all like that. They thought they were better than everybody else. This was the way things were. There was nothing could be done about it. What was he getting angry at McCausiland for? This was the way things were. He had to accept it. That was that. It was those boys O'Donnell and McGinn who were to blame. Trying to stir things up. Trying to change things. Like herself she was trying to change things and get the better of himself.

He felt the anger and the stress reduce in him. He felt the balance that he had created in himself come back. Aye, there was no sense in getting mad at the McCausilands of this world. They were who they were and they were in charge. He accepted that. The problem was that the O'Donnells and the McGinns and herself did not, this was what caused the problems. He would see to it that they were all kept in their place to the extent that it was in his power. Gradually he felt the balance return to him. There was no way out by challenging those above them.

CHAPTER THIRTY ONE

Campbell was off to Donegal Town with Brown. He would be away for two to three days. He was looking at some cattle that Brown wanted to buy there. If he bought them Campbell would be walking them back home. Margaret had been waiting for just such a break as this. She was finished her work around the house and she called Victoria in from the front yard where she was playing. It was a beautiful summer day.

'Victoria, we are going to the lake today. We want to take your wee sister Anne to see the lake for the first time. You and Mary have already been there. But I am going to go every year so that all my children can see it. We have to get Mary and Anne. Will you help me, Victoria? I need your help.'

'I help Mammy.' Margaret looked at her wee girl as she said this and felt all her warmth and solidarity go out to her. They got Mary who was able to walk a little by this stage and Margaret lifted Anne onto her haunch and they set off. Margaret knew that Mary would never be able to walk all the way but she had decided that she was going to the lake every year. Partly for her own mother and partly for her children. As they set off the sun was shining from a perfectly clear sky and it was warm. enough after a few hundred yards Mary had to be carried too. Victoria toddled at Margaret's side holding on to her skirt and Margaret carried the two younger children one on each haunch. It was not easy but Margaret was young and strong. She was able to carry the two young ones. As she walked she talked to the children.

'Victoria, that is a benweed, that is a thistle, do not touch it, it is sharp, that is a nettle do not touch it, it will sting you. There is a whole lot of crows, Victoria, look at them flying off as they have seen us coming.' Victoria would repeat some of the words of each sentence Margaret would say and in this way she was learning to speak.

'Mammy look, more birds, what are they?'

'They are thrushes, Victoria. See their kind of speckled front. They are scratching in the ground trying to catch some worms to eat.'

'Worms to eat Mammy,' Victoria said.

Then, 'Worms worms.' This was Mary she was saying her first words.

'Yes, Mary,' Margaret said. 'Worms. The birds eat them.'

'Eat,' Mary said.

Then it was Victoria. 'The birds eat them. Mammy, the birds eat them. Mary, birds eat them.'

'Worm,' Mary replied. Margaret was almost overcome with emotion. Her two oldest children and herself were for the first time talking to each other as a group. Her life was worth living after all. If only for this moment.

Anne was sleeping in her arms but Mary was awake and looking around her. 'Look, Mary, there is the lake. Over there we can see the first part of it. It's called Proctor's rock. That is the lake.' In five more minutes they were at the lake's edge. Margaret laid Anne down asleep on the soft warm grass between the rocks where she had taken to sitting now on her visits there. Victoria was already putting her wee feet in the water and yelling in delight.

Margaret took Mary and held her and together they walked into the water and Victoria and Mary screamed with pleasure as the soft warm water tickled their legs. As she played with the children and walked in the water, Margaret felt the terrible tension of her life fall away. Life was so hard that every six months or so at most, there were a few moments to relax and be at peace. The last time she remembered was when she and Katie had biscuits together when she had sold her first eggs to McDaid.

What kind of a life was it when only every six months or so was there a moment, or a few moments, of peace? Margaret sighed deeply as she thought of this. Yes only a few minutes of peace every year. She would come up here every year with all the children and the new one every year. This was for her mother and the weans and herself. She would make this a high point of each year. A yearly ceremony. Something to look forward to. Each new child would see the lake for the first time in its first year and every year after that.

The weans were feeling the effects of the walk and were quieting down. Victoria and Mary came and joined Anne in the little grassy hollow. In a few minutes they were asleep lying warm in the summer sun. Margaret looked at her three children lying at peace. They were so young. So vulnerable. They lay there with their little arms and legs trusting that they were safe. Trusting that Margaret would keep them safe. She had done so this far in their lives.

They were growing up quick. The time was going on. Margaret was now the mother of three children and very soon would be pregnant with the fourth. She sat up straighter as she realised that she could no longer be considered a child. It was true she was only seventeen. But what she had come through, what she had experienced, made her a grown woman. She sighed as she thought about her last five years. Life was not easy. Life for her had not been easy. Her father, Allen, Campbell.

But she would not let what happened to her happen to her three wee ones and the ones to come. She would not let Campbell hire them out so there would be more money. She would not let this happen. She would not let them be put in her situation. She would stop it. Look at the wee legs of them, the wee arms, the wee mouths on them, no she would not let the Allens of this world get their hands on them. She would .... But and then she pulled herself up. How could she stop it?

She was protecting them now by doing what Campbell needed of her, the work around the house with the cow and calf, the work in the house, the food and fire and letting him come to her when he wanted. She was doing all this so the children could survive, so they would not be harmed. But they were too young to work anyway. What would happen when they grew up, when they got to eleven and twelve and thirteen and were old enough to work? And the house was full of children as she was having one every year. What would happen then? How would she be able to protect them then?

With that many in the house there would be no room. Somebody, more than somebody, would have to move out. Where would they go to? Who would take them? There would be no place for them to go but to be hired out. To go to work for the Allens and their kind. Margaret rebelled against her own thinking. No, they could stay at home even if there were twelve, thirteen, fourteen, of them. They could stay at home. But then she thought. How would they be fed? There would never be enough to feed them all. She might get one or two of them jobs where they could still live at home, maybe in Browns. But there would never be enough room and food for them all at home.

Margaret went round and round this in her mind. She could see no way out. What could she do? She was not going to sit and do nothing. She resolved that as soon as Victoria got up and old enough to work she would walk to Brown's and ask them to take her on as a servant in their house. That was what she would do. Then she would try others like the Brown's and see if they could be taken on as servants in the big houses.

She knew that the possibility of placing them all in the big houses as servants was very small. But she could not do nothing. And this was better than them going to work for some farmer like Allen and sleeping in his barn and being attacked. She had to fight and she would fight to protect them. They were her children. She had had them. She would fight for them. Whatever happened they must not go to the Allens of the area. This must not be allowed to happen.

If only she owned something, some bit of land, some house, if only she owned the house and not Campbell. She owned nothing but the clothes on her back. And even those, he owned everything. She only had the few pence from the eggs. She owned nothing. If you did not own anything in this country then you were stuck. It was only men that owned things. Women did not own things. This was not fair. But how could she change this? She could not do it. She did not even know how people got to own things. So how could she change this?

Maybe she could stop having babies. Then if she had only four or five they would all be able to stay in the house until they got men of their own and got married. But even then Campbell would want them out and want their earnings just like her own father had done. But anyway she could not stop having babies. If she refused Campbell there would be nothing but trouble and maybe he would put her out and the wee ones with her. She could not stop him doing it to her.

Was there a way to let him do it and not have a baby? She had never heard of such a thing. If he put his thing in her she got pregnant. That was the way it was. She knew of no way out of this. She looked down at the three sleeping children. She felt herself go weak as she looked at them and felt her heart and her warmth go out to them. She would have to find some way to protect them.

If things went on as they were doing she would have twenty-five or more weans before she was too old to have any more. How was she going to manage? Yes the older ones would help her. Victoria was already helping her. That was the only way it would work. With over twenty weans she could not do everything herself. And the good thing is that Victoria likes helping her. This is very good. She would have to bring them all up to help. They could not expect her to do everything.

But was there some way to keep him from putting a new wean in her every year? If there were this would be such a burden off her back. Maybe she would ask Katie. She had no weans at all. Maybe she would know. She brightened up as even this smallest of plans was better than having no plan at all. That is what she would do, she would ask Katie. She would know if anybody would.

She lay down beside the children. She watched the sky and the sun above her. There were no clouds at all. It was a beautiful day. How did her mother do it? She had only five of them. Was she able to stop her father or did she know how not to have weans? She thought of her mother and father. She did not think her mother was able to stop him putting his thing in her. Her father was too much like Allen and like Campbell.

Why was it that men seemed to be so set on putting their things in women? What was it they got out of it? She got nothing out if it. Allen had definitely got something out of it or he would not have forced her again and again to let him. But what? When Allen was forcing her he always had that look on his face. Like he was attacking her, that cruel look, that mean vicious look. Then when he was finished he had that other look. Like disgust with her and everything including himself. And he would spit out the words. 'That will teach her.'

Campbell, when he did it? Well she never saw Campbell's face after he did it. It was always dark. But from what she could see and what she could hear he did not seem to be too happy doing it or after doing it either. It was like a bit of him was determined to do it to her and to make her let him do it. This seemed to be the main thing. Dominating and controlling her. Like he had to do it rather than he wanted to do it.

She got nothing out of it. It was like that piece of her had been killed off when Allen had attacked her. Even before that with all the talk of her mother and the church and sin and women. To the extent she felt anything when they were doing it she felt pain. She got no pleasure out of any of it. Was this it all the time for every woman? That the men forced all the women to do it? Either by physical force as in the case of Allen and her, or by owning things and controlling women, and that was force too, as in the case of Campbell and her.

So would there be no weans at all if the men did not force the women? Was that it? She could not believe that. She loved her weans. She would do anything for them. She would never want a life without weans. But she wanted nothing to do with men putting their things in her and giving her weans. There must be something wrong somewhere. Why could she not like to make the weans when she liked to have them so much? There was something she did not know. There must be a way to like making weans when she liked having them and bringing them up so much.

She lay down beside the children in the little grassy hollow by the lake. The sun was shining and warming her body. She could feel the slightest wee breeze on her but it was not enough to do away with the heat of the sun. She could hear the little waves of the lake rolling up on the shore. She was tired trying to think out all the issues. She was tired and needed to rest. She felt at peace as she felt the heat of her children as they snuggled into her. She slept.

As she did so she dreamt. She dreamt that she was at home in the cottage. That Campbell was dead. That she owned the cottage and her fourth wean had been born. She was no longer forced to do everything he wanted. To cook and work for him and let him do it to her. She was on her own with the weans. She felt like smiling in her sleep. But then her dream took a turn. How would she live? Where would she get any money?

She awoke with a start. The dream had made her happy and then dashed her happiness. She was trapped. Even if she could get rid of Campbell and she had no more weans and was left with the cottage, she would need more than she could grow and raise for the children. She was trapped. There was no way out. She would have to continue to endure the conditions of her life.

She looked down at her three children sleeping in the sun. This was what would give her the strength. This was what would keep her from drying up and dying inside completely. This was what would keep her human. The children. In spite of all the rest, in spite of all the suffering, the children made her life worth continuing with. This was the certainty in her life. This was the foundation in her life.

She watched as a great hawk rested in the air motionless looking down at its prey. It must be a small rabbit or mouse or something like that. Then it moved off in the sky. Its prey must have seen it and moved out of reach. She saw the flock of sheep on the side of the hill that stretched down to the other side of the lake. They seemed at peace as they ate the grass. She watched as two black crows flew over the lake and over her head and disappeared over the hill behind her.

Victoria woke and looked up at her. 'Mammy. Mammy.' And she moved to lie closer to her and put out her tiny hand and took Margaret's. The touch of her tiny fingers. The feel of her tiny hand. These were the things that healed Margaret from the wounds of her life enough to allow her to go on. She held Victoria's hand and looked at the fingers and the little palm. How was it made? That was what she did not know. This wonderful little thing.

She lay back again and slowly drifted off to sleep herself. As she did so she felt again the heat of the sun penetrating into her body. It was healing her. As was the sound of the lake. Coming to the lake every year with her new child this helped to heal her. This helped to keep her going. This peacefulness and the beauty of the lake and the hills and mountains around her, this helped to heal her enough to keep her going on. And the time away from Campbell, not waiting for him to appear, knowing he was not going to appear and shout at her, or ignore her or even hit her. This was also a part of it. His absence made it possible for her to appreciate the wonders of the nature around her and the wonder of her little children and to feel at peace for a while. She fell asleep in the summer sun and with the clear sky above her head. She would survive.

CHAPTER THIRTY TWO

'Look at the three of them lying there sleeping. Sure you are a lucky woman, Margaret. Myself and Shanks sure we would have given anything for the children. To have a wheen of children. But it was not to be. It was the Lord's will. That is what it was. If it wasn't, I could not live with it, Margaret. That is how much I love weans. But you have to accept the Lord's will. There is no getting around it. Myself and Shanks, we were heartbroken but now we know it is the Lord's will. We help other people with the spare time we would have used if we had been looking after the children.'

Margaret was disappointed. So Katie did not know the secret of keeping babies away at all. She and Shanks had just been unlucky. That is what it was. They had just been unlucky. Margaret and Katie were standing in the doorway to the bedroom where the three children slept on the bed. She would just have to go on having babies.

'Margaret, they are doing terribly well. The three weans they are a credit to you. It will not be long to the winter again, Margaret. Now with the two eldest of them able to paddle about you will need more clothes for them. I could show you how to do a bit of knitting. That would be easy enough. You can get the wool and the needles in McDaid's with the egg money. That old swindler he would be good for nothing if it wasn't for that he sold some house things along with the drink.

'Next time you are down there with the eggs buy yourself a couple of needles and some wool. I will get you started. There is nothing like a bit of a wool jumper to get you through the winter. To get the weans through the winter. Sure I tell you what, Margaret, why do you not run on down there now and get yourself some and I will look after the weans?'

Margaret looked at her and did not speak.

'Go on ahead, Margaret, I will look after the weans.' Still Margaret did not move or speak.

It dawned on Katie. 'What is the matter, Margaret? Maybe you have no eggs to sell to him today. That does not matter. He will give you those few things on tick. He will take the price of them out of the next eggs you take in. He knows that you are not going to up and leave the country, that he will get his money all right.'

Margaret understood the idea all right but she could not bring herself to do it. It would take too many words to a stranger, to McDaid.

Katie then realised this too. 'Come on then, Margaret. Gather them up, get them up and the two of us will take them down to McDaid's and we will get you the wool and the needles.' Katie put her arm around Margaret and pushed her into action. Pushed her towards the children. Once she got moving she was okay. The children awoke to her touch and Katie took Victoria by the hand and Mary in her other hand and with Margaret carrying Anne, they set out.

Victoria's eyes were like two saucers as she looked around her as they set off down the road. She had never been there before. Only around the cottage and up to the lake. There were two other places on the way to McDaid's. Tinneys and the Reids. They were wee cottages like their own. They both had dogs and Reids had a couple of old goats. One was tied to the tree in front of the house. The dogs came out and ushered them past Tinney's but nobody appeared.

At Reid's it was a different case altogether. The dogs announced their presence on the road. They barked and barked and jumped around them. The children were not afraid as they were used to their own dog. The goat reared up on its back legs and made efforts to jump at them. The children stared at it and held Margaret's and Katie's hands. Then old man Reid came out. 'Sure it is yourself, Katie. How are you anyway? And Missus Campbell. It is not often we see you and the weans down this far. Won't you come in and have a cup of tea?'

'We are on our way down to McDaid's to buy a couple of things, Liam, if it was not for that, and that Margaret here has to get back to do the milking and see to things, we would be more than glad to come in and sit a while. But we have to be going on. How are you keeping yourself and all your ones? Are they well.?'

'Aye, God be praised, Katie, everybody is grand. Everybody is grand.'

'I thought that you would not want to go in and sit there for an hour, Margaret.' Margaret looked at her and her expression told it all. She was rigid with stress. The thought of having to go in to a stranger's house and sit there and talk. And talk! She would be forever thankful to Katie who understood her so well. 'Aye you would never get away from that Reid man. He is a very nice man but he does not know when to stop the talking. But he knows a lot about these parts and who lived here before we were around. His missus is passed on.'

'How are youse doing, Missus? It is a grand day. And a great day to bring the children down for their first time.' It was McDaid himself. Sometimes McDaid's wife was in the shop but only if he was too busy in the bar or away on some job or other. McDaid did not trust her. The last thing he wanted was for her to get an idea how much he took in and how much he had put away. Then she would be up for trying to get more out of him. Aye, the best place for her was in the kitchen at the back, keeping her nose out of things that were none of her affair.

But this time she heard the talk and the children and she came out. 'How are you, Katie and how are you, Margaret? And look at the weans. Sure they are fine young ones altogether. Here let me see you,' and she reached out for Victoria who held tighter to her mother's hand and tried to hide behind her legs. 'Well then you are shy now. How old is she, Margaret?' But it was all too much for Margaret, it was too much happening together with too many strangers. She could not speak. She could not speak.

The McDaid woman did not know what to do. Katie filled the gap. 'She is three, Mrs McDaid.'

'Well, she is a great big girl for three. And the others?'

Katie took over again. 'Two and almost one.'

'Sure they are great weans. Margaret, you have done a great job bringing them up so fine.' The McDaid woman called her Margaret. There was no way she would call her Mrs Campbell. After all she did not own a bar and shop. But the talking was too much for Margaret.

'Wool, needles. Wool, needles.' She looked around her as she stood there holding Anne. 'Wool, needles.' She was speaking out to halt the other chat.

Both the McDaids straightened up from where they were bent over with the children. They did not understand why Margaret was being so impolite.

'Aye, Missus McDaid, Margaret here wants to get some wool off you and some needles so she can get started with knitting a few jumpers for the young ones for the winter. You never know how soon it will come on us and Margaret wants to be sure she has them done well in time. Have you got any wool and needles?'

McDaid recovered. It never took him long to recover when there was money to be made. 'Aye, we have this wool, made down there in the mill, it's from our own sheep and our own mill. But here is some other stuff from over in Antrim. I have the needles here too. What size do you want?'

Katie picked the middle size needles and she offered the wool to Margaret. 'What colour would you like, Margaret?' But Margaret stood quiet and unmoving.

This time Katie would not go along. The truth was she was getting a bit angry and impatient with Margaret. 'No, Margaret, you will have to choose. These are for your children and so you have to choose which colour you want them in. Here look, there are the two colours. Have a look at them here and see. Which do you want, the more greenish one or the more brown one?' The local mill never made anything but brown and green tweeds and very dark navy blues. These were the colours of the clothes of the Protestant squires and yeomen. The followers of the landlords. No exotic colours allowed. The Antrim mill must have been Protestant too.

Margaret stood holding Victoria and looking down at her feet. She would not look up or look at the wool or talk.

'Here, Margaret, I am not going to choose for you. This is important to the children and to you. You have to choose the colour that is best for you and for the weans. I am not doing it. Which do you want?' McDaid started to speak and then kept quiet. He was not sure what it was but something was going on and he wanted to see what it was and also to see if he could get something from it.

As it turned out he got nothing but the sale of the balls of wool. Margaret heard the tone of strength in Katie's voice. She also was moved by the talk of the children. She had to do this, she had to pick what was best for the children, what she liked best for them. It was mainly the presence of others and the oppression of the past that kept her from speaking. But that was not the only thing. She was stunned by the understanding that she had the right to choose something for herself. This was almost too overwhelming. She had had few times to make choices for herself over the past years.

Only on a few occasions could she do it. When she decided to speak out, when she had decided to sell the eggs, these were choices she had made, and now which wool. Now again it was to do with the children's welfare and future. What colour of jumpers would they wear? This was the question today. In a way this was much more difficult for her than the decisions about speaking out and keeping the egg money. Because this was not a matter of crucial importance to them, it was a matter of colour, of taste.

It was even more shocking to her that she should be given the chance to choose on such an unimportant thing. The colour of the jumpers. 'Margaret, we will have to be getting back soon. Have you...?'

'The brown one.'

They were all shocked. But Katie recovered quickly. 'The brown one it is. Mr McDaid, do you have by any chance a dozen balls of that brown stuff. That is what we will need just for starters. To get you started, Margaret, and to get you on the way.'

'Aye, here there are a dozen. I have plenty more too. Maybe you should take another dozen. You will go through the first dozen quicker than you think.'

'Margaret does not have any money with her today, Mr. McDaid. She will be wanting you to take it out of the egg money. I told her that you did this with all of us. That you were an accommodating man with a wee bit of credit.'

When he heard this McDaid made no more mention of the second dozen.

'Aye, I suppose the one dozen will do you to get her started, Katie, all right. I will take this out of the eggs. Margaret is bringing me down a dozen and a half to two dozen every week. Sure at that rate this will be paid off in four weeks.'

'Four weeks, Mr McDaid? That sounds a long time. Are you sure? Margaret cannot afford to be out more than is fair.'

'Well, let me see again. Well, do you know but you are right Katie. Six dozen will cover the whole thing and an extra pair of needles.'

'What would Margaret be doing with an extra pair of needles, Mr McDaid? It is not like she will be travelling or anything and loss them. Naw, give her an extra ball of wool up front now instead. Look, Mr McDaid, she is a good customer and her husband is a good customer. Be fair now. Three weeks eggs, that will cover it.'

McDaid knew what she was doing, three weeks instead of six dozen eggs. Going by the weeks and not the eggs helped Margaret. But it was not the time to argue. Who knows what that Campbell woman will get up to? Faint or have a fit or something? At the end of it he was glad to see the two of them with the three children leave his shop.

The children were asleep in the bed again. They were exhausted from their travels. Margaret and Katie sat by the fire on two three legged stools. The light came in through the open door and the one window. They could see what they were doing. 'Look here, Margaret, the first thing is to get it cast on. To get it onto the needle.' Katie worked slowly and cast the wool onto the first needle.

'See that is easy now.' Then she pulled it off again. 'Here now, Margaret, you do it.'

In less than an hour Margaret was knitting away. 'That is great, Margaret, you are a fast learner. But here now, what are you going to knit?'

Margaret looked up at her. She had not thought of that in her excitement at learning to knit. She said nothing.

'Look maybe for the wee one first. Naw, that would not be best. For Victoria first then you can have it to pass down when she grows out of it. Well, let's get started on Victoria.'

'Here is what you do. You have to measure Victoria. Come on over and we will get her measured. You have no tape? Well that is not a problem. We will use a bit of wool.' She took a bit of wool and tied a knot in the end. Victoria was lying on her front. 'Look here, you will need it to be big enough to fit on her. But you will have to knit it in two parts.'

Katie held the knot in the piece of wool to Victoria's side and stretched it across her back to the middle of her other side. 'Don't wake her, the front will be the same size. Now, Margaret, you will have to knit a piece this wide and then another piece the same and then we will sew them together and this way we will have a jumper for her. Sure it will be no trouble at all. I will help you with the small things when you get there. The thing is to get you started on the back and the front. Then we can do the sleeves the same way. In two pieces.'

They went back to the fire and Katie stretched the piece of wool out along the needle. She then noted the length she wanted on the needle and then had Margaret cast on enough stitches to cover this length of the needle. She then took the second needle and helped Margaret knit along this length and then back along the same length on the other needle, then back along the original needle, and back and again and on.

After six rows you could see the shape of the back of the jumper take form. 'Carry on now, Margaret, and in no time at all you will have it done. When you get near it, have Victoria stand up and you can measure her so it's the right length. Anyway I will help you also especially when it comes for you to have to finish it and cast off. Between us we will have jumpers for your whole family including yourself and Campbell by the winter. You see, did I not tell you that it was easy? All those nights here yourself and you will knit any amount. After a while you won't even need the light to knit with.'

Katie got up to leave but this time Margaret was more up to what should be done. She got up along with Katie. 'Sit down, Katie.' This was only the second time she had ever called Katie by her name. 'I will get some tea.'

'Naw, naw, not at all, Margaret. I will be going.'

'Naw, Katie. Some tea.' They went back and forward a few more times, Katie saying no out of politeness and Margaret saying yes in determination and meaning it. After a reasonable time, Katie sat down in agreement.

Margaret threw some sticks and then some turf on the fire and pushed the water over the flames. In no time at all it was boiling and Margaret made the tea and got out some bread and together they sat and drank and ate. They also had some biscuits. 'Margaret, thanks for the drop of tea. It will get me home. There is nothing like a good cup of strong tea to send you on your way. Shanks will be home by now and him and my father will be ready for theirs. It will not take me long to get it for them.'

Margaret sat in conflict with herself about how much and what she should say. She could not chat on about nothing like Katie. But she had to speak more for the children's sake. She had to get practice in talking more. It did not need to have every word meaning something important.

'Thank you, Katie.'

She blurted this out and felt relieved on the one hand and embarrassed on the other. Katie was shocked at this unusual outburst from Margaret.

'Margaret, you do not have to thank me. Sure what did I do? I was only a good neighbour, only being what a good neighbour should do. What any good Christian should do. Now you will be able to get wee jumpers for all three of them and for yourself too. And I suppose one for your husband also. You will need all of them before the winter is out. There is no need to go round with that shawl all the time. It is far too awkward and gets in the way of everything.

'You know getting the knitting needles and the spools of wool like this. It is a great thing. It allows us to sit at home and make ourselves some warm clothes. That is why some do not like us knitting. It does them out of a market for the sale of shawls. But the jumpers are far better anyway. They let us have our hands free and we can work far better. On the other hand that is why some of the big boys are for it too. We can work harder for them.

'I will be off now, Margaret. I will be off up the road. Its a beautiful evening.' The sun was going down over the back of the mountain into the Atlantic even though they could not see the ocean. It was a beautiful evening all right. There was a peacefulness about it all. This is what was so good about it. But it was not only the weather. For Margaret it was that she was learning the skills to become a better mother. That is what her life was about. She was so happy when she thought about the three young ones with knit sweaters. She saw Katie out and both of them were subdued as they realised that the day had been special for both of them.

CHAPTER THIRTY THREE

'Look at the three of them. Look at the three of them.' Margaret found herself talking out loud to herself recently. Talking to her self out loud when Campbell was not there. Maybe this would help her talk better to everybody. 'Look at the three of them. The three of them and their wee jumpers.' They looked so well. It was winter now and the three of them were well out of the cold with their jumpers.

Talking out loud to herself was also increasingly talking to the children. When she said 'Look at the three of them.' Victoria turned her head around and looked at her. 'Mammy, Mammy, three of them, Mammy.' Margaret smiled to herself and her inner smile began to appear on her face. But she stopped it as she had learnt to do over the last years. As a poor and powerless young woman in rural Ireland in the early twentieth century, life had taught her not to smile. She had learned not to smile. Not to show anything on her face.

But wait, there was nobody here but the children and her. There was no men about, no Allen, no Campbell, nobody to attack her, to hurt her. There was no danger for the minute. There was only the children and herself. The three of them and her. Look at the three of them. Their wee legs. There was the terrible vulnerability of them, of their wee skinny legs. But wait there was also the possibility of beautiful charming laughter in their wee legs.

She could talk out loud, she could talk out loud to the children, then she could smile, she could smile out loud too. Holding her breath, frightened by what she was about to do, glancing around to see there was nobody around except her and the children, she let the smallest glimpse of a smile come on her face. The three of them and their jumpers and their wee legs. Her life was for them, her life was them.

It had been worth it in spite of everything. Her life was them. She drew the breath deeply into her lungs, her shoulders rose up and tried to straighten back against the round protective shape that had come about on her as one blow followed the other. In spite of it all it had been worth it. It had been worth it. She went over to the bed where the children were lying. And she got into the bed and put her arms around all three of them and lay there and let the touch of them heal her.

After a while she fell asleep with them. After a while the itch of the wool of their jumpers on her skin woke her. She had knit these jumpers. It had taken a few weeks and a lot of help from Katie but she had learnt to knit. She had been able to make skirts and dresses for the children before because there was no alternative, she had seen her mother do it and it was not a difficult task. The knitting was more difficult but she had done it. Aye, she had done it. She lay there with them thinking about her knitting and then her hand went down and she felt the new child in her belly. She sighed and felt more relaxed than at any time in her memory.

'Mammy, Mammy.' She turned her head to Victoria. 'Mammy Mammy, Mary is sleep, Anne is sleep. What is sleep, Mammy? Here, Mammy.'

Margaret did not know how to answer this. She did not know herself what sleep was. 'It's just sleep, Victoria. We need to do it to be able to work. You need to do it to be able to walk around and to play.'

'Why Mammy, why need to sleep?'

'Victoria, I do not know. But we have to do it. Look at Mary and Anne, they are sleeping. You were sleeping. I was sleeping. We have to do it.'

Victoria looked at her without understanding but she could not think of more questions on sleeping. She lay back down beside her mother. Slowly she drifted off to sleep. Margaret held her and the other children in her arms. She too began to drift off to sleep. She thought of Campbell and the children. He never came near them or acknowledged them.

The last time he had come to her she had realised that very soon the noise and disturbance he made when he came to her would waken the children. What would happen if this kept on and the children grew up? They would know what was going on. She could not have that but what could she do? There was nothing she could do. Maybe Campbell himself would do something about it?

The winter was closing in on them. The problem about the winter, besides the cold, was that Campbell was in the house more. She had less time of peace to herself and the weans. The summer was the best. He was out late nearly every night and out early in the morning. If that could only last all year. If she only could have a place of her own that she could have nobody but her and the weans. That was what she needed. But she could never have it. She needed Campbell to have this place.

She shrank in on herself when she thought of the alternative. The workhouse. She had never seen the workhouse but it had been one of the great fears of her mother when she was growing up at home. 'The workhouse, that is where we will end up if your father does not stop spending his money on that drink. And nobody would want to be there. It might be all right for the other kind, half of them did not want to work anyway. But it was no place for our kind, we are hard workers.'

What was the workhouse anyway? The English governments set them up to control the starving poor and to try and get work out of them. They were big buildings around the country where they threw too many people into and where these people had to work to they nearly killed themselves and they all lived together and got disease and died. If they owned anything at all they could not get into the workhouse. No matter how small a piece of land, they had to give this up to get into it. As well as a way to get cheap labour, it was also a way to take land off poor people. It sounded a terrible place to Margaret. Her mother was always afraid she would end up there and she always made Margaret and her brothers afraid and she also made their father feel guilty for not working hard enough in case they would have to go to it.

She always explained that the laws governing the workhouse said that the people who entered it had to have it worse than the starving poor outside. She knew that they kept the terror in people. The fear they created meant that people would work for almost nothing rather than risk the two alternatives: starvation, homelessness and death outside the workhouse, or overcrowding, fourteen-hour days, disease and death inside the workhouse.

Her mother's life was not right, there was no way it was right. She lived and worked all her days and died too young. What about her mother's sister in America? What was she doing? Was her life as hard? Was she still alive? She saw her mother's feet sticking up under the bed clothes as she lay dead. She had never seen her father or brothers since. What were they doing? The donkey and the dog? She felt the glimpse of a smile as she thought of the two animals.

Her new baby kicked her then. She put down her hands and felt for its next kick. She lay waiting with her hands on her belly. It did not kick again. Slowly she became drowsy and drifted off to sleep. She lay there with her three children, all of them were sleeping. She began to dream. Like all her dreams they were outside and up in the air as a bird or in the lake as a fish. To be free , to be wild. That was it.

She dreamt she was hiding in the hedge at the bottom corner of the potato ground. That it was a spring evening and the dusk was just coming on. A rabbit came slowly out of the hedge. Stopping every few inches to sniff to smell if it was safe. A few sniffs and a few steps and a few sniffs and slowly he came out into the open grass and began to eat. Then a hare appeared from the top of the potato ground making its way down the side along the hedge.

They looked at each other and they began to eat the grass. Then, from along the bottom of the potato ground, a fox came loping. It was a beautiful creature with its fine fur and clever alert head. The rabbit and the hare looked up and then ignoring it they went back to their eating. The fox approached where they were and lay down beside them. It began to lick itself and clean its coat. Meanwhile the other two animals went on eating.

Margaret then came out from the hedge where she had been hiding and sat down beside the fox. But Margaret was not Margaret in the dream. She was a badger. She went over and lay down beside the fox. They both lay there cleaning themselves and at times watching the rabbit and the hare who were entirely unperturbed by these two larger, stronger, normally predatory, animals.

Then a crow landed beside them and lay back in the sun. It paid no attention to its four neighbors. After some time when the rabbit, the hare and the crow had eaten their fill they lay down beside the fox and the badger to rest. All five of them now lay close together although not touching each other. They all drifted off to sleep.

Margaret sat up in the bed with a start. What the ....? She took a time to realise where she was and what she was doing. The fox had begun to lick her, the crow to peck gently at her, the rabbit and the hare to lie up against her to keep her quiet. The fox licking her had been what had made her wake with a jerk. She looked around her and slowly she began to realise that it was all a dream. The children were there with her. She was not a badger.

She hugged the children. She was not lying out in the potato ground she was in her warm bed. She was not a badger. She was Margaret and she was lying in bed with her three children. They were all still asleep. What made her dream about that? About being a badger and all the animals being friends among themselves.

She felt good as she came awake. All the animals together, this was the way it should be, everybody and everything together. We could all be friends and look out for each other. This would be the way it should be. This would be very good. Everybody and all the animals stop attacking each other. Just do our work and get together and rest together. This should be the way it should be.

Why was it not like that? Why did she always have to watch out to see if she was going to be attacked? It was living the life of the animals, not the ones in her dream but the ones who were like humans, always ready to turn on each other, to attack each other. Nobody could ever rest, everybody had to be on the alert, just like the wild animals. The way it was in her dreams was the way it should be. Nobody to hit or attack anybody else, nobody to eat anybody else.

It was not right the way everybody was out to get everybody else. Well not everybody but nearly everybody she corrected herself as she thought of Shanks and Katie. It was more like some kind of men who were the worst always trying to control everybody and to attack everybody. This was not right. Look at the little animals in her dream. She lay back and tried to rest.

But it was not right. It was not right for all people. Why could people not be kind to each other, have some solidarity with each other, lie down together and be companions to each other like the animals in her dream? But then in real life animals were not like that either, it was only in her dream. Was there something wrong with herself that she wanted something that she did not have, was this what the matter was? Was there something wrong with her, that she wanted things that could not be?

The children gradually came awake. Victoria first then Mary and Anne began to stir. She hugged them close to her. Well they were all together and not trying to be bad to each other at least. The four of them. She would try and see that they stayed that way. She would try and stop the outside world from changing them. But how could she when she had nothing of her own?

He would be wanting them to go and get hired out as soon as they were able so he could get the money they would earn. It would be just like her and her father. She would have to try and stop that. Whatever else that was no way. Look at her own life. Allen had ruined it. He had ruined it. Aye, she loved Victoria. but those years at Allen's had left her not able to speak, not able to smile, not able to laugh, not able to play and ended up with her being given to Campbell.

She searched in her mind for ways to protect her children from this. But how? Try as she did she could not see how to do it. When they got closer to it then she might be able to have a plan. In the meantime she would speak against doing it if it ever came up. She would have to find a way to stop these wee skinny legs from being forced to work far too hard, forced to accept the dirt and the cold of sleeping in some farmer's barn, forced to bend their knees to some hateful force, forced to be open to some man's brutality.

But her own brothers? They were all hired out just like she had been. They were hired out by the Kilgores. So how could she stop this happening to her three daughters when her older brothers could not stop this happening to them? She loved her daughters, and she would soon have another one, or maybe a boy, they could not be hired out, she could not let them be hired out. That was no life for anybody, especially girls. The farmers would put their hands on them.

There would have to be some way to do it. There would have to be. She could not watch her daughters being sent down the road like she was. Down to some Allen. Her face went dead again as she relived the mornings, it was always the mornings when he came to her, especially the first morning when he tore her insides so bad she could barely walk. Her upper lip twisted up in disgust and rage at the memory of it. And she remembered too the terrible loneliness of it, not knowing if it would ever end, the abuse she had to endure.

There had to be some way to stop all this happening to her children. Her own mother had said she should have done more to stop her father sending her to Allen. Margaret remembered her crying when she told her this and that she was sorry for not doing more. But what could she have done? Well she could have fought with Margaret's father. But then what would this have done?

She did not own the cottage, she did not have any of the money that they made from selling the odd calf and the odd bag of spuds, and from working to the bigger farmers. She would have been helpless to do anything. And Margaret was in the same situation. But she would not be helpless. This was her vow to herself. She did not know what she would do but she would not be helpless. She would do something. Anything was better than to watch her daughters go down the road and then come back a couple of years later exhausted, raped and brutalized by some farmer.

She could not live with this. And the thought struck her like a blow. She half sat up in bed to deal with it. She realised that this was why her own mother had died so young, why her heart had given out so young. Her mother could not live with what had happened and what she had not done. She could not live thinking about what happened to Margaret and that she had not opposed it. None of this was right. None of this was right that her father could send her to Allen, that Allen could attack and abuse her, that her father could then send her to Campbell.

Why was it always the men who decided these things? But then look at her brothers. They were men and they could not stop themselves being hired out and being treated bad by the Kilgores. It was not enough to be a man. It seems that you had to be a man who owned something. Men with nothing were not much better off than herself. But then that was not it all either.

The Browns. That Brown woman, that wee Brown girl, they would never have to be hired out. They were the women of rich men. That was it. All men had power over women, but some men had more power than other men. The more they owned the more they had power. But then the Brown woman had more power than her own brothers. She looked down at her daughters. They would own nothing and on top of that they were girls. She looked at them enraged. There had to be some way to protect them from being hired out.

She would be prepared to die to stop them being hired out. That was it, she would die to stop it. But what, how, what way could she die that would stop it? She sat up. Her mouth was closed tight. Her breathing stopped. How could she die in a way that would stop it? It came down on her like a great weight and slowly crushed her spirit. There was no way that she, even by dying, could stop the children from being hired out. She was so powerless that even her death, no matter what form this took, would not be enough to stop this happening. She felt that she was crushed and hopeless. She hugged her three girls and cried. She felt her heart breaking. She felt like she was going to have a heart attack and die. She had come up against the system in all its power.

CHAPTER THIRTY FOUR

Margaret was still in this bleak state later that day when Campbell was sitting in McDaid's. Things had been better than he had feared they would be after that Dublin fighting. The killing of the leaders had been the right thing to do. It taught the rest of them a lesson. The O'Donnells and the McGinns had not been so quick to talk after that. He had not heard so much talk. But was he missing something? Was there something shifting amongst the rest of them? They did not seem to talk to him so straight anymore, to look him in the eye so much. The talk in McDaid's seemed less natural when he was in it.

He was into his third whisky. He drank scotch, none of that Fenian Irish whiskey for him. McDaid brought it over to him where he sat at his usual seat at the wee table by the door. What was this? What? McDaid pulled a seat over and sat down with him. There was nobody else in the bar. That was it. It was Wednesday, a quiet night. With nobody else in the bar McDaid was not afraid of seeming to be too friendly to him. 'Well, Campbell, how have you been keeping? How is the work going and Lord Taverstock, he is a lucky man to have you to look after things in the bog for him?'

Campbell grunted. He recognized soft soap when he heard it and he waited for what would follow. 'I am glad that there was no follow up from that Dublin business. I mean that trouble around the Easter time. It is a good job it did not spread. And they did the right thing teaching them a lesson. I mean you cannot go starting fighting when the country is at war. Aye, I am glad that it did not spread and it has died down.

'Look at these boys O'Donnell and McGinn. They were all big men for it when it happened but they soon shut their mouths when things got rough. When they shot them and especially when they shot that Connolly boy at the end, wounded and all as he was. You don't hear them so much now. Anyway I will leave you to have your drink in peace. Here let me bring you another one. It will keep the cold out. I am only sorry for them boys in the trenches, if there was anything I could do for them.'

McDaid got up and Campbell grunted. He took another sip from his whisky while McDaid brought him down another and set it in front of him. 'Give me a shout if you need anything else. I will be in the back with the missus having a bite to eat.' This was more of the soft soap, this leaving him alone in the bar. They were the best of friends now this was meant to say. Aye, McDaid was laying it on all right. He wanted Brown to know what he thought and he wanted to keep in with Campbell.

Was something about to happen? This was what was worrying Campbell about McDaid's actions. Was there something about to happen that McDaid knew about in advance and was wanting to make sure he was not tied up with it. Could that be it? Whatever it was it was not out of the goodness of his heart that he gave the extra whisky and left him alone in the bar. Aye, and do something for the men in the trenches. Hah! the only chance of McDaid doing that would be if there was money in it for him.

Well he would tell Brown and keep himself covered. He would tell him that he was worried that something was going to happen, that things were not as quiet as they seemed. He would keep himself

covered this way too. Aye, things were going well for him. He had
more money than before, the work in the bog and the few bits of
things about his own place and the extras he got from Brown, things
were all right. And for sure he was not away getting frozen and shot
at in the trenches. He would make sure that he kept Brown informed.

He got up after finishing the whisky and headed up the road for
home. Would she be up? This was it. Would she be up? He hoped she
would not. He did not want to have to see her making him his tea and
him feeling there was something else he should be doing for her. This
was something new, something that had only come on him recently
when he had a few drinks. He felt that there was something more he
should be doing for her. To hell with the drink anyway.

And to hell with her as well. That was more to the point of it. To
hell with her. More and more recently she was getting him mixed up.
Did he not give her all she needed? A roof over her head, clothes on
her back, food for herself and the young ones. Sure where would she
be if it was not for him? In the workhouse, that is where. She was a
lucky woman that he took her in. Yet she was not content. He knew
she was not. She was not content. But without him she could be in the
workhouse.

Look at her now with the knitting. He hoped that she was not up
knitting when he got back. There was something about the noise of
the needles that made him ready to go off his head. He did not know
what it was. But she was getting more and more annoying. It had
started with her building that lavatory and it had gone on from there.
Building the lavatory, planting the spuds, selling the eggs and keeping the money, then with the money buying the wool and the needles
and then the knitting. Doing more and more for herself.

What would it be next? It was a good job she had no say over the
cottage or the animals or the few fields or you would never know
what she would be up to. That knitting. The tick, tick, tick of it. Her

sitting there. She did not even have to have any light. She could do it in the dark. Sometimes he would be in the bed and he would hear her tick, tick, ticking away. That was it, it was the noise that was the worst. And to have to listen to it when he was lying on his bench trying to sleep in the dark. Nothing could be worse than that.

The tick, tick, tick of it. But it was not only that. It was a lot more than that. It was just her, that was what it was. That tick, tick, ticking and the weans with jumpers and the spuds planted, and the eggs and her keeping the money, and the lavatory she built. The thing about it was she was too above herself, that was what it was about the noise of the knitting, it made him realise that she was too above herself. If she had to ask him for everything this would be better, this would keep her in her place better.

Maybe it was also that he had nothing to say to her about knitting. He knew nothing about it. How to do it. Well he knew what it should look like at the end but he did not know how to do it. That was not right her knowing and him not. This was more of her being above herself, thinking she was above herself. Next she would be wanting more off him, trying to push more out of him. That was what was going on. He would have to watch.

He pushed the door open and went in letting his breath out in relief when he saw she was in her bed. There were a few live embers in the fire. He went over and took the wedge of bread from the box and began to eat. He threw off his coat and went and sat on the bench he slept on beside the fire. Aye, she thought she was above herself that was it. He took off his boots. He turned and lay over on his side with his face to the wall.

Would he go to her? Her and her big belly. But that would be all right. He would as usual open up her legs and stand and get into her that way. Her big belly would not be in the way if he did it that way. The big belly was not that bad anyway. He almost looked around him to be sure nobody could see his thoughts as he remembered that the last time he went to her, and had accidentally touched her big belly, he had been shocked how good it had made him feel.

He had liked the feel of it to an extent that he had never experienced before. It was the powerful softness and smoothness of it. Aye, it was terrible soft and smooth. And the curve on it. The feel of the curve of it. There was something about that curve that fitted so well into the centre of his palm, that seemed to change the way the points of his fingers touched her. He would maybe feel it again tonight. The last night it was by accident that he had felt it. This night he would feel it again, this time more. The curve of it seemed to change his hand and fit in the new shape of it.

He took off his coat and his trousers and boots and got up and went to her. He reached under the covers and took her legs at the back of her knees and pulled them round to where they were over the side of the bed. His thing stuck out in front of him. He pulled her legs apart and put one on each side of him and pushed forward to get into her. He did not like it when he had to put his hand down and part her to get in. That was getting too intimate with her. Why could she not just let him in?

He liked it better when he could just push at her until he found the entrance to her and then he would push on in. Tonight he could not get into her. He did not know that it was the terrible mood she was in after thinking how helpless she was to stop her children being hired out that had taken all the moistness out of her. That was holding her tight and dry against him as he pushed to get into her.

After holding her by the knees and pushing and pushing and angling and pushing he could not get into her. He was getting angry and frustrated. Aye, she was doing this deliberately. Keeping herself closed up and dry. Keeping him out. He knew she was. It was deliberate, she was keeping him out, she was trying to get him mad, that was what it was.

After trying and trying he gave up and let go her left leg and put his hand in between her legs to try and open her body to him. He did not like doing this. This was uncalled for. To hell with her anyway for making him do this. This was something he should not have to do. It was not right he had to do this. He should be able to put his thing in her without this. To hell with her anyway and her thing and her keeping him out.

Then he felt the entrance to her. It was warmer and softer and with the slightest bit of moistness on it. There it was. He pointed himself at it by angling his body and stooping down a bit and he could feel the heat of her engulf the head of his thing. To hell with her. To hell with this. But then the heat of her, aye, the heat of her. It felt so good around his thing that he began to forget about what she was up to, about her thinking she was somebody, about how she was always trying to get above herself, about her keeping him out of her.

But that was no good. That was it. He had to watch out for this too, this pleasure, aye, it could take a man unawares. This heat, this pleasure. But he could not resist, he pushed on into her. He bent further at the knees and let a groan that started at his lips and went in to the inside of him rather than going out. It started under its own steam, it was the pleasure of her forcing the noise out of him, but this was more of her getting at him, she was getting at him. The groan changed in tone to one of aggression and instead of going into him he forced it out of him, he forced it out at her. To hell with her anyway as he pushed in and out of her.

He pushed and pushed at her. Aye, to hell with her anyway. He pounded at her. But he was having difficulty tonight. He would not be quick in ending it this night. It was the drink. It made him have less feeling in his thing and everything was dulled and there was less energy in him. He pushed away and tried to focus on what he was doing to her. He pushed and pushed. He felt himself standing up straight, aye, he was in charge here, he was the boss, he was doing her and she had no say in it. Aye, take that then 'til you see what is what.

But it was not only the drink. It was more than that. He could not keep it simple like he used to be able to do. The very heat of her, the very pleasure of it, these raised themselves up against him. They threatened him. They made him let her and her hopes and fears and dreams threaten to get into him. It was her and he had to watch her, the more he was pleasured the more he was in danger of her taking advantage of him. He was in control, he had to stay in control. That was it. There was no room here for him letting the heat of her and the pleasure of her take over.

He stood up to reassert himself. Aye, he was in control, she was nothing. But as he stood he felt himself slipping out of her. Felt his pleasure of being in her body threatening to escape from him. He found himself bending lower again to try and keep the heat and the pleasure, he found himself drawn into her again and being absorbed by her again. He pushed into her harder and this let his thoughts about him and her and how he was the boss, drift away. Aye, he felt the heat of her around him as he pushed and pushed into her. That heat, she, that heat, her heat. He felt his body and mind move away from all other things and focus on her heat. The pleasure of her.

Then as he tried to get more and more into her he remembered her belly. How round and soft it was. How it was in there in front of him under the bedclothes, under the bedclothes, there it was, big and round and soft and warm. He felt the enriching of the desire in him, he felt the powerful urge in him to put his hand in and feel the warmth, the softness the roundness of her. Aye, that was it. He began to shift his hand. He moved it under the edge of the bedclothes and in until it touched the rising swell of her body. He moved his hand slowly, for the first time there was no aggression in it unlike his movements on all other occasions.

The breath escaped from his mouth. A low groan started in him again and went deeper inside him. The warm soft roundness of her. Aye, that was it. He moved his hand on her. Moving it on up and up towards the top of her rounded belly that rose like a mountain in front of him. Aye, aye, this time he almost murmured out loud. The soft round warmth of it. He moved his hand around and felt her more thoughtfully. He moved his other hand to join the other on the wonder of her belly. He moved one of his hands to hold the wonderful roundness of her full breasts.

He began to feel his own hand in his mind, he began to feel his hand where it touched her skin. He began to think of the feeling that was in his hand and the feeling that was in her skin. He began to let this powerful physical feeling enter into his brain unopposed. She herself, the whole person of her began to enter into his mind also. It was not just a round soft warm belly, it was her and all her person with it that he was touching. His defences were all dismantling.

The way he was touching her now was different. It was something entirely new. It was not only that he was touching her belly which he did not have to touch to enter her. But he was touching differently. When he used the tips of his fingers they were no longer pointed and holding and controlling and aggressive. Now it was the soft inside palms of his finger tips that touched and felt her. His fingers were no longer probing and holding and aggressively aimed at her, they were no longer doing to her, no longer controlling her. Now they were being felt by her as much as they were feeling her. There was a tenderness in it all. It was like she was feeling his fingers with her belly as much as he was feeling her belly. For the first time ever there was a tenderness between them.

It was her and her life, the hard time she had had with Allen, the hard time she had had with the weans and having them, the hard time she had had with all the work she did, the hard times, the new baby in her womb, but she was a person, she was a good person, the feeling went back and forth for a few seconds between her and him. But then he became terrified and he panicked and he leapt back out of her, and he roared at her in aggression and terrified panic. 'To hell with this. To hell with you.' He was out of her and his thing stuck up wet and now cold in the air. He was taking in great deep pants of air. 'Aye, to hell with you. I am not stupid, I know you are up to something.'

He stood there back three feet from where her legs were bent and open on the bed and her sex exposed. 'Aye, I know what it is that you are up to. I am giving you all that you need and deserve. Stop wanting for more. Stop trying to get more. Lying there open to the world. Cover yourself up. What kind of a woman are you anyway? Well you will not fool me. You and your belly and the rest of you. you will not fool me. I am well able for you and your tricks. You will not fool me.' He turned away from her. To hell with her, to hell with her.

He stamped outside the cottage as he was, in his shirttails. He stood by the edge of the yard looking down over the spud ground and the valley stretching way out in the distance. He took his penis in his hand and as it softened he urinated out in front of him. Aye, that will be the end of that. Her and her belly. He shook his penis dry. Aye, her and her belly and her round softness and her. He grunted to himself and he shook his head as he turned to go in again. Aye, to hell with her. But in spite of himself, that moment when he was touching her belly hung on somewhere deep down in his mind as one of the most wonderful moments of his life.

Chapter Thirty Five

'Come on, Victoria. I have Mary and Anne. We have to milk the cow. You like milk, Victoria. If we do not milk we will have none to drink.'

'Milk the cow, Mammy. I will help you. I will watch Mary and Anne.'

'That is good, Victoria, you are a good wee girl to help Mammy. Come and bring Mary, take her hand. See how good she can walk now. The two of you are walking and soon you will be able to help with Anne as I have the new baby.'

The cow was lying down in the stall. It was chained to a post in front of it, which went from the floor to the roof. Margaret tipped its back end with her toe. 'Get up now girl. I have to milk you. Come on now.'

'Milk the cow Mammy.'

'Get up, get up.' Margaret smiled to herself as Victoria helped her and repeated what she said. 'Now, Victoria, you stay back there with Mary and Anne in the pile of hay and look after them. That will be the best way to help Mammy.'

Victoria sat down beside Mary and Anne. She leaned over towards them and put her arm out around their heads and leaned on her elbow. 'Mammy, the cow is not up. Why Mammy?' Margaret turned round and more harshly spoke to the cow and prodded it in the back end with her toe. This time the cow knew that it had to rise and this is what it did. Rising on its back end first it then got up on its front knees and stretched. Margaret did not know if it was true but she had always been told that if an animal stretched when it got up then it was not sick.

Margaret leaned into the cow's side. She pushed herself in close. She got her left elbow in front of the cow's leg to help hold off any kick it might try to give her. By the time Margaret was finished and had the milk back in the house and the children fed and in bed, it was dark. She was very tired with one child in her belly, and Victoria, Mary and Anne too. It was Wednesday and Campbell would have been down with Brown so he would not be back for a while. Anyway almost every night now he went into McDaid's and came home late. Tonight especially she was glad that she would have some time to herself. She put a few extra turf on the fire and sat by it on the stool.

It had been with her all day. It had been irritating her mind all day. She hardly slept the rest of the night last night. She could think of nothing else but what had happened last night when he touched her belly and breasts and then got frightened and angry. What was it that had frightened him that had made him get that angry at her? What was it that had got him like that? She shook her head to herself as she thought about him and his shouts and his pulling out of her and leaving her. And then going outside.

But that was not the main thing that was getting at her. It was something that had happened in herself that was the real thing that she was struggling with. It was the time when he had put one hand then the other hand up on her belly, then on her breasts, and felt her there. He had never felt her like that before. For a few seconds then he had felt her without aggression and violence and brutality. Before he had always felt her the way that he spoke to her. On the very few times that he had spoken to her at all that is. He always felt her the way he spoke to her and treated her. With aggression, with ignorance. with ownership, ordering her, without kindness. For a few seconds last night it had been different.

That was it. Yes for a few seconds last night it had been different. His hands, first the right and then the left, on her belly, on her breasts. What was it? He never used his hands on her when he put his thing in her except to pull her or push her into position so he could get into her. His hands were always used crudely to get him into her. Then there was also that when he touched her those times, his fingers dug into her, caught hold of her, held her down, pushed her down, con-trolled her. That was it, she was used to that. She was used to that aggressive controlling angry way that he did it. The brutal, control-ling way he did it.

She was always under attack. With Allen when he put his thing in her she was under attack, he was always hurting her, always attack-ing her. That was it. Under this assault she would close up and dry up her body. She would have no co-operation with his attack in any way. She was closed and dry to him. That was what her body tried to do to keep him out, to guard herself against his attack.

Allen attacked her by hitting her and by the control he had over her life, and by who he was. He had over fifty good acres she had nothing, he was a man, she was a girl. She had nowhere else to go except his barn. When she saw over his shoulder and past him when he was attacking her all she could see was that she had nothing, she had no power, and he had his fifty good acres and he had his connec-tions. She could not stop him.

Campbell was attacking her too. The first night she had held her legs together. Married, wife, he had snarled at her. This great power-ful organization of the church had told her that Campbell owned her body, that he was the boss. This confused her and weakened her resistance. Married meant something about the man being in charge. Meant something about the church sanctioning whatever the man wanted to do. Wife meant something about doing what the man said. This was it. She was married, she was a wife, This is what he snarled at her. She did not think she could defend herself when she was married and a wife. He owned her.

Ever since then he had been putting his thing in her whenever he wanted to. Like Allen he too had been attacking her. Whenever she saw over his shoulder and past him she could see married and a wife and the church and she had nothing and he had the cottage and the money. And as each child was born she could see that without him she would be in the workhouse with her children. That was it, that was it. She could not defend herself against him, because she had nothing and also being married and a wife, she was not supposed to.

Allen and Campbell. They were both attackers. To both of them her body tried to close itself up against them, to keep them out, to dry itself up, to close itself tight. All of her got pulled together to do this, to dry herself, to close herself. There was to be no welcome to either of them and to their attacks. She was breathing deeply as she sat by the fire and remembered Allen and then Campbell and the pain and the hurt as they forced themselves into her dry tightness.

This was what was confusing her now. Last night for a few seconds, for a few seconds last night things were different. Campbell was not attacking her, was not coming at her. He was not coming at her with his thing stuck out in front of him like a weapon that he stuck in her, that he used to ram and ram at her, and with his hands with their hard fingers and their hard nails digging at her and holding her down so that his attack would work, so that his attack would succeed.

This was the way it was every time except for a few seconds last night. Every time her body would dry itself up, and would close itself up to keep him out. All her energies went to try and keep him out.

There was no welcome in her for his sticking out attacking thing, for his hard holding fingers, for his hard digging nails, for his snarling, attacking everything, that he came at her with. For his property and power and his church sanction that he came at her with, none of which she had. She did not have.

But for a minute last night something else had happened. His hands on her belly were not holding and controlling, his fingers not digging, his nails not cutting. Instead his hands were feeling, and sensing. It was like they were trying to touch her and join with her rather than hold her and control her. It was like they were trying to feel her and to understand her. It was also that they for a moment wanted her body to touch him so that they would exchange touches. Trying to let her skin touch his skin. It was something very different. For a minute there, she was not under attack.

She had not felt that she had to keep all the defences up in her mind and body. For a moment she was able to forget all those things that were used to control her. That she was married to him, that she was his wife, that he had a cottage and she had nothing, that he was something out there in the world and she was nothing, that she had been hired and he was something out there in the world and she was nothing. She had not been under attack for a few seconds last night and this had allowed her to let her defences down.

But it was not only that she had let her defences down. She had responded with a welcome. When his new touchings registered in her mind, her body followed after. She felt her thing open up to him. Welcoming him, letting him in. But not only that. She also felt her thing become moist and wet to welcome him in. And as this happened she also felt the beginnings of the most powerful pleasure such as she had never felt before. It was shocking, frightening, in its power. She braced herself to accept it and to let it flow over her. In doing so she was letting him into her and welcoming him into her more and more.

She breathed out as she grasped the enormity of it all. It was powerful, she struggled to allow a word like wonderful into her mind. She struggled with the gushing wet openness of her body as she welcomed him.

Before last night whenever he came to her all she had felt was pain or nothing. It was as if her place down there was not for him. It was not right for him. It was as if her place down there was dead to him or closed to him. Never had there been any feeling down there that came with him that was good for her. Until that few seconds last night.

When she felt the different touch of him last night. When she felt that she was not under attack, when she felt she could let him touch her belly, that her belly was not under attack, when she felt her belly for a second, want to reach out to touch him, and the same with her breasts, when this happened then that great rush of wetness had come down into her. And for that briefest of few seconds she had felt the first hint of the first beginnings of what she knew could be a great and powerful pleasure, a shocking newness of desire and pleasure and passion.

She had felt it come to her. She had felt her opened up and wetted passage and then all of her body turned to this. It was as if all her body's power, that in the past went to closing up and drying up to keep him out, was turned into its opposite, to opening up and wetting to let him in. And with it came the hint of the shocking power of the greatest physical pleasure that she had ever known. She had never even imagined such pleasure.

Things for a second seemed to have moved into their right place. He was not attacking her, she was not defending herself. He was not holding and probing and controlling her. She was not tightening and closing and drying. Things seemed to have moved into their right place. He was coming to her feeling for her body and its wants and pleasures. She was welcoming him to her, together with his desires and feelings, and feeling for them and responding to them. And that extraordinary pleasure came from this.

But then it was gone. He had roared at her and pulled himself out of her. Then he had grabbed his hands back from her belly. They had closed into fists at his side as he had roared at her standing away back from her with his thing up. His hands were no more open to her and her touch. The inner tips of his fingers were no longer there for her. They were fists again, they were along with his roar again, they were along with his sticking out angry aggressive attacking thing again.

Then it died in her. Then the greatest, most wonderful pleasure that had been only beginning to hint at its presence in her, that had begun to come with her opening up of her passage, that had begun to come come with the lubricating, the wetting of her passage to him, that had begun to come with her move from bitter defence to rushing welcome, then this had died in her. It had died before it had even properly managed to come alive in her.

As she sat and thought of these events of the last night Margaret realised how deep an anger and rage she held for Campbell. He was able to keep alive within himself all of the most nasty and destructive and cruel feelings for her. But when the wonderful sharing nurturing feelings of the night before had developed, he roared his opposition and destroyed them. It was clear he was terrified of them.

She sat at the fire with the embers of the turf fire dying in front of her. She let the breath out of her body with a deep sigh. She was exhausted with the concentration that her last minutes of thinking had demanded from her. That thing had died in her before it was born. That pleasure of opening and wetting and welcoming. It was dead in her again. He had killed it in her. The realization that he had killed it in her hit her very very hard.

Him, with his roars and his anger and his fear. For some reason she suddenly knew that he was afraid of something. That was what had done it. He was afraid. Him and his roars and his pulling out of her and his anger and his killing of the welcoming she had for him for a minute. That was it, he was afraid of the welcoming. He was terrified. She sat as this understanding roamed in her head searching for something to connect with that would make it more understandable. Something that would let her understand why. Why he was afraid.

Then as she found nothing to connect it with, the anger began to rise in her. He was not afraid to attack her. He was not afraid to put his thing in her when she did not want him to put it in her. But when she was welcoming him into her, for some reason that she did not know, when he had stopped attacking her and when he had been seeking to be together with her, and when she had welcomed him, then he was afraid. Then he had panicked and pulled out of her, roaring and turned his hands into fists.

Her hatred of him then broke through. She had been holding it down in her. She had not been letting it come alive in her. She had concluded that she could not afford to hate him because she could not endure having to do what she had to do to live with him if she hated him. But now the hatred came again. With a power, it rose in her. He had killed her pleasure, he had killed her welcoming, he wanted to keep on attacking her instead. He was destroying that which was beautiful and nurturing and pleasuring, and keeping alive all that was destructive. He was killing the possibility of her having pleasure when she was making her children not just bringing them up.

Yes, this is what she suddenly understood now. For years she had been unable to understand how she could love her children so much as she brought them up but at the same time hate the act of the man coming to her, an act which was necessary for the making of her children. She understood now. It was the way they did it. They came to her in brutality and violence and control and aggression. In the face of this it was impossible to do anything else but to close up and try and defend herself. It was impossible to have any pleasure. But last night for a few seconds he came to her with just the hint of tenderness and without aggression. She had responded, from her came the welcoming and the great pleasure. It was, she now understood, possible to make children with great pleasure, just as it was to bring up children with great pleasure.

But she could not do it with him. She understood it now. He was afraid of her. But even more he was afraid of himself. To enter into a tender and loving and warm act with her, opened himself up to her. It demanded a change in their way of interacting with each other. He could no longer give her the orders and hit her. He could no longer be sure that he could order her and control her. This is why he panicked and ran. This is why he roared and ran. The few seconds of pleasure of last night would, if continued with, threaten his whole control of her, his whole view of her, but not only her, but also his control of his world around him and his view of that world and how he related to it.

She slowly turned her head to the door of the room where her children slept. It was only that. It was only them. This was all that made it possible. They were all that made it possible. That was it. She had to do whatever it was for them. She had to live with him and let him attack her and let him kill the welcome in her. Stop it dead. She had to let it happen. She had to let him do it. She had nothing. She had to do whatever was necessary so the children could live. Let him kill the welcoming, and the pleasure she had got the hint of, the living life of her. She would have to live without it. As she sat there and the turf burned down she pushed her hatred for him back down into a manageable place again. For the children's sake.

CHAPTER THIRTY SIX

It had never happened before. Campbell was not sure how to react so he stood motionless thinking about what he was witnessing. Brown had come in his horse and trap to Campbell's cottage looking for him. He pulled the trap around at the end of the yard next to the road and called, 'Campbell! Campbell!'. He did not want to come all the way for Campbell. He wanted to stay on the road and make Campbell come the last few steps to him. In this way the illusion could be at least partially maintained that Campbell was coming to him, that Campbell needed him, not the other way around. This illusion was important to the system of control. Campbell appeared out of the byre.

'Campbell, they are striking. They are striking. The farmers all over the district are all being left without help. Get in. We are going to meet with a few men down at the village. The Sergeant will be there. We are going to have to put an end to this. These boys must be taught their place.'

Campbell had never seen Brown like this before. He could barely breathe and he was white in the face.

'Get in, get in.' They headed off at a trot over the rough road. Campbell was ready for whatever they wanted him to do against the strike. He knew what would happen if they would not obey orders.

347

Look what would happen at his own place if she would not obey orders. The whole thing would fall apart. It was the same with these farm labourers. They had to do what they were told. They would have to learn that striking was no good. They would have to go back to work. They would have to be taught their place.

Rounding a corner a mile from his cottage, Campbell and Brown saw a crowd of about twenty people at the small crossroads up ahead. When they came closer they saw it was labourers. O'Donnell and Brennan were there, and it would have to be, yes, herself's brother was there too. They stopped talking and turned to look at the horse and trap. The tension and hostility in them was obvious. But they did not move to block the road.

Brown slowed but kept the trap moving on. As the horse and trap came abreast of them, they moved a little aside to let it through. Campbell and Brown did not speak. Then as the trap passed through and out of the clump of men O'Donnell shouted: 'Hey, Campbell! You keep out of this! You keep out of this! And that Brown man beside you, if he and his kind paid decent wages this would never happen! You keep out of it, Campbell! Your own wife was hired out and treated bad! You keep out of this!'

There it was again. She was always being thrown up in his face. Campbell raged. But then when Brown did not say anything he began to remember that it was Brown got him linked up with her. But this did not get rid of all the anger in him. He pushed the thoughts away and concentrated on the job ahead. In less than half-an-hour they pulled into the police station in the village. When they entered there were five farmers there and the Sergeant and two policemen.

Brown took charge. 'Well, Sergeant and men, we have to do something to put a stop to this. Otherwise these men will begin to think they are worth more than they are getting. I have spoken to Campbell here and he says he can get some men together from around the area by himself who will help out in the fields. Tomorrow we can get these together and spread them out to where they are most needed. Sergeant, can you give protection to these men?'

Knowing that he could not but not wanting to be seen as blocking the effort, the Sergeant answered, 'Aye, sir, we can do that. We will keep an eye on things.' Then, trying to get some way to undermine his own answer, he said. 'Now, how many men did you say you would be getting, Campbell? Will they be all scattered out across the place? What are the plans?'

'Twenty or thirty or so.' Campbell replied.

'What about if we cycle up tomorrow morning to the wee cross-roads in the bog at Meenticat and meet you there with your men around seven? How would this sound?'

Brown intervened. 'I think the top priority should be those places where the hay is still in the fields. Unless it is worked at in this weath-er, it will rot. There are four of five places, McCausiland's, Magee's, Robinson's, Anderson's and McCrossan's.' It did not occur as strange to anybody that these were all Protestant farmers, like the men that were in charge in the room. That was the way things were.

It was well after midnight when Campbell got home. He had gone to five different houses to get help for the morning and the men in four of these were to get the word out to twenty or so others. He was confident he would have a good squad in the morning. After five hours sleep he was on the road again on the way down to the Meentikat crossroads. It was close to seven when he got there. After more than half an hour the Sergeant and the policemen arrived. And after another half-hour or more, the total men who had turned up ready to work against the strike, were Campbell and three others.

Campbell was angry. But there was nothing he could do. The men he had tried to recruit were all small farmers with bits of land like himself. Far too little to have a labourer work for them. They too were feeling the pinch of the increased prices of the war. Maybe they were even in sympathy with the striking labourers in some cases. One of them as much as told Campbell that last night. When asked to help he turned and walked into his cottage closing the door on Campbell. As he did so he said, 'Men have to eat. I am not taking the food out of any man's mouth.'

Another had been even more clear. He said: 'Look at them farmers. They are hoarding what is left of the bad spud crop from last year. I know many of them won't sell the spuds they have because they think they will get more than the fixed price for them later. This is not right. People are near starving. They are putting up prices of milk and everything. Now you cannot get any flour or meal either. What are we supposed to do? Naw, I am with them strikers.' There was nothing Campbell could do.

'Well let's go then,' the Sergeant said. 'Mr Brown told me that the first place to get covered was McCausiland's. He has over ten acres of hay lying in the ground going bad. It should take us an hour to get there.' The police got on their government issued bicycles. Campbell and the three others walked. 'Look! Look, over there, Campbell. Over there, Sergeant.' They all turned and looked in the direction the man had pointed. It was a group of labourers with O'Donnell at their head. They were strikers and they were coming across the bog towards them. It was a good job the Sergeant was with them.

'Hey!' O'Donnell shouted, 'taking men's jobs. Taking the food out of their mouths. Have you no shame?' The Sergeant intervened. 'Now stay back there, O'Donnell. These men have nothing to do with you.'

A young man no more than a boy stepped up beside O'Donnell, his face tight with rage. 'Aye, what are you doing? I have been working for Magee there for five years, since I was eight. Sleeping in the barn. Nothing but stirabout and spuds to eat. From six in the morning to eight at night. What are you crowd going to do about that?

Sergeant, what are you going to do about that?'

'Go on now, boy. Go about your business. Go back to work and I am sure if you worked hard Magee looked after you. He is a good man with nearly a hundred acres.'

The boy was white with rage. O'Donnell went to speak but before he could say anything the boy shouted. 'I hope the Sinn Fein boys get you. I hope the IRB boys get you. Then you will know what's sticking to you.' The men around O'Donnell were silent at this declaration of all-out hatred by the boy and his threatening of the Sergeant with the IRB. O'Donnell looked at the boy by his side in amazement.

This boy had more audacity than he himself. He was prepared to go all the way. O'Donnell with his few fields and living with his mother, was not as radical and enraged as he thought. O'Donnell thought of this as he considered why he had not said what the boy had said first. The boy had threatened the Sergeant with war and death. O'Donnell was shaken. He thought about his own commitment to the struggle for the first time. Would he be lagging behind? How did this boy go first? As he thought of these things, he gathered himself and shouted at the Sergeant. 'You are well fed. Lying up in that police station. You never have to break your back.'

By this time the police and the strikebreakers had gone on past O'Donnell, the boy and the strikers. Not knowing exactly what to do, the strikers slowed down and then gathered round to talk things over. O'Donnell and all of them were still somewhat overcome by the young boy's words. He knew the boy's name was Kerr.

'Kerr, you shook that Sergeant up when you threatened him with the IRB.' The boy looked at O'Donnell. His expression said that he did not think he had done anything special.

'Kerr, you have been over at Magee's for how long?'

'Since I was eight. I am thirteen now. Five years. My folks live over towards Dungloe. I have not seen them for five years. Magee says he paid my father in the fairs. I suppose he must have or my father would have come to Magee's. But what good is that to me? Living in the barn and half starving. I should have burnt that place down.'

The Sergeant, the two police and the strikebreakers were even more affected by the boy's remarks. They were subdued as they walked and thought of the implications of what he said. This could become more than just a few days working at hay. Campbell was the only one of them that was not regretting having come. The others wished they were at home. It was not worth keeping in with the powers that be if they were going to be shot by the powers that wanted to be.

McCausiland had ten acres of hay. They worked at it all day. Turning it in the swathe to let the sun and the wind at all sides of it. And by the evening they had it up in hand cocks. They had got tea in a tin can and tin mugs and slices of bread from McCausiland's servant. McCausiland had met them when they arrived and thanked them and told them how great men they were but they did not see him again. He was above working in the fields. Him and Brown and Wilson were big together. All of them thought they were above working in the fields.

The police had gone off back to their barracks when there was no sign of any strikers turning up. Before they left they told Campbell that tomorrow morning they should go to Magee's and get his hay up. There was no talk of the police meeting them again in the morning to escort them past any strikers. The men's mood was somber all day. All but Campbell had decided that they would not be doing any scabbing the next day. They were surprised when McCausiland arrived as the sun was going down in a big trap pulled by one of his horses.

'Get in, men. I will take you up as far as the Meentikat cross roads. It will take a bit of the weight of your feet. You have done a good job here today. Those striking labourers have no gratitude. After the way I have looked after them, given them work, fed and housed them, without me they would be in Belgium in the trenches. And then to do this. And just at the time the hay has to be got in. You men have done me a great service. Do not worry I will look after you.'

They were rounding a corner in the road which was lined on both sides by ash bushes. When they got round the corner they saw the strikers that had confronted them that morning on both sides of the road. This time they moved out to block the road. O'Donnell was at their head. Spurred on by the young Kerr boy's words that morning he grabbed at the horse's bridle and pulled its head across into the hedge.

'Come on get out of that trap. You are taking men's jobs. You are taking the food out of men's mouths.' Margaret's brother was there and in the forefront. He shouted at Campbell.

'What are you doing here, Campbell? Sure Margaret was hired out and look at the way she was treated by Allen. Why are you doing our work? We need better money. Less hours.' Campbell glowered but did not speak. 'But then you took the pay off from Allen. You got a cow out of it.'

Young Kerr picked up a stone off the road and threw it at the men in the trap. It struck the side of the trap. The rest of the strikers followed his lead again and reached down for stones. At this point McCausiland reached into the waistband of his trousers and brought out a revolver. He pointed it at the strikers and then pointed it higher into the sky and fired two shots. Everybody stopped. What was this? What? Then McCausiland whipped the horse and the trap and the men in it were taken out of the group of strikers as the horse galloped up the road.

The strikers stared after them. This time it was O'Donnell who took the lead. 'Look they have to go round the long way. We can watch our steps and get up across the bog and the hill and get them at Meentikat crossroads. That McCausiland will not take them any further as he will not want to risk his trap wheels on that bad road.' They ran off across the bog with O'Donnell and Kerr at their head. It took them almost half-an-hour to get to the top of the hill where they could see the crossroads.

It was as O'Donnell had said. McCausiland had left them off and was already turned round and on the way back down again. The four strikebreakers were hurrying up the road in the direction of Campbell's cottage. They all lived on up the side of the mountain past Campbell. It was clear that they were too far away and the strikers would not be able to catch them. They slowed down. They took their time and headed down to the crossroads. They spoke amongst themselves with excitement about attacking McCausiland's trap. They were proud they had gone past the talking stage.

Some of them had no place to stay. Since they were hired out and striking they could not stay in the barns they were used to sleeping in. Some of them had families not far away and made in that direction. Before they parted all of them agreed to meet in the morning at the crossroads to tackle the strike-breakers again. O'Donnell, Brennan and young Kerr, on O'Donnell's invitation, set off in the direction of O'Donnell's cottage.

Campbell in the meantime was pushing the door open into his cottage. Margaret did not know what he had been doing all day but she could see that he was deep in himself. She served up his food and realised that he was not aware of her. He ate and went and lay on his bench. He was no sooner down than a voice shouted outside his door. 'Campbell! Campbell!' He sat up with a worried look on his face.

'Who is it?'

'It's me. O'Neill.'

Campbell relaxed as it was one of the men who had been with him all day. He opened the door.

354

'Campbell, I am not coming tomorrow. I am not coming.'
Margaret was in her room with her, by now, four children and could
hear everything.

'I am not coming. Look at that young Kerr boy what he said about
the IRB. Then that McCausiland fires his gun. Then the police, they
do not even come back with us. And to tell you the truth my heart is
not in it. I know for a fact that Kerr was working over at Magee's and
instead of the agreement he had to work from six to six they made
him work from six to eight. This is not right. Things have to change.

'I have not got two pennies to rub together myself. I cannot afford
to pay the prices for a bit of flour or meal if you could get it. And
them big farmers are hoarding the spuds. I am as bad off nearly as
them labourers. And I am out doing their work, doing them out of a
job. It is not right. Them farmers should pay them better. Look, all the
boys are asking for is the same as in Lifford district. Look, it's not
right. I am not coming anymore, Campbell.'

'Whatever you think,' Campbell grunted and slammed the door in
O'Neil's face. He went and lay on his bench.

Margaret lay with her children. The fourth had been born in the
spring. It was another girl and she called it Martha. She lay in bed
now with her four girls. Martha on one side and Victoria, Mary and
Anne on the other. She needed Campbell more than ever if she was
to be able to feed all her children, and to be able to stay out of the
workhouse. She raised her head and looked at his back where he was
lying on the bench. She knew from what she had heard of the conversation that he was doing the labourers' work and somebody had
fired a shot. He could be shot. She was worried.

But Margaret also struggled to connect this with her years at
Allen's. But her isolation had been so great, and she had been so
young, she could not. The only place she had ever got together with
people other than her family, was at church where she had to sit and

listen like the rest. They may have been together physically but they were still isolated in their fear of the threat of hell and trying to follow the preacher's words to learn how each, by individual effort, could get out of burning forever. And this was before she had been hired out.

Margaret could see no way she could connect with the labourers' collective action that could help her with her children and her position now. Only Campbell could help her by letting her stay in the cottage and bringing in the food. She could not see how she could support herself and the children no matter how hard she worked. She would have to keep in with him to get him to do that. She wondered about him and what would happen to him tomorrow. She worried about what O'Neill had said about somebody firing a gun. She needed Campbell if her children were to be looked after. She fell asleep without seeing any other road for her to take.

Chapter Thirty Seven

'Look, let him sleep. He is only a boy.' O'Donnell was talking quietly to Brennan in his mother's cottage. 'We will take care of it. We will fix Campbell. Do not get him into it.'

Brennan looked at O'Donnell. 'I suppose you are right. It's a job for grown men.'

O'Donnell was still disturbed by Kerr's audacity the day before. He was not sure why he was letting the boy sleep on in his cottage while they went out to do Campbell. Was he trying to make sure that he himself was seen as the real fighter or was he concerned for the young boy's safety?

He knew why it had to be done, that was a different matter. All over the country the unions were growing and strikes taking place. The rich farmers of all religions were hoarding and profiteering out of the war while the poor folks were near starvation and the poor men who had gone to fight were being slaughtered. The rage was still in him that he could do nothing at the time of the Dublin uprising and the killing of the leaders. Then he had been hearing about a revolution that had taken place in Russia. He had to do something to change things.

They hurried along the dirt road from his mother's cottage. Brennan was not sure about what they had decided to do.

'So are we going to kill him or just give him a beating? What do you think? Eh, O'Donnell?'

O'Donnell was not sure either what he had in mind. Spurred on by the events of yesterday, thinking of the murder of the Dublin rising leaders, enraged at the way the farmers treated the hired laborers, he knew he had to do something. Campbell was the closest to hand and the leader of the strike-breakers.

'But if he sees us then we will be done for. So maybe we will have to kill him. They killed Connolly and Pearse and the boys.' O'Donnell was angry because he also was unsure. 'We will hide behind that big turf stack of Farron's and if we step out quick behind him and give it to him with this swingletree I brought he will be down and out and never see us.' O'Donnell had brought a swingletree which was used to attach the plough to the chains pulled by the horse. It had a metal covered tip at both ends.

They hid behind the turf stack without any more conversation and waited. Shortly they heard Campbell approaching. As he passed the end of the stack, O'Donnell stepped out and struck him with all his strength on the head with the swingletree. Campbell went down with a grunt. O'Donnell hit him again and again. He lay unconscious on the road. They both stood back and looked in shock at what they had done.

Then Brennan broke the silence. 'I think you have killed him, O'Donnell. I think he is dead.'

They bent over him and the blood was running out of the wounds to Campbell's head. O'Donnell was shocked by what he had done and what he was looking at. 'Aye, he is done for. Let's get out of here.'

They both ran off quickly across the bog in the direction of O'Donnell's cottage. 'What about the swingletree? Get rid of that, O'Donnell. The bog hole . Put it in that and it will sink. There is no bottom to that bog hole.' They took a detour and dumped the weapon.

Campbell lay unconscious and bleeding on the dirt road. But his wounds were not as bad as they had seemed to O'Donnell and Brennan. His skull was not crushed. None of his arteries had been severed. While he still bled, the stream of blood was slowing and beginning to dry up. He was this way when Shanks came on him as he made his way home from checking his rabbit snares. He stood still with the dead rabbit in his hand when he saw the form of Campbell on the road.

Then he ran to him. 'Ah man look at that. Ah man he is killed.' But then he saw the rise and fall of Campbell's chest and knew he was alive. He must do something to save him. What would Margaret do without him? He must do something. He got up and ran towards Campbell's cottage. This was much closer than his own. He banged on the door of the cottage and called to Margaret. She opened the door and looked at him without speaking.

'It's Campbell, Margaret, he is badly hurt on the road down by Farron's turf stack. I need the wee donkey to get him up and if you have a few cloths to wrap his head where he is bleeding.'

Margaret stood still and never answered.

Shanks for once lost his polite manner. 'Margaret!' he shouted 'I need some cloths. Get me some cloths. I am going to get the donkey.'

Shanks ran down to the field where the donkey was grazing and caught it by the bridle which was never taken off its head. He ran up clicking at it to make it trot to the door of the cottage. Margaret had disappeared inside. He put his head in and saw she was coming to him with cloths. 'You stay here with the weans, Margaret, and I will bring him up.' He turned and ran off out of the yard and down the road with the donkey trotting at his heels with its ears back with annoyance.

Campbell was moaning when he got to him. He was a big man and Shanks would have his work cut out for him to get him on the donkey's back. He put the rope from the donkey's bridle on the ground and tramped on it. Holding the donkey in place in this way he put his arms under Campbell's shoulders and tried to lift him. Campbell groaned with pain and Shanks could not get him up. He was too heavy. What would he do? The bleeding was slowed up from what it was before. Some of the wounds had even dried up altogether.

Shanks was stuck. He would have to get help. But who was close? Then he remembered that he had seen Campbell once with an old sheet of corrugated tin that he had tied behind the donkey and used to put bags of turf on and pull them out of the bog. He must have this above at the cottage. Campbell was too big a believer that everybody was a thief, to leave it in the bog. He ran off back up the road.

Sure enough there it was behind the byre. He held it under one arm and ran back again to Campbell. He threw the piece of tin on the ground beside Campbell. The ropes and the collar that Campbell used to attach it to the donkey were all there. Shanks put the collar on the donkey and fastened it across the top of its neck. The donkey was then standing in front of the sheet of tin with two ropes going from its collar back to the one end of the tin.

Shanks then rolled Campbell onto the tin. He settled him on his back on it. This had reopened the wounds again but none of them was bleeding too badly. He took the donkey by the head and urged it on. It felt the weight and tried to stand against Shank's urgings but Shanks was at it and made it move forward. Slowly the tin began to move and the donkey with the makeshift stretcher behind it with Campbell on board, began to move slowly up the road.

At the cottage door Shanks shouted for Margaret. She came out. 'Give me a lift, Margaret. Take his feet.' With Shanks taking his head they carried him into the cottage and laid him up on the bench by the fire where he always lay. He was still unconscious. But his bleeding had mostly stopped and his groaning had become less. He did not look too bad Shanks thought. His colour could have been worse. And he was breathing regularly.

He would go and get Katie. She would be able to help better now. 'Margaret, I am going to get Katie. She will help.' Margaret did not speak. She just looked at Shanks and followed him with her eyes as he went out the door. She was on her own with Campbell for the first time since he had been attacked. She looked at him lying there unconscious. She heard Victoria chortle to herself in the bed. She was awake.

She went into the room to see if the children were all right. She stood and looked at them. Victoria was awake and frightened. Mary, Anne and Martha were still asleep. For a while she stood there. Campbell had to get better. She needed his support for the children. She turned and went over to him. The cloths she had given Shanks were there on the bench beside him. She took these and took some hot water from the hanging can above the fire. She wet them and she began to wash Campbell's wounds. She felt as if she was attending to one of her children. This was how she managed to help this man who had brought her so little help in her life and so much pain. By imagining he was a child.

The blood began to seep from the main wound and she kept pressing the cloth against it and it began to slow again. She sat there on his bench and worked at him. This was the first time she had ever sat on his bench. The first time she had ever touched his head or touched him anywhere. She had always been touched by him before. By his fist, or his thing. Now she was touching him. And her touch was helping him.

When the blood had stopped, Margaret wrapped a strip of cloth around his head and fastened it by tucking in its end. He was lying on his back breathing regularly. He did not look bad. His colour was good. At this point Katie and Shanks arrived. 'The bleeding has stopped, Margaret?' Katie asked. She looked at them and nodded. 'That's good. He does not look bad. Do you think you should get the doctor, Margaret?'

Margaret did not know what to say. She did not know how to get a doctor. She did not know if they had any money to pay a doctor. She thought of her father not getting the doctor for her mother. She did not answer Katie.

'Well if the bleeding has stopped, Margaret, and he seems to be breathing all right and his colour is not bad then maybe we could wait a bit. Save the expense. Anyway you never know how long it would take that Doctor Johnston to get here. It might be days. Can we help you in any way, Margaret?'

As Katie was speaking Campbell began to stir on the bench. He groaned and opened his eyes. He looked around him. The blows had partially concussed him. His vision was damaged and his awareness distorted. He could see Margaret and Shanks and Katie but he could not make out how far they were from him. They also seemed distorted. Katie came to him with a tin mug of water. She put her hand behind the back of his neck and held the mug to his lips and he drank. His eyes opened and closed and he lay back resting.

'You will be all right, Campbell. I found you on the road down by Farron's turf stack. Your head is badly cut. But the bleeding has stopped, Margaret here bandaged you. You are going to be all right. You just need a bit of time and rest. What happened you anyway? Somebody must have hit you. Did you see anybody? Do you remember what happened?'

Campbell did not answer. He was not going to answer anybody's questions. Instead he fell back into sleep again. 'I think he will be all right, Margaret. He just needs some sleep and rest and his bandages changed. Come on, Katie, we will go and leave Margaret here to get on with whatever she has to do.'

'If you need us, Margaret, come up and get us. We will always be here to give you a hand anytime you need it. Your children are doing okay? They look well anyway,' Katie said as she looked round the door into the room where they were lying on the bed.

It was later in the morning and Campbell was still sleeping or semi-conscious, it was not clear which, when Margaret heard a man's voice calling; 'Campbell! Campbell!' She went out to the door and saw Brown sitting in his trap and the Sergeant standing by his bicycle. Margaret had no idea of the role that Brown had played in her life. 'Girl,' the Sergeant addressed Margaret, the mother of four children, 'we are here to see Campbell.' The Sergeant wheeled his bicycle into the yard and leaned it against the cottage wall. Brown drove the trap in.

Margaret went back into the cottage and stood in front of the doorway to her room where the children lay. The two men entered without being asked and saw Campbell lying bandaged and asleep. 'Well that's too bad. What happened to him anyway, girl?' Margaret did not answer. So Brown went on, 'we heard that Shanks found him beaten on the road. We will look into this. Sergeant, you must find out what happened to this man.' The Sergeant nodded.

Brown reached out and shook Campbell. 'Campbell. Campbell. Wake up man . We are here to see you. The Sergeant wants to know what happened to you.' Campbell opened his eyes. 'Campbell, what happened to you?'

Campbell had recovered from the concussion by now. His head hurt bad but other than that he could not feel any great after-effects. 'I do not remember anything. I was walking down the road and then I was lying here. My head, it's not good.'

The Sergeant spoke up. 'Campbell, somebody attacked you that is clear. You did not see anybody? Can you help us at all with who it might be? Do you remember anything at all?' Campbell said he did not. 'Well then we will be on our way. We had no men to help out today at all. The farmers are meeting tonight and they are going to pay the same rate as in Lifford and Murlog districts. The strike should be over tomorrow. Campbell, you did a good job for us yesterday. You will be better soon.' And the two men left and Margaret could hear them move off down the road.

Margaret had boiled some spuds and eggs and set these on the table. He slowly rose from the bench, groaning with the pain, and sat at the table and ate the food. When he was finished, he slowly and unsteadily went outside. Margaret could hear him cross the yard. He must be going. When he came back in he went back and lay on his bench and in a few minutes he was asleep again. Margaret breathed again with relief and lay on the bed with her babies and fell asleep.

In the pub O'Donnell, Brennan and young Kerr had arrived and joined the rest of the men at the fire. 'O'Donnell, did you hear about Campbell? They found him badly wounded on the road this morning. The Sergeant and Brown were up seeing him. It appears that he can remember nothing about what happened. Whoever did it are lucky men.' Everybody was watching O'Donnell closely while McDaid was talking.

O'Donnell was giving nothing away. 'Aye, we heard about it. I wonder what that was about. Well, he treated a lot of men badly so he must have a lot of enemies.'

'Aye, that he has,' Brennan joined in.

'Aye. And on the strike, I hear they are going to pay what we are asking, the Lifford and Murlog rates. This is good.' O'Donnell was cleverly changing the subject. All eyes turned to him when he said this.

'They are,' Brennan said. 'Well that's only right. They should have done it without the men having to strike. They always say we are only a pair of hands. But this shows what happens when they do not have their hands.'

Young Kerr was the only one who did not appear happy about the news. The rest of them were laughing and celebrating. O'Donnell noticed Kerr.

'What is wrong with you Kerr?'

'Ten shillings a week, eight with food. It is still nothing. And now

I have to go back and slave for that Magee again. If I do not, he will say that I broke the contract and I will get nothing for the months I have worked since the start of the season.'

This sobered the men. It made them realise how little had been won. They looked at Kerr.

'What about your folks, Kerr? Can you not go back to them?'

'I have not seen them for five years. I have nothing to bring them, no money. They would be expecting me to bring back something. No. I have to go back to that Magee's. That is all that is for it. I will have to go back to Magee's.'

O'Donnell and Brennan had told nobody about their assault on Campbell. Kerr had still been sleeping when they had got back to the cottage that morning. Brennan would have to go back to work for Murphy to finish out his contract to the autumn. Kerr would have to go back to Magee's. O'Donnell lived with his mother in the cottage and made a living out of the three fields, the bit of bog and poaching, and the odd job he would pick up driving to Derry and surrounding towns for some of the farmers.

Brennan turned to Kerr. 'Look, Kerr, when the time is up with you at Magee's it will be up for me at Murphy's. I will come and look for you there. Do not hire on with him again. The two of us can head over to Scotland for the spud gathering and we can see if we get work over there after and stay there. Leave this bloody country. What do you think? Come on, Kerr.' Kerr looked up and with an effort he nodded his head in agreement.

'All right, but it will be even worse now back at Magee's because I was out on the strike. They will be looking to get their own back.'

CHAPTER THIRTY EIGHT

It was the morning after Campbell was attacked. Margaret came in from milking the cow. Victoria had been looking after the other three weans who were still asleep on the bed. Campbell was sitting up on the bench. The bandage had become unravelled and one end of it was hanging down his back. He was feeling carefully at the back of his head through the bandage. Margaret went to the fire which she had stirred into life before she went out, and lifted off the hanging can of water.

Campbell did not speak to her or look at her. She felt the water and it was not too hot to her touch. She got a cloth from the room where the children slept and went and stood in front of Campbell with the can in one hand and the cloth in the other. She did not speak. Nor did he. Then he turned around and sat with his back to her on the bench. He offered his back and head to her. She unwound the bandage the rest of the way and washed his wounds. Then she bandaged him again with another cloth.

No words were exchanged throughout this process. Campbell occasionally groaned in pain. He was numbed with the attack and the after-shock. He did not know what he thought of her at this time. He lay back down on the bench and drifted off to sleep. Margaret washed out the cloths and hung them on the couple of bushes outside to dry.

She felt stronger in herself after tending to him, more confident. She felt that Campbell was not so much in control of her as before.

As time went on, there were more occasions when she was acting on others rather than she was being acted on. Her children were the most important in this regard. She gave birth to them, she fed them, she looked after them in every way. She grew in strength as she did so. Now with Campbell injured she was looking after his wounds. She already made his food. She had built the toilet, she planted the potatoes, she milked the cow, she had got the rooster and now was able to breed young chicks and sell the eggs. She was getting control over more aspects of her life.

But she had to be careful as much of this was built on sand. She owned nothing. He owned the cottage and the piece of land and without these she was powerless. She had to go along with his wishes because he owned everything. But it was not totally one sided, she had been making gains. She had been getting his control slackened if only by a minor degree. But this made life easier for her and for her children.

It was a week later and Campbell had recovered enough to be able to get about. He left to go to see Brown. Margaret and he had never spoken during the previous days as she had tended his wounds. But he had been more passive and showed none of the antagonism to her that he usually did. During these days he sat outside when it was not raining, or sat in the byre. The children saw more of him during this time and Victoria would regularly go and hold onto his knee when he ate. He showed no resentment to this.

Campbell knocked at Brown's door. 'Well it's good to see you on your feet again, Campbell. You are looking well recovered. Come on into the harness room here. I knew you were coming and the Sergeant is on his way up so we can have a chat about who did this. There he is now. Sergeant,' he called and the Sergeant saw them and crossed the yard into the harness room.

'How are you, Mister Brown? How are you, Campbell?'

'He is looking well is he not, Sergeant?'

'Aye, he is that. He is looking well.' Campbell did not speak because he recognized the old soft soap for what it was. 'Now, Campbell, I hope that your memory has come back and that you can help us with who did this to you. We cannot let somebody think they can take the law into their own hands and attack people who are only going about their work and helping keep things going when those strikers were going to ruin the hay.'

'I can remember nothing,' Campbell grunted.

'Nothing at all?' The Sergeant queried as he looked at Brown and then again at Campbell. 'I think that O'Donnell was at the centre of it, Campbell. He is not a good boy. He is involved in that Sinn Fein business and he never shuts his mouth about that Connolly the Socialist who was a leader in the Dublin treachery. We want to put a stop to O'Donnell. And remember it was O'Donnell who shouted at you and warned you not to help us against the strikers.'

Campbell sat there. 'I saw nothing, nobody. I remember nothing.'

Brown intervened this time. 'Look Campbell, even if you did not get a proper look. Even if you did not see clearly that it was O'Donnell, we are sure he was involved. And anyway we want him out of the way. If you can help us here we will appreciate it. The Sergeant can arrest him and you can explain that it was him who did it and that will be the end of it. He will be out of the way for years.'

Campbell realised what they were trying to do. They were trying to get him to say it was O'Donnell whether it was O'Donnell or not. They did not care who did it. They wanted O'Donnell. It would be simple for him to say he saw O'Donnell and give them what they wanted. This is what he always did. He gave the powers that be what they wanted. He knew his place. But for some reason he could not understand he felt a stubborn determination not to go along with them on this.

He had gone along with Brown on everything for years. Harassing the tenants who rented the bog banks. Cutting the banks down smaller and charging the same rents. Spying on those he met on a day-to-day basis and reporting back to Brown. Then taking herself in and marrying her. And now organizing the men to do the work when the labourers were on strike. He had done everything that Brown had asked him.

But there was something stopping him saying that he had seen O'Donnell. It was not because he had any love for O'Donnell. Far from it. It was something in himself. They did not even ask him into the house, even now with his injuries, or even offer him a glass of water. Then they wanted him to do anything they suggested. They wanted him to swear lies as well as everything else. He felt a dogged determination rise in him. He was not their slave. They left him alone after a while when it was clear he was not going to do what they wanted.

He headed back up the road with his donkey and the dog. He had brought the donkey to lean on in his weakness. He was still feeling weak. When he was over half way home he went in over a hedge and lay down and rested. He drifted in and out of sleep and the sun heated him as he lay. He began to dream. It had to do with himself, Brown, the Sergeant and Lord Taverstock whom he had never met.

They were all in the church together and the four of them were singing in the choir. Every few bars they would stop and the other three would turn on Campbell and in unison they would shout. 'Campbell, you are not singing our tune.' He awoke with a start. Not singing their tune. What did that mean? He always sang their tune. He always sang their tune. This was the truth. He lay back down again and drifted off to sleep once more. But the dream had frightened him. Had he ruined things with Brown and the Sergeant?

This time he dreamt of her at home. She was bandaging his head.

As she was doing this she was singing and dancing around him. In his dream he got more and more worried. Why was she singing and dancing? Anybody who was singing and dancing was not doing enough work. Or she was up to something and trying to hide this. In his dream she shouted 'I am a good woman.' He awoke with a start. The sweat was running down his face.

What, what was this? She was a good woman. Singing and dancing. What was she saying? Then he remembered it was a dream. But it left him disturbed. He knew that she was still doing what she was told but he also knew that she was not doing it in the same way as before. He knew that there was a bit of her that he did not control as before. The fourth baby made it worse. This bit of her was growing. She had been bandaging him all week. She need not think that she would get away with anything because of that. It was her job to bandage him.

He felt under pressure from all sides. She was pushing on him at one end, pressurizing him from below. She never said it but she wanted more room to breathe. She wanted more from him for her children and herself. Just like those strikers and those Dublin boys had tried to rise up against things from below. Why would they not learn? Why would they not learn? They had to know their place. They had to stay in their place. Look at him, he knew his place. He stayed in his place. There was no point in trying to change things from below.

Then he had Brown and the Sergeant pressurizing from above. Trying to get him to say he had seen O'Donnell and to get him to do the strikers' work and to spy on O'Donnell and everybody he met. Well that was only their job to keep him in his place. To get him to do what made things run best for them. It would be better if O'Donnell was away out the area. He would not be there to stir up the other boys. Brown and the Sergeant were right. But then why did he not give them what they wanted? He squelched the thought that, by not naming O'Donnell, maybe he too was slipping the controls. He could not afford to entertain that thought.

He sat there thinking about things. Her at home, the tenants, his job was to keep control of them, to teach them their place. This was his job and he did it well. If they would only accept their place it would be better for them and for him, for everybody. Then there was Brown and the Sergeant. Why would he not give them what they wanted? That was his place to do this. Why would he not? He felt that he was going to burst as he thought about the pressures on him and worried about his refusal to go along and name O'Donnell. He held his head with both hands as he tried to escape from the pressure.

Later, as he was on his way home again and he neared McDaid's, he felt he wanted a drink. He tied the donkey outside and went in. The bandage was off his head but there were wounds in the back of his head still and his hair was matted around them. There was the usual crowd around the fire and they stopped talking when they saw it was him. McDaid broke the silence. 'It's good to see you again, Campbell. How are you feeling? I hope you are feeling better.'

Campbell grunted in reply and sat at the door. The crowd around the fire resumed their talking. O'Donnell was holding forth. 'Look, everybody has the right to live. Everybody has the right to a bite to eat and a place to sleep. Us labourers we are not treated right. Twelve hours and fourteen hours a day and sleeping in the barn. We should not have had to strike to get the same pay as the boys in the Lifford district. That was not right. Look at the trouble they caused by trying to stop us getting the raise.' Campbell heard this and for a minute thought yes if they had not forced them to strike he would never have been beaten up. But he quickly pushed this thought away.

O'Donnell went on: 'They came here and stole the land. They took the other crops and starved us when the spuds failed. They forced us off to the boat. They jailed or killed those that fought them. This is not right. And it's not only the other kind that do this. Our own kind do it too. Look at Murphy in Dublin and look at our own kind around here who hire out labourers. They treat them just as bad as the other kind does.'

Campbell listened to O'Donnell and as he did so he reassured himself that there was no way for him to find a way out upwards. His refusal to name O'Donnell was only an episode. It was not the beginning of a rebellion. He had his cottage, his few fields, his bog lettings, his cow and few animals. He could not be risking all this. Naw, there was no way out upwards. He was going to carry on as before. He had the few fields, the bog lettings, the cow and herself working around the place. This was the best way for him to continue. If he went up against Brown and them he would pay. He might squeeze a little extra here and there from them. This was possible. But not take them on openly.

Now for a second he wished he had told them it was O'Donnell. He could have got something out of it. But he still felt he could not do this. There was something else that held him back. It was about her, something about the way she had treated him, looking after his wounds and feeding him without a word since he was attacked. There was something about this. She had acted right to him. It seemed like this meant he had to do something right now too or she would get even more out of his control. She would be better than him and if he knew she was better than him, and if he thought he was obliged to her, it would be even harder to control her. This was also involved in his refusal to lie about O'Donnell for them. Margaret had acted right to him, he had to act right if only for once and even if it involved O'Donnell.

He pushed in the door of the cottage. The fire was low and she and the weans were in bed. He went and lay on the bench. After a while he got up and went to her, pulled her legs to the side of the bed and entered her body. He pushed at her and his sperm went up inside her. He pulled his thing out of her and went back to his bench. He felt disturbed by what he had done. He felt that he should have touched her easier. He did not feel that putting his thing in her and doing what he wanted and taking it out and walking away from her, was right.

He swore to himself as he went back to his bench and realised why he was feeling disturbed. He was thinking of what she thought and felt. He was thinking about her as a person. This was bad. He would have to stop it. It did not mean anything what she thought or felt, or what he thought and felt. They had to know their place. He had to know his place. He had to do what they wanted. He did not lie for them today. That was just an isolated incident. He knew his place.

She would have to know her place, he would have to keep her in her place. To do that he would have to stop thinking of what she was feeling and of what she wanted. What she thought and what she felt had no place in the way things were. Who did she think she was? She would do what he said and like it. Did he not feed her and give her a roof over her head? She should be glad of everything he had done for her.

He lay down on the bench. His head hurt. He touched it and thought of her again. It was her job to bandage him. She was here to work and to look after him. She had her place and she would have to do as she was told. He hardened himself up again against her and his own better feelings. He wished he could go back and put his thing in her again and pull it out and turn away and feel nothing.

Chapter Thirty Nine

Margaret's four children, her work in the house and with the animals around the cottage, her putting in of the spuds and vegetables, left her little time for anything else. She made her weekly visits to McDaid's to sell her eggs and buy the odd thing for the children, either for them to eat or wool to knit them clothes. She and the children went with Katie and gradually she became more comfortable with Katie in spite of the fact she could not hold up her end of the conversation. She was able to save a few pence every month out of the egg sales and she hid it in a hole at the bottom of the wall behind the outhouse. Campbell no longer attacked her about the money.

Without Victoria she would not have been able to cope with all her work. She had turned into a great wee girl who loved to help out. She was four and with Mary almost three, Margaret did not have to do everything. She was getting help especially in looking after the two younger children. Victoria would hold them and make sure they did not hurt themselves when Margaret was working.

Margaret also found that Campbell seemed to be less antagonistic to her and the children since the attack was made on him. Or maybe it was because she had looked after him so well. He had healed up and seemed to have completely recovered. Nobody had ever been found responsible. He still came to her on some nights. He never repeated the more gentle touching of her of that one night but he was not so crude and brutal either. It was as if the beating had taken some of the edge off him.

Margaret struggled with herself to deal with this new situation. She was glad he was less harsh but she was also angry that he could not sort out whatever was his problem and try to be more human both to the children and herself. Why could he not talk to the children and herself and why could he not touch her again the way he had that night when he had got frightened and ran outside? But she did not dwell on these issues much. Her life was filled with unrelenting work. In spite of the help from Victoria and Mary, her new baby Martha and also Anne took every minute of her day. Not that she resented that in any way. She felt for them the way she felt for the others. They had brought her more of the only good thing she had in her life. Without them she would never have been able to get over the terrible brutalization of her spirit that had occurred at Allen's.

When she came from there she could not laugh or smile or talk. But her babies and what she had to do for them had changed that. But it was not only that. It was also their spirit and their laughter and their gentle skins which had evoked in her a renewed hidden laughter. She thought of this as she was in the bed with them one night when Campbell had still not come home. Looking at them she wondered what happened to people who had no children or who had children who were killed or who died. Thinking about this she sat up with a start. What would happen if any of her children were killed or died? She was stricken with horror as she thought of it. It would be a disaster for all of them. For her children. For herself. Would it kill her spirit? But she would not let anything happen to any of them, she would make sure of that.

Thinking of this she thought about the fact that she was already pregnant again. It was early 1918. She would have it in early summer.

That would be five babies she would have and she was still only nineteen years old. But she loved them all and without them she would be in a terrible mess altogether. She would most likely still be hired out. Five babies. This made her think about the bed. She would have to do something. They would never all fit. She could no longer put off making a new mattress for a couple of them. She liked sleeping in the one bed with them all so much. This is what she was doing but with five this would be impossible.

Ever since she had got the rooster from Katie and Shanks and had been getting the new chicks along with the new eggs, she had been killing one of the older hens for eating every few months. She would pluck it and save the feathers. She had a bag of them saved up now. It was not enough to make a small mattress on the floor for Victoria and Mary but she would take some from the large mattress to fill it out. But the problem was she needed a cover to put them in. Any cloth would not do as they would work their way out. She needed the special bed tic material that McDaid sold. Would she have enough money? She would ask Katie.

She thought about Katie and Shanks and how much they helped her even though they were not ones of her own. Katie's father had died the year before. Margaret was ashamed she had not been able to go to the wake or to speak properly to Katie when she saw her next. She had to recognize that she would never be able to speak properly, that she would never be able to relate properly to others even those who helped most like Katie and Shanks. Something must be broken in her. She would wait and see Katie some day going past and ask her about the bed material.

She thought more about this. This was the greatest damage that Allen had done to her. Not the physical damage of her rapes as horrific as they were, but the destruction of her ability to speak properly. She could not say what she thought to her friends, Katie and Shanks.

Especially she could not say when she had good feelings. Only to her children when she was alone could she express good thoughts. And even there she still worried that they were not hearing her talk properly to other people and that this could prevent them talking properly. Yes, this was the greatest damage that Allen had done to her, he had damaged her ability to speak and express positive feelings.

On the day of their next weekly visit to McDaid's, which was always a Wednesday as this was when Campbell went to Brown and Katie and Shanks had fitted in with this without asking, Margaret managed to ask about the bed.

'I need a new bed for two of the children. I have the feathers but need the cover. Do McDaid's have this? How much is it? I have some money and I hope it is enough'.

This was the most Margaret had ever said to Katie and Shanks. They were taken by surprise. Margaret was ashamed again thinking she could have spoken to them better about Katie's father's death. She was wrong not to have tried harder. When her children needed something she tried harder.

Shanks recovered and answered. 'Aye, McDaid has it. But he will try and make you pay too much for it or buy too much. We will have to keep him in his place. He is one miserable boy. Just about everything he sells he tries to give low weight or water down. He would be trying to water the drink if there were not so many experts who drink in that pub who would be able to taste it and know. And they would not take well to their drink being watered. McDaid is afraid of them. Aye, that McDaid boy. He is so tight he squeaks. But come along with us and you will be all right.'

'Hello, Katie and Shanks, Hello, Mrs Campbell.' McDaid was recognizing Campbell's so-called superior status in the community. It had never struck Margaret before but this time it did. Why did McDaid not call Shanks and Katie Mr and Mrs? This was not right that she should be treated better than them. They were good people. They had helped her out and treated her better than anybody. They were as good as her. Yet McDaid wanted to put them down. He wanted to put them in what he thought was their place. He wanted to make sure everybody knew he thought they were not as important as her. She was ashamed by this action of McDaid and for herself for being treated better.

'Aye, McDaid,' Shanks said getting his own back by calling him McDaid, 'Margaret wants some bed tic. She wants to make a mattress for her two oldest ones. And she wants it at a fair price too.'

'Sure Shanks, everything here is at a fair price. You know that. Come on over here. This is where we have it.' McDaid was putting on a good front but inside he was fuming because he knew he would have to charge Margaret the right price with Shanks and Katie there. If he did not they would spread the word all over the country.

'You will probably want enough to make a mattress that can do them when they grow up, Mrs. Campbell?' he said trying to get something out of the situation.

'Now why would she need that, McDaid?' Shanks said. 'Sure when that time comes she can use what she has in this wee mattress and get some more from you then. Naw, she only needs enough for the two young ones. Maybe about eight foot by four foot will do. That should do. What do you think of this, Margaret? Would this do?'

Margaret nodded her head and murmured 'Aye' in agreement.

'And do you need a needle and some thread?'

'Some thread, that will be all.' Shanks answered McDaid.

'Margaret, you will need that tough thread but the needle you have is all right.' Katie advised her.

'How much is that, McDaid? And now do not be doing this woman here. It would not do if it got about that she was not treated fair. And with what happened to her poor husband only a while ago.'

McDaid said nothing but he was enraged as he cut the cloth and got the thread for Margaret. They even threw Campbell's beating up at him, he thought, as he watched the three of them as they sold him their eggs, bought a few other odds and ends and headed back up the hill.

'Margaret, how are you getting on with the four weans now? It must be hard work and on top of that the yard work and the house-work. You must be near killed altogether.'

Margaret did not speak. She had not managed to be able to carry on a conversation with others except her children. Only if Shanks confronted her directly, and then only to answer with one or two words or only if she had a very specific need for the children, did she speak in any kind of way. It was only at home with the children when Campbell was not there that she carried on a full conversation. Shanks had given up trying as he felt too sorry for her when he tried to force her to answer direct.

As they walked, Katie and Shanks talked between themselves for Margaret's benefit. Shanks liked to tell her stories and see if he could get a response. 'Margaret, you know what happened last week? You know the Apache boy I have told you about a few times. Well he came up to our house and he was full. He had been drinking all day. He goes on the tear for weeks at a time until his money runs out. Then he goes around and borrows to keep going another while. Well he came up to our place and came in. He was well on. He is one funny man when he is well on. He can come out with them. "Shanks" he said to me "what are you doing up there at the fire? You look like the ember of a turf. Katie, what are you up to these days? I do not know how you can put up with a man like Shanks here. What you need is a real man like myself."

'That Apache is some boy.' Shanks and Katie both laughed togeth-er, remembering what had happened. 'We got him to take a bite to eat at the end of it but we could loan him nothing as we have nothing at the moment. And he only got bread and tea as things are tight these days. There is not much to spare.'

Margaret thought about the story and how Katie and Shanks must be short of food. When they got back to Margaret's cottage she said 'Wait. Wait.'

Katie and Shanks were surprised. Margaret left the children with Katie and Shanks and quickly ran in and wrapped a dozen eggs in a flour bag and ran back out and gave them to Katie.

'Eggs. Eat them.' she said.

Katie and Shanks were shocked. Shanks went to give them back but Katie knew it was important for Margaret to be able to help them. It would make her feel better about herself. They thanked Margaret and went on up towards their home while she went into her cottage.

Margaret went inside and held her children and looked at the cloth for the new bed. She also felt a strong contentment that she had been able to help Shanks and Katie. And from the eggs that she was getting from her hens. She had the smallest bit of independence and she was able to help Katie and Shanks. She hugged her children and they broke free from her and the two oldest played around the floor while she put the two youngest onto the bed and then lay down herself and breastfed Martha. Breastfeeding her baby always renewed her spirit and laid her down content.

CHAPTER FORTY

Margaret woke to hear the knocking on the door. Campbell got up and pulled on his trousers and shouted 'Who is there?'

'It's me for Margaret. The old man is dying. He will probably be gone when I get back. Margaret you should come over.'

Margaret could not see how she could go with the children. Anyway she had long lost any good feeling for her father. Campbell opened the door and her brother James came in.

Campbell continued dressing and grunted. 'I'll go'. It was the closest thing to speaking directly to her and doing anything personal for her that she had ever heard. And it had to come with death. With that he and James turned and left. James was looking round to see what would Margaret do.

Margaret lay and thought about her mother's death and how they had let her die without a doctor. She wondered if they had got a doctor for him. She felt nothing for him. He had sent her to Allen's and took her money and if Allen had not raped her and she had not got pregnant she might be there yet. And they were able to do without her money when she was no longer hired out so she did not have to go through that misery. He had just wanted something extra. She was sure that her mother did not see anything of the money she had earned at Allen's.

Margaret could not leave the house with the weans alone. She went about her usual work and waited to hear what was going on. That night Katie and Shanks came to her door and told her that her father was dead. She asked them in and she made them tea. She felt a powerful warmth in this act of hospitality to them, she felt more for their help than about the death of her father. She did not cry.

'Aye, he died a couple of hours ago, Margaret. Pneumonia it was in the end. He went very quickly and there was no pain. He was a hard working man. We are very sorry for your trouble.' Margaret said nothing. She just sat down and held her youngest child while Shanks and Katie ate.

They realised that she did not want to talk and said they would come down tomorrow if she wanted to go over, and help her with the children. Margaret shook her head from side to side.

'You do not want to go, Margaret?'

Margaret spoke, 'Just to the funeral, that is all.'

Katie and Shanks looked at each other and for a moment were quiet. They thought also about how Margaret's father had sent her to Allen's and taken her money and treated her mother. They did not try to get her to change her mind.

'Well, Margaret, we will be going over to the funeral too so we will call in and help you over with the children. There is a service at the house and then it goes to the church. We will be going to the house.'

On the day of the funeral Campbell went off early without any talk with her about was she going and, if so, how was she getting there. He was no sooner gone than Shanks and Katie came. Katie said, 'Margaret why don't I stay here with the youngest ones and you go with Victoria and Shanks? Or if you want to leave Victoria too this is okay with me. Whatever you think is for the best.'

Margaret did not know what to do. She had to decide about leaving her children behind. Could she not take them with her? But they were too heavy to carry and only Victoria could walk any distance.

Katie resolved it for her. 'Here, Margaret, you take Victoria. I will stay here with Mary, Anne and Martha. We will be great here and keep ourselves company. You and Shanks and Victoria be off with you.'

Shanks replied, 'That is a good idea, Katie. Come, Margaret.'

And before she could think about it much more, Margaret found herself being bundled out the door. Martha and Anne were still asleep but Mary was up and began to cry as Margaret started to walk down the yard to the road. Katie took Mary up in her arms and called to Margaret, 'Don't worry we will all be okay here'.

Margaret's heart was pounding as she walked. Victoria held her hand and skipped. This was all that kept her going. The three of them, Victoria, herself and Shanks, walked along, with Victoria asking questions and Shanks answering them and Margaret silent and almost in a state of shock. But gradually she recovered and thought about Katie looking after her children before and how they would be all right. She braced herself and strengthened herself. She did not know why she was going to the funeral anyway. It was just because so many people expected her to go.

Margaret's father's cottage was surrounded by a large crowd of men talking. Inside were the women making tea and serving up bread and butter and carrying it out. The men were eating and also drinking either from a bottle of stout or from small bottles of whisky they kept in their pockets. They approached Margaret when she came and told her they were sorry for her trouble. Her two brothers were there amongst them. They just looked at her. Margaret said nothing.

Two of her father's neighbours had taken over when her father had died and laid him out in his best set of clothes and put him in the coffin. She went inside and looked at him in the coffin and thought very little. His actions towards her had long ago killed any feelings she had for him. She looked at him again and then two women she did not know came and took her arms on both sides and led her away. 'They are going to close him up now.'

The room went silent as a couple of men with hammers lifted the lid of the coffin from beside the coffin, and began to hammer it into place. Margaret looked around and thought about how things worked. The women who came to the wake had brought donations of food and some of the men brought donations of cigarettes or tobacco or alcohol. In this way her father had been waked. There was only herself living away in Campbell's place and her two brothers and they were not capable of putting such an event together.

Margaret was sat down by some of the women who brought her food and she ate. Many women and men came and offered their sympathy. She would nod and say nothing. She had a cup of tea and a slice of buttered bread. She was astonished and also guilty how good she felt to be served rather than having to serve herself. She sat and drank and ate and looked around her. One of the woman she knew from when she was a very young child, sat with her and held Victoria and made a fuss of her. Victoria too had tea and buttered bread.

After some time Margaret realised that there was some kind of trouble about the service. A woman came to her and said that the minister had been supposed to be there over one hour before for the service but there was no sign of him. If the funeral did not leave soon then it would be too late for the people who were waiting at the church where the main service was to be held. A general agreement developed that the minister had lost his way and could not find the cottage. It was also agreed that Margaret's father's body would have to be taken off without a service at his home. 'What can be done?' one of the neighbours said, 'There is no minister'.

A number of men gathered round the coffin where it was set on wooden supports in the kitchen and carried it outside and put it into the back of the horse drawn hearse. There was a pause as nobody felt comfortable with what was going on. There was no minister. There would be no service. The body would be being taken away from the home place without any kind of words being said over it. This was not good. People looked at each other but could see no way out. There was no minister.

Then to everybody's astonishment Shanks stepped forward. 'Look boys this is no good. Taking a man away from his home place with no words being said over him. Some of you boys say something.' and he gestured to a number of men who included Margaret's brothers who were Protestants like Margaret's father. They stood there shuffling their feet and looking down. They did not answer. They made no move to do anything. 'Come on now,' Shanks said again to them but still they did nothing.

'Well no man should be taken from his own home without a couple of words said over him so if you won't do it I will do it. I will.'

And stepping up to a high spot on the rocky yard outside of the cottage Shanks said: 'Good God. All of us here may see some small things different about you but we all here believe you are God Almighty. So we ask you today to look down upon this man, our neighbour, and look after him from now on. He tried his best to get through this hard world. With your help we look forward to him joining you in the next. Look after his children also, and we look forward to all being together in the next world.'

The gathering were frozen in place for a moment at Shanks' audacity. Here he was stepping forward to take the minister's place, but not only that, here he was stepping forward as a Catholic to say the service over a Protestant at the Protestant's funeral. Nobody said a word. The hearse driver went to the horses' head and led it out of the yard to break the paralysis that Shanks' actions had brought. The men who were going to the service at the church, fell in and walked behind the hearse. The women stayed behind as was the custom.

As the funeral moved off all present were thinking of Shanks' actions. Why had he been able to act when the Protestants had not? Shanks had spent years on the drink. He had come to be looked down on during that time but he had also come to be able to look up and see that society was not what it made itself out to be. It was full of hypocrisy and phony people and institutions. The landlords, the priests, the ministers, the shopkeepers, none of them were any better than anybody else. And he was no worse than any of them. He was just as able to talk to God as any of them. Having been at the so-called very bottom of society for a time, having been looked down on and scorned by society for a while, had enabled Shanks to see and criticize that society much more clearly.

But for those who saw things as fixed and who wanted to be accepted by that society, it was a different thing. They did not want to break the rules. Speaking to God was the job for the minister or the priest. It did not do to usurp their position. To do so would mean that the powers that be in society would not trust them anymore. The Protestant peasants were indoctrinated into believing that their marginally privileged place in society was secure only if they knew and kept their place. And for the better off farmers and landowners, both Catholic and Protestant, and for McDaid who was also at the funeral, it would not do to take over the minister's job as they too believed their privileged place in society was secure only if they kept their particular allotted slot in it,

This would go round the country now like wildfire. That Shanks had done the service at Wallace's house. Aye, Shanks would be looked at even more as an outsider and a character than before. His years lying drunk had made him an object of mild contempt but harmless. But now he would be seen as mildly suspect and somebody to be watched. If there were anything to be given out in the future this would be remembered. Shanks would be at the back of the line. Aye, you would never know what he would do. Did he not take over the minister's place at Wallace's funeral? The others who stood with their heads down shuffling their feet, they were safe, they would be nearer the front of the line.

But Shanks did not care. He was very content. He had spent years on the drink and in misery. Now he was out of it and he had his few fields and a good woman and was able to get by. He wanted nothing from anybody. Not only did he not care but as he walked with the funeral procession he felt that he had done the right thing. And that is a powerful feeling. That he had stepped forward and done the right thing without thinking about it, he was proud of himself. He would tell Katie when he got back. None of the rest of them had the guts. He was proud of himself.

CHAPTER FORTY ONE

Margaret's fifth child was born in the spring of 1918. She named her Kathleen. She thought it was because of all the help Katie had given her but she did not think of this until after she had named it. It seemed the children were coming quicker now. But she was able to cope with them better as she had become more skilled and the older ones were also able to help her a little. But one of the things she regretted about having five was that the last year she had not been able to make her yearly visit to the lake. This had become like a pilgrimage to her mother as well as an annual excursion for the children. She wanted to go this year with her new baby and also to take Martha for the first time. Katie? Would taking Katie spoil it?

The next day when she saw Katie she went out on the road and spoke as she had never spoken to Katie before.

'I want to go up for a walk to the lake. Would you help me and come and we could take the children? Would Shanks like to come and be with us and the children too? Tomorrow the weather looks like being good.'

Katie glowed. 'We will do that, we will do it.'

Margaret was very pleased as Campbell would be away at Brown's the next day. 'That is good,' Margaret said, speaking out better than she had for some time. Again it was when the needs of her children were at stake.

'Tomorrow morning then, Margaret ,we will be down around twelve or so. Will that do?'

The next day Margaret, Katie, Shanks and the five children set off for the lake. Margaret carrying her newest born child, Katie the next and Shanks carrying Martha. The other two, Victoria and Mary scampered along ahead and wondered and asked non-stop questions about everything they saw. Margaret was bursting with happiness at their joy and at being able to make the trip again after missing it last year. Now two of her children would be seeing it for the first time. The only thing was she did not know if she felt so good about Katie and Shanks being there. But they did not talk much, they seemed to know this was something that was almost sacred for her.

Margaret had noticed that Shanks had been carrying a bundle with him and thought it was some fishing or snaring gear but it looked far too big for that. But he made no move to open it when they got to the lake. She forgot about it as the older children paddled in the lake and as she and Katie held the younger ones' feet in it. All the children squealed with delight except the youngest who was too young to really enjoy it. Margaret herself felt wonderful and refreshed as her feet were cooled and cleaned in the water.

Margaret was also wishing that she would see a fish again as they had once before. But none appeared. The seagulls and the crows came and hovered around them to see if there was anything to eat. Again Margaret was struck by how much she liked the dignity of the crows and their black feathers and the way they walked, not exactly strutting, but more carefully putting one foot in front of the other. She wondered if she could get a crow for a pet.

'They are looking for something to eat,' Shanks said, 'I am kind of hungry myself. Maybe it is time to have a bite.'

Margaret did not know what he was talking about. He reached for his bundle and opened it up. Inside were buttered bread, eggs, bits of meat and a couple of bottles of milk with cork tops. 'You see, Margaret, we do not come empty handed. There will be enough for all of us here. Now get stuck in. We will have a great picnic here at the lake.'

Margaret was too overcome with it all to reach out and take something. She also could not believe she was being given food that somebody else had prepared for her. But the children had no such hesitations. They took the food that Shanks and Katie handed them and ate happily. Katie made a sandwich for her and she also was able to take it and eat.

Gradually the newness and the fear of taking food from somebody else left her, gradually the defensive methods she had built up over the previous years to protect herself weakened. She even felt like abandoning her straight up posture and leaning back against the rocks while she ate. But this was a bit far for her yet. But she ate the sandwich and watched the children and their great enjoyment at the food they were eating and she looked out over the lake and felt that this was the best day of her life. She lowered her head as she thought of Katie and Shanks and how much she owed them. She was thankful to them in her heart. And 'Thank you,' she said out loud.

That night she and all the children slept well after their day out. Campbell did not come to her either as he was probably tired after being down to Brown's. But in her sleep she dreamt. Again her mother came to her. This was usual after she went to the lake. But this was only for a short time. Her mother faded from the dream and was replaced by her children. Then she herself became the only person in her dream. She dreamt she was at the lake having left all the children in the cottage with Shanks and Katie. It was a beautiful summer day.

She dreamt that she had brought food and had a picnic by herself. And when she was finished she had laid back and rested on the soft green moss by the bank of the lake. The sun shone on her and warmed her and a little breeze ruffled her hair and her dress. And then she dreamt that she arose and took off her dress and walked slowly into the lake and stood there naked. She felt the sun and the breeze on her. She looked out over the lake and the mountains. She worshipped the land in which she stood and it in turn worshipped her with its breeze and sun. She felt freer than she had ever felt before. She made a noise to herself.

But then she dreamt that she became afraid, afraid that somebody would see her. Especially that Campbell would see her. She thought that it was ridiculous that it was him she feared the most. But he would be most angry as he considered that he owned her and nobody else should be able to have her body, either to touch it or to see it, or should be able to have any of the results of the work her body did. She thought he would hit her if he saw her.

Then she thought again maybe he would not care if anybody saw her or not. He just took her like a bit of meat. Ever since that one brief time, he had returned again to his coming in his aggression and controlling when he came to her. So maybe he would not care. But what he would definitely be angry about was if she worked for anybody else, if her labour went to anybody else. She knew for certain that this would make him very angry. When she dreamt of this she awoke with a start and looked around her expecting to see him coming to hit her. But he was asleep in his bench.

The next morning Campbell had to go to Donegal Town to bring some cattle that Brown had bought. He would be away for two days at least. She looked forward to it. The first evening he was gone she took her one chair out to the door of the cottage, sat down with her knitting and looked out over the valley. It was beautiful. Her life was marginally better and she could now see that beauty. Some of the worst pressures had lessened. Her father was dead. Her brothers now lived in the cottage. Campbell was no longer as aggressive since he got beaten up, the tension in the cottage was not so great. The five children were a lot of work but she was getting more and more help and love from the older ones.

As she sat she thought again about how she could go on and on to have twenty-five or thirty children. What would she do then? How would she cope? But also how would they feed them on the bit of land they had? They would never be able to do it. If they planted it all in spuds she supposed they could but then there would be nothing for anything else or for the few animals. She refused to consider the idea of any of the children being hired out. Maybe they would get married young. But then she shrugged that idea aside. It was very unlikely that enough would go this way.

As she knit she tried to push this idea from her head. Then she heard the clatter of horse's hooves on the road outside. She wondered who it could be. They stopped at the cottage. She got very nervous. Then round the corner came the minister from the church she had been married in. Not Wilson but the other one, the assistant who had married her. He stopped in his tracks. The expression on his face made it clear he wished he had stopped at some other cottage where he would not see her. But he was too late to go back now.

He had stopped to ask for a drink of water. But he was ashamed when he saw Margaret. Ashamed of his role in marrying her at the back of the church and then rushing her and her family out the side door and he going out the main door. But it was not only shame. This struggled in him with contempt for her and all the poor. He had been brought up in wealth and anybody who was poor it was their own fault according to his beliefs. Look at her there with four or five children. It's her own fault that she is the way she is.

Look at himself. He would be married soon to his betrothed and they would be living in the second manse. And they would have only two or three children. He knew how to control his urges. He was on the way to being a bishop later. He gave no thought to the fact that his position in life gave him so many more outlets for his creativity than Margaret's, nor that he had so much more power to say yes or no to what was demanded of him. And not only that, he had also begun to take care of his urges when he made those trips to Derry and Dublin for the church events. The urges could always be taken care of there for a small amount of money. Those women there that his uncle had set him up with. He wondered did Wilson do this too.

He asked Margaret for a drink of water and examined the mug to see if it was clean. He was not too happy about it but he drank it down. 'How are you, Mrs Campbell?' He cringed to even call her that. Had she not come with her big belly and with her poverty to the back of the church? Mrs. indeed. She kept her head bent forward and did not look him in the eye. 'Well thank you for the drink and I hope to see you in church soon.' He was very glad to be away. He was very glad that she had not spoken to him and that it was easy to get away. These people. Living in filth and squalor and their own urges. Just like animals.

Margaret was equally glad that he was gone. He had interrupted the bit of peace that she had been feeling. And he had reminded her of her marriage when she had been treated so badly. She could also see in his eyes that he thought of her today what he had thought of her then. That is that she was some kind of animal. She felt like he wanted to go and wash his hands after he had anything to do with her. But she had done nothing wrong, it was wrong that had been done to her. Her father, Allen, Campbell, that minister himself and his treatment of her in the church. Why did he think she was the animal and not the others including himself, who had abused her? She could not understand this.

Campbell himself never attended church. He saw the ministers and the parishioners as hypocrites and wanted nothing to do with them. He never mentioned to her that she should go. There was no pressure from the church on her to go. They had slotted her into the marriage with Campbell and out of sight. They did not want to be reminded of the base way in which they had treated her. Sometime in the future they would make a move to have her children baptized but the present bishop and minister who had treated her so badly, were in no hurry to have to look her in the face.

As she sat there knitting, the dusk of the summer evening gradually fell over the valley. It became even more beautiful and peaceful. The disruption of the minister slowly dissipated and she got back some peace again. She thought of what she had seen in McDaid's last week when she was down with Katie. There was a big woman there called Mrs. Shanaghan. She was a very loud person shouting at McDaid and dominating the whole shop. Margaret was afraid of her and wished she could be her at the same time.

'Now, McDaid, do not be giving me any low weights or I will go in behind that counter and give it to you. Aye, and no one will stop me either. I am just the one to do it.' Mrs Shanaghan had looked at Margaret and when she spoke she had a glint of humour in her eyes. 'I will tell you, McDaid, what I have been hearing about you watering the drink and giving low weights, is enough to get you shot. It is not beyond happening you know the days that's in it, you keep yourself straight from now on, you hear me.'

Katie and Margaret and Mrs. Shanaghan had left the shop together and Katie who knew her stopped to talk.

'You have to keep that boy in his place.' Mrs Shanaghan explained. 'He will be feared now that the boys out there will be thinking of shooting him for his dirty business. I made it all up. Not that he might not get it some time. He is far too close to the powers that be for my liking. He hears everything in there and who knows who he tells. I would not trust him as far as I could throw him. The two of you be careful with him and always keep an eye on him when he weights up your stuff'.

Katie and Margaret walked back up the road with the children. Katie said: 'Aye she is a character that one, Mrs Shanaghan. She was married a while ago but she treated him so bad, she used to batter him about the place, he was a terrible wee man altogether, he was no match for her at all, she just battered him about the place. He upped and left her for Scotland. She lives on down the road towards the village. She is an awful woman altogether. She hangs out over her half door and watches for people walking down to the village and she will call them over and tell them some yarn about somebody else. There would not be a word of truth to it. She would have made it all up. She would then see how long it took to come back up to her. Till somebody came back up and told it to her again and also how and if it had been changed. She is a wild women altogether.' Katie laughed.

Margaret thought about Mrs. Shanaghan and the more she did, the more she wished she was like her. Able to shout at McDaid and threaten. Able to dominate her husband and chase him out of the house. Maybe not hit him. And able to make up schemes like telling yarns to people going to the village and waiting till they were told back to her by people coming back up. But she did not think she could ever be like her. She had been beat down too much for that. She could not change enough now. She tried to imagine herself shouting at McDaid. As she did so the image came so clear in her mind that for a few seconds it seemed real and when she realised what she was thinking, a couple of ripples of laughter escaped her mouth and the briefest glimmer of a smile crossed her face.

Katie could not believe it. She was astounded. 'Margaret, what is it? Are you all right?'

Margaret was embarrassed. What right had she to smile never mind laugh? She had five children to look after.

'Margaret, what were you smiling about?' Katie wanted to know what miracle had brought this about so she could try and get it to happen again. 'Come on, Margaret, tell me'.

Margaret was silent and in a state of confusion about what had just gone on. But then her mind cleared a little. She was glad she had almost laughed, she was glad she had smiled. She had the right. She turned to Katie and lifted her head and looked up into Katie's eyes and said, 'Mrs Shanaghan'.

Katie did not ask any more. She knew what Margaret meant. That Mrs Shanaghan is a terrible woman. She could make you laugh, she could get you going. And that was what she had done here with Margaret today. Katie vowed to never condemn Mrs Shanaghan again. She had done what nobody else could do for Margaret and she vowed to tell Shanks when she got home. He would be mad that he missed hearing Margaret laugh. Aye, he would be mad indeed but he would also be overjoyed. That Mrs. Shanaghan is a good one.

CHAPTER FORTY TWO

Margaret was picking nettles along the inside of the hedge running along the side of the spud ground and the road. She put these in stews to supplement the food now that things were tighter. The spud crop had not been good and money was tight with the rising prices of the war. She had the children and Campbell and herself to feed. She did not cut back on his food for fear of angering him but she cut back on her own. She tried everything bar starving herself completely not to cut back on the children's.

She had thought about taking up the snaring as Shanks had suggested but she could not as she felt too sorry for the rabbits. This did not make sense as she had the chickens and she killed them to eat. But what seemed different was that the rabbits were free and also that they looked so beautiful and gentle. When she looked at them she wanted to pet them instead of kill and eat them. But she knew that if things got so bad that the children were going hungry then she would get some snares from Shanks and snare them. She would never let anything come before the children.

As she was picking the nettles, she heard Campbell and another man come up the road. She recognized the other man's voice as that of the man who had bought the calf from Campbell. She stopped her picking as she knew Campbell would be angry for her to be seen doing this. This was what the starving Fenians did. Not the Protestants. Protestants were above this. And the other man was one of their own. She stayed motionless and quiet. They did not know she was there.

'Campbell, what do you think of the state of things? You are always talking with Brown.' Campbell thought to himself that he did not talk to Brown. He only listened to Brown. 'What does Brown think is going to happen? Look at this. They want conscription and there is a lot of boys against it. I see that them Republican boys are getting a lot more support. Did you see the big meeting over in Glenfinn last weekend? It is not good. I mean that's where those boys should be, over in the trenches. It would put manners on them. Teach them to respect their betters.' Campbell grunted in agreement.

'Did you see too, Campbell, that they are trying to keep the spuds from being exported? They are trying to say that because they are scarce and people are hungry that they should not be exported that we should be forced to sell them right away here at home. What kind of thinking is that? Sure we have to be allowed to make a bit of a profit, we have to be allowed to export our spuds when we want, to sell them when and where we want. It's not our fault that they do not have enough to eat or that the flour and the maize are scarce in the shops.

'And you know what I am worried about most? The priests. In the past they always had control over their own kind. And the priests in spite of their talk were always for the property man and always for keeping in with London. Sure they supported the execution of the 1916 boys. They know where their bread is buttered. They are always wanting to see if they could get closer to London. So they kept their own boys here down and under control. But the priests are losing control now. You can see it everywhere. This is not good for us either. The ones that will take over could be a lot worse. It could be them Republicans and Socialists.

'Sure look there are strikes everywhere, and not only the Catholics but our own kind are into it as well. Did you see in Derry the Catholic and Protestant labourers got together and struck? We were lucky to get them divided or we could have had real trouble. That would be the worst, the common labourer getting together. Then they would think they were worth more than they are and maybe even think they could run things. Imagine that. Them boys running things. Sure it would never work.

'Did you see what is happening around the milk in Derry? Sure they say that some of the boys are watering the milk. Now you know that this would not be happening, or if it was it would only be a handful of boys would be at it. Sure them Derry farmers, they are ones of our own. They are decent men. But the city crowd is saying the milk is watered. Up in the Fountain area the other day, and you know they are all our own kind up there, the milkman was beat up.

'And do you know what they want? They want the city to set up a dairy, a municipal dairy. Sure how would that work? They would never be able to run it. It takes people like ourselves to run things. If a man is not making a bit of profit he is not going to be looking after things. Aye, a municipal dairy. That is some idea. It will have to be stopped. If they got that they would want more. Next they would want an abattoir, maybe control over the docks. Aye, you know what they say, the appetite comes with the eating. Naw, these boys will have to be stopped. Whatever kind they are, our own kind or the other kind.

'It's that Russia that has got them all stirred up too. Them Lenins and Trotskys and Bolsheviks or whatever you call them. Taking the land off the people and taking over the factories. They are a godless bunch too. That is where we need the priests as well. To tell this to their own kind and to keep them in control. Naw, we have to be careful. If we can help them priests to get in control of their own kind this would be a good job. Things are not as simple as they were before.'

Margaret had been listening to all this from inside the hedge. She could not make much sense out of it all. She had been hearing all her life how bad the priests were. Now it seemed they were good as long as they controlled their own people. When Campbell and the other man passed where she was, she walked quickly across the spud ground and up to the cottage and inside and got the fire stirred up to boil the spuds for Campbell. He was still outside talking to the other man. She was still going over the conversation she had heard, in her head.

Had she been lied to all her life? Had her own kind been no better than the other kind? Were the priests and the ministers no different from each other and no better than each other? She thought about how none of them had ever helped or protected her. The minister the other day could not wait to get away from her quick enough. He had married her and put her with Campbell but he showed no sense of responsibility to see if she was all right. What kind of an attitude was that?

What was she going to teach her children? Was she going to teach them that Catholics were bad and Protestants were good? How could she do this? Look at Allen, how bad he was to her and look at Katie and Shanks, how good they were to her. She was sure it could be the other way around for a Catholic girl sent to a Catholic farm house to be hired out. How could she teach her children this when she could see it was not true? She resolved not to do this. She thought that not only was it her duty to feed her children well but also to tell them the truth.

Campbell came in and ate and left right away. She was glad for the peace this gave her. The children were lying down with the exception of Kathleen who she was feeding at her breast. She sat at the fire. The autumn was coming in and it was cool at the door. The turf was burning and its smell and red embers were very comforting. She sat and rocked with Kathleen and felt the peace of feeding her. The peace that came from being able to provide for this child she had brought into the world.

Then she thought of Campbell. He was the father to all but one of her children. He was not so aggressive to her since he had been beaten. He still came to her in the night and while he never showed any of the more gentle feeling he had for her that few seconds on that one night, he was no longer so brutal with her. Where was he now? Was he in the bog even though it was dark and late? Or was he in the pub? She thought he did not go to the pub so often as she did not smell the whisky so much. Only a few times now and then.

Then she began to worry about Campbell. What would happen to her if anything happened to him? Without him she would be in the workhouse. She put the thought out of her mind. Instead she just allowed herself the comfort of sitting there with her child and nursing it at her breast. She wished she could sing. She wished she could be like Mrs Shanaghan. She knew she must be able to sing. She smiled again to herself as she thought of Mrs Shanaghan and McDaid. Then it came to her with a shock. McDaid was afraid of Mrs Shanaghan. A man afraid of a woman? She was very surprised by the whole idea of it but she also thought that it was not bad. She liked it.

How did it work? Mrs Shanaghan scared him with her tongue. She shouted out loud and everybody heard what she said. McDaid did not want everybody to hear as it was about his crooked weights and knowledge of this would be bad for his business. So he was afraid of her. Margaret also supposed that he could not hit her to silence her as he owned the pub and shop and everybody would hear about it and this would be bad for his business. Margaret thought about this in relation to Campbell. But she had nobody to hear her in the cottage. She was isolated. He had the power over her. She sat in silence and felt her powerlessness. No property and no public to appeal to.

Margaret heard Campbell's boots on the yard outside and got up to make him his tea and get out of his way. He came in and ate and went and lay on his bench and slept. Margaret also went to bed. But as she did the dog crept over to her and raised its head. It wanted her petting and approval. She petted it on the top of its head. It looked up at her. She thought about its life. It went with Campbell wherever he went but he never spoke to it except to give it orders. When it was back at the cottage it lay by Campbell but it also would come to her and come to lick the children's hands and legs.

Margaret looked down at the dog where it lay beside the bed. She thought about it and what went on in its head. The dog looked up at her and its eyes met hers. She liked the dog. She then realised that the dog was maybe the freest of all of them. It could go with Campbell to the different places he went, it could go anywhere in the cottage, it felt at ease to go over to her room and bed, and to lick her and the children. This thought surprised her. How could the dog be freer than anybody else in the house? It was not even human. She could not figure it out.

Campbell came to her that night. She thought she was already pregnant with her sixth child. Afterwards she lay there more relaxed than usual. The thoughts that had been going round in her head all day were still there. Especially about Mrs Shanaghan. She thought about what Katie said, that she used to beat up her husband. She let this idea circulate in her mind for a while and she smiled and even laughed a little secretly and silently to herself. Then it connected itself with Campbell directly. If only she was bigger and not such a wee thin thing. She had this vision of slapping him around the room and kicking him out of the cottage.

Suddenly this was not just a dull thought. Suddenly it was full of life and laughter and vitality in her head. She could actually see herself do it. She took him by the scruff of the neck and kicked him in the ass while opening the door with the other hand and out he went. The image was so vivid in her mind that she could not stop herself. She burst out laughing and started to shake. The children stirred around her as she did so. But with a great effort she stifled it. There were too many obstacles in her life to be laughing like this. The biggest one was that she was afraid that Campbell would hear and think she was laughing at him and maybe realise what she was thinking.

But there were others. She was just not used to laughing. It scared her somehow. It had been beaten out of her by her life. To laugh was to open herself up to attack. She had to keep closed and on the defensive. There was no laughter in battle and her life was an unrelenting battle. She had to keep on the alert. Soon she would have her sixth baby and things would become even harder. There would be no time for laughter. She killed the idea off before it even got started. She hated to do it because it felt so good. All the great things, like the smallest flicker of explosive pleasure she had felt that night when Campbell had treated her gently, like the great bursting pleasure she had just felt when she had broke out with laughter, she could not afford these, her life was too hard, she was too much under attack.

CHAPTER FORTY THREE

'Mammy, Mammy. I like school, but that boy Holmes, he is very bad to me and calls me names. The teacher told him to stop but when we get out he starts again. Why does he do that Mammy? It is not fair.'

This was Margaret's great new opening in her life. Victoria was now at school and coming home and wanting to talk. She was also learning to read and write and she was full of excitement about these new experiences.

Margaret glowed with pride as she looked at Victoria. 'Just ignore him, Victoria'. She said, 'He is just stupid.'

Margaret saw in Victoria the bright and smart child that she was. Bursting with life. Loving to go to school and wanting to tell everything that happened when she came home. Even the bad things.

'Mammy, Mammy,' Mary said, 'I want to go to school too'.

'Yes, Mary, you will go when the new year starts in September. You will be old enough then and they will have room for you. You and Victoria will be able to go together. You will be able to stand up for each other and not let people call you names.'

But Margaret's pride that day was not just for Victoria and her going to school. She had given birth to her sixth child in the late autumn. She had never thought about it in advance. She had just taken it for granted that it would be a girl. All the others were. But it was not. It was a boy. On the other occasions when she had given birth Campbell had never mentioned or taken any note of it. This time when he heard from Katie that it was a boy he grunted in response. And when he came home that night he came over to the bed and while not touching her or the baby he grunted in some sort of acknowledgement. Like she had done better this time.

She did not know exactly what he was saying but he was saying something when he grunted at her. She knew it must be to do with the child being a boy. That was all that was different this time. Also he did not seem angry. He just grunted at her. She hoped that he was pleased. Not that she felt anything for him anymore but because it might make her life easier. If he was pleased he had a son, he might think that his own life was better and therefore not be so aggressive and antagonistic to others. She herself was glad it was a son because now she would have a boy to go with the girls.

Margaret wondered was he angry all this time because she had only had girls. But then she thought of everything else. It was not anything she had done that made him the way he was. But even so maybe the boy baby would help him be more kind to her. But then she thought more about it. It would not. He was just the person he was and he would be the same in the future. She could not afford to hope that things would change for the better. She had to keep her expectations low. Life was too hard otherwise.

Margaret called her new baby James. It was all she could think of and it was her husband's name and her brother's name. She was intrigued with her first baby boy as she looked after him and cleaned him. He fed at her breast just like the girls and he made her feel at peace and needed her just like the girls. In his looks he looked more like Campbell than any of the girls. They looked more like her. She did not care about this as she held them all equally precious. Each one strengthened her in her mind as she was needed more when each one came and she responded to that need.

But Margaret was wearing herself down in other ways. The shortage of food, a new baby each year and feeding each new baby, the constant stress of trying to not provoke Campbell while at the same time making sure she protected the children. She was wearing herself down. When she was nursing this new baby she found it the hardest she had yet. Living on less food than any of them she lost weight and strength. Sometimes she wondered if she would be able to go on. A terrible weakness descended on her sometimes.

Katie noticed it one day when she saw her in the potato ground trying to get a meal of potatoes out of the pit. 'Margaret, you should not be doing that. You are not looking too well. You need to get yourself strengthened up after the baby. Leave that for a while.' Margaret looked round and looked Katie in the face. She said nothing but her colour and her eyes frightened Katie.

'Margaret, come on now. Get into the house and rest. You will get exhausted out here. I will bring you in a meal of spuds.'.

Margaret allowed herself to be led into the cottage by Katie. That was how weak she was.

Then she realised it was not only that she felt weak. She did not feel well. She felt hot. She held onto Katie's hand and arm and sat down on the stool at the fire.

Katie looked at her with increasing concern. 'You sit there and I will go and wash these spuds and put them on so you do not have to worry.'

The older children were around Margaret and leaning against her legs. The new baby James, and Kathleen and Martha were asleep on the bed. Margaret felt she should go and feed James but she was feeling so bad that she put it off. He was not yet crying for milk.

'There, the spuds are on now, Margaret. They will be ready for your man. I will make you a cup of tea and a bit of bread before I go.'

Katie was getting more worried by the minute as Margaret would usually never let anybody help her, let alone anybody serve her. As Katie went about the work there was one worry she kept trying to keep buried in her mind. But she could not. It kept pushing to the surface. The big flu. For nearly a year now the country and the world had been hit by a flu epidemic.

'Aw God, let it not be. After all she has been through. Do not let her now be struck down with that. Aw God, do not allow this to happen to her,' Katie thought to herself.

She buttered some bread and gave it to Margaret with the tea. Margaret drank the tea and ate the bread and refused any more. She sat at the fire with her head forward while the oldest of the children leaned against her and talked to her. Katie did not want to be there when Campbell came but she was worried about Margaret. She did not know what to do. But Margaret seemed to be wide enough awake, she was able to sit up and get about. Katie decided to go.

'Margaret, I am off now, is there anything else you would want me to do before I go? I will be going down to McDaid's tomorrow so I will call in and see you.'

Margaret did not answer just looked up at Katie for a while. Katie left and Margaret sat alone until she heard Campbell's feet come up the yard. She was barely able to do it but she managed to get up and get him his food. She then went and lay in the bed with the children around her and she managed to feed James at her breast. It was all she could do. She asked Victoria and Mary and Anne and Martha to be good and to watch in case any of the others was going to fall out of the bed during the night. She was feeling feverish and she felt that she could maybe loss consciousness.

And that of all nights he came to her. She felt the heat of her skin as he handled her. Other than that, she felt nothing when he was in her. When he was finished she lay there as she did not have the strength to pull herself back into bed for nearly half-an-hour. There was something wrong with her, this was what she suddenly realised, there was something bad wrong with her. She had never been sick in her life, her trouble had always been brought on by somebody else. But now there was something wrong with her. She was sick. She was sick.

More than ever before she was terrified. More than when she was sent away by her father, more than when she was attacked by Allen, more than when she was married off to Campbell, more than when she had had the pain of Victoria being born. This was the worst. Now she had the children to look after. If anything happened to her what would happen to the children? This was the nightmare that ripped through her mind and would not go away. It was only interrupted by her own illness as she drifted in and out of consciousness and she realised she had a fever and it was worsening.

The sweat poured off Margaret as the night went on. She was soaked and the children in the bed with her were getting soaked too. She worried if she was going to make them sick as well. But what could she do? There was nowhere else for her or them to sleep. She threw the clothes off herself and tried to let the heat go straight up from her body and leave the children alone. While this helped they could not escape the heat, they were lying sweltering in a bed that was becoming increasingly soaked. Margaret's heat combined with her feverish dreams, were turning her sleep into a nightmare.

She dreamt but she did not know of what. Just visions and frightening episodes running through her mind. She had to hang on to herself to keep from groaning and crying out. She did not want to wake anybody, any of the children. But half way through the night Victoria awoke and asked her what was wrong.

'Nothing, Victoria. Nothing.'

'But, Mammy, you are all warm and wet. What is wrong, Mammy?'

'Please, Victoria. It is nothing. Just go back to sleep. Everything will be all right. Do not waken your sisters and brother. I do not want them to waken.'

Victoria went back to sleep and Margaret eventually also drifted into a delirious sleep. When she woke she could see it was getting clear outside. She had to get up. She had to get up and make his breakfast. She could not let it go. Victoria also had to go to school. With a terrible effort she dragged herself out of the bed and put on her other dress, which was dry. She herself felt cold now as she got up from the wet bed. Victoria rose with her and helped make the breakfast and dressed herself for school. Campbell got up, ate his breakfast and left. Victoria left soon after. Margaret lay back down in the bed. She felt the hot fever strike her again. But she was too exhausted to move. She just lay there.

'Look Shanks, you have to come with me. She was very sick last night. I went with you when she was pregnant with the first baby to see her mother. You have to come with me. Come on now.' Shanks got himself up and complaining followed her out the door.

'Margaret, Margaret,' they called and then knocked on the door of Margaret's cottage. There was no answer. Katie pushed the door and the top half opened in. She called again. 'Margaret. Margaret.'

Mary's little voice answered. 'Mammy is sleeping, Mammy is sleeping.'

Katie reached over and opened the bottom half of the door and went in. Shanks followed her.

'Mary, we are here to see how your mother is. If she is all right. Last night she did not seem well.' Then walking over to their room Katie looked in and asked, 'Margaret, Margaret how are you? Are you all right. Are you all right?'

But in spite of seeing Margaret's shape in the bed, she got no answer. The rest of the children were stirring now. The new baby

James was by Margaret's side asleep, the next one was also asleep on the other side of Margaret. The other two were rising from the mattress on the floor. They looked up at Katie and looked at their Mammy in the bed.

Mary the oldest at home who was standing by the bed asked,

'Is Mammy sick. Is Mammy sick?'

Katie did not answer. Instead she reached out to touch Margaret's forehead. It was burning and wet.

'Shanks, Shanks, she is very sick. She is very sick. We need to get help for her, we need to get the doctor from Stranorlar, that Dr Johnston. We have to be quick. She has been sick since yesterday. You know how quick this flu can go with people. It can be only a matter of a day or two for some people. We need to get off and get that doctor right away. Will you go and get him and I will stay here? I know it is a long way and Campbell should be doing it but we cannot just let her lie here and maybe die. Aw Shanks, this cannot happen to Margaret now after all she has been through.'

'Sure I will go,' Shanks said and with that he was out the door and down the road.

It was over ten miles to where the doctor lived but Shanks hoped to get a lift, or lifts part of the way, on carts. He knew that that Doctor Johnston had a motor car, one of the only ones in the county and maybe he would even get a lift back in that. But for the minute he was walking and he put a spurt on as he'd promised Katie. Margaret was sick. There was something serious wrong with her. 'Aw, do not let anything happen to her after all she has been through.' Shanks clenched his teeth with anger at how cruel the world was.

CHAPTER FORTY FOUR

Shanks was a couple of miles on his way when he heard a pony and trap come clattering on the road behind him. He hoped it was not full and whoever it was would give him a lift. Looking over his shoulder he eventually saw it come into view. Then he saw who it was. Aye, he would be all right here. He would get a lift. It was Kelly, the one who had sold him the new rooster that he had kept and then given their own to Margaret. Kelly was not bad, a bit of a bitter boy, but he had nothing against Shanks.

'Shanks, where are you off to this morning? Getting a bit of exercise? Is that what you are up to? Or did Katie throw you out?' Shanks then sobered Kelly by telling him where he was going and why.

'Ah, that is bad. That wee girl has had a tough time of it all right. I will give you a lift all the way. I am going into Stranorlar myself. I am wanting to get a few things from Brennan's. And maybe I will have a wee drink or two to myself when I am in there.

'Why did that Campbell boy not go to get the doctor for his own wife, Shanks? Why do you have to do it?'

Shanks shook his head, he did not want to say much but he had accumulated a lot of anger against Campbell over the years and could not help himself.

'That boy, Kelly. He treats her like dirt, she is just somebody to work for him and he never gives her a kind word. I have never heard him speak to her ever. Nor has Katie. It is like she is not there except to do his work for him. I do not know if he will even be there tonight when we get back and if she is still sick.'

'He has not many friends, Shanks, neither amongst his own kind or our kind. Mind that beating he got? Sure nobody had any sympathy for him. And this is a bad time to have no friends. Look at what is happening. Everywhere there are strikes and now you see there are some of the boys getting out the guns. Before it is over a lot of these Protestant boys will pay the price of what they have done. Some of our own kind will pay the price for their informing too. Campbell would need to be careful. Even his own kind do not like him.

'What do you think about it all, Shanks? Sure now that the war is over do you think we will get the independence?'

Shanks normally did not give an opinion on things but he was angry about Margaret.

'I do not think these English boys will give anything up unless they are forced to. They are too greedy and too used to being the bosses and running things. It will have to be taken off them.'

Kelly was very surprised to hear Shanks speak out so strong.

'Shanks, you are a man after my own opinion. We will have to take it off them.'

They talked of the countryside and the crops and the different people whose houses they drove past, as they made their way into Stranorlar. They made it in over an hour. Kelly left Shanks off at the house of Dr Johnston saying he would be going back in a few hours and would give him a lift. It was impossible to miss the doctor's house as his brand new motor car was sitting outside. He was the only one in the town with a car. Shanks walked up the drive way and followed the sign 'Patients' round to the side. He knocked at the door. In a short time a woman came out and asked him what he wanted. He explained about Margaret and she told him to wait.

In a few minutes, she came out again and told him to come in. She told him to sit in a small room with basic wooden furniture. He waited there for close to half-an-hour. He was getting very anxious. But he did not have the confidence to get up and demand to see the doctor. Then the door opened and the doctor came in. He was tall and overweight with a chain and key fob on his waistcoat

To intimidate the rest of us who cannot afford one, Shanks thought.

'Well what is it that you want, my man?' he asked Shanks.

Shanks explained about Margaret, laying emphasis on how bad she was. The doctor, later to become famous as the Johnston in 'Johnston's Motorcar', said nothing for a minute. He just looked in a calculating way at Shanks.

'Who is she again, man?'

Shanks explained she was married to Campbell and the doctor asked who Campbell was. Shanks wondered why this was important to Margaret's health until he realised it was to see if he would get paid.

'That is a very bad road up there to their place, is it not? Very rough.'

Now he was thinking about his new car too. Shanks got more and more angry. He spoke out.

'She is very sick, Doctor, she needs your help fast. She has six children. What will happen to them if anything happens to her? She needs your help fast.'

The doctor grew uncomfortable under the pressure from Shanks and spoke out.

'I have a few other patients to see today and when I am finished with them I will get up to her.' And with that he turned and left the room before Shanks could speak again. The same woman ushered him out.

'That dirty cur. That is what he is. A dirty cur.'

'What are you talking about man?' Kelly asked Shanks as he picked him up in his trap again from where Shanks had been sitting waiting on the edge of town.

'That doctor! He wanted to know who Margaret was and about the state of the road, wanting to know if he would get paid and would his car get bumped. And all the time Margaret is very sick. What kind of people are they anyway? These ones who have money. They get greedier and greedier. It's us poor folk who are more inclined to help each other. That is the truth.'

'Look, Shanks, when they get a bit behind them they are afraid to loose it. But it's not only their kind, it's our own kind also. Look at your man Fitzgerald, one of our own kind, over by the big forest. He has over two hundred acres. He would not give you a spud if you were starving. He was keeping his men sleeping in the barns the whole winter. And he hired out a young one and encouraged the boys to do her. This kept them quieter and he was able to pay them less. When she was beginning to swell up with the wean he put her out. You could not get worse than that and he was one of our own.

'If we ever get the independence we will have to watch out for our own kind too. They are just as bad when they get their hands on money and land. The only people you can trust is the poor. They have nothing to loss. Who was it said, the rich always betray the poor. I think it was Henry Joy McCracken. He was a fighter to the end and he was a Protestant. Naw, we have to keep an eye out for all of them who have the money and the power.

'That doctor he will be in it too. He has the knowledge to help people but look at how he is with Margaret. You can be sure that he would be in that car and up that road in a minute if it was Brown who was sick or the Bishop Wilson. There would be stones flying and bits flying off his brand new car as he headed up to see them. There would be no weighing it up like he is doing with Margaret. Something has to change in this country, Shanks, something has to change.'

'Aye, you are right, Kelly. Look at that McDaid up here. Sure he is fleecing everybody. Giving low weights and low measures and watering the drink. Look at him, he is one of our own and yet he is at this. The more somebody gets drunk the more he waters it. And he is always trying to do the women when they come in there with the eggs, trying to get them to spend all he gives them for the eggs before they leave the shop. Katie had to go down with Margaret to keep him from robbing her.'

'And you know what I heard, Shanks, do not let this out. But I heard that that McDaid, when he goes down to Stranorlar, passes on all he hears to Craig the shopkeeper whose brother is the Sergeant there. That he is an informer. That is what I hear. I would not say it to anybody else but you. But I know I can trust you to keep your mouth shut. But that is what I heard.'

Shanks looked at Kelly and said nothing. He knew they were getting into dangerous ground. Informers did not fare well if they were caught. And McDaid did not have many friends to start with. Shanks decided to say as little as possible.

'Well is that what you heard, Kelly? That he is an informer. That is not good. A man would have to watch what he said when he would get a few drinks around the bar at night. Anything could slip out and it might mean nothing but he could make a big thing of it and pass it on. He will be wanting to pass on as much as he can whether it's true or not. That boy, aye, you would have to watch him. There is nothing worse than an informer.'

By this time they were at Margaret's cottage and Kelly pulled in to let Shanks off and he got out of the trap himself. Katie came out of the door when she heard them arrive.

'What happened, Shanks? What did the doctor say? She is not any better. She has a fever and does not hardly know what is going on. I think it is not good.' Katie looked at Kelly and addressed him. 'We are worried she might have the flu. You know that that is dangerous. And Margaret is not that healthy. She is worn down and half starved with all the work and the children one after another.'

She turned again to Shanks and as she did, Margaret's three oldest children came out the door and clung onto to Katie's dress.

'What did he say, Shanks?'

'He says that he has a few more patients to see and then he will come up. But I could see he was wondering would he get paid and about how rough the road would be on his new car. He is one miserable boy, Katie. As I was saying to Kelly here if it was Brown or the Bishop Wilson he would be up the road in a flash. But let us go in and see her.'

Kelly spoke up. He was afraid he would get the flu. 'I won't. I will be on my way. I hope she gets better. That Johnston he will probably be up soon.'

Katie and Shanks went into the cottage with the children following them. They went over to where Margaret was lying on the bed in the small room, which she had shared with all her children since she had come there. She was hotter than ever. The sweat was running off her. She seemed to be semi-conscious at best.

'Margaret, Margaret,' Katie said, 'I have a cup of water here for you.'

Katie put her arm around her and lifted her up and Shanks helped her hold the cup and get her to drink. But she only sipped a few sips.

'Shanks, can we do anything more for her? I feel helpless just sitting here giving her drinks of water.'

The children were watching Katie help their mother and every now and then they would run out and play in the yard. But Victoria, the oldest, never left Katie's side as she helped Margaret. She was helping hold the cup of water and helping raise her mother up. All the children except the two youngest were looking at their mother and worried about what was going on. They knew whatever it was, it was not good.

Shanks was only back a few minutes and the darkness was falling when they heard Campbell's feet on the yard. Shanks and Katie went outside. Campbell looked up at them and girned.

'She is very sick, Campbell,' Shanks said, 'I was in Stranorlar today and I told Doctor Johnston. He is coming up. She is very sick.'

Campbell was enraged when he heard this. Shanks had no right to do this. Who was going to pay? But he felt he could say nothing. He would be condemned by everybody if he did not get the doctor and she died.

Katie then spoke. 'Campbell, she is very sick. She has been in a fever now for over twentyfour hours. It has not broken. This is very dangerous with this flu going round. I will stay here and help all night if you want me to. I would like to. Margaret needs help. She needs to be dried down and to be given water and drinks regularly or she will get all dried out. Campbell, she is in a very dangerous state. She needs looking after. I will stay and Shanks also will stay if that will help.'

Campbell grunted 'Naw.' And gestured at the children. The oldest of them, Victoria, was only six years old. 'Naw, them.' And again gestured at the children.

Katie and Shanks felt enraged now. They were being blocked. It was his house. It was his house and Margaret was his wife. And he would not let them help her. They wanted to just ignore him and stay. But it was his house and his wife, how could they do this? They stood, all of them silent and motionless for a few minutes. Margaret's heavy breathing could be heard from the bed.

'Plenty of water and keep her covered up,' Katie said as they gave up and she and Shanks turned towards the door.

As they walked up towards their own place Shanks and Katie were in a state of shock. They were silent. How could a man do that? They had been driven out of the house. They could not help Margaret. They would never forget it. They would never forgive him for it even if Margaret got better. This was the worst thing Campbell had ever done. As they walked Katie put her hand through Shank's arm. They both needed the comfort and warmth of each other after the brutality of what they had just come through.

'I hope the doctor comes,' said Shanks. 'I hope Margaret lives. I hope that Campbell dies and I never have to look at him again.' And they both wept and sobbed.

CHAPTER FORTY FIVE

Campbell knew Margaret was very sick when he saw she had not milked the cow nor made him his tea. This is all that restrained him from taking out his anger on her. He held this anger inside as he went about doing these jobs himself. 'Who does she think she is?' he kept saying to himself. He made himself some boiled eggs and bread and tea. It did not occur to him to make her any. She lay there surrounded by the children. Victoria and Mary were doing what they had seen Katie do, trying to give her a drink now and then and wiping the sweat off her brow. Campbell got up from his food and walked over to the room and looked at Margaret.

'Aw, she is all right,' he grunted. 'It's just a cold.'

He turned and went back to his bench and lay down with his face to the wall and went to sleep. The children were still awake except for the two youngest who were asleep on the floor mattress in the small room. They knew there was something wrong with their mother because she was different from she had ever been before. She was not watching out for them at every move.

As Margaret lay there breathing heavily and sweating, Victoria and Mary tried to help her. They got on each side of her and tried to lift her up a bit on the bolster that her head was on. When they managed this a bit, they then tried to get her to drink some water.

Margaret would only take the smallest of sips and then her head would slip to the side and Victoria and Mary could not get her straightened up again. Even though their mother was very thin she was too much for the two young ones.

The other two younger children grew very tired and gradually settled down on the ground mattress and drifted off to sleep also. Everybody was asleep now except Victoria and Mary. They did not really know it but their mother was not so much asleep as drifting into unconsciousness. They lay beside her and put their arms around her. She was partly aware of this and it comforted her. But she was also aware that she was very sick and that she was sweating non-stop and only partly conscious.

She had the dreams that come with this. Some dreams but more hallucinations and nightmares. She tried to fight them off and be clear in her head but she could not manage this. She would keep slipping into horrible images and fears. The fever and the sweat in which she was trapped made it worse as she was in terrible physical discomfort. The children were not strong enough nor did they have the sheets to change the bed and keep her dry.

Then things began to change. Margaret began to come out of the hallucinations and the nightmares. And she began to feel as if the fever was passing. She looked around and Victoria and Mary helped her sit up better in the bed. She felt their love in their help and felt her love in her need of them. She looked down and saw the other children asleep and reached out one hand but she was too weak. Victoria reached a cup of water to her mouth.

'Mammy, Mammy, here, take some water.' Margaret drank.

Victoria then thought that maybe her mother needed food. She went to the milk bench and got a cup of milk and then reached up to the tin and took out a packet of rich tea biscuits that her mother had bought at McDaid's and which she liked. Coming back to the bed

Victoria found her mother had slipped down in the bed again. She could not get her pulled up and hold the milk and biscuits at the one time. So instead she took a biscuit and dipped it in the milk and put it to her mother's mouth. Her mother opened her mouth and took in a little bit in an unenthusiastic way. She was too weak to even eat the biscuit. She took it more in appreciation of Victoria giving it to her than anything else.

Victoria and Mary together helped her mother take some milk-dipped biscuit and then they wiped their mother's chin. They had never seen their mother helpless like this before. They felt powerful love for her and a terrible need to help her. She was sick, she was helpless. They must help her and save her. They felt something new and deep and powerful growing inside themselves as they fought to help their mother live.

Their mother only managed to take a few pieces of the biscuit dipped in milk. She turned her head away and closed her mouth. When Victoria and Mary tried to get their mother to drink the milk on its own or eat a biscuit on its own she did the same. Turned her head away and closed her mouth. Margaret did not feel like eating or drinking anymore. She was not feeling hungry or thirsty. She was not feeling feverish and sweaty and warm.

An exhaustion, a powerful powerful exhaustion was overcoming her. Like she could not go on any more. And as she lay there the exhaustion became so great it began to blot out everything else. Blotting out the desire to go on anymore. Blotting out the thought that her children would be left behind. In some way the exhaustion was so great that it seemed to encompass the children and they were with her in it. The children were with her in her exhaustion. They were no longer out there for her to worry about.

She lay back and the fight left her with the exhaustion. All her fight since her father had sent her away, since the Allens had worked her like a slave, since Allen had raped her, since she had been brought back and given to Campbell by the words of a church at its back door. But now all the fight was draining out of her. In its place a great exhausted dark peacefulness was taking over. She was finding herself drifting into a peacefulness she had never felt before.

This also brought its own hallucinations. She dreamt she was with her mother and they were at the lake and paddling in its shallow waters. It was a beautiful summer day and they rested away from the orders and attacks of any man. But she was not only with her mother. Her own children and Katie were there with them. Margaret lay in the bed and saw this go before her eyes. She felt like smiling and reached out and touched Victoria and Mary.

But then her hallucination left her and she came back with all her knowledge, to the room and the cottage and the children and Campbell and herself. She could feel the sweat pour off her body again and the weakness of her. She thought of the 'flu and how people were dying all over of it. For the first time she was now convinced. She was dying of the flu. That was it. She was dying of the 'flu. And there was nothing she could do about it. She was at death's door.

But what about the children? She had worried about how she could stop them being hired out. Now she would not even be able to help them get old enough to be able to worry about this. What would happen to them? She was dying. That was what was happening. She turned her head and looked at Victoria and Mary. She was too weak to hug or kiss them. She tried to get up enough to look down and see the rest of the children on the floor mattress. But she could only see the side of it. She was dying.

The effort took the last remaining strength out of her. She lay back. Victoria and Mary held her and looked at her and cried with great sobs to their mother. Margaret herself for the first time since she had got sick, broke down and began to cry in deep sobs to herself. But these were barely audible as she was so weak. And they got weaker. Then they finally stopped. And then Margaret turned to try and look at Victoria again but she was not able to do it. She did not have the strength. She just lay back on the bed.

Victoria and Mary lay there with her. Holding her and weeping and weeping. They did not know anything else to do. Her breathing was changing from being heavy and laboured to shallow. They did not know what this meant but they were scared. They knew their mother was very sick. They wished that Katie was there to help but their father had sent her and Shanks away. But they needed help. When would the doctor come? Would he get there in time? Why was he not there already? Shanks had went for him and told him. He should have come last night.

Should they wake their father? But what would he do? He would just probably leave. That was what he would probably do. That was what he always did in any sort of crisis and he just saw their mother as something to be used. He never looked to see how he could help her. No, it would not help to waken up their father, he would not be of any use, he would only make things worse. He would be angry at them. He lay with his face to the wall every night for a purpose. To tell them to leave him alone.

The girls lay there with their mother. What could they do? As they considered all this they grew up and matured more in those few hours than they had in all their previous years. They began to see their father in a different and clearer light, they began to think about the doctor and the world in a more questioning way, they began to feel their own nourishing qualities and powers and how they were able to comfort their mother and they began to feel they were no longer just very young children but that they were growing up.

Victoria and Mary lay in their mother's arms and holding her in their arms, drifted off to sleep. They did not realise it but their mother was unconscious. The three of them lay there unaware that the night was passing. Then Margaret's breathing began to change and she began to struggle in the bed. Gradually this awoke Victoria and Margaret. They could see that something was different. That their mother was not the same. She was breathing differently. Her breath was catching in her throat.

Both of them sat up in the bed and tried to get their mother up too and take a drink of water. But they could not get her up. Then her breath began to come in deeper more guttural sounds. Then it began to come intermittently, choking for ever longer times in her throat. The children did not know it but they were watching the last battle of their mother to stay alive. And she was losing. Each gasp got shorter, with a greater space between them. Then there was a long space, followed by a deep, deep gasp.

Victoria and Mary were sitting up in the bed crying and watching their mother and trying to get her to sit up and stay alive. But it was not to be. There in front of their eyes, their mother breathed her last breath and sank back into death. She was only twenty years old, she had had six children, she had been abused and controlled all her life, and she had never been outside a ten-mile radius from where she was born in the hills of East Donegal, in her life. Victoria and Mary wept, this wakened the other children, the older two climbed weeping up on the bed while the younger two lay crying on their mattress.

Their mother lay dead on the bed. By her side and in her small room with her were her six children all of whom were now weeping. In one way she would have been happy. She was surrounded by the love of her children whom she had brought into the world and nurtured. In another way she would have been horrified as they had nobody now to protect them from the fathers, the Allens and the Campbells and the world that was out there waiting for them.

Margaret and her love and protection were gone.

AFTERWORD

Readers of this book may want to know what happened to my grandmother's six children. They all survived and grew up healthy. My grandfather changed and accepted the help of neighbours and relatives. My mother was the second oldest of the six children. She lived until her nineties and had five children of which I am the youngest. All my other grandmother's children lived into their late middle and old age. With one exception they had children of their own.

Four went to work in the homes of rich families as servants and two into the local woollen mill. None had to go to work in the hiring out system. My grandmother would have been overjoyed about that. It breaks my heart when I think that she did not survive to see any of them grow up, to see her grandchildren come into the world and to sit with them in her old age.

The cottage in which she lived and in which her children were born no longer stands. Up to twenty years ago its ruins were visible. Now it has been bulldozed and made into a graveyard. My sister and I visited the old ruins once and took a stone away as a commemoration to my grandmother and the years and struggle she went through within its walls. This book is also a memorial.

The author John Throne - Born in Lifford ,
Co Donegal, in 1944 - first became involved in
politics in the tumultuous events in Derry in 1968.
He has spent all his life since then working full-time
in socialist/Marxist politics and the labour movement in Ireland and abroad.
The Donegal Woman is his first novel.